GARDEN CITY PUBLISHING Co. Reprint Edition 1946, by special
arrangement with DOUBLEDAY & COMPANY, INC.

ADVENTURES IN CONTENTMENT

ADVENTURES IN FRIENDSHIP

THE FRIENDLY ROAD

Formerly published as
ADVENTURES OF DAVID GRAYSON

(ADVENTURES OF DAVID GRAYSON)

DAVID GRAYSON
OMNIBUS

ADVENTURES IN CONTENTMENT

ADVENTURES IN FRIENDSHIP

THE FRIENDLY ROAD

ILLUSTRATED BY THOMAS FOGARTY

GARDEN CITY PUBLISHING CO., INC.

Garden City   New York

CONTENTS

BOOK I

CONTENTS

BOOK III

INTRODUCTION

ALTHOUGH the first book of the "Adventures of David Grayson," which was called "Adventures in Contentment," was published eighteen years ago, the demand for this and for the succeeding volumes—to the astonishment of the author—has continued unabated.

While these books have been published in a set, in separate volumes, there has recently been a demand for a more compact and cheaper edition. This project of bringing three of the early volumes together between one set of covers therefore seems to the author and to the publisher an interesting experiment.

We are therefore calling the present volume the "David Grayson Omnibus," and including in it three of the earlier books, each complete, as follows:

"Adventures in Contentment"
"Adventures in Friendship"
"The Friendly Road"

It is the hope of the author that in this convenient and beautiful form the book may reach many new readers.

DAVID GRAYSON

I

"THE BURDEN OF THE VALLEY OF VISION"

I CAME HERE eight years ago as the renter of this farm, of which soon afterward I became the owner. The time before that I like to forget. The chief impression it left upon my memory, now happily growing indistinct, is of being hurried faster than I could well travel. From the moment, as a boy of seventeen, I first began to pay my own way, my days were ordered by an inscrutable power which drove me hourly to my task. I was rarely allowed to look up or down, but always forward, toward that vague Success which we Americans love to glorify.

My senses, my nerves, even my muscles were continually strained to the utmost of attainment. If I loitered or paused by the wayside, as it seems natural for me to do, I soon heard the sharp crack of the lash. For many years, and I can say it truthfully, I never rested. I neither thought nor reflected. I had no pleasure, even though I pursued it fiercely during the brief respite of vacations. Through many feverish years I did not work: I merely produced.

The only real thing I did was to hurry as though every moment were my last, as though the world, which now seems so rich in everything, held only one prize which might be seized

3

upon before I arrived. Since then I have tried to recall, like one who struggles to restore the visions of a fever, what it was that I ran to attain, or why I should have borne without rebellion such indignities to soul and body. That life seems now, of all illusions, the most distant and unreal. It is like the unguessed eternity before we are born: not of concern compared with that eternity upon which we are now embarked.

All these things happened in cities and among crowds. I like to forget them. They smack of that slavery of the spirit which is so much worse than any mere slavery of the body.

One day—it was in April, I remember, and the soft maples in the city park were just beginning to blossom—I stopped suddenly. I did not intend to stop. I confess in humiliation that it was no courage, no will of my own. I intended to go on toward Success: but Fate stopped me. It was as if I had been thrown violently from a moving planet: all the universe streamed around me and past me. It seemed to me that of all animate creation, I was the only thing that was still or silent. Until I stopped I had not known the pace I ran; and I had a vague sympathy and understanding, never felt before, for those who left the running. I lay prostrate with fever and close to death for weeks and watched the world go by: the dust, the noise, the very colour of haste. The only sharp pang that I suffered was the feeling that I should be broken-hearted and that I was not; that I should care and that I did not. It was as though I had died and escaped all further responsibility. I even watched with dim equanimity my friends racing past me, panting as they ran. Some of them paused an instant to comfort me where I lay, but I could see that their minds were still upon the running and I was glad when they went away. I cannot tell with what weariness their haste oppressed me. As for them, they somehow blamed me for dropping out. I knew. Until we ourselves understand, we accept no excuse from the man who stops. While I felt it all, I was not bitter. I did not seem to care. I said to myself: "This is Unfitness. I survive no longer. So be it."

Thus I lay, and presently I began to hunger and thirst. Desire rose within me: the indescribable longing of the convalescent for the food of recovery. So I lay, questioning wearily what it was that I required. One morning I wakened with a strange, new joy in my soul. It came to me at that moment with indescribable poignancy, the thought of walking barefoot in cool, fresh plow furrows as I had once done when a boy. So vividly the memory came to me—the high airy world as it was at that moment, and the boy I was walking free in the furrows—that the weak tears filled my eyes, the first I had shed in many years. Then I thought of sitting in quiet thickets in old fence corners, the wood behind me rising still, cool, mysterious, and the fields in front stretching away in illimitable pleasantness. I thought of the good smell of cows at milking—you do not know, if you do not know!—I thought of the sights and sounds, the heat and sweat of the hay fields. I thought of a certain brook I knew when a boy that flowed among alders and wild parsnips, where I waded with a three-foot rod for trout. I thought of all these things as a man thinks of his first love. Oh, I craved the soil. I hungered and thirsted for the earth. I was greedy for growing things.

And thus, eight years ago, I came here like one sore-wounded creeping from the field of battle. I remember walking in the sunshine, weak yet, but curiously satisfied. I that was dead lived again. It came to me then with a curious certainty, not since so assuring, that I understood the chief marvel of nature hidden within the Story of the Resurrection, the marvel of plant and seed, father and son, the wonder of the seasons, the miracle of life. I, too, had died: I had lain long in darkness, and now I had risen again upon the sweet earth. And I possessed beyond others a knowledge of a former existence, which I knew, even then, I could never return to.

For a time, in the new life, I was happy to drunkenness—working, eating, sleeping. I was an animal again, let out to run in green pastures. I was glad of the sunrise and the sunset. I was glad at noon. It delighted me when my muscles ached with work and when, after supper, I could not keep my eyes open for sheer weariness. And sometimes I was awakened in the night out of a sound sleep—seemingly by the very silences—

and lay in a sort of bodily comfort impossible to describe.

I did not want to feel or to think: I merely wanted to live. In the sun or the rain I wanted to go out and come in, and never again know the pain of the unquiet spirit. I looked forward to an awakening not without dread for we are as helpless before birth as in the presence of death.

But like all birth, it came, at last, suddenly. All that summer I had worked in a sort of animal content. Autumn had now come, late autumn, with coolness in the evening air. I was plowing in my upper field—not then mine in fact—and it was a soft afternoon with the earth turning up moist and fragrant. I had been walking the furrows all day long. I had taken note, as though my life depended upon it, of the occasional stones or roots in my field, I made sure of the adjustment of the harness, I drove with peculiar care to save the horses. With such simple details of the work in hand I had found it my joy to occupy my mind. Up to that moment the most important things in the world had seemed a straight furrow and well-turned corners—to me, then, a profound accomplishment.

I cannot well describe it, save by the analogy of an opening door somewhere within the house of my consciousness. I had been in the dark: I seemed to emerge. I had been bound down: I seemed to leap up—and with a marvellous sudden sense of freedom and joy.

I stopped there in my field and looked up. And it was as if I had never looked up before. I discovered another world. It had been there before, for long and long, but I had never seen nor felt it. All discoveries are made in that way: a man finds the new thing, not in nature but in himself.

It was as though, concerned with plow and harness and furrow, I had never known that the world had height or colour or sweet sounds, or that there was *feeling* in a hillside. I forgot myself, or where I was. I stood a long time motionless. My dominant feeling, if I can at all express it, was of a strange new friendliness, a warmth, as though these hills, this field about me, the woods, had suddenly spoken to me and caressed me. It was as though I had been accepted in membership, as though I was now recognised, after long trial, as belonging here.

Across the town road which separates my farm from my nearest neighbour's, I saw a field, familiar, yet strangely new and unfamiliar, lying up to the setting sun, all red with autumn, above it the incalculable heights of the sky, blue, but not quite clear, owing to the Indian summer haze. I cannot convey the sweetness and softness of that landscape, the airiness of it, the mystery of it, as it came to me at that moment. It was as though, looking at an acquaintance long known, I should discover that I loved him. As I stood there I was conscious of the cool tang of burning leaves and brush heaps, the lazy smoke of which floated down the long valley and found me in my field, and finally I heard, as though the sounds were then made for the first time, all the vague murmurs of the country side—a cow-bell somewhere in the distance, the creak of a wagon, the blurred evening hum of birds, insects, frogs. So much it means for a man to stop and look up from his task. So I stood, and I looked up and down with a glow and a thrill which I cannot now look back upon without some envy and a little amusement at the very grandness and seriousness of it all. And I said aloud to myself: "I will be as broad as the earth. I will not be limited."

Thus I was born into the present world, and here I continue, not knowing what other world I may yet achieve. I do not know, but I wait in expectancy, keeping my furrows straight and my corners well turned. Since that day in the field, though my fences include no more acres, and I still plow my own fields, my real domain has expanded until I crop wide fields and take the profit of many curious pastures. From my farm I can see most of the world; and if I wait here long enough all people pass this way.

And I look out upon them not in the surroundings which they have chosen for themselves, but from the vantage ground of my familiar world. The symbols which meant so much in cities mean little here. Sometimes it seems to me as though I saw men naked. They come and stand beside my oak, and the oak passes solemn judgment; they tread my furrows and the clods give silent evidence; they touch the green blades of my corn, the corn whispers its sure conclusions. Stern judgments that will be deceived by no symbols!

Thus I have delighted, secretly, in calling myself an unlimited farmer, and I make this confession in answer to the inner and truthful demand of the soul that we are not, after all, the slaves of things, whether corn, or banknotes, or spindles; that we are not the used, but the users; that life is more than profit and loss. And so I shall expect that while I am talking farm some of you may be thinking of dry goods, banking, literature, carpentry, or what-not. But if you can say: I am an unlimited dry goods merchant, I am an unlimited carpenter, I will give you an old-fashioned country hand-shake, strong and warm. We are friends; our orbits coincide.

Thomas Fogarty

II

I BUY A FARM

As I have said, when I came here I came as a renter, working all of the first summer without that "open vision" of which the prophet Samuel speaks. I had no memory of the past and no hope of the future. I fed upon the moment. My sister Harriet kept the house and I looked after the farm and the fields. In all those months I hardly knew that I had neighbours, although Horace, from whom I rented my place, was not infrequently a visitor. He has since said that I looked at him as though he were a "statute." I was "citified," Horace said; and "citified" with us here in the country is nearly the limit of invective, though not violent enough to discourage such a gift of sociability as his. The Scotch Preacher, the rarest, kindest man I know, called once or twice, wearing the air of formality which so ill becomes him. I saw nothing in him: it was my fault, not his, that I missed so many weeks of his friendship. Once in that time the Professor crossed my fields with his tin box slung from his shoulder; and the only feeling I had, born of crowded cities, was that this was an intrusion upon my property. Intrusion: and the Professor! It is now unthinkable. I often passed the Carpentry Shop on my way to town. I saw Baxter many times at his bench. Even then Baxter's eyes attracted me: he always glanced up at me as I passed, and his look had in it something of a caress. So the home of Starkweather, standing aloof among its broad lawns and tall trees, carried no meaning for me.

Of all my neighbours, Horace is the nearest. From the back door of my house, looking over the hill, I can see the two red chimneys of his home, and the top of the windmill. Horace's barn and corn silo are more pretentious by far than his house, but fortunately they stand on lower ground, where they are not visible from my side of the hill. Five minutes' walk in a straight line across the fields brings me to Horace's door; by the road it takes at least ten minutes.

In the fall after my arrival I had come to love the farm and its surroundings so much that I decided to have it for my own. I did not look ahead to being a farmer. I did not ask Harriet's advice. I found myself sitting one day in the justice's office. The justice was bald and as dry as corn fodder in March. He sat with spectacled impressiveness behind his ink-stained table. Horace hitched his heel on the round of his chair and put his hat on his knee. He wore his best coat and his hair was brushed in deference to the occasion. He looked uncomfortable, but important. I sat opposite him, somewhat overwhelmed by the business in hand. I felt like an inadequate boy measured against solemnities too large for him. The processes seemed curiously unconvincing, like a game in which the important part is to keep from laughing; and yet when I thought of laughing I felt cold chills of horror. If I had laughed at that moment I cannot think what that justice would have said! But it was a pleasure to have the old man read the deed, looking at me over his spectacles from time to time to make sure I was not playing truant. There are good and great words in a deed. One of them I brought away with me from the conference, a very fine, big one, which I love to have out now and again to remind me of the really serious things of life. It gives me a peculiar dry, legal feeling. If I am about to enter upon a serious bargain, like the sale of a cow, I am more avaricious if I work with it under my tongue.

Hereditaments! Hereditaments!

Some words need to be fenced in, pig-tight, so that they cannot escape us; others we prefer to have running at large, indefinite but inclusive. I would not look up that word for anything: I might find it fenced in so that it could not mean to me all that it does now.

Hereditaments! May there be many of them—or it!

Is it not a fine Providence that gives us different things to love? In the purchase of my farm both Horace and I got the better of the bargain—and yet neither was cheated. In reality a fairly strong lantern light will shine through Horace, and I could see that he was hugging himself with the joy of his bargain; but I was content. I had some money left—what more does anyone want after a bargain?—and I had come into possession of the thing I desired most of all. Looking at bargains from a purely commercial point of view, someone is always cheated, but looked at with the simple eye both seller and buyer always win.

We came away from the gravity of that bargaining in Horace's wagon. On our way home Horace gave me fatherly advice about using my farm. He spoke from the height of his knowledge to me, a humble beginner. The conversation ran something like this:

HORACE: Thar's a clump of plum trees along the lower pasture fence. Perhaps you saw 'm——

MYSELF: I saw them: that is one reason I bought the back pasture. In May they will be full of blossoms.

HORACE: They're *wild* plums: they ain't good for nothing.

MYSELF: But think how fine they will be all the year round.

HORACE: Fine! They take up a quarter-acre of good land. I've been going to cut 'em myself this ten years.

MYSELF: I don't think I shall want them cut out.

HORACE: Humph.

After a pause:

HORACE: There's a lot of good body cord-wood in that oak on the knoll.

MYSELF: Cord-wood! Why, that oak is the treasure of the

whole farm. I have never seen a finer one. I could not think of cutting it.

HORACE: It will bring you fifteen or twenty dollars cash in hand.

MYSELF: But I rather have the oak.

HORACE: Humph.

So our conversation continued for some time. I let Horace know that I preferred rail fences, even old ones, to a wire fence, and that I thought a farm should not be too large, else it might keep one away from his friends. And what, I asked, is corn compared with a friend? Oh, I grew really oratorical! I gave it as my opinion that there should be vines around the house (Waste of time, said Horace), and that no farmer should permit anyone to paint medicine advertisements on his barn (Brings you ten dollars a year, said Horace), and that I proposed to fix the bridge on the lower road (What's a path-master for? asked Horace). I said that a town was a useful adjunct for a farm; but I laid it down as a principle that no town should be too near a farm. I finally became so enthusiastic in setting forth my conceptions of a true farm that I reduced Horace to a series of humphs. The early humphs were incredulous, but as I proceeded, with some joy, they became humorously contemptuous, and finally began to voice a large, comfortable, condescending tolerance. I could fairly feel Horace growing superior as he sat there beside me. Oh, he had everything in his favour. He could prove what he said: One tree + one thicket = twenty dollars.

One landscape = ten cords of wood = a quarter-acre of corn = twenty dollars. These equations prove themselves. Moreover, was not Horace the "best off" of any farmer in the country? Did he not have the largest barn and the best corn silo? And are there better arguments?

Have you ever had anyone give you up as hopeless? And is it not a pleasure? It is only after people resign you to your fate that you really make friends of them. For how can you win the friendship of one who is trying to convert you to his superior beliefs?

As we talked, then, Horace and I, I began to have hopes of him. There is no joy comparable to the making of a friend, and the more resistant the material the greater the triumph. Baxter, the carpenter, says that when he works for enjoyment he chooses curly maple.

When Horace set me down at my gate that afternoon he gave me his hand and told me that he would look in on me occasionally, and that if I had any trouble to let him know.

A few days later I heard by the round-about telegraph common in country neighbourhoods that Horace had found a good deal of fun in reporting what I said about farming and that he had called me by a highly humorous but disparaging name. Horace has a vein of humour all his own. I have caught him alone in his fields chuckling to himself, and even breaking out in a loud laugh at the memory of some amusing incident that happened ten years ago. One day, a month or more after our bargain, Horace came down across his field and hitched his jean-clad leg over my fence, with the intent, I am sure, of delving a little more in the same rich mine of humour.

"Horace," I said, looking him straight in the eye, "did you call me an—Agriculturist!"

I have rarely seen a man so pitifully confused as Horace was at that moment. He flushed, he stammered, he coughed, the perspiration broke out on his forehead. He tried to speak and could not. I was sorry for him.

"Horace," I said, "you're a Farmer."

We looked at each other a moment with dreadful seriousness,

and then both of us laughed to the point of holding our sides. We slapped our knees, we shouted, we wriggled, we almost rolled with merriment. Horace put out his hand and we shook heartily. In five minutes I had the whole story of his humorous reports out of him.

No real friendship is ever made without an initial clashing which discloses the metal of each to each. Since that day Horace's jean-clad leg has rested many a time on my fence and we have talked crops and calves. We have been the best of friends in the way of whiffle-trees, butter tubs and pig killings—but never once looked up together at the sky.

The chief objection to a joke in the country is that it is so imperishable. There is so much room for jokes and so few jokes to fill it. When I see Horace approaching with a peculiar, friendly, reminiscent smile on his face I hasten with all ardour to anticipate him:

"Horace," I exclaim, "you're a Farmer."

feeling of proprietorship. I could do anything I liked. The farm was *mine*.

How sweet an emotion is possession! What charm is inherent in ownership! What a foundation for vanity, even for the greater quality of self-respect, lies in a little property! I fell to thinking of the excellent wording of the old books in which land is called "real property," or "real estate." Money we may possess, or goods or chattels, but they give no such impression of mineness as the feeling that one's feet rest upon soil that is his: that part of the deep earth is his with all the water upon it, all small animals that creep or crawl in the holes of it, all birds or insects that fly in the air above it, all trees, shrubs, flowers, and grass that grow upon it, all houses, barns and fences— all, his. As I strode along that afternoon I fed upon possession. I rolled the sweet morsel of ownership under my tongue. I seemed to set my feet down more firmly on the good earth. I straightened my shoulders: *this land was mine*. I picked up a clod of earth and let it crumble and drop through my fingers: it gave me a peculiar and poignant feeling of possession. I can understand why the miser enjoys the very physical contact of his gold. Every sense I possessed, sight, hearing, smell, touch, fed upon the new joy.

At one corner of my upper field the fence crosses an abrupt ravine upon leggy stilts. My line skirts the slope halfway up. My neighbour owns the crown of the hill which he has shorn until it resembles the tonsured pate of a monk. Every rain brings the light soil down the ravine and lays it like a hand of infertility upon my farm. It had always bothered me, this wastage; and as I looked across my fence I thought to myself:

"I must have that hill. I will buy it. I will set the fence farther up. I will plant the slope. It is no age of tonsures either in religion or agriculture."

The very vision of widened acres set my thoughts on fire. In imagination I extended my farm upon all sides, thinking how much better I could handle my land than my neighbours. I dwelt avariciously upon more possessions: I thought with discontent of my poverty. More land I wanted. I was enveloped in clouds of envy. I coveted my neighbour's land: I felt myself superior and Horace inferior: I was consumed with black vanity.

So I dealt hotly with these thoughts until I reached the top of the ridge at the farther corner of my land. It is the highest point on the farm.

For a moment I stood looking about me on a wonderful prospect of serene beauty. As it came to me—hills, fields, woods—the fever which had been consuming me died down. I thought how the world stretched away from my fences—just such fields —for a thousand miles, and in each small enclosure a man as hot as I with the passion of possession. How they all envied, and hated, in their longing for more land! How property kept them apart, prevented the close, confident touch of friendship, how it separated lovers and ruined families! Of all obstacles to that complete democracy of which we dream, is there a greater than property?

I was ashamed. Deep shame covered me. How little of the earth, after all, I said, lies within the limits of my fences. And I looked out upon the perfect beauty of the world around me, and I saw how little excited it was, how placid, how undemanding.

I had come here to be free and already this farm, which I thought of so fondly as my possession, was coming to possess me. Ownership is an appetite like hunger or thirst, and as we may eat to gluttony and drink to drunkenness so we may possess to avarice. How many men have I seen who, though they regard themselves as models of temperance, wear the marks of unbridled indulgence of the passion of possession, and how like gluttony or licentiousness it sets its sure sign upon their faces.

I said to myself, Why should any man fence himself in? And why hope to enlarge one's world by the creeping acquisition of a few acres to his farm? I thought of the old scientist, who, laying his hand upon the grass, remarked: "Everything under my hand is a miracle"—forgetting that everything outside was also a miracle.

"How graceful climb these shadows on my hill"

As I stood there I glanced across the broad valley wherein lies the most of my farm, to the field of buckwheat which belongs to Horace. For an instant it gave me the illusion of a hill on fire: for the late sun shone full on the thick ripe stalks of the buckwheat, giving forth an abundant red glory that blessed the eye. Horace had been proud of his crop, smacking his lips at the prospect of winter pancakes, and here I was entering his field and taking without hindrance another crop, a crop gathered not with hands nor stored in granaries: a wonderful crop, which, once gathered, may long be fed upon and yet remain unconsumed.

So I looked across the countryside; a group of elms here, a tufted hilltop there, the smooth verdure of pastures, the rich brown of new-plowed fields—and the odours, and the sounds of the country—all cropped by me. How little the fences keep me out: I do not regard titles, nor consider boundaries. I enter either by day or by night, but not secretly. Taking my fill, I leave as much as I find.

And thus standing upon the highest hill in my upper pasture, I thought of the quoted saying of a certain old abbot of the middle ages—"He that is a true monk considers nothing as belonging to him except a lyre."

What finer spirit? Who shall step forth freer than he who goes with nothing save his lyre? He shall sing as he goes: he shall not be held down nor fenced in.

With a lifting of the soul I thought of that old abbot, how smooth his brow, how catholic his interest, how serene his outlook, how free his friendships, how unlimited his whole life. Nothing but a lyre!

So I made a covenant there with myself. I said: "I shall use, not be used. I do not limit myself here. I shall not allow possessions to come between me and my life or my friends."

For a time—how long I do not know—I stood thinking. Presently I discovered, moving slowly along the margin of the field below me, the old professor with his tin botany box. And somehow I had no feeling that he was intruding upon my new land. His walk was slow and methodical, his head and even his shoulders were bent—almost habitually—from looking close upon the earth, and from time to time he stooped, and once he knelt to examine some object that attracted his eye. It seemed appropriate that he should thus kneel to the earth. So he gathered *his* crop and fences did not keep him out nor titles disturb him. He also was free! It gave me at that moment a peculiar pleasure to have him on my land, to know that I was, if unconsciously, raising other crops than I knew. I felt friendship for this old professor: I could understand him, I thought. And I said aloud but in a low tone, as though I were addressing him:

—Do not apologise, friend, when you come into my field. You do not interrupt me. What you have come for is of more importance at this moment than corn. Who is it that says I must plow so many furrows this day? Come in, friend, and sit here on these clods: we will sweeten the evening with fine words. We will invest our time not in corn, or in cash, but in life.—

I walked with confidence down the hill toward the professor. So engrossed was he with his employment that he did not see me until I was within a few paces of him. When he looked up at me it was as though his eyes returned from some far journey. I felt at first out of focus, unplaced, and only gradually coming into view. In his hand he held a lump of earth containing a thrifty young plant of the purple cone-flower, having several blossoms. He worked at the lump deftly, delicately, so that the earth, pinched, powdered and shaken out, fell between his fingers, leaving the knotty yellow roots in his hand. I marked how firm, slow, brown, the old man was, how little obtrusive in my field. One foot rested in a furrow, the other was set among the grass of the margin, near the fence—his place, I thought.

His first words, though of little moment in themselves, gave me a curious satisfaction, as when a coin, tested, rings true gold, or a hero, tried, is heroic.

"I have rarely," he said, "seen a finer display of rudbeckia than this, along these old fences."

If he had referred to me, or questioned, or apologised, I should have been disappointed. He did not say, "your fences," he said "these fences," as though they were as much his as mine. And he spoke in his own world, knowing that if I could enter I would, but that if I could not, no stooping to me would avail either of us.

"It has been a good autumn for flowers," I said inanely, for so many things were flying through my mind that I could not at once think of the great particular words which should bring us together. At first I thought my chance had passed, but he seemed to see something in me after all, for he said:

"Here is a peculiarly large specimen of the rudbeckia. Observe the deep purple of the cone, and the bright yellow of the petals. Here is another that grew hardly two feet away, in the grass near the fence where the rails and the blackberry bushes have shaded it. How small and undeveloped it is."

"They crowd up to the plowed land," I observed.

"Yes, they reach out for a better chance in life—like men. With more room, better food, freer air, you see how much finer they grow."

It was curious to me, having hitherto barely observed the coneflowers along my fences, save as a colour of beauty, how simple we fell to talking of them as though in truth they were people like ourselves, having our desires and possessed of our capabilities. It gave me then, for the first time, the feeling which has since meant such varied enjoyment, of the peopling of the woods.

"See here," he said, "how different the character of these individuals. They are all of the same species. They all grow along this fence within two or three rods; but observe the difference not only in size but in colouring, in the shape of the petals, in the proportions of the cone. What does it all mean? Why, nature trying one of her endless experiments. She sows here broadly, trying to produce better cone-flowers. A few she plants on the edge of the field in the hope that they may escape the plow. If they grow, better food and more sunshine produce more and larger flowers."

So we talked, or rather he talked, finding in me an eager listener. And what he called botany seemed to me to be life. Of birth, of growth, of reproduction, of death, he spoke, and his flowers became sentient creatures under my eyes.

And thus the sun went down and the purple mists crept silently along the distant low spots, and all the great, great mysteries came and stood before me beckoning and questioning. They came and they stood, and out of the cone-flower, as the old professor spoke, I seemed to catch a glimmer of the true light. I reflected how truly everything is in anything. If one could really understand a cone-flower he could understand this Earth. Botany was only one road toward the Explanation.

Always I hope that some traveller may have more news of the way than I, and sooner or later, I find I must make inquiry of the direction of every thoughtful man I meet. And I have always had especial hope of those who study the sciences: they ask such intimate questions of nature. Theology possesses a vain-gloriousness which places its faith in human theories; but science, at its best, is humble before nature herself. It has no thesis to defend: it is content to kneel upon the earth, in the way of my friend, the old professor, and ask the simplest questions, hoping for some true reply.

I wondered, then, what the professor thought, after his years of work, of the Mystery; and finally, not without confusion, I asked him. He listened, for the first time ceasing to dig, shake out and arrange his specimens. When I had stopped speaking he remained for a moment silent, then he looked at me with a new regard. Finally he quoted quietly, but with a deep note in his voice:

"Canst thou by searching find God? Canst thou find out the Almighty unto perfection? It is as high as heaven: what canst thou do? deeper than hell, what canst thou know?"

When the professor had spoken we stood for a moment silent, then he smiled and said briskly:

"I have been a botanist for fifty-four years. When I was a boy I believed implicitly in God. I prayed to him, having a vision of him—a person—before my eyes. As I grew older I concluded that there was no God. I dismissed him from the universe. I believed only in what I could see, or hear, or feel. I talked about Nature and Reality."

He paused, the smile still lighting his face, evidently recalling to himself the old days. I did not interrupt him. Finally he turned to me and said abruptly,

"And now—it seems to me—there is nothing but God."

As he said this he lifted his arm with a peculiar gesture that seemed to take in the whole world.

For a time we were both silent. When I left him I offered my hand and told him I hoped I might become his friend. So I turned my face toward home. Evening was falling, and as I walked I heard the crows calling, and the air was keen and cool, and I thought deep thoughts.

And so I stepped into the darkened stable. I could not see the outlines of the horse or the cow, but knowing the place so well I could easily get about. I heard the horse step aside with a soft expectant whinny. I smelled the smell of milk, the musty, sharp odour of dry hay, the pungent smell of manure, not unpleasant. And the stable was warm after the cool of the fields with a sort of animal warmth that struck into me soothingly. I spoke in a low voice and laid my hand on the horse's flank. The flesh quivered and shrunk away from my touch—coming back confidently, warmly. I ran my hand along his back and up his hairy neck. I felt his sensitive nose in my hand. "You shall have your oats," I said, and I gave him to eat. Then I spoke as gently to the cow, and she stood aside to be milked.

And afterward I came out into the clear bright night, and the air was sweet and cool, and my dog came bounding to meet me. —So I carried the milk into the house, and Harriet said in her heartiest tone:

"You are late, David. But sit up, I have kept the biscuits warm."

And that night my sleep was sound.

IV

ENTERTAIN AN AGENT UNAWARES

With the coming of winter I thought the life of a farmer might lose something of its charm. So much interest lies in the growth not only of crops but of trees, vines, flowers, sentiments and emotions. In the summer the world is busy, concerned with many things and full of gossip: in the winter I anticipated a cessation of many active interests and enthusiasms. I looked forward to having time for my books and for the quiet contemplation of the life around me. Summer indeed is for activity, winter for reflection. But when winter really came every day discovered some new work to do or some new adventure to enjoy. It is surprising how many things happen on a small farm. Examining the book which accounts for that winter, I find the history of part of a forenoon, which will illustrate one of the curious adventures of a farmer's life. It is dated January 5.

I went out this morning with my axe and hammer to mend the fence along the public road. A heavy frost fell last night and the brown grass and the dry ruts of the roads were powdered white. Even the air, which was perfectly still, seemed full of frost crystals, so that when the sun came up one seemed to walk in a magic world. I drew in a long breath and looked out across the wonderful shining country and I said to myself:

"Surely, there is nowhere I would rather be than here." For I could have travelled nowhere to find greater beauty or a better enjoyment of it than I had here at home.

As I worked with my axe and hammer, I heard a light wagon come rattling up the road. Across the valley a man had begun to chop a tree. I could see the axe steel flash brilliantly in the sunshine before I heard the sound of the blow.

The man in the wagon had a round face and a sharp blue eye. I thought he seemed a businesslike young man.

"Say, there," he shouted, drawing up at my gate, "would you mind holding my horse a minute? It's a cold morning and he's restless."

"Certainly not," I said, and I put down my tools and held his horse.

He walked up to my door with a brisk step and a certain jaunty poise of the head.

"He is well contented with himself," I said. "It is a great blessing for any man to be satisfied with what he has got."

I heard Harriet open the door—how every sound rang through the still morning air!

The young man asked some question and I distinctly heard Harriet's answer:

"He's down there."

The young man came back: his hat was tipped up, his quick eye darted over my grounds as though in a single instant he had appraised everything and passed judgment upon the cash value of the inhabitants. He whistled a lively little tune.

"Say," he said, when he reached the gate, not at all disconcerted, "I thought you was the hired man. Your name's Grayson, ain't it? Well, I want to talk with you."

After tying and blanketing his horse and taking a black satchel from his buggy he led me up to my house. I had a pleasurable sense of excitement and adventure. Here was a new character come to my farm. Who knows, I thought, what he may bring with him: who knows what I may send away by him? Here in the country we must set our little ships afloat on small streams, hoping that somehow, some day, they will reach the sea.

It was interesting to see the busy young man sit down so confidently in our best chair. He said his name was Dixon, and he took out from his satchel a book with a fine showy cover. He said it was called "Living Selections from Poet, Sage and Humourist."

"This," he told me, "is only the first of the series. We publish six volumes full of literchoor. You see what a heavy book this is?"

I tested it in my hand: it was a heavy book.

"The entire set," he said, "weighs over ten pounds. There are 1,162 pages, enough paper if laid down flat, end to end, to reach half a mile."

I cannot quote his exact language: there was too much of it, but he made an impressive showing of the amount of literature that could be had at a very low price per pound. Mr. Dixon was a hypnotist. He fixed me with his glittering eye, and he talked so fast, and his ideas upon the subject were so original that he held me spellbound. At first I was inclined to be provoked: one does not like to be forcibly hypnotised, but gradually the situation began to amuse me, the more so when Harriet came in.

"Did you ever see a more beautiful binding?" asked the agent, holding his book admiringly at arm's length. "This up here," he said, pointing to the illuminated cover, "is the Muse of Poetry. She is scattering flowers—poems, you know. Fine idea, ain't it? Colouring fine, too."

He jumped up quickly and laid the book on my table, to the evident distress of Harriet.

"Trims up the room, don't it?" he exclaimed, turning his head a little to one side and observing the effect with an expression of affectionate admiration.

"How much," I asked, "will you sell the covers for without the insides?"

"Without the insides?"

"Yes," I said, "the binding will trim up my table just as well without the insides."

I thought he looked at me a little suspiciously, but he was evidently satisfied by my expression of countenance, for he answered promptly:

"Oh, but you want the insides. That's what the books are for. The bindings are never sold alone."

He then went on to tell me the prices and terms of payment, until it really seemed that it would be cheaper to buy the books than to let him carry them away again. Harriet stood in the doorway behind him frowning and evidently trying to catch my eye. But I kept my face turned aside so that I could not see her signal of distress and my eyes fixed on the young man Dixon. It was as good as a play. Harriet there, serious-minded, thinking I was being befooled, and the agent thinking he was befooling me, and I, thinking I was befooling both of them—and all of us wrong. It was very like life wherever you find it.

Finally, I took the book which he had been urging upon me, at which Harriet coughed meaningly to attract my attention. She knew the danger when I really got my hands on a book. But I made up as innocent as a child. I opened the book almost at random—and it was as though, walking down a strange road, I had come upon an old tried friend not seen before in years. For there on the page before me I read:

> "The world is too much with us; late and soon,
> Getting and spending we lay waste our powers:
> Little we see in Nature that is ours;
> We have given our hearts away, a sordid boon!
> The sea that bares her bosom to the moon;
> The winds that will be howling at all hours,
> But are up-gathered now like sleeping flowers;
> For this, for everything, we are out of tune;
> It moves us not."

And as I read it came back to me—a scene like a picture— the place, the time, the very feel of the hour when I first saw those lines. Who shall say that the past does not live! An odour will sometimes set the blood coursing in an old emotion, and a line of poetry is the resurrection and the life. For a moment I forgot Harriet and the agent, I forgot myself, I even forgot the book on my knee—everything but that hour in the past—a view of shimmering hot housetops, the heat and dust and noise of an August evening in the city, the dumb weariness of it all, the loneliness, the longing for green fields; and then these great lines of Wordsworth, read for the first time, flooding in upon me:

> *"Great God! I'd rather be*
> *A pagan suckled in a creed outworn:*
> *So might I, standing on this pleasant lea,*
> *Have glimpses that would make me less forlorn;*
> *Have sight of Proteus rising from the sea;*
> *And hear old Triton blow his wreathèd horn."*

When I had finished I found myself standing in my own room with one arm raised, and, I suspect, a trace of tears in my eyes—there before the agent and Harriet. I saw Harriet lift one hand and drop it hopelessly. She thought I was captured at last. I was past saving. And as I looked at the agent I saw "grim conquest glowing in his eye!" So I sat down not a little embarrassed by my exhibition—when I had intended to be self-poised.

"You like it, don't you?" said Mr. Dixon unctuously.

"I don't see," I said earnestly, "how you can afford to sell such things as this so cheap."

"They *are* cheap," he admitted regretfully. I suppose he wished he had tried me with the half-morocco.

"They are priceless," I said, "absolutely priceless. If you were the only man in the world who had that poem, I think I would deed you my farm for it."

Mr. Dixon proceeded, as though it were all settled, to get out his black order book and open it briskly for business. He drew his fountain pen, capped it, and looked up at me expectantly. My feet actually seemed slipping into some irresistible whirlpool. How well he understood practical psychology! I struggled within myself, fearing engulfment: I was all but lost.

"Shall I deliver the set at once," he said, "or can you wait until the first of February?"

At that critical moment a floating spar of an idea swept my way and I seized upon it as the last hope of the lost.

"Did you ever see a more beautiful binding?"

"I don't understand," I said, as though I had not heard his last question, "how you dare go about with all this treasure upon you. Are you not afraid of being stopped in the road and robbed? Why, I've seen the time when, if I had known you carried such things as these, such cures for sick hearts, I think I should have stopped you myself!"

"Say, you *are* an odd one," said Mr. Dixon.

"Why do you sell such priceless things as these?" I asked, looking at him sharply.

"Why do I sell them?" and he looked still more perplexed. "To make money, of course; same reason you raise corn."

"But here is wealth," I said, pursuing my advantage. "If you have these you have something more valuable than money."

Mr. Dixon politely said nothing. Like a wise angler, having failed to land me at the first rush, he let me have line. Then I thought of Ruskin's words, "Nor can any noble thing be wealth except to a noble person." And that prompted me to say to Mr. Dixon:

"These things are not yours; they are mine. You never owned them; but I will sell them to you."

He looked at me in amazement, and then glanced around—evidently to discover if there were a convenient way of escape. "You're all straight, are you?" he asked, tapping his forehead; "didn't anybody ever try to take you up?"

"The covers are yours," I continued as though I had not heard him, "the insides are mine and have been for a long time: that is why I proposed buying the covers separately."

I opened his book again. I thought I would see what had been chosen for its pages. And I found there many fine and great things.

"Let me read you this," I said to Mr. Dixon; "it has been mine for a long time. I will not sell it to you. I will give it to you outright. The best things are always given."

Having some gift in imitating the Scotch dialect, I read:

> "November chill blaws loud wi' angry sugh;
>   The short'ning winter day is near a close;
> The miry beasts retreating frae the pleugh;
>   The black'ning trains o' craws to their repose:
> The toil-worn Cotter frae his labour goes,
>   This night his weekly moil is at an end,
> Collects his spades, his mattocks and his hoes,
>   Hoping the morn in ease and rest to spend,
> And weary, o'er the moor, his course does hameward bend."

So I read "The Cotter's Saturday Night." I love the poem very much myself, sometimes reading it aloud, not so much for the tenderness of its message, though I prize that, too, as for the wonder of its music:

"Compar'd with these, Italian trills are tame;
The tickl'd ear no heart-felt raptures raise."

I suppose I showed my feeling in my voice. As I glanced up
from time to time I saw the agent's face change, and his look
deepen and the lips, usually so energetically tense, loosen with
emotion. Surely no poem in all the language conveys so perfectly

the simple love of the home, the quiet joys, hopes, pathos of
those who live close to the soil.

When I had finished—I stopped with the stanza beginning:

"Then homeward all take off their sev'ral way";

the agent turned away his head trying to brave out his emotion. Most of us, Anglo-Saxons, tremble before a tear when we
might fearlessly beard a tiger.

I moved up nearer to the agent and put my hand on his knee;
then I read two or three of the other things I found in his wonderful book. And once I had him laughing and once again I had
the tears in his eyes. Oh, a simple young man, a little crusty without, but soft inside—like the rest of us.

Well, it was amazing once we began talking not of books but
of life, how really eloquent and human he became. From being
a distant and uncomfortable person, he became at once like a

near neighbour and friend. It was strange to me—as I have thought since—how he conveyed to us in a few words the essential emotional note of his life. It was no violin tone, beautifully complex with harmonics, but the clear simple voice of the flute. It spoke of his wife and his baby girl and his home. The very incongruity of detail—he told us how he grew onions in his back yard—added somehow to the homely glamour of the vision which he gave us. The number of his house, the fact that he had a new cottage organ, and that the baby ran away and lost herself in Seventeenth Street—were all, curiously, fabrics of his emotion.

It was beautiful to see commonplace facts grow phosphorescent in the heat of true feeling. How little we may come to know Romance by the cloak she wears and how humble must be he who would surprise the heart of her!

It was, indeed, with an indescribable thrill that I heard him add the details, one by one—the mortgage on his place, now rapidly being paid off, the brother who was a plumber, the mother-in-law who was not a mother-in-law of the comic papers. And finally he showed us the picture of the wife and baby that he had in the cover of his watch; a fat baby with its head resting on its mother's shoulder.

"Mister," he said, "p'raps you think it's fun to ride around the country like I do, and be away from home most of the time. But it ain't. When I think of Minnie and the kid——"

He broke off sharply, as if he had suddenly remembered the shame of such confidences.

"Say," he asked, "what page is that poem on?"

I told him.

"One forty-six," he said. "When I get home I'm going to read that to Minnie. She likes poetry and all such things. And where's that other piece that tells how a man feels when he's lonesome? Say, that fellow knew!"

We had a genuinely good time, the agent and I, and when he finally rose to go, I said:

"Well, I've sold you a new book."

"I see now, mister, what you mean."

I went down the path with him and began to unhitch his horse.

"Let me, let me," he said eagerly.

Then he shook hands, paused a moment awkwardly as if about to say something, then sprang into his buggy without saying it.

When he had taken up his reins he remarked:

"Say! but you'd make an agent! You'd hypnotise 'em."

I recognised it as the greatest compliment he could pay me: the craft compliment.

Then he drove off, but pulled up before he had gone five yards. He turned in his seat, one hand on the back of it, his whip raised.

"Say!" he shouted, and when I walked up he looked at me with fine embarrassment.

"Mister, perhaps you'd accept one of these sets from Dixon free gratis, for nothing."

"I understand," I said, "but you know I'm giving the books to you—and I couldn't take them back again."

"Well," he said, "you're a good one, anyhow. Good-bye again," and then, suddenly, business naturally coming uppermost, he remarked with great enthusiasm:

"You've given me a new idea. *Say,* I'll sell 'em."

"Carry them carefully, man," I called after him; "they are precious."

So I went back to my work, thinking how many fine people there are in this world—if you scratch 'em deep enough.

"Horace 'hefted' it"

V

THE AXE-HELVE

April the 15th.

THIS MORNING I broke my old axe handle. I went out early while the fog still filled the valley and the air was cool and moist as it had come fresh from the filter of the night. I drew a long breath and let my axe fall with all the force I could give it upon a new oak log. I swung it unnecessarily high for the joy of doing it and when it struck it communicated a sharp yet not unpleasant sting to the palms of my hands. The handle broke short off at the point where the helve meets the steel. The blade was driven deep in the oak wood. I suppose I should have regretted my foolishness, but I did not. The handle was old and somewhat worn, and the accident gave me an indefinable satisfaction: the culmination of use, that final destruction which is the complement of great effort.

This feeling was also partly prompted by the thought of the new helve I already had in store, awaiting just such a catastrophe.

36

Having come somewhat painfully by that helve, I really wanted to see it in use.

Last spring, walking in my fields, I looked out along the fences for a well-fitted young hickory tree of thrifty second growth, bare of knots at least head high, without the cracks or fissures of too rapid growth or the doziness of early trans-gression. What I desired was a fine, healthy tree fitted for a great purpose and I looked for it as I would look for a perfect man to save a failing cause. At last I found a sapling growing in one of the sheltered angles of my rail fence. It was set about by dry grass, overhung by a much larger cherry tree, and bear-ing still its withered last year's leaves, worn diaphanous but curled delicately, and of a most beautiful ash gray colour, something like the fabric of a wasp's nest, only yellower. I gave it a shake and it sprung quickly under my hand like the muscle of a good horse. Its bark was smooth and trim, its bole well set and solid.

A perfect tree! So I came up again with my short axe and after clearing away the grass and leaves with which the wind had mulched it, I cut into the clean white roots. I had no twinge of compunction, for was this not fulfillment? Nothing comes of sorrow for worthy sacrifice. When I had laid the tree low, I clipped off the lower branches, snapped off the top with a single clean stroke of the axe, and shouldered as pretty a second-growth sapling stick as anyone ever laid his eyes upon.

I carried it down to my barn and put it on the open rafters over the cow stalls. A cow stable is warm and not too dry, so that a hickory log cures slowly without cracking or checking. There it lay for many weeks. Often I cast my eyes up at it with satisfaction, watching the bark shrink and slightly deepen in colour, and once I climbed up where I could see the minute seams making way in the end of the stick.

In the summer I brought the stick into the house, and put it in the dry, warm storeroom over the kitchen where I keep my seed corn. I do not suppose it really needed further attention, but sometimes when I chanced to go into the storeroom, I turned it over with my foot. I felt a sort of satisfaction in knowing that it was in preparation for service: good material for useful work. So it lay during the autumn and far into the winter.

One cold night when I sat comfortably at my fireplace, listening to the wind outside, and feeling all the ease of a man at peace with himself, my mind took flight to my snowy field sides and I thought of the trees there waiting and resting through the winter. So I came in imagination to the particular corner in the fence where I had cut my hickory sapling. Instantly I started up, much to Harriet's astonishment, and made my way mysteriously up the kitchen stairs. I would not tell what I was after: I felt it a sort of adventure, almost like the joy of seeing a friend long forgotten. It was as if my hickory stick had cried out at last, after long chrysalishood:

"I am ready."

I stood it on end and struck it sharply with my knuckles: it rang out with a certain clear resonance.

"I am ready."

I sniffed at the end of it. It exhaled a peculiar good smell, as of old fields in the autumn.

"I am ready."

So I took it under my arm and carried it down.

"Mercy, what are you going to do?" exclaimed Harriet.

"Deliberately, and with malice aforethought," I responded, "I am going to litter up your floor. I have decided to be reckless. I don't care what happens."

Having made this declaration, which Harriet received with becoming disdain, I laid the log by the fireplace—not too near —and went to fetch a saw, a hammer, a small wedge, and a draw-shave.

I split my log into as fine white sections as a man ever saw— every piece as straight as morality, and without so much as a sliver to mar it. Nothing is so satisfactory as to have a task come out in perfect time and in good order. The little pieces of bark and sawdust I swept scrupulously into the fireplace, looking up from time to time to see how Harriet was taking it. Harriet was still disdainful.

Making an axe-helve is like writing a poem (though I never

wrote one). The material is free enough, but it takes a poet to use it. Some people imagine that any fine thought is poetry, but there was never a greater mistake. A fine thought, to become poetry, must be seasoned in the upper warm garrets of the mind for long and long, then it must be brought down and slowly carved into words, shaped with emotion, polished with love. Else it is no true poem. Some people imagine that any hickory stick will make an axe-helve. But this is far from the truth. When I had whittled away for several evenings with my draw-shave and jack-knife, both of which I keep sharpened to the keenest edge, I found that my work was not progressing as well as I had hoped.

"This is more of a task," I remarked one evening, "than I had imagined."

Harriet, rocking placidly in her arm-chair, was mending a number of pairs of new socks. Poor Harriet! Lacking enough old holes to occupy her energies, she mends holes that may possibly appear. A frugal person!

"Well, David," she said, "I warned you that you could buy a helve cheaper than you could make it."

"So I can buy a book cheaper than I can write it," I responded.

I felt somewhat pleased with my return shot, though I took pains not to show it. I squinted along my hickory stick which was even then beginning to assume, rudely, the outlines of an axe-handle. I had made a prodigious pile of fine white shavings and I was tired, but quite suddenly there came over me a sort of love for that length of wood. I sprung it affectionately over my knee, I rubbed it up and down with my hand, and then I set it in the corner behind the fireplace.

"After all," I said, for I had really been disturbed by Harriet's remark—"after all, power over one thing gives us power over everything. When you mend socks prospectively—into futurity —Harriet, that is an evidence of true greatness."

"Sometimes I think it doesn't pay," remarked Harriet, though she was plainly pleased.

"Pretty good socks," I said, "can be bought for fifteen cents a pair."

Harriet looked at me suspiciously, but I was as sober as the face of nature.

For the next two or three evenings I let the axe-helve stand alone in the corner. I hardly looked at it, though once in a while, when occupied with some other work, I would remember, or rather half remember, that I had a pleasure in store for the evening. The very thought of sharp tools and something to make with them acts upon the imagination with peculiar zest. So we love to employ the keen edge of the mind upon a knotty and difficult subject.

One evening the Scotch preacher came in. We love him very much, though he sometimes makes us laugh—perhaps, in part, because he makes us laugh. Externally he is a sort of human cocoanut, rough, brown, shaggy, but within he has the true milk of human kindness. Some of his qualities touch greatness. His youth was spent in stony places where strong winds blew; the trees where he grew bore thorns; the soil where he dug was full of roots. But the crop was human love. He possesses that quality, unusual in one bred exclusively in the country, of magnanimity toward the unlike. In the country we are tempted to throw stones at strange hats! But to the Scotch preacher every man in one way seems transparent to the soul. He sees the man himself, not his professions any more than his clothes. And I never knew anyone who had such an abiding disbelief in the wickedness of the human soul. Weakness he sees and comforts; wickedness he cannot see.

When he came in I was busy whittling my axe-helve, it being my pleasure at that moment to make long, thin, curly shavings so light that many of them were caught on the hearth and bowled by the draught straight to fiery destruction.

There is a noisy zest about the Scotch preacher: he comes in "stomping" as we say, he must clear his throat, he must strike his hands together; he even seems noisy when he unwinds the thick red tippet which he wears wound many times around his neck. It takes him a long time to unwind it, and he accomplishes the task with many slow gyrations of his enormous rough head. When he sits down he takes merely the edge of the chair, spreads his stout legs apart, sits as straight as a post, and blows his nose with a noise like the falling of a tree.

His interest in everything is prodigious. When he saw what I was doing he launched at once upon an account of the methods of axe-helving, ancient and modern, with true incidents of his childhood.

"Man," he exclaimed, "you've clean forgotten one of the preenciple refinements of the art. When you chop, which hand do you hold down?"

At the moment, I couldn't have told to save my life, so we both got up on our feet and tried.

"It's the right hand down," I decided; "that's natural to me."

"You're a normal right-handed chopper, then," said the Scotch preacher, "as I was thinking. Now let me instruct you in the art. Being right-handed, your helve must bow out—so. No first-class chopper uses a straight handle."

He fell to explaining, with gusto, the mysteries of the bowed handle, and as I listened I felt a new and peculiar interest in my task. This was a final perfection to be accomplished, the finality of technique!

So we sat with our heads together talking helves and axes, axes with single blades and axes with double blades, and hand axes and great choppers' axes, and the science of felling trees, with the true philosophy of the last chip, and arguments as to the best procedure when a log begins to "pinch"—until a listener would have thought that the art of the chopper included the whole philosophy of existence—as indeed it does, if you look at it in that way. Finally I rushed out and brought in my old axe-handle, and we set upon it like true artists, with critical proscription for being a trivial product of machinery.

"Man," exclaimed the preacher, "it has no character. Now your helve here, being the vision of your brain and work of your hands, will interpret the thought of your heart."

Before the Scotch preacher had finished his disquisition upon the art of helve-making and its relations with all other arts, I felt like Peary discovering the Pole.

In the midst of the discourse, while I was soaring high, the Scotch preacher suddenly stopped, sat up, and struck his knee with a tremendous resounding smack.

"Spoons!" he exclaimed.

Harriet and I stopped and looked at him in astonishment.

"Spoons," repeated Harriet.

"Spoons," said the Scotch preacher. "I've not once thought of my errand; and my wife told me to come straight home. I'm more thoughtless every day!"

Then he turned to Harriet:

"I've been sent to borrow some spoons," he said.

"Spoons!" exclaimed Harriet.

"Spoons," answered the Scotch preacher. "We've invited friends for dinner to-morrow, and we must have spoons."

"But why—how—I thought——" began Harriet, still in astonishment.

The Scotch preacher squared around toward her and cleared her throat.

"It's the baptisms," he said: "when a baby is brought for baptism, of course it must have a baptismal gift. What is the best gift for a baby? A spoon. So we present it with a spoon. To-day we discovered we had only three spoons left, and company coming. Man, 'tis a proleefic neighbourhood."

He heaved a great sigh.

Harriet rushed out and made up a package. When she came in I thought it seemed suspiciously large for spoons, but the Scotch preacher having again launched into the lore of the chopper, took it without at first perceiving anything strange. Five minutes after we had closed the door upon him he suddenly returned holding up the package.

"This is an uncommonly heavy package," he remarked; "did I say table-spoons?"

"Go on!" commanded Harriet; "your wife will understand."

"All right—good-bye again," and his sturdy figure soon disappeared in the dark.

"The impractical man!" exclaimed Harriet. "People impose on him."

"Let my axe fall"

"What was in that package, Harriet?"

"Oh, I put in a few jars of jelly and a cake of honey."

After a moment Harriet looked up from her work.

"Do you know the greatest sorrow of the Scotch preacher and his wife?"

"What is it?" I asked.

"They have no chick nor child of their own," said Harriet.

It is prodigious, the amount of work required to make a good axe-helve—I mean to make it according to one's standard. I had times of humorous discouragement and times of high elation when it seemed to me I could not work fast enough. Weeks passed when I did not touch the helve but left it standing quietly in the corner. Once or twice I took it out and walked about with it as a sort of cane, much to the secret amusement, I think, of Harriet. At times Harriet takes a really wicked delight in her superiority.

Early one morning in March the dawn came with a roaring wind, sleety snow drove down over the hill, the house creaked and complained in every clapboard. A blind of one of the upper windows, wrenched loose from its fastenings, was driven shut with such force that it broke a window pane. When I rushed up to discover the meaning of the clatter and to repair the damage, I found the floor covered with peculiar long fragments of glass—the pane having been broken inward from the centre.

"Just what I have wanted," I said to myself.

I selected a few of the best pieces and so eager was I to try them that I got out my axe-helve before breakfast and sat scratching away when Harriet came down.

Nothing equals a bit of broken glass for putting on the final perfect touch to a work of art like an axe-helve. Nothing will so beautifully and delicately trim out the curves of the throat or give a smoother turn to the waist. So with care and an indescribable affection, I added the final touches, trimming the helve until it exactly fitted my hand. Often and often I tried it in pantomime, swinging nobly in the centre of the sitting-room (avoiding the lamp), attentive to the feel of my hand as it ran along the helve. I rubbed it down with fine sandpaper until it fairly shone with whiteness. Then I borrowed a red flannel cloth of Harriet and having added a few drops—not too much—of boiled oil, I rubbed the helve for all I was worth. This I continued for upward of an hour. At that time the axe-helve had taken on a yellowish shade, very clear and beautiful.

I do not think I could have been prouder if I had carved a statue or built a parthenon. I was consumed with vanity; but I set the new helve in the corner with the appearance of utter unconcern.

"There," I remarked, "it's finished."

I watched Harriet out of the corner of my eye: she made as if to speak and then held silent.

That evening friend Horace came in. I was glad to see him. Horace is or was a famous chopper. I placed him at the fireplace where his eye, sooner or later, must fall upon my axe-helve. Oh, I worked out my designs! Presently he saw the helve, picked it up at once and turned it over in his hands. I had a suffocating, not unhumorous, sense of self-consciousness. I know how a poet must feel at hearing his first poem read aloud by some other person who does not know its authorship. I suffer and thrill with the novelist who sees a stranger purchase his book in a book-shop. I felt as though I stood that moment before the Great Judge.

Horace "hefted" it and balanced it, and squinted along it; he rubbed it with his thumb, he rested one end of it on the floor and sprung it roughly.

"David," he said severely, "where did you git this?"

Once when I was a boy I came home with my hair wet. My father asked:

"David, have you been swimming?"

I had exactly the same feeling when Horace asked his question. Now I am, generally speaking, a truthful man. I have written a good deal about the immorality, the unwisdom, the shortsightedness, the sinful wastefulness of a lie. But at that moment, if Harriet had not been present—and that illustrates one of the purposes of society, to bolster up a man's morals—I should have evolved as large and perfect a prevarication as it lay within me to do—cheerfully. But I felt Harriet's moral eye upon me: I was a coward as well as a sinner. I faltered so long that Horace finally looked around at me.

Horace has no poetry in his soul, neither does he understand the philosophy of imperfection nor the art of irregularity.

It is a tender shoot, easily blasted by cold winds, the creative instinct: but persistent. It has many adventitious buds. A late frost destroying the freshness of its early verdure, may be the means of a richer growth in later and more favourable days.

For a week I left my helve standing there in the corner. I did not even look at it. I was slain. I even thought of getting up in the night and putting the helve on the coals—secretly. Then, suddenly, one morning, I took it up not at all tenderly, indeed with a humorous appreciation of my own absurdities, and carried it out into the yard. An axe-helve is not a mere ornament but a thing of sober purpose. The test, after all, of axe-helves is not sublime perfection, but service. We may easily find flaws in the verse of the master—how far the rhythm fails of the final perfect music, how often uncertain the rhyme—but it bears within it, hidden yet evident, that certain incalculable fire which kindles and will continue to kindle the souls of men. The final test is not the perfection of precedent, not regularity, but life, spirit.

It was one of those perfect, sunny, calm mornings that sometimes come in early April: the zest of winter yet in the air, but a promise of summer.

I built a fire of oak chips in the middle of the yard, between two flat stones. I brought out my old axe, and when the fire had burned down somewhat, leaving a foundation of hot coals, I thrust the eye of the axe into the fire. The blade rested on one of the flat stones, and I kept it covered with wet rags in order that it might not heat sufficiently to destroy the temper of the steel. Harriet's old gray hen, a garrulous fowl, came and stood on one leg and looked at me first with one eye and then with the other. She asked innumerable impertinent questions and was generally disagreeable.

"I am sorry, madam," I said finally, "but I have grown adamant to criticism. I have done my work as well as it lies in me to do it. It is the part of sanity to throw it aside without compunction. A work must prove itself. Shoo!"

I said this with such conclusiveness and vigour that the critical old hen departed hastily with ruffled feathers.

So I sat there in the glorious perfection of the forenoon, the great day open around me, a few small clouds abroad in the highest sky, and all the earth radiant with sunshine. The last snow of winter was gone, the sap ran in the trees, the cows fed further afield.

When the eye of the axe was sufficiently expanded by the heat I drew it quickly from the fire and drove home the helve which I had already whittled down to the exact size. I had a hickory wedge prepared, and it was the work of ten seconds to drive it into the cleft at the lower end of the helve until the eye of the axe was completely and perfectly filled. Upon cooling the steel shrunk upon the wood, clasping it with such firmness that nothing short of fire could ever dislodge it. Then, carefully, with knife and sandpaper I polished off the wood around the steel of the axe until I had made as good a job of it as lay within my power.

So I carried the axe to my log-pile. I swung it above my head and the feel of it was good in my hands. The blade struck deep into the oak wood. And I said to myself with satisfaction:

"It serves the purpose."

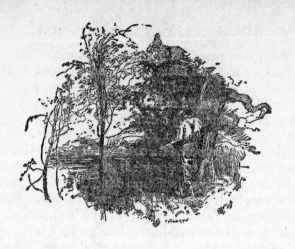

VI

THE MARSH DITCH

"If the day and the night are such that you greet them with joy and life emits a fragrance like flowers and sweet-smelling herbs—is more elastic, more starry, more immortal—that is your Success."

IN ALL THE DAYS of my life I have never been so well content as I am this spring. Last summer I thought I was happy, the fall gave me a finality of satisfaction, the winter imparted perspective, but spring conveys a wholly new sense of life, a quickening the like of which I never before experienced. It seems to me that everything in the world is more interesting, more vital, more significant. I feel like "waving aside all roofs," in the way of Le Sage's Asmodeus.

I even cease to fear Mrs. Horace, who is quite the most formidable person in this neighbourhood. She is so avaricious in the saving of souls—and so covetous of mine, which I wish especially to retain. When I see her coming across the hill I feel like running and hiding, and if I were as bold as a boy, I should do it, but being a grown-up coward I remain and dissemble.

She came over this morning. When I beheld her afar off, I drew a long breath: "One thousand," I quoted to myself, "shall flee at the rebuke of one."

In calmness I waited. She came with colours flying and hurled her biblical lance. When I withstood the shock with unexpected jauntiness, for I usually fall dead at once, she looked at me with severity and said:

"Mr. Grayson, you are a materialist."

"You have shot me with a name," I replied. "I am unhurt."

It would be impossible to slay me on a day like this. On a day like this I am immortal.

It comes to me as the wonder of wonders, these spring days, how surely everything, spiritual as well as material, proceeds out of the earth. I have times of sheer Paganism when I could bow and touch my face to the warm bare soil. We are so often ashamed of the Earth—the soil of it, the sweat of it, the good common coarseness of it. To us in our fine raiment and soft manners, it seems indelicate. Instead of seeking that association with the earth which is the renewal of life, we devise ourselves distant palaces and seek strange pleasures. How often and sadly we repeat the life story of the yellow dodder of the moist lanes of my lower farm. It springs up fresh and clean from the earth itself, and spreads its clinging viny stems over the hospitable wild balsam and golden rod. In a week's time, having reached the warm sunshine of the upper air, it forgets its humble beginnings. Its roots wither swiftly and die out, but the sickly yellow stems continue to flourish and spread, drawing their nourishment not from the soil itself, but by strangling and sucking the life juices of the hosts on which it feeds. I have seen whole byways covered thus with yellow dodder—rootless, leafless, parasitic—reaching up to the sunlight, quite cutting off and smothering the plants which gave it life. A week or two it flourishes and then most of it perishes miserably. So many of us come to be like that: so much of our civilization is like that. Men and women there are—the pity of it—who, eating plentifully, have never themselves taken a mouthful from the earth. They have never known a moment's real life of their own.

Lying up to the sun in warmth and comfort—but leafless—they do not think of the hosts under them, smothered, strangled, starved. They take *nothing* at first hand. They experience described emotion, and think prepared thoughts. They live not in life, but in printed reports of life. They gather the odour of odours, not the odour itself: they do not hear, they overhear. A poor, sad, second-rate existence!

Bring out your social remedies! They will fail, they will fail, every one, until each man has his feet somewhere upon the soil!

My wild plum trees grow in the coarse earth, among excrementitious mould, a physical life which finally blossoms and exhales its perfect odour: which ultimately bears the seed of its immortality.

Human happiness is the true odour of growth, the sweet exhalation of work: and the seed of human immortality is borne secretly within the coarse and mortal husk. So many of us crave the odour without cultivating the earthly growth from which it proceeds: so many, wasting mortality, expect immortality!

——"Why," asks Charles Baxter, "do you always put the end of your stories first?"

"You may be thankful," I replied, "that I do not make my remarks all endings. Endings are so much more interesting than beginnings."

Without looking up from the buggy he was mending, Charles Baxter intimated that my way had at least one advantage: one always knew, he said, that I really had an end in view—and hope deferred, he said——

——How surely, soundly, deeply, the physical underlies the spiritual. This morning I was up and out at half-past four, as perfect a morning as I ever saw: mists yet huddled in the low spots, the sun coming up over the hill, and all the earth fresh with moisture, sweet with good odours, and musical with early bird-notes.

It is the time of the spring just after the last seeding and before the early haying: a catch-breath in the farmer's year. I have been utilising it in digging a drainage ditch at the lower end of my farm. A spot of marsh grass and blue flags occupies nearly half an acre of good land and I have been planning ever since I bought the place to open a drain from its lower edge to the creek, supplementing it in the field above, if necessary, with submerged tiling. I surveyed it carefully several weeks ago and drew plans and contours of the work as though it were an inter-oceanic canal. I find it a real delight to work out in the earth itself the details of the drawing.

This morning, after hastening with the chores, I took my bag and my spade on my shoulder and set off (in rubber boots) for the ditch. My way lay along the margin of my cornfield in the deep grass. On my right as I walked was the old rail fence full of thrifty young hickory and cherry trees with here and there a clump of blackberry bushes. The trees beyond the fence cut off the sunrise so that I walked in the cool broad shadows. On my left stretched the cornfield of my planting, the young corn well up, very attractive and hopeful, my really frightful scarecrow standing guard on the knoll, a wisp of straw sticking up through a hole in his hat and his crooked thumbs turned down—"No mercy."

"Surely no corn ever before grew like this," I said to myself. "To-morrow I must begin cultivating again."

So I looked up and about me—not to miss anything of the morning—and I drew in a good big breath and I thought the world had never been so open to my senses.

I wonder why it is that the sense of smell is so commonly under-regarded. To me it is the source of some of my greatest pleasures. No one of the senses is more often allied with robustity of physical health. A man who smells acutely may be set down as enjoying that which is normal, plain, wholesome. He does not require seasoning: the ordinary earth is good enough for him. He is likely to be sane—which means sound, healthy—in his outlook upon life.

Of all hours of the day there is none like the early morning for downright good odours—the morning before eating. Fresh from sleep and unclogged with food a man's senses cut like knives. The whole world comes in upon him. A still morning is best, for the mists and the moisture seem to retain the odours which they have distilled through the night. Upon a breezy morning one is likely to get a single predominant odour as of clover when the wind blows across a hay field or of apple blossoms when the wind comes through the orchard, but upon a perfectly still morning, it is wonderful how the odours arrange themselves in upright strata, so that one walking passes through them as from room to room in a marvellous temple of fragrance. (I should have said, I think, if I had not been on my way to dig a ditch, that it was like turning the leaves of some delicate volume of lyrics!)

So it was this morning. As I walked along the margin of my field I was conscious, at first, coming within the shadows of the wood, of the cool, heavy aroma which one associates with the night: as of moist woods and earth mould. The penetrating scent of the night remains long after the sights and sounds of it have disappeared. In sunny spots I had the fragrance of the open cornfield, the aromatic breath of the brown earth, giving curiously the sense of fecundity—a warm, generous odour of daylight and sunshine. Down the field, toward the corner, cutting in sharply, as though a door opened (or a page turned to another lyric), came the cloying, sweet fragrance of wild crab-apple blossoms, almost tropical in their richness, and below that, as I came to my work, the thin acrid smell of the marsh, the place of the rushes and the flags and the frogs.

How few of us really use our senses! I mean give ourselves fully at any time to the occupation of the senses. We do not expect to understand a treatise on Economics without applying our minds to it, nor can we really smell or hear or see or feel without every faculty alert. Through sheer indolence we miss half the joy of the world!

Often as I work I stop to see: really see: see everything, or to listen, and it is the wonder of wonders, how much there is in this old world which we never dreamed of, how many beautiful, curious, interesting sights and sounds there are which ordinarily make no impression upon our clogged, overfed and preoccupied minds. I have also had the feeling—it may be unscientific but it is comforting—that any man might see like an Indian or smell like a hound if he gave to the senses the brains which the Indian and the hound apply to them. And I'm pretty sure about the Indian! It is marvellous what a man can do when he puts his entire mind upon one faculty and bears down hard.

So I walked this morning, not hearing nor seeing, but smelling. Without desiring to stir up strife among the peaceful senses, there is this further marvel of the sense of smell. No other possesses such an after-call. Sight preserves pictures: the complete view of the aspect of objects, but it is photographic and external. Hearing deals in echoes, but the sense of smell, while saving no vision of a place or a person, will re-create in a way almost miraculous the inner *emotion* of a particular time or place. I know of nothing that will so "create an appetite under the ribs of death."

Only a short time ago I passed an open doorway in the town. I was busy with errands, my mind fully engaged, but suddenly I caught an odour from somewhere within the building I was passing. I stopped! It was as if in that moment I lost twenty years of my life: I was a boy again, living and feeling a particular instant at the time of my father's death. Every emotion of that occasion, not recalled in years, returned to me sharply and clearly as though I experienced it for the first time. It was a peculiar emotion: the first time I had ever felt the oppression of space—can I describe it?—the utter bigness of the world and the aloofness of myself, a little boy, within it—now that my father was gone. It was not at that moment sorrow, nor remorse, nor love: it was an inexpressible cold terror—that anywhere I might go in the world, I should still be alone!

And there I stood, a man grown, shaking in the sunshine with that old boyish emotion brought back to me by an odour! Often and often have I known this strange rekindling of dead fires. And I have thought how, if our senses were really perfect, we might lose nothing, out of our lives: neither sights, nor sounds, nor emotions: a sort of mortal immortality. Was not Shakespeare great because he lost less of the savings of his senses than other men? What a wonderful seer, hearer, smeller, taster, feeler, he must have been—and how, all the time, his mind must have played upon the gatherings of his senses! All scenes, all men, the very turn of a head, the exact sound of a voice, the taste of food, the feel of the world—all the emotions of his life must he have had there before him as he wrote, his great mind playing upon them, reconstructing, re-creating and putting them down hot upon his pages. There is nothing strange about great men; they are like us, only deeper, higher, broader: they think as we do, but with more intensity: they suffer as we do, more keenly: they love as we do, more tenderly.

I may be over-glorifying the sense of smell, but it is only because I walked this morning in a world of odours. The greatest of the senses, of course, is not smell or hearing, but sight. What would not any man exchange for that: for the faces one loves, for the scenes one holds most dear, for all that is beautiful and changeable and beyond description? The Scotch Preacher says that the saddest lines in all literature are those of Milton, writing of his blindness.

> *"Seasons return; but not to me returns*
> *Day, or the sweet approach of even or morn,*
> *Or sight of vernal bloom or Summer's rose,*
> *Or flocks, or herds, or human face divine."*

——I have wandered a long way from ditch-digging, but not wholly without intention. Sooner or later I try to get back into the main road. I throw down my spade in the wet trampled grass at the edge of the ditch. I take off my coat and hang it over a limb of the little hawthorn tree. I put my bag near it. I roll up the sleeves of my flannel shirt: I give my hat a twirl: I'm ready for work.

——The senses are the tools by which we lay hold upon the world: they are the implements of consciousness and growth. So long as they are used upon the good earth—used to wholesome weariness—they remain healthy, they yield enjoyment, they nourish growth; but let them once be removed from their natural employment and they turn and feed upon themselves, they seek the stimulation of luxury, they wallow in their own corruption, and finally, worn out, perish from off the earth which they have not appreciated. Vice is ever the senses gone astray.

——So I dug. There is something fine in hard physical labour, straight ahead: no brain used, just muscles. I stood ankle-deep in the cool water: every spadeful came out with a smack, and as I turned it over at the edge of the ditch small turgid rivulets coursed back again. I did not think of anything in particular. I dug. A peculiar joy attends the very pull of the muscles. I drove the spade home with one foot, then I bent and lifted and turned with a sort of physical satisfaction difficult to describe. At first

I had the cool of the morning, but by seven o'clock the day was hot enough! I opened the breast of my shirt, gave my sleeves another roll, and went at it again for half an hour, until I dripped with perspiration.

"I will knock off," I said, so I used my spade as a ladder and climbed out of the ditch. Being very thirsty, I walked down through the marshy valley to the clump of alders which grows along the creek. I followed a cow-path through the thicket and came to the creek side, where I knelt on a log and took a good long drink. Then I soused my head in the cool stream, dashed the water upon my arms and came up dripping and gasping! Oh, but it was fine!

So I came back to the hawthorn tree, where I sat down comfortably and stretched my legs. There is a poem in stretched legs—after hard digging—but I can't write it, though I can feel it! I got my bag and took out a half loaf of Harriet's bread. Breaking off big crude pieces, I ate it there in the shade. How rarely we taste the real taste of bread! We disguise it with butter, we toast it, we eat it with milk or fruit. We even soak it with gravy (here in the country where we aren't at all polite—but very comfortable), so that we never get the downright delicious taste of the bread itself. I was hungry this morning and I ate my half loaf to the last crumb—and wanted more. Then I lay down for a moment in the shade and looked up into the sky through the thin outer branches of the hawthorn. A turkey buzzard was lazily circling cloud-high above me: a frog boomed intermittently from the little marsh, and there were bees at work in the blossoms.

——I had another drink at the creek and went back somewhat reluctantly, I confess, to the work. It was hot, and the first joy of effort had worn off. But the ditch was to be dug and I went at it again. One becomes a sort of machine—unthinking, mechanical: and yet intense physical work, though making no immediate impression on the mind, often lingers in the consciousness. I find that sometimes I can remember and enjoy for long afterward every separate step in a task.

It is curious, hard physical labour! One actually stops thinking. I often work long without any thought whatever, so far as I know, save that connected with the monotonous repetition of the labour itself—down with the spade, out with it, up with it, over with it—and repeat. And yet sometimes—mostly in the forenoon when I am not at all tired—I will suddenly have a sense as of the world opening around me—a sense of its beauty and its meanings—giving me a peculiar deep happiness, that is near complete content——

Happiness, I have discovered, is nearly always a rebound from hard work. It is one of the follies of men to imagine that they can enjoy mere thought, or emotion, or sentiment! As well try to eat beauty! For happiness must be tricked! She loves to see men at work. She loves sweat, weariness, self-sacrifice. She will be found not in palaces but lurking in cornfields and factories and hovering over littered desks: she crowns the unconscious head of the busy child. If you look up suddenly from hard work you will see her, but if you look too long she fades sorrowfully away.

——Down toward the town there is a little factory for barrel hoops and staves. It has one of the most musical whistles I ever heard in my life. It toots at exactly twelve o'clock: blessed sound! The last half-hour at ditch-digging is a hard, slow pull. I'm warm and tired, but I stick down to it and wait with straining ear for the music. At the very first note of that whistle I drop my spade. I will even empty out a load of dirt half way up rather than expend another ounce of energy; and I spring out of the ditch and start for home with a single desire in my heart —or possibly lower down. And Harriet, standing in the doorway, seems to me a sort of angel—a culinary angel!

Talk of joy: there may be things better than beef stew and baked potatoes and homemade bread—there may be——

VII

AN ARGUMENT
WITH A MILLIONNAIRE

"Let the mighty and great
Roll in splendour and state,
I envy them not, I declare it.
I eat my own lamb,
My own chicken and ham,
I shear my own sheep and wear it.

I have lawns, I have bowers,
I have fruits, I have flowers.
The lark is my morning charmer;
So you jolly dogs now,
Here's God bless the plow—
Long life and content to the farmer."
—RHYME ON AN OLD PITCHER OF ENGLISH POTTERY.

I HAVE BEEN HEARING of John Starkweather ever since I came here. He is a most important personage in this community. He is rich. Horace especially loves to talk about him. Give Horace half a chance, whether the subject be pigs or churches, and he will break in somewhere with the remark: "As I was saying to

58

Mr. Starkweather—" or, "Mr. Starkweather says to me—" How we love to shine by reflected glory! Even Harriet has not gone unscathed; she, too, has been affected by the bacillus of admiration. She has wanted to know several times if I saw John Starkweather drive by: "the finest span of horses in this country," she says, and *did* you see his daughter?" Much other information concerning the Starkweather household, culinary and otherwise, is current among our hills. We know accurately the number of Mr. Starkweather's bedrooms, we can tell how much coal he uses in winter and how many tons of ice in summer, and upon such important premises we argue his riches.

Several times I have passed John Starkweather's home. It lies between my farm and the town, though not on the direct road, and it is really beautiful with the groomed and guided beauty possible to wealth. A stately old house with a huge end chimney of red brick stands with dignity well back from the road; round about lie pleasant lawns that once were cornfields: and there are drives and walks and exotic shrubs. At first, loving my own hills so well, I was puzzled to understand why I should also enjoy Starkweather's groomed surroundings. But it came to me that after all, much as we may love wildness, we are not wild, nor our works. What more artificial than a house, or a barn, or a fence? And the greater and more formal the house, the more formal indeed must be the nearer natural environments. Perhaps the hand of man might well have been less evident in developing the surroundings of the Starkweather home—for art, dealing with nature, is so often too accomplished!

But I enjoy the Starkweather place and as I look in from the road, I sometimes think to myself with satisfaction: "Here is this rich man who has paid his thousands to make the beauty which I pass and take for nothing—and having taken, leave as much behind." And I wonder sometimes whether he, inside his fences, gets more joy of it than I, who walk the roads outside. Anyway, I am grateful to him for using his riches so much to my advantage.

On fine mornings John Starkweather sometimes comes out in his slippers, bare-headed, his white vest gleaming in the sunshine, and walks slowly around his garden. Charles Baxter says that on these occasions he is asking his gardener the names of the vegetables. However that may be, he has seemed to our community the very incarnation of contentment and prosperity —his position the acme of desirability.

What was my astonishment, then, the other morning to see John Starkweather coming down the pasture lane through my farm. I knew him afar off, though I had never met him. May I express the inexpressible when I say he had a rich look; he walked rich, there was richness in the confident crook of his elbow, and in the positive twitch of the stick he carried: a man accustomed to having doors opened before he knocked. I stood there a moment and looked up the hill at him, and I felt that profound curiosity which every one of us feels every day of his life to know something of the inner impulses which stir his nearest neighbour. I should have liked to know John Starkweather; but I thought to myself as I have thought so many times how surely one comes finally to imitate his surroundings. A farmer grows to be a part of his farm; the sawdust on his coat is not the most distinctive insignia of the carpenter; the poet writes his truest lines upon his own countenance. People passing in my road take me to be a part of this natural scene. I suppose I seem to them as a partridge squatting among dry grass and leaves, so like the grass and leaves as to be invisible. We all come to be marked upon by nature and dismissed—how carelessly!—as genera or species. And is it not the primal struggle of man to escape classification, to form new differentiations?

Sometimes—I confess it—when I see one passing in my road, I feel like hailing him and saying:

"Friend, I am not all farmer. I, too, am a person; I am different and curious. I am full of red blood, I like people, all sorts of people; if you are not interested in me, at least I am intensely interested in you. Come over now and let's talk!"

So we are all of us calling and calling across the incalculable gulfs which separate us even from our nearest friends!

Once or twice this feeling has been so real to me that I've been near to the point of hailing utter strangers—only to be instantly overcome with a sense of the humorous absurdity of such an enterprise. So I laugh it off and I say to myself:

"Steady now: the man is going to town to sell a pig; he is coming back with ten pounds of sugar, five of salt pork, a can of coffee and some new blades for his mowing machine. He hasn't time for talk"—and so I come down with a bump to my digging, or hoeing, or chopping, or whatever it is.

——Here I've left John Starkweather in my pasture while I remark to the extent of a page or two that I didn't expect him to see me when he went by.

I assumed that he was out for a walk, perhaps to enliven a worn appetite (do you know, confidentially, I've had some pleasure in times past in reflecting upon the jaded appetites of millionnaires!), and that he would pass out by my lane to the country road; but instead of that, what should he do but climb the yard fence and walk over toward the barn where I was at work.

Perhaps I was not consumed with excitement: here was fresh adventure!

"A farmer," I said to myself with exultation, "has only to wait long enough and all the world comes his way."

I had just begun to grease my farm wagon and was experiencing some difficulty in lifting and steadying the heavy rear axle while I took off the wheel. I kept busily at work, pretending (such is the perversity of the human mind) that I did not see Mr. Starkweather. He stood for a moment watching me; then he said:

"Good morning, sir."

I looked up and said:

"Oh, good morning!"

"Nice little farm you have here."

"It's enough for me," I replied. I did not especially like the "little." One is human.

Then I had an absurd inspiration: he stood there so trim and jaunty and prosperous. So rich! I had a good look at him. He was dressed in a woollen jacket coat, knee-trousers and leggins; on his head he wore a jaunty, cocky little Scotch cap; a man, I should judge, about fifty years old, well-fed and hearty in appearance, with grayish hair and a good-humoured eye. I acted on my inspiration:

"You've arrived," I said, "at the psychological moment."

"How's that?"

"Take hold here and help me lift this axle and steady it. I'm having a hard time of it."

The look of astonishment in his countenance was beautiful to see.

For a moment failure stared me in the face. His expression said with emphasis: "Perhaps you don't know who I am." But I looked at him with the greatest good feeling and my expression said, or I meant it to say: "To be sure I don't: and what difference does it make, anyway!"

"You take hold there," I said, without waiting for him to catch his breath, "and I'll get hold here. Together we can easily get the wheel off."

Without a word he set his cane against the barn and bent his back, up came the axle and I propped it with a board.

"Now," I said, "you hang on there and steady it while I get the wheel off"—though, indeed, it didn't really need much steadying.

As I straightened up, whom should I see but Harriet standing transfixed in the pathway half way down to the barn, transfixed with horror. She had recognised John Starkweather and had heard at least part of what I said to him, and the vision of that important man bending his back to help lift the axle of my old wagon was too terrible! She caught my eye and pointed and mouthed. When I smiled and nodded, John Starkweather straightened up and looked around.

"Don't, on your life," I warned, "let go of that axle."

He held on and Harriet turned and retreated ingloriously. John Starkweather's face was a study!

"Did you ever grease a wagon?" I asked him genially.

"Never," he said.

"There's more of an art in it than you think," I said, and as I worked I talked to him of the lore of axle-grease and showed him exactly how to put it on—neither too much nor too little, and so that it would distribute itself evenly when the wheel was replaced.

"There's a right way of doing everything," I observed.

"That's so," said John Starkweather: "if I could only get workmen that believed it."

By that time I could see that he was beginning to be interested. I put back the wheel, gave it a light turn and screwed on the nut. He helped me with the other end of the axle with all good humour.

"Perhaps," I said, as engagingly as I knew how, "you'd like to try the art yourself? You take the grease this time and I'll steady the wagon."

"All right!" he said, laughing, "I'm in for anything."

He took the grease box and the paddle—less gingerly than I thought he would.

"Is that right?" he demanded, and so he put on the grease. And oh, it was good to see Harriet in the doorway!

"Steady there," I said, "not so much at the end: now put the box down on the reach."

And so together we greased the wagon, talking all the time in the friendliest way. I actually believe that he was having a pretty good time. At least it had the virtue of unexpectedness. He wasn't bored!

When he had finished we both straightened our backs and looked at each other. There was a twinkle in his eye: then we both laughed. "He's all right," I said to myself. I held up my hands, then he held up his: it was hardly necessary to prove that wagon-greasing was not a delicate operation.

"It's a good wholesome sign," I said, "but it'll come off. Do you happen to remember a story of Tolstoi's called 'Ivan the Fool'?"

("What is a farmer doing quoting Tolstoi!" remarked his countenance—though he said not a word.)

"In the kingdom of Ivan, you remember," I said, "it was the rule that whoever had hard places on his hands came to table, but whoever had not must eat what the others left."

Thus I led him up to the back steps and poured him a basin of hot water—which I brought myself from the kitchen, Harriet having marvellously and completely disappeared. We both washed our hands, talking with great good humour.

When we had finished I said:

"Sit down, friend, if you've time, and let's talk."

So he sat down on one of the logs of my woodpile: a solid sort of man, rather warm after his recent activities. He looked me over with some interest and, I thought, friendliness.

"Why does a man like you," he asked finally, "waste himself on a little farm back here in the country?"

For a single instant I came nearer to being angry than I have been for a long time. *Waste* myself! So we are judged without knowledge. I had a sudden impulse to demolish him (if I could) with the nearest sarcasms I could lay hand to. He was so sure of himself! "Oh well," I thought, with vainglorious superiority, "he doesn't know." So I said:

"What would you have me be—a millionnaire?"

He smiled, but with a sort of sincerity.

"You might be," he said: "who can tell!"

I laughed outright: the humour of it struck me as delicious. Here I had been, ever since I first heard of John Starkweather, rather gloating over him as a poor suffering millionnaire (of course millionnaires *are* unhappy), and there he sat, ruddy of face and hearty of body, pitying *me* for a poor unfortunate farmer back here in the country! Curious, this human nature of ours, isn't it? But how infinitely beguiling!

So I sat down beside Mr. Starkweather on the log and crossed my legs. I felt as though I had set foot in a new country.

"Would you really advise me," I asked, "to start in to be a millionnaire?"

He chuckled:

"Well, that's one way of putting it. Hitch your wagon to a star; but begin by making a few dollars more a year than you spend. When I began——" he stopped short with an amused smile, remembering that I did not know who he was.

"Of course," I said, "I understand that."

"What would you have me be—a millionnaire?"

THOMAS FOGARTY

"A man must begin small"—he was on pleasant ground—"and anywhere he likes, a few dollars here, a few there. He must work hard, he must save, he must be both bold and cautious. I know a man who began when he was about your age with total assets of ten dollars and a good digestion. He's now considered a fairly wealthy man. He has a home in the city, a place in the country, and he goes to Europe when he likes. He has so arranged his affairs that young men do most of the work and he draws the dividends—and all in a little more than twenty years. I made every single cent—but as I said, it's a penny business to start with. The point is, I like to see young men ambitious."

"Ambitious," I asked, "for what?"

"Why, to rise in the world; to get ahead."

"I know you'll pardon me," I said, "for appearing to cross-examine you, but I'm tremendously interested in these things. What do you mean by rising? And who am I to get ahead of?"

He looked at me in astonishment, and with evident impatience at my consummate stupidity.

"I am serious," I said. "I really want to make the best I can of my life. It's the only one I've got."

"See here," he said: "let us say you clear up five hundred a year from this farm——"

"You exaggerate—" I interrupted.

"Do I?" he laughed; "that makes my case all the better. Now, isn't it possible to rise from that? Couldn't you make a thousand or five thousand or even fifty thousand a year?"

It seems an unanswerable argument: fifty thousand dollars!

"I suppose I might," I said, "but do you think I'd be any better off or happier with fifty thousand a year than I am now? You see, I like all these surroundings better than any other place I ever knew. That old green hill over there with the oak on it is an intimate friend of mine. I have a good cornfield in which every year I work miracles. I've a cow and a horse, and a few pigs. I have a comfortable home. My appetite is perfect, and I have plenty of food to gratify it. I sleep every night like a boy, for I haven't a trouble in this world to disturb me. I enjoy the mornings here in the country: and the evenings are pleasant.

Some of my neighbours have come to be my good friends. I like them and I am pretty sure they like me. Inside the house there I have the best books ever written and I have time in the evenings to read them—I mean *really* read them. Now the question is, would I be any better off, or any happier, if I had fifty thousand a year?"

John Starkweather laughed.

"Well, sir," he said, "I see I've made the acquaintance of a philosopher."

"Let us say," I continued, "that you are willing to invest twenty years of your life in a million dollars." ("Merely an illustration," said John Starkweather.) "You have it where you can put it in the bank and take it out again, or you can give it form in houses, yachts, and other things. Now twenty years of my life—to me—is worth more than a million dollars. I simply can't afford to sell it for that. I prefer to invest it, as somebody or other has said, unearned in life. I've always had a liking for intangible properties."

"See here," said John Starkweather, "you are taking a narrow view of life. You are making your own pleasure the only standard. Shouldn't a man make the most of the talents given him? Hasn't he a duty to society?"

"Now you are shifting your ground," I said, "from the question of personal satisfaction to that of duty. That concerns me, too. Let me ask you: Isn't it important to society that this piece of earth be plowed and cultivated?"

"Yes, but——"

"Isn't it honest and useful work?"

"Of course."

"Isn't it important that it shall not only be done, but well done?"

"Certainly."

"It takes all there is in a good man," I said, "to be a good farmer."

"But the point is," he argued, "might not the same faculties applied to other things yield better and bigger results?"

"That is a problem, of course," I said. "I tried money-making once—in a city—and I was unsuccessful and unhappy; here I am both successful and happy. I suppose I was one of the young men who did the work while some millionnaire drew the dividends." (I was cutting close, and I didn't venture to look at him). "No doubt he had his houses and yachts and went to Europe when he liked. I know I lived upstairs—back—where there wasn't a tree to be seen, or a spear of green grass, or a hill, or a brook: only smoke and chimneys and littered roofs. Lord be thanked for my escape! Sometimes I think that Success has formed a silent conspiracy against Youth. Success holds up a single glittering apple and bids Youth strip and run for it; and Youth runs and Success still holds the apple."

John Starkweather said nothing.

"Yes," I said, "there are duties. We realise, we farmers, that we must produce more than we ourselves can eat or wear or burn. We realise that we are the foundation: we connect human life with the earth. We dig and plant and produce, and having eaten at the first table ourselves, we pass what is left to the bankers and millionnaires. Did you ever think, stranger, that most of the wars of the world have been fought for the control of this farmer's second table? Have you thought that the surplus of wheat and corn and cotton is what the railroads are struggling to carry? Upon our surplus run all the factories and mills; a little of it gathered in cash makes a millionnaire. But we farmers, we sit back comfortably after dinner, and joke with our wives and play with our babies, and let all the rest of you fight for the crumbs that fall from our abundant tables. If once we really cared and got up and shook ourselves, and said to the maid: 'Here, child, don't waste the crusts: gather 'em up and to-morrow we'll have a cottage pudding,' where in the world would all the millionnaires be?"

Oh, I tell you, I waxed eloquent. I couldn't let John Starkweather, or any other man, get away with the conviction that a millionnaire is better than a farmer. "Moreover," I said, "think of the position of the millionnaire. He spends his time playing not with life, but with the symbols of life, whether cash or houses. Any day the symbols may change; a little war may happen along, there may be a defective flue or a western breeze, or even a panic because the farmers aren't scattering as many crumbs as usual (they call it crop failure, but I've noticed that the farmers still continue to have plenty to eat) and then what happens to your millionnaire? Not knowing how to produce anything himself, he would starve to death if there were not always, somewhere, a farmer to take him up to the table."

"You're making a strong case," laughed John Starkweather.

"Strong!" I said. "It is simply wonderful what a leverage upon society a few acres of land, a cow, a pig or two, and a span of horses gives a man. I'm ridiculously independent. I'd be the hardest sort of a man to dislodge or crush. I tell you, my friend, a farmer is like an oak, his roots strike deep in the soil, he draws a sufficiency of food from the earth itself, he breathes the free air around him, his thirst is quenched by heaven itself—and there's no tax on sunshine."

I paused for very lack of breath. John Starkweather was laughing.

"When you commiserate me, therefore" ("I'm sure I shall never do it again," said John Starkweather)—"when you commiserate me, therefore, and advise me to rise, you must give me really good reasons for changing my occupation and becoming a millionnaire. You must prove to me that I can be more independent, more honest, more useful as a millionnaire, and that I shall have better and truer friends!"

John Starkweather looked around at me (I knew I had been absurdly eager and I was rather ashamed of myself) and put his hand on my knee (he has a wonderfully fine eye!).

"I don't believe," he said, "you'd have any truer friends."

"Anyway," I said repentantly, "I'll admit that millionnaires have their place—at present I wouldn't do entirely away with them, though I do think they'd enjoy farming better. And if I were to select a millionnaire for all the best things I know, I should certainly choose you, Mr. Starkweather."

He jumped up.

"You know who I am?" he asked.

I nodded.

"And you knew all the time?"

I nodded.

"Well, you're a good one!"

We both laughed and fell to talking with the greatest friendliness. I led him down my garden to show him my prize pie-plant, of which I am enormously proud, and I pulled for him some of the finest stalks I could find.

"Take it home," I said, "it makes the best pies of any pie-plant in this country."

He took it under his arm.

"I want you to come over and see me the first chance you get," he said. "I'm going to prove to you by physical demonstration that it's better sport to be a millionnaire than a farmer—not that I am a millionnaire: I'm only accepting the reputation you give me."

So I walked with him down to the lane.

"Let me know when you grease up again," he said, "and I'll come over."

So we shook hands: and he set off sturdily down the road with the pie-plant leaves waving cheerfully over his shoulder.

"Somehow, and suddenly, I was a boy again"

VIII

A BOY AND A PREACHER

THIS MORNING I went to church with Harriet. I usually have some excuse for not going, but this morning I had them out one by one and they were altogether so shabby that I decided not to use them. So I put on my stiff shirt and Harriet came out in her best black cape with the silk fringes. She looked so immaculate, so ruddy, so cheerfully sober (for Sunday) that I was reconciled to the idea of driving her up to the church. And I am glad I went, for the experience I had.

It was an ideal summer Sunday: sunshiny, clear and still. I believe if I had been some Rip Van Winkle waking after twenty years' sleep I should have known it for Sunday. Away off over the hill somewhere we could hear a lazy farm boy singing at the top of his voice: the higher cadences of his song reached us pleasantly through the still air. The hens sitting near the lane fence, fluffing the dust over their backs, were holding a small

71

and talkative service of their own. As we turned into the main road we saw the Patterson children on their way to church, all the little girls in Sunday ribbons, and all the little boys very uncomfortable in knit stockings.

"It seems a pity to go to church on a day like this," I said to Harriet.

"A pity!" she exclaimed. "Could anything be more appropriate?"

Harriet is good because she can't help it. Poor woman!—but I haven't any pity for her.

It sometimes seems to me the more worshipful I feel the less I want to go to church. I don't know why it is, but these forms, simple though they are, trouble me. The moment an emotion, especially a religious emotion, becomes an institution, it somehow loses life. True emotion is rare and costly and that which is awakened from without never rises to the height of that which springs spontaneously from within.

Back of the church stands a long low shed where we tied our horse. A number of other buggies were already there, several women were standing in groups, preening their feathers, a neighbour of ours who has a tremendous bass voice was talking to a friend:

"Yas, oats is showing up well, but wheat is backward."

His voice, which he was evidently trying to subdue for Sunday, boomed through the still air. So we walked among the trees to the door of the church. A smiling elder, in an unaccustomed long coat, bowed and greeted us. As we went in there was an odour of cushions and our footsteps on the wooden floor echoed in the warm emptiness of the church. The Scotch preacher was finding his place in the big Bible; he stood solid and shaggy behind the yellow oak pulpit, a peculiar professional look on his face. In the pulpit the Scotch preacher is too much minister, too little man. He is best down among us with his hand in ours. He is a sort of human solvent. Is there a twisted and hardened heart in the community he beams upon it from his cheerful eye, he speaks out of his great charity, he gives the friendly pressure of his large hand, and that hardened heart dissolves and its frozen hopelessness loses itself in tears. So he goes through life, seeming always to understand. He is not surprised by wickedness nor discouraged by weakness: he is so sure of a greater Strength!

But I must come to my experience, which I am almost tempted to call a resurrection—the resurrection of a boy, long since gone away, and of a tall lank preacher who, in his humility, looked upon himself as a failure. I hardly know how it all came back to me; possibly it was the scent-laden breeze that came in from the woods and through the half-open church window, perhaps it was a line in one of the old songs, perhaps it was the droning voice of the Scotch preacher—somehow, and suddenly, I was a boy again.

——To this day I think of death as a valley: a dark shadowy valley: the Valley of the Shadow of Death. So persistent are the impressions of boyhood! As I sat in the church I could see, as distinctly as though I were there, the church of my boyhood and the tall dyspeptic preacher looming above the pulpit, the peculiar way the light came through the coarse colour of the windows, the barrenness and stiffness of the great empty room, the raw girders overhead, the prim choir. There was something in that preacher, gaunt, worn, sodden though he appeared: a spark somewhere, a little flame, mostly smothered by the gray dreariness of his surroundings, and yet blazing up at times to some warmth.

As I remember it, our church was a church of failures. They sent us the old gray preachers worn out in other fields. Such a succession of them I remember, each with some peculiarity, some pathos. They were of the old sort, indoctrinated Presbyterians, and they harrowed well our barren field with the tooth of their hard creed. Some thundered the Law, some pleaded Love; but of all of them I remember best the one who thought himself the greatest failure. I think he had tried a hundred churches—a hard life, poorly paid, unappreciated—in a new country. He had once had a family, but one by one they had died. No two were buried in the same cemetery; and finally, before he came to our village, his wife, too, had gone. And he

was old, and out of health, and discouraged: seeking some final
warmth from his own cold doctrine. How I see him, a trifle
bent, in his long worn coat, walking in the country roads: not
knowing of a boy who loved him!

He told my father once: I recall his exact words:

"My days have been long, and I have failed. It was not given
me to reach men's hearts."

Oh, gray preacher, may I now make amends? Will you forgive me? I was a boy and did not know; a boy whose emotions
were hidden under mountains of reserve: who could have stood
up to be shot more easily than he could have said: "I love you!"

Of that preacher's sermons I remember not one word, though
I must have heard scores of them—only that they were inter-
minably long and dull and that my legs grew weary of sitting
and that I was often hungry. It was no doubt the dreadful old
doctrine that he preached, thundering the horrors of disobedience, urging an impossible love through fear and a vain belief
without reason. All that touched me not at all, save with a sort
of wonder at the working of his great Adam's apple and the
strange rollings of his cavernous eyes. This he looked upon as
the work of God; thus for years he had sought, with self-
confessed failure, to touch the souls of his people. How we
travel in darkness and the work we do in all seriousness counts
for naught, and the thing we toss off in play-time, unconsciously,
God uses!

One tow-headed boy sitting there in a front row dreaming
dreams, if the sermons touched him not, was yet thrilled to the
depths of his being by that tall preacher. Somewhere, I said,
he had a spark within him. I think he never knew it: or if he
knew it, he regarded it as a wayward impulse that might lead
him from his God. It was a spark of poetry: strange flower in
such a husk. In times of emotion it bloomed, but in daily life it
emitted no fragrance. I have wondered what might have been
if some one—some understanding woman—had recognised his
gift, or if he himself as a boy had once dared to cut free! We do
not know: we do not know the tragedy of our nearest friend!

By some instinct the preacher chose his readings mostly from the Old Testament—those splendid, marching passages, full of oriental imagery. As he read there would creep into his voice a certain resonance that lifted him and his calling suddenly above his gray surroundings.

How vividly I recall his reading of the twenty-third Psalm—a particular reading. I suppose I had heard the passage many times before, but upon this certain morning——

Shall I ever forget? The windows were open, for it was May, and a boy could look out on the hillside and see with longing eyes the inviting grass and trees. A soft wind blew in across the church; it was full of the very essence of spring. I smell it yet. On the pulpit stood a bunch of crocuses crowded into a vase: some Mary's offering. An old man named Johnson who sat near us was already beginning to breathe heavily, preparatory to sinking into his regular Sunday snore. Then those words from the preacher, bringing me suddenly—how shall I express it?— out of some formless void, to intense consciousness—a miracle of creation:

"Yea though I walk through the valley of the shadow of death, I will fear no evil: for thou art with me; thy rod and thy staff they comfort me."

Well, I saw the way to the place of death that morning; far more vividly I saw it than any natural scene I know: and myself walking therein. I shall know it again when I come to pass that way; the tall, dark, rocky cliffs, the shadowy path within, the overhanging dark branches, even the whitened dead bones by the way—and as one of the vivid phantasms of boy- hood—cloaked figures I saw, lurking mysteriously in deep re- cesses, fearsome for their very silence. And yet I with magic rod and staff walking within—boldly, fearing no evil, full of faith, hope, courage, love, invoking images of terror but for the joy of braving them. Ah, tow-headed boy, shall I tread as lightly that dread pathway when I come to it? Shall I, like you, fear no evil!

So that great morning went away. I heard nothing of singing or sermon and came not to myself until my mother, touching my arm, asked me if I had been asleep! And I smiled and thought how little grown people knew—and I looked up at the sad sick face of the old preacher with a new interest and friendliness. I felt, somehow, that he too was a familiar of my secret valley. I should have liked to ask him, but I did not dare. So I followed my mother when she went to speak to him, and when he did not see, I touched his coat.

After that how I watched when he came to the reading. And one great Sunday, he chose a chapter from Ecclesiastes, the one that begins sonorously:

"Remember now thy creator in the days of thy youth."

Surely that gaunt preacher had the true fire in his gray soul. How his voice dwelt and quivered and softened upon the words!

"While the sun, or the light, or the moon, or the stars, be not darkened, nor the clouds return after the rain——"

Thus he brought in the universe to that small church and filled the heart of a boy.

"In the days when the keepers of the house shall tremble, and the strong men shall bow themselves, and the grinders cease because they are few, and those that look out of the windows be darkened.
"And the doors shall be shut in the streets, when the sound of the grinding is low, and he shall rise up at the voice of the bird and all the daughters of music shall be brought low."

Do not think that I understood the meaning of those passages: I am not vain enough to think I know even now—but the *sound* of them, the roll of them, the beautiful words, and above all, the pictures!

Those Daughters of Music, how I lived for days imagining them! They were of the trees and the hills, and they were very beautiful but elusive; one saw them as he heard singing afar off, sweet strains fading often into silences. Daughters of Music! Daughters of Music! And why should they be brought low?

Doors shut in the street—how I *saw* them—a long, long street,

silent, full of sunshine, and the doors shut, and no sound anywhere but the low sound of the grinding: and the mill with the
wheels drowsily turning and no one there at all save one boy
with fluttering heart, tiptoeing in the sunlit doorway.

And the voice of the bird. Not the song but the *voice*. Yes,
a bird had a voice. I had known it always, and yet somehow I had
not dared to say it. I felt that they would look at me with that
questioning, incredulous look which I dreaded beyond belief.
They might laugh! But here it was in the Book—the voice of a
bird. How my appreciation of that Book increased and what a
new confidence it gave me in my own images! I went about for
days, listening, listening, listening—and interpreting.

So the words of the preacher and the fire in them:

"And when they shall be afraid of that which is high and fears
shall be in the way——"

I knew the fear of that which is high: I had dreamed of it
commonly. And I knew also the Fear that stood in the way: him
I had seen in a myriad of forms, looming black by darkness in
every lane I trod; and yet with what defiance I met and slew
him!

And then, more thrilling than all else, the words of the
preacher:

"Or ever the silver cord be loosed, or the golden bowl be broken,
or the pitcher be broken at the fountain, or the wheel broken at
the cistern."

Such pictures: that silver cord, that golden bowl! And why
and wherefore?

A thousand ways I turned them in my mind—and always
with the sound of the preacher's voice in my ears—the resonance
of the words conveying an indescribable fire of inspiration.
Vaguely and yet with certainty I knew the preacher spoke out of
some unfathomable emotion which I did not understand—which
I did not care to understand. Since then I have thought what
those words must have meant to him!

Ah, that tall lank preacher, who thought himself a failure: how long I shall remember him and the words he read and the mournful yet resonant cadences of his voice—and the barren church, and the stony religion! Heaven he gave me, unknowing, while he preached an ineffectual hell.

As we rode home Harriet looked into my face.

"You have enjoyed the service," she said softly.

"Yes," I said.

"It *was* a good sermon," she said.

"Was it?" I replied.

IX

THE TRAMP

I HAVE HAD a new and strange experience—droll in one way, grotesque in another and when everything is said, tragic: at least an adventure. Harriet looks at me accusingly, and I have had to preserve the air of one deeply contrite now for two days (no easy accomplishment for me!), even though in secret I have smiled and pondered.

How our life has been warped by books! We are not contented with realities: we crave conclusions. With what ardour our minds respond to real events with literary deductions. Upon a train of incidents, as unconnected as life itself, we are wont to clap a booky ending. An instinctive desire for completeness animates the human mind (a struggle to circumscribe the infinite). We would like to have life "turn out"—but it doesn't—it doesn't. Each event is the beginning of a whole new genealogy of events. In boyhood I remember asking after every story I heard: "What happened next?" for no conclusion ever quite satisfied me—even when the hero died in his own gore. I always knew there was something yet remaining to be told. The only sure conclusion we can reach is this: Life changes. And what is more enthralling to the human mind than this splendid, boundless, coloured mutability!—life in the making? How strange it is, then, that we should be contented to take such small parts of it as we can grasp, and to say, "This is the true explanation." By such devices we seek to bring infinite existence within our finite egoistic grasp. We solidify and define where solidification means loss of interest; and loss of interest, not years, is old age.

So I have mused since my tramp came in for a moment out of the Mystery (as we all do) and went away again into the Mystery (in our way, too).

There are strange things in this world!

As I came around the corner I saw sitting there on my steps the very personification of Ruin, a tumble-down, dilapidated wreck of manhood. He gave one the impression of having been dropped where he sat, all in a heap. My first instinctive feeling was not one of recoil or even of hostility, but rather a sudden desire to pick him up and put him where he belonged, the instinct, I should say, of the normal man who hangs his axe always on the same nail. When he saw me he gathered himself together with reluctance and stood fully revealed. It was a curious attitude of mingled effrontery and apology. "Hit me if you dare," blustered his outward personality. "For God's sake, don't hit me," cried the innate fear in his eyes. I stopped and looked at him sharply. His eyes dropped, his look slid away, so that I experienced a sense of shame, as though I had trampled upon him. A damp rag of humanity! I confess that my first impulse, and a strong one, was to kick him for the good of the human race. No man has a right to be like that.

And then, quite suddenly, I had a great revulsion of feeling. What was I that I should judge without knowledge? Perhaps, after all, here was one bearing treasure. So I said:

"You are the man I have been expecting."

He did not reply, only flashed his eyes up at me, wherein fear deepened.

"I have been saving up a coat for you," I said, "and a pair of shoes. They are not much worn," I said, "but a little too small for me. I think they will fit you."

He looked at me again, not sharply, but with a sort of weak cunning. So far he had not said a word.

"I think our supper is nearly ready," I said: "let us go in."

"No, mister," he mumbled, "a bite out here—no, mister"— and then, as though the sound of his own voice inspired him, he grew declamatory.

"I'm a respectable man, mister, plumber by trade, but——"

"But," I interrupted, "you can't get any work, you're cold and you haven't had anything to eat for two days, so you are walking out here in the country where we farmers have no plumbing to do. At home you have a starving wife and three small children——"

"Six, mister——"

"Well, six— And now we will go in to supper."

I led him into the entry way and poured for him a big basin of hot water. As I stepped out again with a comb he was slinking toward the doorway.

"Here," I said, "is a comb; we are having supper now in a few minutes."

I wish I could picture Harriet's face when I brought him into her immaculate kitchen. But I gave her a look, one of the commanding sort that I can put on in times of great emergency, and she silently laid another place at the table.

When I came to look at our Ruin by the full lamplight I was surprised to see what a change a little warm water and a comb had wrought in him. He came to the table uncertain, blinking, apologetic. His forehead, I saw, was really impressive—high, narrow and thin-skinned. His face gave one somehow the impression of a carving once full of significant lines, now blurred and worn as though Time, having first marked it with the lines of character, had grown discouraged and brushed the hand of forgetfulness over her work. He had peculiar thin, silky hair of no particular colour, with a certain almost childish pathetic waviness around the ears and at the back of the neck. Something, after all, about the man aroused one's compassion.

I don't know that he looked dissipated, and surely he was not as dirty as I had at first supposed. Something remained that suggested a care for himself in the past. It was not dissipation, I decided; it was rather an indefinable looseness and weakness, that gave one alternately the feeling I had first experienced, that of anger, succeeded by the compassion that one feels for a child. To Harriet, when she had once seen him, he was all child, and she all compassion.

We disturbed him with no questions. Harriet's fundamental quality is homeliness, comfortableness. Her tea-kettle seems always singing; an indefinable tabbiness, as of feather cushions, lurks in her dining-room, a right warmth of table and chairs, indescribably comfortable at the end of a chilly day. A busy good-smelling steam arises from all her dishes at once, and the light in the middle of the table is of a redness that enthralls the human soul. As for Harriet herself, she is the personification of comfort, airy, clean, warm, inexpressibly wholesome. And never in the world is she so engaging as when she ministers to a man's hunger. Truthfully, sometimes, when she comes to me out of the dimmer light of the kitchen to the radiance of the table with a plate of muffins, it is as though she and the muffins were a part of each other, and that she is really offering some of herself. And down in my heart I know she is doing just that!

Well, it was wonderful to see our Ruin expand in the warmth of Harriet's presence. He had been doubtful of me; of Harriet, I could see, he was absolutely sure. And how he did eat, saying nothing at all, while Harriet plied him with food and talked to me of the most disarming commonplaces. I think it did her heart good to see the way he ate; as though he had had nothing before in days. As he buttered his muffin, not without some refinement, I could see that his hand was long, a curious, lean, ineffectual hand, with a curving little finger. With the drinking of the hot coffee colour began to steal up into his face, and when Harriet brought out a quarter of pie saved over from our dinner and placed it before him—a fine brown pie with small hieroglyphics in the top from whence rose sugary bubbles—he seemed almost to escape himself. And Harriet fairly purred with hospitality.

The more he ate the more of a man he became. His manners improved, his back straightened up, he acquired a not unimpressive poise of the head. Such is the miraculous power of hot muffins and pie!

"As you came down," I asked finally, "did you happen to see old man Masterson's threshing machine?"

"A big red one, with a yellow blow-off?"

"That's the one," I said.

"Well, it was just turning into a field about two miles above here," he replied.

"Big gray, banked barn?" I asked.

"Yes, and a little unpainted house," said our friend:

"That's Parsons'," put in Harriet, with a mellow laugh. "I wonder if he ever *will* paint that house. He builds bigger barns every year and doesn't touch the house. Poor Mrs. Parsons——"

And so we talked of barns and threshing machines in the way we farmers love to do and I lured our friend slowly into talking about himself. At first he was non-committal enough and what he said seemed curiously made to order; he used certain set phrases with which to explain simply what was not easy to explain—a device not uncommon to all of us. I was fearful of not getting within this outward armouring, but gradually as we talked and Harriet poured him a third cup of hot coffee he dropped into a more familiar tone. He told with some sprightliness of having seen threshings in Mexico, how the grain was beaten out with flails in the patios, and afterwards thrown up in the wind to winnow out.

"You must have seen a good deal of life," remarked Harriet sympathetically.

At this remark I saw one of our Ruin's long hands draw up and clinch. He turned his head toward Harriet. His face was partly in the shadow, but there was something striking and strange in the way he looked at her, and a deepness in his voice when he spoke:

"Too much! I've seen too much of life." He threw out one arm and brought it back with a shudder.

"You see what it has left me," he said, "I am an example of too much life."

In response to Harriet's melting compassion he had spoken with unfathomable bitterness. Suddenly he leaned forward toward me with a piercing gaze as though he would look into my soul. His face had changed completely; from the loose and vacant mask of the early evening it had taken on the utmost tensity of emotion.

"You do not know," he said, "what it is to live too much—and to be afraid."

"Live too much?" I asked.

"Yes, live too much, that is what I do—and I am afraid."

He paused a moment and then broke out in a higher key:

"You think I am a tramp. Yes—you do. I know—a worthless fellow, lying, begging, stealing when he can't beg. You have taken me in and fed me. You have said the first kind words I have heard, it seems to me, in years. I don't know who you are. I shall never see you again."

I cannot well describe the intensity of the passion with which he spoke, his face shaking with emotion, his hands trembling.

"Oh, yes," I said easily, "we are comfortable people here—and it is a good place to live."

"No no," he returned. "I know, I've got my call—" Then leaning forward he said in a lower, even more intense voice—"I live everything beforehand."

I was startled by the look of his eyes: the abject terror of it: and I thought to myself, "The man is not right in his mind." And yet I longed to know of the life within this strange husk of manhood.

"I know," he said, as if reading my thought, "you think"—and he tapped his forehead with one finger—"but I'm not. I'm as sane as you are."

It was a strange story he told. It seems almost unbelievable to me as I set it down here, until I reflect how little any one of us knows of the deep life within his nearest neighbour—what stories there are, what tragedies enacted under a calm exterior! What a drama there may be in this commonplace man buying ten pounds of sugar at the grocery store, or this other one driving his two old horses in the town road! We do not know. And how rarely are the men of inner adventure articulate! Therefore I treasure the curious story the tramp told me. I do not question its truth. It came as all truth does, through a clouded and unclean medium: and any judgment of the story itself must be based upon a knowledge of the personal equation of the Ruin who told it.

"I am no tramp," he said, "in reality, I am no tramp. I began as well as anyone— It doesn't matter now, only I won't have any of the sympathy that people give to the man who has seen better days. I hate sentiment. *I hate it——*"

I cannot attempt to set down the story in his own words. It was broken with exclamations and involved with wandering sophistries and diatribes of self-blame. His mind had trampled upon itself in throes of introspection until it was often difficult to say which way the paths of the narrative really led. He had thought so much and acted so little that he travelled in a veritable bog of indecision. And yet, withal, some ideas, by constant attrition, had acquired a really striking form. "I am afraid before life," he said. "It makes me dizzy with thought."

At another time he said, "If I am a tramp at all, I am a mental tramp. I have an unanchored mind."

It seems that he came to a realisation that there was something peculiar about him at a very early age. He said they would look at him and whisper to one another and that his sayings were much repeated, often in his hearing. He knew that he was considered an extraordinary child: they baited him with questions that they might laugh at his quaint replies. He said that as early as he could remember he used to plan situations so that he might say things that were strange and even shocking in a child. His father was a small professor in a small college—a "worm" he called him bitterly—"one of those worms that bores in books and finally dries up and blows off." But his mother—he said she was an angel. I recall his exact expression about her eyes that "when she looked at one it made him better." He spoke of her with a softening of the voice, looking often at Harriet. He talked a good deal about his mother, trying to account for himself through her. She was not strong, he said, and very sensitive to the contact of either friends or enemies— evidently a nervous, high-strung woman.

"You have known such people," he said, "everything hurt her."

He said she "starved to death." She starved for affection and understanding.

One of the first things he recalled of his boyhood was his passionate love for his mother.

"I can remember," he said, "lying awake in my bed and thinking how I would love her and serve her—and I could see myself in all sorts of impossible places saving her from danger. When she came to my room to bid me good night, I imagined how I should look—for I have always been able to see myself doing things—when I threw my arms around her neck to kiss her."

Here he reached a strange part of his story. I had been watching Harriet out of the corner of my eye. At first her face was tearful with compassion, but as the Ruin proceeded it became a study in wonder and finally in outright alarm. He said that when his mother came in to bid him good night he saw himself so plainly beforehand ("more vividly than I see you at this moment") and felt his emotion so keenly that when his mother actually stooped to kiss him, somehow he could not respond. He could not throw his arms around her neck. He said he often lay quiet, in waiting, trembling all over until she had gone, not only suffering himself but pitying her, because he understood how she must feel. Then he would follow her, he said, in imagination through the long hall, seeing himself stealing behind her, just touching her hand, wistfully hoping that she might turn to him again—and yet fearing. He said no one knew the agonies he suffered at seeing his mother's disappointment over his apparent coldness and unresponsiveness.

"I think," he said, "it hastened her death."

He would not go to the funeral; he did not dare, he said. He cried and fought when they came to take him away, and when the house was silent he ran up to her room and buried his head in her pillows and ran in swift imagination to her funeral. He said he could see himself in the country road, hurrying in the cold rain—for it seemed raining—he said he could actually feel the stones and the ruts, although he could not tell how it was possible that he should have seen himself at a distance and *felt* in his own feet the stones of the road. He said he saw the box taken from the wagon—*saw* it—and that he heard the sound of the clods thrown in, and it made him shriek until they came running and held him.

As he grew older he said he came to live everything beforehand, and that the event as imagined was so far more vivid and affecting that he had no heart for the reality itself.

"It seems strange to you," he said, "but I am telling you exactly what my experience was."

It was curious, he said, when his father told him he must not do a thing, how he went on and imagined in how many different ways he could do it—and how, afterward, he imagined he was punished by that "worm," his father, whom he seemed to hate bitterly. Of those early days, in which he suffered acutely—in idleness, apparently—and perhaps that was one of the causes of his disorder—he told us at length, but many of the incidents were so evidently worn by the constant handling of his mind that they gave no clear impression.

Finally, he ran away from home, he said. At first he found

that a wholly new place and new people took him out of himself ("surprised me," he said, "so that I could not live everything beforehand"). Thus he fled. The slang he used, "chased himself all over the country," seemed peculiarly expressive. He had been in foreign countries; he had herded sheep in Australia (so he said), and certainly from his knowledge of the country he had wandered with the gamboleros of South America; he had gone for gold to Alaska, and worked in the lumber camps of the Pacific Northwest. But he could not escape, he said. In a short time he was no longer "surprised." His account of his travels, while fragmentary, had a peculiar vividness. He *saw* what he described, and he saw it so plainly that his mind ran off into curious details that made his words strike sometimes like flashes of lightning. A strange and wonderful mind—uncontrolled. How that man needed the discipline of common work!

I have rarely listened to a story with such rapt interest. It was not only what he said, nor how he said it, but how he let me see the strange workings of his mind. It was continuously a story of a story. When his voice finally died down I drew a long breath and was astonished to perceive that it was nearly midnight—and Harriet speechless with her emotions. For a moment he sat quiet and then burst out:

"I cannot get away: I cannot escape," and the veritable look of some trapped creature came into his eyes, fear so abject that I reached over and laid my hand on his arm:

"Friend," I said, "stop here. We have a good country. You have travelled far enough. I know from experience what a cornfield will do for a man."

"I have lived all sorts of life," he continued as if he had not heard a word I said, "and I have lived it all twice, and I am afraid."

"Face it," I said, gripping his arm, longing for some power to "blow grit into him."

"Face it!" he exclaimed, "don't you suppose I have tried. If I could do a thing—anything—a few times without thinking—*once* would be enough—I might be all right. I should be all right."

He brought his fist down on the table, and there was a note of resolution in his voice. I moved my chair nearer to him, feeling as though I were saving an immortal soul from destruction. I told him of our life, how the quiet and the work of it would solve his problems. I sketched with enthusiasm my own experience and I planned swiftly how he could live, absorbed in simple work—and in books.

"Try it," I said eagerly.

"I will," he said, rising from the table, and grasping my hand. "I'll stay here."

I had a peculiar thrill of exultation and triumph. I know how the priest must feel, having won a soul from torment!

He was trembling with excitement and pale with emotion and weariness. One must begin the quiet life with rest. So I got him off to bed, first pouring him a bathtub of warm water. I laid out clean clothes by his bedside and took away his old ones, talking to him cheerfully all the time about common things. When I finally left him and came downstairs I found Harriet standing with frightened eyes in the middle of the kitchen.

"I'm afraid to have him sleep in this house," she said.

But I reassured her. "You do not understand," I said.

Owing to the excitement of the evening I spent a restless night. Before daylight, while I was dreaming a strange dream of two men running, the one who pursued being the exact counterpart of the one who fled, I heard my name called aloud:

"David, David!"

I sprang out of bed.

"The tramp has gone," called Harriet.

He had not even slept in his bed. He had raised the window, dropped out on the ground and vanished.

X

THE INFIDEL

I FIND THAT WE HAVE an infidel in this community. I don't know that I should set down the fact here on good white paper; the walls, they say, have eyes, the stones have ears. But consider these words written in bated breath! The worst of it is—I gather from common report—this infidel is a Cheerful Infidel, whereas a true infidel should bear upon his face the living mark of his infamy. We are all tolerant enough of those who do not agree with us, provided only they are sufficiently miserable! I confess when I first heard of him—through Mrs. Horace (with shudders)—I was possessed of a consuming secret desire to see him. I even thought of climbing a tree somewhere along the public road—like Zaccheus, wasn't it?—and watching him go by. If by any chance he should look my way I could easily avoid discovery by crouching among the leaves. It shows how pleasant must be the paths of unrighteousness that we are tempted to climb trees to see those who walk therein. My imagination busied itself with the infidel. I pictured him as a sort of Moloch treading our pleasant countryside, flames and smoke proceeding from his nostrils, his feet striking fire, his voice like the sound of a great wind. At least that was the picture I formed of him from common report.

And yesterday afternoon I met the infidel and I must here set down a true account of the adventure. It is, surely, a little new door opened in the house of my understanding. I might travel a whole year in a city, brushing men's elbows, and not once have such an experience. In country spaces men develop sensitive surfaces, not calloused by too frequent contact, accepting the new impression vividly and keeping it bright to think upon.

I met the infidel as the result of a rather unexpected series of incidents. I don't think I have said before that we have for some time been expecting a great event on this farm. We have raised corn and buckwheat, we have a fertile asparagus bed and onions and pie-plant (enough to supply the entire population of this community) and I can't tell how many other vegetables. We have had plenty of chickens hatched out (I don't like chickens, especially hens, especially a certain gaunt and predatory hen named [so Harriet says] Evangeline, who belongs to a neighbour of ours) and we have had two litters of pigs, but until this bright moment of expectancy we never have had a calf.

Upon the advice of Horace, which I often lean upon as upon a staff, I have been keeping my young heifer shut up in the cow-yard now for a week or two. But yesterday, toward the middle of the afternoon, I found the fence broken down and the cow-yard empty. From what Harriet said, the brown cow must have been gone since early morning. I knew, of course, what that meant, and straightway I took a stout stick and set off over the hill, tracing the brown cow as far as I could by her tracks. She had made way toward a clump of trees near Horace's wood lot, where I confidently expected to find her. But as fate would have it, the pasture gate, which is rarely used, stood open and the tracks led outward into an old road. I followed rapidly, half pleased that I had not found her within the wood. It was a promise of new adventure which I came to with downright en-

joyment (confidentially—I should have been cultivating corn!).
I peered into every thicket as I passed: once I climbed an old
fence and, standing on the top rail, intently surveyed my neighbour's pasture. No brown cow was to be seen. At the crossing
of the brook I shouldered my way from the road down a path
among the alders, thinking the brown cow might have gone that
way to obscurity.

It is curious how, in spite of domestication and training, Nature in her great moments returns to the primitive and instinctive! My brown cow, never having had anything but the kindest
treatment, is as gentle an animal as could be imagined, but she
had followed the nameless, ages-old law of her breed: she had
escaped in her great moment to the most secret place she
knew. It did not matter that she would have been safer in my
yard—both she and her calf—that she would have been surer
of her food; she could only obey the old wild law. So turkeys
will hide their nests. So the tame duck, tame for unnumbered
generations, hearing from afar the shrill cry of the wild drake,
will desert her quiet surroundings, spread her little-used wings
and become for a time the wildest of the wild.

So we think—you and I—that we are civilised! But how often,
how often, have we felt that old wildness which is our common
heritage, scarce shackled, clamouring in our blood!

I stood listening among the alders, in the deep cool shade.
Here and there a ray of sunshine came through the thick
foliage: I could see it where it silvered the cobweb ladders of
those moist spaces. Somewhere in the thicket I heard an un-
alarmed catbird trilling her exquisite song, a startled frog leaped
with a splash into the water; faint odours of some blossoming
growth, not distinguishable, filled the still air. It was one of
those rare moments when one seems to have caught Nature un-
aware. I lingered a full minute, listening, looking; but my brown
cow had not gone that way. So I turned and went up rapidly to
the road, and there I found myself almost face to face with a
ruddy little man whose countenance bore a look of round astonishment. We were both surprised. I recovered first.

"Have you seen a brown cow?" I asked.

He was still so astonished that he began to look around him; he thrust his hands nervously into his coat pockets and pulled them out again.

"I think you won't find her in there," I said, seeking to relieve his embarrassment.

But I didn't know, then, how very serious a person I had encountered.

"No—no," he stammered, "I haven't seen your cow."

So I explained to him with sobriety, and at some length, the problem I had to solve. He was greatly interested and inasmuch as he was going my way he offered at once to assist me in my search. So we set off together. He was rather stocky of build, and decidedly short of breath, so that I regulated my customary stride to suit his deliberation. At first, being filled with the spirit of my adventure, I was not altogether pleased with this arrangement. Our conversation ran something like this:

STRANGER: Has she any spots or marks on her?

MYSELF: No, she is plain brown.

STRANGER: How old a cow is she?

MYSELF: This is her first calf.

STRANGER: Valuable animal?

MYSELF (*fencing*): I have never put a price on her; she is a promising young heifer.

STRANGER: Pure blood?

MYSELF: No, grade.

After a pause:

STRANGER: Live around here?

MYSELF: Yes, half a mile below here. Do you?

STRANGER: Yes, three miles above here. My name's Purdy.

MYSELF: Mine is Grayson.

He turned to me solemnly and held out his hand. "I'm glad to meet you, Mr. Grayson," he said. "And I'm glad," I said, "to meet you, Mr. Purdy."

I will not attempt to put down all we said: I couldn't. But by such devices is the truth in the country made manifest.

So we continued to walk and look. Occasionally I would unconsciously increase my pace until I was warned to desist by the puffing of Mr. Purdy. He gave an essential impression of genial timidity: and how he *did* love to talk!

We came at last to a rough bit of land grown up to scrubby oaks and hazel brush.

"This," said Mr. Purdy, "looks hopeful."

We followed the old road, examining every bare spot of earth for some evidence of the cow's tracks, but without finding so much as a sign. I was for pushing onward but Mr. Purdy insisted that this clump of woods was exactly such a place as a cow would like. He developed such a capacity for argumentation and seemed so sure of what he was talking about that I yielded, and we entered the wood.

"We'll part here," he said: "you keep over there about fifty yards and I'll go straight ahead. In that way we'll cover the ground. Keep a-shoutin'."

So we started and I kept a-shoutin'. He would answer from time to time: "Hulloo, hulloo!"

It was a wild and beautful bit of forest. The ground under the trees was thickly covered with enormous ferns or bracken, with here and there patches of light where the sun came through the foliage. The low spots were filled with the coarse green verdure of skunk cabbage. I was so sceptical about finding the cow in a wood where concealment was so easy that I confess I rather idled and enjoyed the surroundings. Suddenly, however, I heard Mr. Purdy's voice, with a new note in it:

"Hulloo, hulloo——"

"What luck?"

"Hulloo, hulloo——"

"I'm coming—" and I turned and ran as rapidly as I could through the trees, jumping over logs and dodging low branches, wondering what new thing my friend had discovered. So I came to his side.

"Have you got trace of her?" I questioned eagerly.

"Sh!" he said, "over there. Don't you see her?"

"Where, where?"

He pointed, but for a moment I could see nothing but the trees and the bracken. Then all at once, like the puzzle in a picture, I saw her plainly. She was standing perfectly motionless, her head lowered, and in such a peculiar clump of bushes and ferns that she was all but indistinguishable. It was wonderful, the perfection with which her instinct had led her to conceal herself.

All excitement, I started toward her at once. But Mr. Purdy put his hand on my arm.

"Wait," he said, "don't frighten her. She has her calf there."

"No!" I exclaimed, for I could see nothing of it.

We went, cautiously, a few steps nearer. She threw up her head and looked at us so wildly for a moment that I should hardly have known her for my cow. She was, indeed, for the time being, a wild creature of the wood. She made a low sound and advanced a step threateningly.

"Steady," said Mr. Purdy, "this is her first calf. Stop a minute and keep quiet. She'll soon get used to us."

Moving to one side cautiously, we sat down on an old log. The brown heifer paused, every muscle tense, her eyes literally blazing. We sat perfectly still. After a minute or two she lowered her head, and with curious guttural sounds she began to lick her calf, which lay quite hidden in the bracken.

"She has chosen a perfect spot," I thought to myself, for it was the wildest bit of forest I had seen anywhere in this neighbourhood. At one side, not far off, rose a huge gray rock, partly covered on one side with moss, and round about were oaks and a few ash trees of a poor scrubby sort (else they would long ago have been cut out). The earth underneath was soft and springy with leaf mould.

Mr. Purdy was one to whom silence was painful; he fidgeted about, evidently bursting with talk, and yet feeling compelled to follow his own injunction of silence. Presently he reached into his capacious pocket and handed me a little paper-covered booklet. I took it, curious, and read the title:

"Is There a Hell?"

It struck me humorously. In the country we are always—at least some of us are—more or less in a religious ferment. The city may distract itself to the point where faith is unnecessary;

but in the country we must, perforce, have something to believe in. And we talk about it, too! I read the title aloud, but in a low voice:

"Is There a Hell?" Then I asked: "Do you really want to know?"

"The argument is all there," he replied.

"Well," I said, "I can tell you off-hand, out of my own experience, that there certainly is a hell——"

He turned toward me with evident astonishment, but I proceeded with tranquillity:

"Yes, sir, there's no doubt about it. I've been near enough myself several times to smell the smoke. It isn't around here," I said.

As he looked at me his china-blue eyes grew larger, if that were possible, and his serious, gentle face took on a look of pained surprise.

"Before you say such things," he said, "I beg you to read my book."

He took the tract from my hands and opened it on his knee.

"The Bible tells us," he said, "that in the beginning God created the heavens and the earth, He made the firmament and divided the waters. But does the Bible say that He created a hell or a devil? Does it?"

I shook my head.

"Well, then!" he said triumphantly, "and that isn't all, either. The historian Moses gives in detail a full account of what was made in six days. He tells how day and night were created, how the sun and the moon and the stars were made; he tells how God created the flowers of the field, and the insects, and the birds, and the great whales, and said, 'Be fruitful and multiply.' He accounts for every minute of the time in the entire six days —and of course God rested on the seventh—and there is not one word about hell. Is there?"

I shook my head.

"Well then—" exultantly, "where is it? I'd like to have any man, no matter how wise he is, answer that. Where is it?"

"That," I said, "has troubled me, too. We don't always know

Thomas Fogarty

"He reached into his pocket and handed me a little
paper-covered booklet"

just where our hells are. If we did we might avoid them. We are not so sensitive to them as we should be—do you think?"

He looked at me intently: I went on before he could answer:

"Why, I've seen men in my time living from day to day in the very atmosphere of perpetual torment, and actually arguing that there was no hell. It is a strange sight, I assure you, and one that will trouble you afterwards. From what I know of hell, it is a place of very loose boundaries. Sometimes I've thought we couldn't be quite sure when we were in it and when we were not."

I did not tell my friend, but I was thinking of the remark of old Swedenborg: "The trouble with hell is we shall not know it when we arrive."

At this point Mr. Purdy burst out again, having opened his little book at another page.

"When Adam and Eve had sinned," he said, "and the God of Heaven walked in the garden in the cool of the evening and called for them and they had hidden themselves on account of their disobedience, did God say to them: Unless you repent of your sins and get forgiveness I will shut you up in yon dark and dismal hell and torment you (or have the devil do it) for ever and ever? Was there such a word?"

I shook my head.

"No, sir," he said vehemently, "there was not."

"But does it say," I asked, "that Adam and Eve had not themselves been using their best wits in creating a hell? That point has occurred to me. In my experience I've known both Adams and Eves who were most adroit in their capacity for making places of torment—and afterwards of getting into them. Just watch yourself some day after you've sown a crop of desires and you'll see promising little hells starting up within you like pigweeds and pusley after a warm rain in your garden. And our heavens, too, for that matter—they grow to our own planting: and how sensitive they are too! How soon the hot wind of a passion withers them away! How surely the fires of selfishness blacken their perfection!"

I'd almost forgotten Mr. Purdy—and when I looked around,

his face wore a peculiar puzzled expression not unmixed with alarm. He held up his little book eagerly, almost in my face.

"If God had intended to create a hell," he said, "I assert without fear of successful contradiction that when God was there in the Garden of Eden it was the time for Him to have put Adam and Eve and all their posterity on notice that there was a place of everlasting torment. It would have been only a square deal for Him to do so. But did He?"

I shook my head.

"He did not. If He had mentioned hell on that occasion I should not now dispute its existence. But He did not. This is what He said to Adam—the very words: 'In the sweat of thy face shalt thou eat bread, till thou return unto the ground: for out of it thou wast taken: for dust thou art, and unto dust shalt thou return.' You see He did not say 'Unto hell shalt thou return.' He said, 'Unto dust.' That isn't hell, is it?"

"Well," I said, "there are in my experience a great many different kinds of hells. There are almost as many kinds of hells as there are men and women upon this earth. Now, your hell wouldn't terrify me in the least. My own makes me no end of trouble. Talk about burning pitch and brimstone: how futile were the imaginations of the old fellows who conjured up such puerile torments. Why, I can tell you of no end of hells that are worse—and not half try. Once I remember, when I was younger——"

I happened to glance around at my companion. He sat there looking at me with horror—fascinated horror.

"Well, I won't disturb your peace of mind by telling *that* story," I said.

"Do you believe that we shall go to hell?" he asked in a low voice.

"That depends," I said. "Let's leave out the question of 'we'; let's be more comfortably general in our discussion. I think we can safely say that some go and some do not. It's a curious and noteworthy thing," I said, "but I've known of cases— There are some people who aren't really worth good honest tormenting— let alone the rewards of heavenly bliss. They just haven't any-

thing to torment! What is going to become of such folks? I confess I don't know. You remember when Dante began his journey
into the infernal regions——"

"I don't believe a word of that Dante," he interrupted ex-
citedly; "it's all a made up story. There isn't a word of truth
in it; it is a blasphemous book. Let me read you what I say
about it in here."

"I will agree with you without argument," I said, "that it is
not *all* true. I merely wanted to speak of one of Dante's experiences as an illustration of the point I'm making. You remember
that almost the first spirits he met on his journey were those who
had never done anything in this life to merit either heaven or
hell. That always struck me as being about the worst plight
imaginable for a human being. Think of a creature not even
worth good honest brimstone!"

Since I came home, I've looked up the passage; and it is a
wonderful one. Dante heard wailings and groans and terrible
things said in many tongues. Yet these were not the souls of the
wicked. They were only those "who had lived without praise
or blame, thinking of nothing but themselves." "Heaven would
not dull its brightness with those, nor would lower hell receive
them."

"And what is it," asked Dante, "that makes them so grievously
suffer?"

"Hopelessness of death," said Virgil. "Their blind existence
here, and immemorable former life, make them so wretched
that they envy every other lot. Mercy and Justice alike disdain
them. Let us speak of them no more. Look, and pass!"

But Mr. Purdy, in spite of his timidity, was a man of much
persistence.

"They tell me," he said, "when they try to prove the reason-
ableness of hell, that unless you show sinners how they're goin'
to be tormented, they'd never repent. Now, I say that if a
man has to be scared into religion, his religion ain't much good."

"There," I said, "I agree with you completely."

His face lighted up, and he continued eagerly:

"And I tell 'em: You just go ahead and try for heaven; don't pay any attention to all this talk about everlasting punishment."

"Good advice!" I said.

It had begun to grow dark. The brown cow was quiet at last. We could hear small faint sounds from the calf. I started slowly through the bracken. Mr. Purdy hung at my elbow, stumbling sideways as he walked, but continuing to talk eagerly. So we came to the place where the calf lay. I spoke in a low voice:

"So boss, so boss."

I would have laid my hand on her neck but she started back with a wild toss of her horns. It was a beautiful calf! I looked at it with a peculiar feeling of exultation, pride, ownership. It was red-brown, with a round curly pate and one white leg. As it lay curled there among the ferns, it was really beautiful to look at. When we approached, it did not so much as stir. I lifted it to its legs, upon which the cow uttered a strange half-wild cry and ran a few steps off, her head thrown in the air. The calf fell back as though it had no legs.

"She is telling it not to stand up," said Mr. Purdy.

I had been afraid at first that something was the matter!

"Some are like that," he said. "Some call their calves to run.

Others won't let you come near 'em at all; and I've even known of a case where a cow gored its calf to death rather than let anyone touch it."

I looked at Mr. Purdy not without a feeling of admiration. This was a thing he knew: a language not taught in the universities. How well it became him to know it; how simply he expressed it! I thought to myself: There are not many men in this world, after all, that it will not pay us to go to school to— for something or other.

I should never have been able, indeed, to get the cow and calf home, last night at least, if it had not been for my chance friend. He knew exactly what to do and how to do it. He wore a stout coat of denim, rather long in the skirts. This he slipped off, while I looked on in some astonishment, and spread it out on the ground. He placed my staff under one side of it and found another stick nearly the same size for the other side. These he wound into the coat until he had made a sort of stretcher. Upon this we placed the unresisting calf. What a fine one it was! Then, he in front and I behind, we carried the stretcher and its burden out of the wood. The cow followed, sometimes threatening, sometimes bellowing, sometimes starting off wildly, head and tail in the air, only to rush back and, venturing up with trembling muscles, touch her tongue to the calf, uttering low maternal sounds.

"Keep steady," said Mr. Purdy, "and everything'll be all right."

When we came to the brook we stopped to rest. I think my companion would have liked to start his argument again, but he was too short of breath.

It was a prime spring evening! The frogs were tuning up. I heard a drowsy cowbell somewhere over the hills in the pasture. The brown cow, with eager, outstretched neck, was licking her calf as it lay there on the improvised stretcher. I looked up at the sky, a blue avenue of heaven between the tree tops; I felt the peculiar sense of mystery which nature so commonly conveys.

"I have been too sure!" I said. "What do we know after all!

Why may there not be future heavens and hells—'other heavens for other earths'? We do not know—we do not *know*——"

So, carrying the calf, in the cool of the evening, we came at last to my yard. We had no sooner put the calf down than it jumped nimbly to its feet and ran, wobbling absurdly, to meet its mother.

"The rascal," I said, "after all our work."

"It's the nature of the animal," said Mr. Purdy, as he put on his coat.

I could not thank him enough. I invited him to stay with us to supper, but he said he must hurry home.

"Then come down soon to see me," I said, "and we will settle this question as to the existence of a hell."

He stepped up close to me and said, with an appealing note in his voice:

"You do not really believe in a hell, do you?"

How human nature loves conclusiveness: nothing short of the categorical will satisfy us! What I said to Mr. Purdy evidently appeased him, for he seized my hand and shook and shook.

"We haven't understood each other," he said eagerly. "You don't believe in eternal damnation any more than I do." Then he added, as though some new uncertainty puzzled him, "Do you?"

At supper I was telling Harriet with gusto of my experiences. Suddenly she broke out:

"What was his name?"

"Purdy."

"Why, he's the infidel that Mrs. Horace tells about!"

"Is that possible?" I said, and I dropped my knife and fork. The strangest sensation came over me.

"Why," I said, "then I'm an infidel too!"

So I laughed and I've been laughing gloriously ever since—at myself, at the infidel, at the entire neighbourhood. I recalled that delightful character in "The Vicar of Wakefield" (my friend the Scotch Preacher loves to tell about him), who seasons error by crying out "Fudge!"

"Fudge!" I said.

We're all poor sinners!

XI

THE COUNTRY DOCTOR

Sunday afternoon, June 9.

We had a funeral to-day in this community and the longest funeral procession, Charles Baxter says, he has seen in all the years of his memory among these hills. A good man has gone away—and yet remains. In the comparatively short time I have been here I never came to know him well personally, though I saw him often in the country roads, a ruddy old gentleman with thick, coarse, iron-gray hair, somewhat stern of countenance, somewhat shabby of attire, sitting as erect as a trooper in his open buggy, one muscular hand resting on his knee, the other holding the reins of his familiar old white horse. I said I did not come to know him well personally, and yet no one who knows this community can help knowing Doctor John North. I never so desired the gift of moving expression as I do at this moment, on my return from his funeral, that I may give some faint idea of what a good man means to a community like ours —as the more complete knowledge of it has come to me to-day.

In the district school that I attended when a boy we used to love to leave our mark, as we called it, wherever our rovings led us. It was a bit of boyish mysticism, unaccountable now that we have grown older and wiser (perhaps); but it had its meaning. It was an instinctive outreaching of the young soul to perpetuate the knowledge of its existence upon this forgetful earth. My mark, I remember, was a notch and a cross. With what secret fond diligence I carved it in the gray bark of beech trees, on fence posts, or on barn doors, and once, I remember, on the roof-ridge of our home, and once, with high imaginings of how long it would remain, I spent hours chiseling it deep in a hard-headed old boulder in the pasture, where, if man has been as kind as Nature, it remains to this day. If you should chance to see it you would not know of the boy who carved it there.

So Doctor North left his secret mark upon the neighbourhood —as all of us do, for good or for ill, upon *our* neighbourhoods, in accordance with the strength of that character which abides within us. For a long time I did not know that it was he, though it was not difficult to see that some strong good man had often passed this way. I saw the mystic sign of him deep-lettered in the hearthstone of a home; I heard it speaking bravely from the weak lips of a friend; it is carved in the plastic heart of many a boy. No, I do not doubt the immortalities of the soul; in this community, which I have come to love so much, dwells more than one of John North's immortalities—and will continue to dwell. I, too, live more deeply because John North was here.

He was in no outward way an extraordinary man, nor was his life eventful. He was born in this neighbourhood: I saw him lying quite still this morning in the same sunny room of the same house where he first saw the light of day. Here among these common hills he grew up, and save for the few years he spent at school or in the army, he lived here all his life long. In old neighbourhoods and especially farm neighbourhoods people come to know one another—not clothes knowledge, or money knowledge—but that sort of knowledge which reaches down into the hidden springs of human character. A country community may be deceived by a stranger, too easily deceived, but not by one of its own people. For it is not a studied knowledge; it resembles that slow geologic uncovering before which not even the deep buried bones of the prehistoric saurian remain finally hidden.

I never fully realised until this morning what a supreme triumph it is, having grown old, to merit the respect of those who know us best. Mere greatness offers no reward to compare with it, for greatness compels that homage which we freely bestow upon goodness. So long as I live I shall never forget this morning. I stood in the door-yard outside of the open window of the old doctor's home. It was soft, and warm, and very still— a June Sunday morning. An apple tree not far off was still in blossom, and across the road on a grassy hillside sheep fed unconcernedly. Occasionally, from the roadway where the horses of the countryside were waiting, I heard the clink of a bit-ring or the low voice of some new-comer seeking a place to hitch. Not half those who came could find room in the house: they stood uncovered among the trees. From within, wafted through the window, came the faint odour of flowers, and the occasional minor intonation of someone speaking—and finally our own Scotch Preacher! I could not see him, but there lay in the cadences of his voice a peculiar note of peacefulness, of finality. The day before he died Dr. North had said:

"I want McAlway to conduct my funeral, not as a minister but as a man. He has been my friend for forty years; he will know what I mean."

The Scotch Preacher did not say much. Why should he? Everyone there *knew*: and speech would only have cheapened what we knew. And I do not now recall even the little he said, for there was so much all about me that spoke not of the death of a good man, but of his life. A boy who stood near me—a boy no longer, for he was as tall as a man—gave a more eloquent tribute than any preacher could have done. I saw him stand his ground for a time with that grim courage of youth which dreads emotion more than a battle: and then I saw him crying behind a tree! He was not a relative of the old doctor's; he was only one of many into whose deep life the doctor had entered.

They sang "Lead, Kindly Light," and came out through the

narrow doorway into the sunshine with the coffin, the hats of the pall-bearers in a row on top, and there was hardly a dry eye among us.

And as they came out through the narrow doorway, I thought how the Doctor must have looked out daily through so many, many years upon this beauty of hills and fields and of sky above, grown dearer from long familiarity—which he would know no more. And Kate North, the Doctor's sister, his only relative, followed behind, her fine old face gray and set, but without a tear in her eye. How like the Doctor she looked: the same stern control!

In the hours which followed, on the pleasant winding way to the cemetery, in the groups under the trees, on the way homeward again, the community spoke its true heart, and I have come back with the feeling that human nature, at bottom, is sound and sweet. I knew a great deal before about Doctor North, but I knew it as knowledge, not as emotion, and therefore it was not really a part of my life.

I heard again the stories of how he drove the country roads, winter and summer, how he had seen most of the population into the world and had held the hands of many who went out! It was the plain, hard life of a country doctor, and yet it seemed to rise in our community like some great tree, its roots deep buried in the soil of our common life, its branches close to the sky. To those accustomed to the outward excitements of city life it would have seemed barren and uneventful. It was significant that the talk was not so much of what the Doctor did as of *how* he did it, not so much of his actions as of the natural expression of his character. And when we come to think of it, goodness *is* uneventful. It does not flash, it glows. It is deep, quiet and very simple. It passes not with oratory, it is commonly foreign to riches, nor does it often sit in the places of the mighty: but may be felt in the touch of a friendly hand or the look of a kindly eye.

Outwardly, John North often gave the impression of brusqueness. Many a woman, going to him for the first time, and until she learned that he was in reality as gentle as a girl, was frightened by his manner. The country is full of stories of such encounters. We laugh yet over the adventure of a woman who formerly came to spend her summers here. She dressed very beautifully and was "nervous." One day she went to call on the Doctor. He made a careful examination and asked many questions. Finally he said, with portentous solemnity:

"Madam, you're suffering from a very common complaint."

The Doctor paused, then continued, impressively:

"You haven't enough work to do. This is what I would advise. Go home, discharge your servants, do your own cooking, wash your own clothes and make your own beds. You'll get well."

She is reported to have been much offended, and yet to-day there was a wreath of white roses in Doctor North's room sent from the city by that woman.

If he really hated anything in this world the Doctor hated whimperers. He had a deep sense of the purpose and need of punishment, and he despised those who fled from wholesome discipline.

A young fellow once went to the Doctor—so they tell the story—and asked for something to stop his pain.

"Stop it!" exclaimed the Doctor: "why, it's good for you. You've done wrong, haven't you? Well, you're being punished; take it like a man. There's nothing more wholesome than good honest pain."

And yet how much pain he alleviated in this community—in forty years!

The deep sense that a man should stand up to his fate was one of the key-notes of his character; and the way he taught it, not only by word but by every action of his life, put heart into many a weak man and woman. Mrs. Patterson, a friend of ours, tells of a reply she once had from the Doctor to whom she had gone with a new trouble. After telling him about it she said:

"I've left it all with the Lord."

"You'd have done better," said the Doctor, "to keep it yourself. Trouble is for your discipline: the Lord doesn't need it."

It was thus out of his wisdom that he was always telling people what they knew, deep down in their hearts, to be true. It sometimes hurt at first, but sooner or later, if the man had a spark of real manhood in him, he came back, and gave the Doctor an abiding affection.

There were those who, though they loved him, called him intolerant. I never could look at it that way. He *did* have the only kind of intolerance which is at all tolerable, and that is the intolerance of intolerance. He always set himself with vigour against that unreason and lack of sympathy which are the essence of intolerance; and yet there was a rock of conviction on many subjects behind which he could not be driven. It was not intolerance: it was with him a reasoned certainty of belief. He had a phrase to express that not uncommon state of mind, in this age particularly, which is politely willing to yield its foothold within this universe to almost any reasoner who suggests some other universe, however shadowy, to stand upon. He called it a "mush of concession." He might have been wrong in his convictions, but he, at least, never floundered in a "mush of concession." I heard him say once:

"There are some things a man can't concede, and one is, that a man who has broken a law, like a man who has broken a leg, has got to suffer for it."

It was only with the greatest difficulty that he could be prevailed upon to present a bill. It was not because the community was poor, though some of our people are poor, and it was certainly not because the Doctor was rich and could afford such philanthropy, for, saving a rather unproductive farm which during the last ten years of his life lay wholly uncultivated, he was as poor as any man in the community. He simply seemed to forget that people owed him.

It came to be a common and humorous experience for people to go to the Doctor and say:

"Now, Doctor North, how much do I owe you? You remember you attended my wife two years ago when the baby came—and John when he had the diphtheria——"

"Yes, yes," said the Doctor, "I remember."

"I thought I ought to pay you."

"Well, I'll look it up when I get time."

But he wouldn't. The only way was to go to him and say:

"Doctor, I want to pay ten dollars on account."

"All right," he'd answer, and take the money.

To the credit of the community I may say with truthfulness that the Doctor never suffered. He was even able to supply himself with the best instruments that money could buy. To him nothing was too good for our neighbourhood. This morning I saw in a case at his home a complete set of oculist's instruments, said to be the best in the county—a very unusual equipment for a country doctor. Indeed, he assumed that the responsibility for the health of the community rested upon him. He was a sort of self-constituted health officer. He was always sniffing about for old wells and damp cellars—and somehow, with his crisp humour and sound sense, getting them cleaned. In his old age he even grew querulously particular about these things— asking a little more of human nature than it could quite accomplish. There were innumerable other ways—how they came out to-day all glorified now that he is gone!—in which he served the community.

Horace tells how he once met the Doctor driving his old white horse in the town road.

"Horace," called the Doctor, "why don't you paint your barn?"

"Well," said Horace, "it *is* beginning to look a bit shabby."

"Horace," said the Doctor, "you're a prominent citizen. We look to you to keep up the credit of the neighbourhood."

Horace painted his barn.

I think Doctor North was fonder of Charles Baxter than of anyone else, save his sister. He hated sham and cant: if a man had a single *reality* in him the old Doctor found it; and Charles Baxter in many ways exceeds any man I ever knew in the downright quality of genuineness. The Doctor was never tired of telling—and with humour—how he once went to Baxter to have a table made for his office. When he came to get it he found the table upside down and Baxter on his knees finishing off the under part of the drawer slides. Baxter looked up and smiled in the engaging way he has, and continued his work. After watching him for some time the Doctor said:

"Baxter, why do you spend so much time on that table? Who's going to know whether or not the last touch has been put on the under side of it?"

Baxter straightened up and looked at the Doctor in surprise. "Why, I will," he said.

How the Doctor loved to tell that story! I warrant there is no boy who ever grew up in this country who hasn't heard it.

It was a part of his pride in finding reality that made the Doctor such a lover of true sentiment and such a hater of sentimentality. I prize one memory of him which illustrates this point. The district school gave a "speaking" and we all went. One boy with a fresh young voice spoke a "soldier piece"—the soliloquy of a one-armed veteran who sits at a window and sees the troops go by with dancing banners and glittering bayonets, and the people cheering and shouting. And the refrain went something like this:

"Never again call 'Comrade'
To the men who were comrades for years;
Never again call 'Brother'
To the men we think of with tears."

I happened to look around while the boy was speaking, and there sat the old Doctor with the tears rolling unheeded down his ruddy face; he was thinking, no doubt, of *his* war time and the comrades *he* knew.

On the other hand, how he despised fustian and bombast. His "Bah!" delivered explosively, was often like a breath of fresh air in a stuffy room. Several years ago, before I came here—and it is one of the historic stories of the county—there was a semi-political Fourth of July celebration with a number of ambitious orators. One of them, a young fellow of small worth who wanted to be elected to the legislature, made an impassioned address on "Patriotism." The Doctor was present, for he liked gatherings: he liked people. But he did not like the young orator, and did not want him to be elected. In the midst of the speech, while the audience was being carried through the clouds of oratory, the Doctor was seen to be growing more and more uneasy. Finally he burst out:

"Bah!"

The orator caught himself, and then swept on again.

"Bah!" said the Doctor.

THOMAS FOGARTY.

By this time the audience was really interested. The orator stopped. He knew the Doctor, and he should have known better than to say what he did. But he was very young and he knew the Doctor was opposing him.

"Perhaps," he remarked sarcastically, "the Doctor can make a better speech than I can."

The Doctor rose instantly, to his full height—and he was an impressive-looking man.

"Perhaps," he said, "I can, and what is more, I will." He stood up on a chair and gave them a talk on Patriotism—real patriotism —the patriotism of duty done in the small concerns of life. That speech, which ended the political career of the orator, is not forgotten to-day.

One thing I heard to-day about the old Doctor impressed me deeply. I have been talking about it ever since: it illuminates his character more than anything I have heard. It is singular, too, that I should not have known the story before. I don't believe it was because it all happened so long ago; it rather remained untold out of deference to a sort of neighbourhood delicacy.

I had, indeed, wondered why a man of such capacities, so many qualities of real greatness and power, should have escaped a city career. I said something to this effect to a group of men with whom I was talking this morning. I thought they exchanged glances; one said:

"When he first came out of the army he'd made such a fine record as a surgeon that everyone urged him to go to the city and practice——"

A pause followed which no one seemed inclined to fill.

"But he didn't go," I said.

"No, he didn't go. He was a brilliant young fellow. He *knew* a lot, and he was popular, too. He'd have had a great success——"

Another pause.

"But he didn't go?" I asked promptingly.

"No; he staid here. He was better educated than any man in this county. Why, I've seen him more'n once pick up a book of Latin and read it *for pleasure.*"

I could see that all this was purposely irrelevant, and I liked them for it. But walking home from the cemetery Horace gave me the story; the community knew it to the last detail. I suppose it is a story not uncommon among men, but this morning, told of the old Doctor we had just laid away, it struck me with a tragic poignancy difficult to describe.

"Yes," said Horace, "he was to have been married, forty years ago, and the match was broken off because he was a drunkard."

"A drunkard!" I exclaimed, with a shock I cannot convey.

"Yes, sir," said Horace, "one o' the worst you ever see. He got it in the army. Handsome, wild, brilliant—that was the Doctor. I was a little boy but I remember it mighty well."

He told me the whole distressing story. It was all a long time ago and the details do not matter now. It was to be expected that a man like the old Doctor should love, love once, and love as few men do. And that is what he did—and the girl left him because he was a drunkard!

"They all thought," said Horace, "that he'd up an' kill himself. He said he would, but he didn't. Instid o' that he put an open bottle on his table and he looked at it and said: 'Which is stronger, now, you or John North? We'll make that the test,' he said, 'we'll live or die by that.' Them was his exact words. He couldn't sleep nights and he got haggard like a sick man, but he left the bottle there and never touched it."

How my heart throbbed with the thought of that old silent struggle! How much it explained; how near it brought all these people around him! It made him so human. It is the tragic necessity (but the salvation) of many a man that he should come finally to an irretrievable experience, to the assurance that everything is lost. For with that moment, if he be strong, he is saved. I wonder if anyone ever attains real human sympathy who has not passed through the fire of some such experience. Or to humour either! For in the best laughter do we not hear constantly that deep minor note which speaks of the ache in the human heart? It seems to me I can understand Doctor North!

He died Friday morning. He had been lying very quiet all night; suddenly he opened his eyes and said to his sister: "Good-bye, Kate," and shut them again. That was all. The last call had come and he was ready for it. I looked at his face after death. I saw the iron lines of that old struggle in his mouth and chin; and the humour that it brought him in the lines around his deep-set eyes.

——And as I think of him this afternoon, I can see him—curiously, for I can hardly explain it—carrying a banner as in battle right here among our quiet hills. And those he leads seem to be the people we know, the men, and the women, and the boys! He is the hero of a new age. In olden days he might have been a pioneer, carrying the light of civilisation to a new land; here he has been a sort of moral pioneer—a pioneering far more difficult than any we have ever known. There are no heroics connected with it, the name of the pioneer will not go ringing down the ages; for it is a silent leadership and its success is measured by victories in other lives. We see it now, only too dimly, when he is gone. We reflect sadly that we did not stop to thank him. How busy we were with our own affairs when he was among us! I wonder is there anyone here to take up the banner he has laid down!

——I forgot to say that the Scotch Preacher chose the most impressive text in the Bible for his talk at the funeral:

"He that is greatest among you, let him be . . . as he that doth serve."

And we came away with a nameless, aching sense of loss, thinking how, perhaps, in a small way, we might do something for somebody else—as the old Doctor did.

XII

AN EVENING AT HOME

"How calm and quiet a delight
   Is it, alone,
To read and meditate and write,
   By none offended, and offending none.
To walk, ride, sit or sleep at one's own ease,
   And, pleasing a man's self, none other to displease."
—CHARLES COTTON, A FRIEND OF IZAAK WALTON, 1650.

DURING THE LAST FEW MONTHS so many of the real adventures
of life have been out of doors and so much of the beauty, too,
that I have scarcely written a word about my books. In the
summer the days are so long and the work so engrossing that a
farmer is quite willing to sit quietly on his porch after supper
and watch the long evenings fall—and rest his tired back, and
go to bed early. But the winter is the true time for indoor enjoyment!

Days like these! A cold night after a cold day! Well wrapped,
you have made arctic explorations to the stable, the chicken-yard
and the pig-pen; you have dug your way energetically to the
front gate, stopping every few minutes to beat your arms around
your shoulders and watch the white plume of your breath in the
still air—and you have rushed in gladly to the warmth of the

116

dining-room and the lamp-lit supper. After such a day how sharp your appetite, how good the taste of food! Harriet's brown bread (moist, with thick, sweet, dark crusts) was never quite so delicious, and when the meal is finished you push back your chair feeling like a sort of lord.

"That was a good supper, Harriet," you say expansively.

"Was it?" she asks modestly, but with evident pleasure.

"Cookery," you remark, "is the greatest art in the world——"

"Oh, you were hungry!"

"Next to poetry," you conclude, "and much better appreciated. Think how easy it is to find a poet who will turn you a presentable sonnet, and how very difficult it is to find a cook who will turn you an edible beefsteak——"

I said a good deal more on this subject which I shall not attempt to repeat. Harriet did not listen through it all. She knows what I am capable of when I really get started; and she has her well-defined limits. A practical person, Harriet! When I have gone about so far, she begins clearing the table or takes up her mending—but I don't mind it at all. Having begun talking, it is wonderful how pleasant one's own voice becomes. And think of having a clear field—and no interruptions!

My own particular room, where I am permitted to revel in the desert of my own disorder, opens comfortably off the sitting-room. A lamp with a green shade stands invitingly on the table shedding a circle of light on the books and papers underneath, but leaving all the remainder of the room in dim pleasantness. At one side stands a comfortable big chair with everything in arm's reach, including my note books and ink bottle. Where I sit I can look out through the open doorway and see Harriet near the fireplace rocking and sewing. Sometimes she hums a little tune which I never confess to hearing, lest I miss some of the unconscious cadences. Let the wind blow outside and the snow drift in piles around the doorway and the blinds rattle— I have before me a whole long pleasant evening.

What a convenient and delightful world is this world of books!—if you bring to it not the obligations of the student, or look upon it as an opiate for idleness, but enter it rather with the enthusiasm of the adventurer! It has vast advantages over the ordinary world of daylight, of barter and trade, of work and worry. In this world every man is his own King—the sort of King one loves to imagine, not concerned in such petty matters as wars and parliaments and taxes, but a mellow and moderate despot who is a true patron of genius—a mild old chap who has in his court the greatest men and women in the world— and all of them vying to please the most vagrant of his moods! Invite any one of them to talk, and if your highness is not pleased with him you have only to put him back in his corner —and bring some jester to sharpen the laughter of your highness, or some poet to set your faintest emotion to music!

I have marked a certain servility in books. They entreat you for a hearing: they cry out from their cases—like men, in an eternal struggle for survival, for immortality.

"Take me," pleads this one, "I am responsive to every mood You will find in me love and hate, virtue and vice. I don't preach: I give you life as it is. You will find here adventures cunningly linked with romance and seasoned to suit the most fastidious taste. Try *me*."

"Hear such talk!" cries his neighbour. "He's fiction. What he says never happened at all. He tries hard to make you believe it, but it isn't true, not a word of it. Now, I'm fact. Everything you find in me can be depended upon."

"Yes," responds the other, "but who cares! Nobody wants to read you, you're dull."

"You're false!"

As their voices grow shriller with argument your highness listens with the indulgent smile of royalty when its courtiers contend for its favour, knowing that their very life depends upon a wrinkle in your august brow.

As for me I confess to being a rather crusty despot. When Horace was over here the other evening talking learnedly about silos and ensilage I admit that I became the very pattern of humility, but when I take my place in the throne of my arm-chair with the light from the green-shaded lamp falling on the open pages of my book, I assure you I am decidedly an autocratic person. My retainers must distinctly keep their places! I have my court favourites upon whom I lavish the richest gifts of my attention. I reserve for them a special place in the worn case nearest my person, where at the mere outreaching of an idle hand I can summon them to beguile my moods. The necessary slavies of literature I have arranged in indistinct rows at the farther end of the room where they can be had if I require their special accomplishments.

How little, after all, learning counts in this world either in books or in men. I have often been awed by the wealth of information I have discovered in a man or a book: I have been awed and depressed. How wonderful, I have thought, that one brain should hold so much, should be so infallible in a world of fallibility. But I have observed how soon and completely such a fount of information dissipates itself. Having only things to give, it comes finally to the end of its things: it is empty. What it has hived up so painfully through many a studious year comes now to be common property. We pass that way, take our share, and do not even say "Thank you." Learning is like money; it is of prodigious satisfaction to the possessor thereof, but once given forth it diffuses itself swiftly.

"What have you?" we are ever asking of those we meet. "Information, learning, money?"

We take it cruelly and pass onward, for such is the law of material possessions.

"What have you?" we ask. "Charm, personality, character, the great gift of unexpectedness?"

How we draw you to us! We take you in. Poor or ignorant though you may be, we link arms and loiter; we love you not for what you have or what you give us, but for what you are.

I have several good friends (excellent people) who act always as I expect them to act. There is no flight! More than once I have listened to the edifying conversation of a certain sturdy old gentleman whom I know, and I am ashamed to say that I have thought:

"Lord! if he would jump up now and turn an intellectual handspring, or slap me on the back (figuratively, of course: the other would be unthinkable), or—yes, swear! I—think I could love him."

But he never does—and I'm afraid he never will!

When I speak then of my books you will know what I mean. The chief charm of literature, old or new, lies in its high quality of surprise, unexpectedness, spontaneity: high spirits applied to life. We can fairly hear some of the old chaps you and I know laughing down through the centuries. How we love 'em! They laughed for themselves, not for us!

Yes, there must be surprise in the books that I keep in the worn case at my elbow, the surprise of a new personality perceiving for the first time the beauty, the wonder, the humour, the tragedy, the greatness of truth. It doesn't matter at all whether the writer is a poet, a scientist, a traveller, an essayist or a mere daily space-maker, if he have the God-given grace of wonder.

"What on *earth* are you laughing about?" cries Harriet from the sitting-room.

When I have caught my breath, I say, holding up my book:

"This absurd man here is telling of the adventures of a certain chivalrous Knight."

"But I can't see how you can laugh out like that, sitting all alone there. Why, it's uncanny."

"You don't know the Knight, Harriet, nor his squire Sancho."

"You talk of them just as though they were real persons."

"Real!" I exclaim, "real! Why they are much more real than most of the people we know. Horace is a mere wraith compared with Sancho."

And then I rush out.

"Let me read you this," I say, and I read that matchless chapter wherein the Knight, having clapped on his head the helmet which Sancho has inadvertently used as a receptacle for a dinner of curds and, sweating whey profusely, goes forth to fight two fierce lions. As I proceed with that prodigious story, I can see Harriet gradually forgetting her sewing, and I read on the more furiously until, coming to the point of the conflict wherein the generous and gentle lion, having yawned, "threw out some half yard of tongue wherewith he licked and washed his face," Harriet begins to laugh.

"There!" I say triumphantly.

Harriet looks at me accusingly.

"Such foolishness!" she says. "Why should any man in his senses try to fight caged lions!"

"Harriet," I say, "you are incorrigible."

She does not deign to reply, so I return with meekness to my room.

The most distressing thing about the ordinary fact writer is his cock-sureness. Why, here is a man (I have not yet dropped him out of the window) who has written a large and sober book explaining life. And do you know when he gets through he is apparently much discouraged about this universe. This is the veritable moment when I am in love with my occupation as a despot! At this moment I will exercise the prerogative of tyranny:

"Off with his head!"

I do not believe this person though he have ever so many titles to jingle after his name, nor in the colleges which gave them, if they stand sponsor for that which he writes. I do not believe he has compassed this universe. I believe him to be an inconsequent being like myself—oh, much more learned, of course—and yet only upon the threshold of these wonders. It goes too deep—life—to be solved by fifty years of living. There is far too much in the blue firmament, too many stars, to be dissolved in the feeble logic of a single brain. We are not yet great enough, even this explanatory person, to grasp the "scheme of things entire." This is no place for weak pessimism—this universe. This is Mystery and out of Mystery springs the fine adventure! What we have seen or felt, what we think we know, are insignificant compared with that which may be known.

What this person explains is not, after all, the Universe—but himself, his own limited, faithless personality. I shall not accept his explanation. I escape him utterly!

Not long ago, coming in from my fields, I fell to thinking of the supreme wonder of a tree; and as I walked I met the Professor.

"How," I asked, "does the sap get up to the top of these great maples and elms? What power is there that should draw it upward against the force of gravity?"

He looked at me a moment with his peculiar slow smile.

"I don't know," he said.

"What!" I exclaimed, "do you mean to tell me that science has not solved this simplest of natural phenomena?"

"We do not know," he said. "We explain, but we do not know."

No, my Explanatory Friend, we do not know—we do not know the why of the flowers, or the trees, or the suns; we do not even know why, in our hearts, we should be asking this curious question—and other deeper questions.

No man becomes a great writer unless he possesses a highly developed sense of Mystery, of wonder. A great writer is never *blasé;* everything to him happened not longer ago than this forenoon.

The other night the Professor and the Scotch Preacher happened in here together and we fell to discussing, I hardly know how, for we usually talk the neighbourhood chat of the Starkweathers, of Horace and of Charles Baxter, we fell to discussing old Izaak Walton—and the nonsense (as a scientific age knows it to be) which he sometimes talked with such delightful sobriety.

"How superior it makes one feel, in behalf of the enlightenment and progress of his age," said the Professor, "when he reads Izaak's extraordinary natural history."

"Does it make you feel that way?" asked the Scotch Preacher. "It makes me want to go fishing."

And he took the old book and turned the leaves until he came to page 54.

"Let me read you," he said, "what the old fellow says about the 'fearfulest of fishes.' "

" '. . . Get secretly behind a tree, and stand as free from motion as possible; then put a grasshopper on your hook, and let your hook hang a quarter of a yard short of the water, to which end you must rest your rod on some bough of a tree; but it is likely that the Chubs will sink down towards the bottom of the water at the first shadow of your rod, for a Chub is the fearfulest of fishes, and will do so if but a bird flies over him and makes the least shadow on the water; but they will presently rise up to the top again, and there lie soaring until some shadow affrights them again; I say, when they lie upon the top of the water, look at the best Chub, which you, getting yourself in a fit place, may very easily see, and move your rod as slowly as a snail moves, to that Chub you intend to catch, let your bait fall gently upon the water three or four inches before him, and he will infallibly take the bait, and you will be as sure to catch him. . . . Go your way presently, take my rod, and do as I bid you, and I will sit down and mend my tackling till you return back——' "

"Now I say," said the Scotch Preacher, "that it makes me want to go fishing."

"That," I said, "is true of every great book: it either makes us want to do things, to go fishing, or fight harder or endure more patiently—or it takes us out of ourselves and beguiles us for a time with the friendship of completer lives than our own."

The great books indeed have in them the burning fire of life;

. . . . "nay, they do preserve, as in a violl, the purest efficacie and extraction of that living intellect that bred them. I know they are as lively, and as vigorously productive, as those fabulous Dragon's teeth; which being sown up and down, may chance to spring up armed men."

How soon we come to distinguish the books of the mere writers from the books of real men! For true literature, like happiness, is ever a by-product; it is the half-conscious expression of a man greatly engaged in some other undertaking; it is the song of one working. There is something inevitable, unrestrainable about the great books; they seemed to come despite the author. "I could not sleep," says the poet Horace, "for the pressure of unwritten poetry." Dante said of his books that they "made him lean for many days." I have heard people say of a writer in explanation of his success:

"Oh, well, he has the literary knack."

"The beauty, the wonder, the humour, the tragedy, the greatness of truth"

It is not so! Nothing is further from the truth. He writes well not chiefly because he is interested in writing, or because he possesses any especial knack, but because he is more profoundly, vividly interested in the activities of life and he tells about them—over his shoulder. For writing, like farming, is ever a tool, not an end.

How the great one-book men remain with us! I can see Marcus Aurelius sitting in his camps among the far barbarians writing out the reflections of a busy life. I see William Penn engaged in great undertakings, setting down "Some of the Fruits of Solitude," and Abraham Lincoln striking, in the hasty paragraphs written for his speeches, one of the highest notes in our American literature.

"David?"
"Yes, Harriet."

"I am going up now; it is very late."

"Yes."

"You will bank the fire and see that the doors are locked?"

"Yes."

After a pause: "And, David, I didn't mean—about the story you read. Did the Knight finally kill the lions?"

"No," I said with sobriety, "it was not finally necessary."

"But I thought he set out to kill them."

"He did; but he proved his valour without doing it."

Harriet paused, made as if to speak again, but did not do so.

"Valour"—I began in my hortatory tone, seeing a fair opening, but at the look in her eye I immediately desisted.

"You won't stay up late?" she warned.

"N-o," I said.

Take John Bunyan as a pattern of the man who forgot himself into immortality. How seriously he wrote sermons and pamphlets, now happily forgotten! But it was not until he was shut up in jail (some writers I know might profit by his example) that he "put aside," as he said, "a more serious and important work" and wrote "Pilgrim's Progress." It is the strangest thing in the world—the judgment of men as to what is important and serious! Bunyan says in his rhymed introduction:

> *"I only thought to make*
> *I knew not what: nor did I undertake*
> *Thereby to please my neighbour; no, not I:*
> *I did it my own self to gratify."*

Another man I love to have at hand is he who writes of Blazing Bosville, the Flaming Tinman, and of The Hairy Ones. How Borrow escapes through his books! His object was not to produce literature but to display his erudition as a master of language and of outlandish custom, and he went about the task in all seriousness of demolishing the Roman Catholic Church. We are not now so impressed with his erudition that we do not smile at his vanity and we are quite contented, even after reading his books, to let the church survive; but how shall we spare our friend with his inextinguishable love of life, his pugilists, his gypsies, his horse traders? We are even willing to plow through arid deserts of dissertation in order that we may enjoy the perfect oases in which the man forgets himself!

Reading such books as these and a hundred others, the books of the worn case at my elbow,

> *"The bulged and the bruised octavos,*
> *The dear and the dumpy twelves——"*

I become like those initiated in the Eleusinian mysteries who, as Cicero tells us, have attained "the art of living joyfully and of dying with a fairer hope."

It is late, and the house is still. A few bright embers glow in the fireplace. You look up and around you, as though coming back to the world from some far-off place. The clock in the dining-room ticks with solemn precision; you did not recall that it had so loud a tone. It has been a great evening, in this quiet room on your farm, you have been able to entertain the worthies of all the past!

You walk out, resoundingly, to the kitchen and open the door. You look across the still white fields. Your barn looms black in the near distance, the white mound close at hand is your wood-pile, the great trees stand like sentinels in the moonlight; snow has drifted upon the doorstep and lies there untracked. It is, indeed, a dim and untracked world: coldly beautiful but silent—and of a strange unreality! You close the door with half a shiver and take the real world with you up to bed. For it is past one o'clock.

XIII

THE POLITICIAN

In the city, as I now recall it (having escaped), it seemed to be the instinctive purpose of every citizen I knew not to get into politics but to keep out. We sedulously avoided caucuses and school-meetings, our time was far too precious to be squandered in jury service, we forgot to register for elections, we neglected to vote. We observed a sort of aristocratic contempt for political activity and then fretted and fumed over the low estate to which our government had fallen—and never saw the humour of it all.

At one time I experienced a sort of political awakening: a "boss" we had was more than ordinarily piratical. I think he had a scheme to steal the city hall and sell the monuments in the park (something of that sort), and I, for one, was disturbed. For a time I really wanted to bear a man's part in helping to correct the abuses, only I did not know how and could not find out.

In the city, when one would learn anything about public matters, he turns, not to life, but to books or newspapers. What we get in the city is not life, but what someone else tells us about life. So I acquired a really formidable row of works on

Political Economy and Government (I admire the word "works" in that application) where I found Society laid out for me in the most perfect order—with pennies on its eyes. How often, looking back, I see myself as in those days, reading my learned books with a sort of fury of interest!—

From the reading of books I acquired a sham comfort. Dwelling upon the excellent theory of our institutions, I was content to disregard the realities of daily practice. I acquired a mock assurance under which I proceeded complacently to the polls, and cast my vote without knowing a single man on the ticket, what he stood for, or what he really intended to do. The ceremony of the ballot bears to politics much the relationship that the sacrament bears to religion: how often, observing the formality, we yet depart wholly from the spirit of the institution.

It was good to escape that place of hurrying strangers. It was good to get one's feet down into the soil. It was good to be in a place where things *are* because they *grow,* and politics, not less than corn! Oh, my friend, say what you please, argue how you like, this crowding together of men and women in unnatural surroundings, this haste to be rich in material things, this attempt to enjoy without production, this removal from first-hand life, is irrational, and the end of it is ruin. If our cities were not recruited constantly with the fresh, clean blood of the country, with boys who still retain some of the power and the vision drawn from the soil, where would they be!

"We're a great people," says Charles Baxter, "but we don't always work at it."

"But we talk about it," says the Scotch Preacher.

"By the way," says Charles Baxter, "have you seen George Warren? He's up for supervisor."

"I haven't yet."

"Well, go around and see him. We must find out exactly what he intends to do with the Summit Hill road. If he is weak on that we'd better look to Matt Devine. At least Matt is safe."

The Scotch Preacher looked at Charles Baxter and said to me with a note of admiration in his voice:

"Isn't this man Baxter getting to be intolerable as a politica' boss!"

Baxter's shop! Baxter's shop stands close to the road and just in the edge of a grassy old apple orchard. It is a low, unpainted building, with generous double doors in front, standing irresistibly open as you go by. Even as a stranger coming here first from the city I felt the call of Baxter's shop. Shall I ever forget! It was a still morning—one of those days of warm sunshine—and perfect quiet in the country—and birds in the branches —and apple trees all in bloom. Baxter was whistling at his work in the sunlit doorway of his shop, in his long, faded apron, much worn at the knees. He was bending to the rhythmic movement of his plane, and all around him as he worked rose billows of shavings. And oh, the odours of that shop! the fragrant, resinous odour of new-cut pine, the pungent smell of black walnut, the dull odour of oak wood—how they stole out in the sunshine, waylaying you as you came far up the road, beguiling you as you passed the shop, and stealing reproachfully after you as you went onward down the road.

Never shall I forget that grateful moment when I first passed Baxter's shop—a failure from the city—and Baxter looking out at me from his deep, quiet, gray eyes—eyes that were almost a caress!

My wayward feet soon took me, unintroduced, within the doors of that shop, the first of many visits. And I can say no more in appreciation of my ventures there than that I came out always with more than I had when I went in.

The wonders there! The long bench with its huge-jawed wooden vises, and the little dusty windows above looking out into the orchard, and the brown planes and the row of shiny saws, and the most wonderful pattern squares and triangles and curves, each hanging on its own peg; and above, in the rafters, every sort and size of curious wood. And oh! the old bureaus and whatnots and high-boys in the corners waiting their turn to be mended; and the sticky glue-pot waiting, too, on the end of the sawhorse. There is family history here in this shop—no end of it—the small and yet great (because intensely human) tragedies and humours of the long, quiet years among these sunny hills. That whatnot there, the one of black walnut with the top knocked off, that belonged in the old days to——

"Charles Baxter," calls my friend Patterson from the roadway, "can you fix my cupboard?"

"Bring it in," says Charles Baxter, hospitably, and Patterson brings it in, and stops to talk—and stops—and stops—There is great talk in Baxter's shop—the slow-gathered wisdom of the country, the lore of crops and calves and cabinets. In Baxter's shop we choose the next President of these United States!

You laugh! But we do—exactly that. It is in the Baxters' shops (not in Broadway, not in State Street) where the presidents are decided upon. In the little grocery stores you and I know, in the blacksmithies, in the schoolhouses back in the country!

Forgive me! I did not intend to wander away. I meant to keep to my subject—but the moment I began to talk of politics in the country I was beset by a compelling vision of Charles Baxter coming out of his shop in the dusk of the evening, carrying his curious old reflector lamp and leading the way down the road to the schoolhouse. And thinking of the lamp brought a vision of the joys of Baxter's shop, and thinking of the shop brought me naturally around to politics and presidents; and here I am again where I started!

Baxter's lamp is, somehow, inextricably associated in my mind with politics. Being busy farmers, we hold our caucuses and other meetings in the evening and usually in the schoolhouse. The schoolhouse is conveniently near to Baxter's shop, so we gather at Baxter's shop. Baxter takes his lamp down from the bracket above his bench, reflector and all, and you will see us, a row of dusky figures, Baxter in the lead, proceeding down the roadway to the schoolhouse. Having arrived, someone scratches a match, shields it with his hand (I see yet the sudden fitful illu-

mination of the brown-bearded, watchful faces of my neighbours!) and Baxter guides us into the schoolhouse—with its
shut-in dusty odours of chalk and varnished desks and—yes,
left-over lunches!

Baxter's lamp stands on the table, casting a vast shadow of
the chairman on the wall.

"Come to order," says the chairman, and we have here at this
moment in operation the greatest institution in this round
world: the institution of free self-government. Great in its simplicity, great in its unselfishness! And Baxter's old lamp with
its smoky tin reflector, is not that the veritable torch of our
liberties?

This, I forgot to say, though it makes no special difference—
a caucus would be the same—is a school meeting.

You see, ours is a prolific community. When a young man and
a young woman are married they think about babies; they want

babies, and what is more, they have them! and love them afterward! It is a part of the complete life. And having babies, there must be a place to teach them to live.

Without more explanation you will understand that we needed an addition to our schoolhouse. A committee reported that the amount required would be $800. We talked it over. The Scotch Preacher was there with a plan which he tacked up on the black-board and explained to us. He told us of seeing the stone-mason and the carpenter, he told us what the seats would cost, and the door knobs and the hooks in the closet. We are a careful people; we want to know where every penny goes!

"If we put it all in the budget this year what will that make the rate?" inquires a voice from the end of the room.

We don't look around; we know the voice. And when the secretary has computed the rate, if you listen closely you can almost hear the buzz of multiplications and additions which is going on in each man's head as he calculates exactly how much the addition will mean to him in taxes on his farm, his daughter's piano, his wife's top-buggy.

And many a man is saying to himself:

"If we build this addition to the schoolhouse, I shall have to give up the new overcoat I have counted upon, or Amanda won't be able to get the new cooking-range."

That's *real* politics: the voluntary surrender of some private good for the upbuilding of some community good. It is in such exercises that the fibre of democracy grows sound and strong. There is, after all, in this world no real good for which we do not have to surrender something. In the city the average voter is never conscious of any surrender. He never realises that he is giving anything himself for good schools or good streets. Under such conditions how can you expect self-government? No service, no reward!

The first meeting that I sat through watching those bronzed farmers at work gave me such a conception of the true meaning of self-government as I never hoped to have.

"This is the place where I belong," I said to myself.

It was wonderful in that school meeting to see how every

essential element of our government was brought into play. Finance? We discussed whether we should put the entire $800 into the next year's budget or divide it, paying part in cash and bonding the district for the remainder. The question of credit, of interest, of the obligations of this generation and the next, were all discussed. At one time long ago I was amazed when I heard my neighbours arguing in Baxter's shop about the issuance of certain bonds by the United States government: how completely they understood it! I know now where they got that understanding. Right in the school meetings and town caucuses where they raise money yearly for the expenses of our small government! There is nothing like it in the city.

The progress of a people can best be judged by those things which they accept as matters-of-fact. It was amazing to me, coming from the city, and before I understood, to see how ingrained had become some of the principles which only a few years ago were fiercely-mooted problems. It gave me a new pride in my country, a new appreciation of the steps in civilisation which we have already permanently gained. Not a question have I ever heard in any school meeting of the necessity of educating every American child—at any cost. Think of it! Think how far we have come in that respect, in seventy—yes, fifty—years. Universal education has become a settled axiom of our life.

And there was another point—so common now that we do not appreciate the significance of it. I refer to majority rule. In our school meeting we were voting money out of men's pockets —money that we all needed for private expenses—and yet the moment the minority, after full and honest discussion, failed to maintain its contention in opposition to the new building, it yielded with perfect good humour and went on with the discussion of other questions. When you come to think of it, in the light of history, is not that a wonderful thing?

One of the chief property owners in our neighbourhood is a rather crabbed old bachelor. Having no children and heavy taxes to pay, he looks with jaundiced eye on additions to schoolhouses. He will object and growl and growl and object, and yet pin him down as I have seen the Scotch Preacher pin him more than once, he will admit that children ("of course," he will say, "certainly, of course") must be educated.

"For the good of bachelors as well as other people?" the Scotch Preacher will press it home.

"Certainly, of course."

And when the final issue comes, after full discussion, after he has tried to lop off a few yards of blackboard or order cheaper desks or dispense with the clothes-closet, he votes for the addition with the rest of us.

It is simply amazing to see how much grows out of those discussions—how much of that social sympathy and understanding which is the very tap-root of democracy. It's cheaper to put up a miserable shack of an addition. Why not do it? So we discuss architecture—blindly, it is true; we don't know the books on the subject—but we grope for the big true things, and by our own discussion we educate ourselves to know why a good building is better than a bad one. Heating and ventilation in their relation to health, the use of "fad studies"—how I have heard those things discussed!

How Dr. North, who has now left us forever, shone in those meetings, and Charles Baxter and the Scotch Preacher—broad men, every one—how they have explained and argued, with what patience have they brought into that small schoolhouse, lighted by Charles Baxter's lamp, the grandest conceptions of human society—not in the big words of the books, but in the simple, concrete language of our common life.

"Why teach physiology?"

What a talk Dr. North once gave us on that!

"Why pay a teacher $40 a month when one can be had for $30?"

You should have heard the Scotch Preacher answer that question! Many a one of us went away with some of the education which we had come, somewhat grudgingly, to buy for our children.

These are our political bosses: these unknown patriots, who preach the invisible patriotism which expresses itself not in flags and oratory, but in the quiet daily surrender of private advantage to the public good.

There is, after all, no such thing as perfect equality; there must be leaders, flag-bearers, bosses—whatever you call them. Some men have a genius for leading; others for following; each is necessary and dependent upon the other. In cities, that leadership is often perverted and used to evil ends. Neither leaders nor followers seem to understand. In its essence politics is merely a mode of expressing human sympathy. In the country many and many a leader like Baxter works faithfully year in and year out, posting notices of caucuses, school meetings and elections, opening cold schoolhouses, talking to candidates, prodding selfish voters—and mostly without reward. Occasionally they are elected to petty offices where they do far more work than they are paid for (we have our eyes on 'em); often they are rewarded by the power and place which leadership gives them among their neighbours, and sometimes—and that is Charles Baxter's case—they simply like it! Baxter is of the social temperament: it is the natural expression of his personality. As for thinking of himself as a patriot, he would never dream of it. Work with the hands, close touch with the common life of the soil, has given him much of the true wisdom of experience. He knows us and we know him; he carries the banner, holds it as high as he knows how, and we follow.

Whether there can be a real democracy (as in a city) where there is not that elbow-knowledge, that close neighbourhood sympathy, that conscious surrender of little personal goods for bigger public ones, I don't know.

We haven't many foreigners in our district, but all three were there on the night we voted for the addition. They are Polish. Each has a farm where the whole family works—and puts on a little more Americanism each year. They're good people. It is surprising how much all these Poles, Italians, Germans and others, are like us, how perfectly human they are, when we know them personally! One Pole here, named Kausky, I have come to know pretty well, and I declare I have forgotten that he *is* a Pole. There's nothing like the rub of democracy! The reason why we are so suspicious of the foreigners in our cities is that they are crowded together in such vast, unknown, undigested masses. We have swallowed them too fast, and we suffer from a sort of national dyspepsia.

Here in the country we promptly digest our foreigners and they make as good Americans as anybody.

"Catch a foreigner when he first comes here," says Charles Baxter, "and he takes to our politics like a fish to water."

The Scotch Preacher says they "gape for education." And when I see Kausky's six children going by in the morning to school, all their round, sleepy, fat faces shining with soap, I believe it! Baxter tells with humour how he persuaded Kausky to vote for the addition to the schoolhouse. It was a pretty stiff tax for the poor fellow to pay, but Baxter "figgered children with him," as he said. With six to educate, Baxter showed him that he was actually getting a good deal more than he paid for!

Be it far from me to pretend that we are always right or that we have arrived in our country at the perfection of self-government. I do not wish to imply that all of our people are interested, that all attend the caucuses and school-meetings (some of the most prominent never come near—they stay away, and if things don't go right they blame Charles Baxter!). Nor must I over-emphasise the seriousness of our public interest. But we certainly have here, if anywhere in this nation, real self-government. Growth is a slow process. We often fail in our election of delegates to State conventions; we sometimes vote wrong in national affairs. It is an easy thing to think school district; difficult, indeed, to think State or nation. But we grow. When we make mistakes, it is not because we are evil, but because we don't know. Once we get a clear understanding of the right or wrong of any question you can depend upon us —absolutely—to vote for what is right. With more education we shall be able to think in larger and larger circles—until we become, finally, really national in our interests and sympathies. Whenever a man comes along who knows how simple we are, and how much we really want to do right, if we can be convinced that a thing *is* right—who explains how the railroad question, for example, affects us in our intimate daily lives, what the rights and wrongs of it are, why, we can understand and do understand—and we are ready to act.

It is easy to rally to a flag in times of excitement. The patriotism of drums and marching regiments is cheap; blood is material and cheap; physical weariness and hunger are cheap. But the struggle I speak of is not cheap. It is dramatised by few symbols. It deals with hidden spiritual qualities within the conscience of men. Its heroes are yet unsung and unhonoured. No combats in all the world's history were ever fought so high upward in the spiritual air as these; and, surely, not for nothing!

And so, out of my experience both in city and country, I feel— yes, I *know*—that the real motive power of this democracy lies back in the little country neighbourhoods like ours where men gather in dim schoolhouses and practice the invisible patriotism of surrender and service.

XIV

THE HARVEST

"Oh, Universe, what thou wishest, I wish."
—MARCUS AURELIUS

I COME TO THE END of these Adventures with a regret I can
scarcely express. I, at least, have enjoyed them. I began setting
them down with no thought of publication, but for my own
enjoyment; the possibility of a book did not suggest itself until
afterwards. I have tried to relate the experiences of that secret,
elusive, invisible life which in every man is so far more real, so
far more important than his visible activities—the real expression of a life much occupied in other employment.

When I first came to this farm, I came empty-handed. I was
the veritable pattern of the city-made failure. I believed that
life had nothing more in store for me. I was worn out physically,

mentally and, indeed, morally. I had diligently planned for Success; and I had reaped defeat. I came here without plans. I plowed and harrowed and planted, expecting nothing. In due time I began to reap. And it has been a growing marvel to me, the diverse and unexpected crops that I have produced within these uneven acres of earth. With sweat I planted corn, and I have here a crop not only of corn but of happiness and hope. My tilled fields have miraculously sprung up to friends!

This book is one of the unexpected products of my farm. It is this way with the farmer. After the work of planting and cultivating, after the rain has fallen in his fields, after the sun has warmed them, after the new green leaves have broken the earth—one day he stands looking out with a certain new joy across his acres (the wind bends and half turns the long blades of the corn) and there springs up within him a song of the fields. No matter how little poetic, how little articulate he is, the song rises irrepressibly in his heart, and he turns aside from his task with a new glow of fulfillment and contentment. At harvest time in our country I hear, or I imagine I hear, a sort of chorus rising over all the hills, and I meet no man who is not, deep down within him, a singer! So song follows work: so art grows out of life!

And the friends I have made! They have come to me naturally, as the corn grows in my fields or the wind blows in my trees. Some strange potency abides within the soil of this earth! When two men stoop (there must be stooping) and touch it together, a magnetic current is set up between them: a flow of common understanding and confidence. I would call the attention of all great Scientists, Philosophers, and Theologians to this phenomenon: it will repay investigation. It is at once the rarest and the commonest thing I know. It shows that down deep within us, where we really live, we are all a good deal alike. We have much the same instincts, hopes, joys, sorrows. If only it were not for the outward things that we commonly look upon as important (which are in reality not at all important) we might come together without fear, vanity, envy, or prejudice and be friends. And what a world it would be! If civilisation means anything at all it means the increasing ability of men to look through material possessions, through clothing, through differences of speech and colour of skin, and to see the genuine man that abides within each of us. It means an escape from symbols!

I tell this merely to show what surprising and unexpected things have grown out of my farm. All along I have had more than I bargained for. From now on I shall marvel at nothing! When I ordered my own life I failed; now that I work from day to day, doing that which I can do best and which most delights me, I am rewarded in ways that I could not have imagined. Why, it would not surprise me if heaven were at the end of all this!

Now, I am not so foolish as to imagine that a farm is a perfect place. In these Adventures I have emphasised perhaps too forcibly the joyful and pleasant features of my life. In what I have written I have naturally chosen only those things which were most interesting and charming. My life has not been without discouragement and loss and loneliness (loneliness most of all). I have enjoyed the hard work; the little troubles have troubled me more than the big ones. I detest unharnessing a muddy horse in the rain! I don't like chickens in the barn. And somehow Harriet uses an inordinate amount of kindling wood. But once in the habit, unpleasant things have a way of fading quickly and quietly from the memory.

And you see after living so many years in the city the worst experience on the farm is a sort of joy!

In most men as I come to know them—I mean men who dare to look themselves in the eye—I find a deep desire for more naturalness, more directness. How weary we all grow of this fabric of deception which is called modern life. How passionately we desire to escape but cannot see the way! How our hearts beat with sympathy when we find a man who has turned his back upon it all and who says "I will live it no longer." How we flounder in possessions as in a dark and suffocating bog, wasting our energies not upon life but upon *things*. Instead of employing our houses, our cities, our gold, our clothing, we let these inanimate things possess and employ us—to what utter

weariness. "Blessed be nothing," sighs a dear old lady of my
knowledge.

Of all ways of escape I know, the best, though it is far from
perfection, is the farm. There a man may yield himself most
nearly to the quiet and orderly processes of nature. He may attain most nearly to that equilibrium between the material and
spiritual, with time for the exactions of the first, and leisure
for the growth of the second, which is the ideal of life.

In times past most farming regions in this country have suffered the disadvantages of isolation, the people have dwelt far
distant from one another and from markets, they have had little
to stimulate them intellectually or socially. Strong and peculiar
individuals and families were often developed at the expense
of a friendly community life: neighbourhood feuds were common. Country life was marked with the rigidity of a hard pro-
vincialism. All this, however, is rapidly changing. The closer
settlement of the land, the rural delivery of mails (the morning
newspaper reaches the tin box at the end of my lane at noon),
the farmer's telephone, the spreading country trolleys, more
schools and churches, and cheaper railroad rates, have all helped
to bring the farmer's life well within the stimulating currents
of world thought without robbing it of its ancient advantages.
And those advantages are incalculable: Time first for thought
and reflection (narrow streams cut deep) leading to the growth
of a sturdy freedom of action—which is, indeed, a natural
characteristic of the man who has his feet firmly planted upon
his own land.

A city hammers and polishes its denizens into a defined
model: it worships standardisation; but the country encourages
differentiation, it loves new types. Thus it is that so many great
and original men have lived their youth upon the land. It would
be impossible to imagine Abraham Lincoln brought up in a
street of tenements. Family life on the farm is highly educative;
there is more discipline for a boy in the continuous care of a
cow or a horse than in many a term of school. Industry, patience,
perseverance are qualities inherent in the very atmosphere of
country life. The so-called manual training of city schools is

only a poor makeshift for developing in the city boy those habits which the country boy acquires naturally in his daily life. An honest, hard-working country training is the best inheritance a father can leave his son.

And yet a farm is only an opportunity, a tool. A cornfield, a plow, a woodpile, an oak tree, will cure no man unless he have it in himself to be cured. The truth is that no life, and least of all a farmer's life, is simple—unless it is simple. I know a man

and his wife who came out here to the country with the avowed purpose of becoming, forthwith, simple. They were unable to keep the chickens out of their summer kitchen. They discovered microbes in the well, and mosquitoes in the cistern, and wasps in the garret. Owing to the resemblance of the seeds, their radishes turned out to be turnips! The last I heard of them they were living snugly in a flat in Sixteenth Street—all their troubles solved by a dumb-waiter.

The great point of advantage in the life of the country is that if a man is in reality simple, if he love true contentment, it is the place of all places where he can live his life most freely and fully, where he can *grow*. The city affords no such opportunity; indeed, it often destroys, by the seductiveness with which it flaunts its carnal graces, the desire for the higher life which animates every good man.

While on the subject of simplicity it may be well to observe that simplicity does not necessarily, as some of those who escape from the city seem to think, consist in doing without things, but rather in the proper use of things. One cannot return, unless with affectation, to the crudities of a former existence. We do not believe in Diogenes and his tub. Do you not think the good Lord has given us the telephone (that we may better reach that elbow-rub of brotherhood which is the highest of human ideals) and the railroad (that we may widen our human knowledge and sympathy)—and even the motor-car? (though, indeed, I have sometimes imagined that the motor-cars passing this way had a different origin!). He may have given these things to us too fast, faster than we can bear; but is that any reason why we should denounce them all and return to the old, crude, time-consuming ways of our ancestors? I am no reactionary. I do not go back. I neglect no tool of progress. I am too eager to know every wonder in this universe. The motor-car, if I had one, could not carry me fast enough! I must yet fly!

After my experience in the country, if I were to be cross-examined as to the requisites of a farm, I should say that the chief thing to be desired in any sort of agriculture, is good health in the farmer. What, after all, can touch that! How many of our joys that we think intellectual are purely physical! This joy o' the morning that the poet carols about so cheerfully, is often nothing more than the exuberance produced by a good hot breakfast. Going out of my kitchen door some mornings and standing for a moment, while I survey the green and spreading fields of my farm, it seems to me truly as if all nature were making a bow to me. It seems to me that there never was a better cow than mine, never a more really perfect horse, and as for pigs, could any in this world herald my approach with more cheerful gruntings and squealings!

But there are other requisites for a farm. It must not be too large, else it will keep you away from your friends. Provide a town not too far off (and yet not too near) where you can buy your flour and sell your grain. If there is a railroad convenient (though not so near that the whistling of the engines reaches you), that is an added advantage. Demand a few good old oak trees, or walnuts, or even elms will do. No well-regulated farm should be without trees; and having secured the oaks—buy your fuel of your neighbours. Thus you will be blessed with beauty both summer and winter.

As for neighbours, accept those nearest at hand; you will find them surprisingly human, like yourself. If you like them you will be surprised to find how much they all like you (and will upon occasion lend you a spring-tooth harrow or a butter tub, or help you with your plowing); but if you hate them they will return your hatred with interest. I have discovered that those who travel in pursuit of better neighbours never find them.

Somewhere on every farm, along with the other implements, there should be a row of good books, which should not be allowed to rust with disuse: a book, like a hoe, grows brighter with employment. And no farm, even in this country where we enjoy the even balance of the seasons, rain and shine, shine and rain, should be devoid of that irrigation from the currents of the world's thought which is so essential to the complete life. From the papers which the postman puts in the box flow the true waters of civilisation. You will find within their columns how to be good or how to make pies: you will get out of them what you look for! And finally, down the road from your farm, so that you can hear the bell on Sunday mornings, there should be a little church. It will do you good even though, like me, you do not often attend. It's a sort of Ark of the Covenant; and when you get to it, you will find therein the True Spirit—if you take it with you when you leave home. Of course you will look for good land and comfortable buildings when you buy your farm: they are, indeed, prime requisites. I have put them last for the reason that they are so often first. I have observed, however, that the joy of the farmer is by no means in proportion to the area of his arable land. It is often a nice matter to decide between acres and contentment: men perish from too much as well as from too little. And if it be possible there should be a long table in the dining-room and little chairs around it, and small beds upstairs, and young voices calling at their play in the fields—if it be possible.

Sometimes I say to myself: I have grasped happiness! Here it is; I have it. And yet, it always seems at that moment of complete fulfillment as though my hand trembled, that I might not take it!

I wonder if you recall the story of Christian and Hopeful, how, standing on the hill Clear (as we do sometimes—at our best) they looked for the gates of the Celestial City (as we look —how fondly!):

"Then they essayed to look, but the remembrance of that last thing that the shepherds had showed them made their hands shake, by means of which impediment they could not look steadily through the glass: yet they thought they saw something like the gate, and also some of the glory of the place."

How often I have thought that I saw some of the glory of the place (looking from the hill Clear) and how often, lifting the glass, my hand has trembled!

BOOK II

ADVENTURES IN FRIENDSHIP

I

AN ADVENTURE IN FRATERNITY

Tᴴɪꜱ, I am firmly convinced, is a strange world, as strange a one as I was ever in. Looking about me I perceive that the simplest things are the most difficult, the plainest things, the darkest, the commonest things, the rarest.

I have had an amusing adventure—and made a friend.

This morning when I went to town for my marketing I met a man who was a Mason, an Oddfellow and an Elk, and who wore the evidences of his various memberships upon his coat. He asked me what lodge I belonged to, and he slapped me on the back in the heartiest manner, as though he had known me intimately for a long time. (I may say, in passing, that he was trying to sell me a new kind of corn-planter.) I could not help feeling complimented—both complimented and abashed. For I am not a Mason, or an Oddfellow, or an Elk. When I told him so he seemed much surprised and disappointed.

"You ought to belong to one of our lodges," he said. "You'd be sure of having loyal friends wherever you go.

He told me all about his grips and passes and benefits; he told me how much it would cost me to get in and how much more to stay in and how much for a uniform (which was not

149

compulsory). He told me about the fine funeral the Masons would give me; he said that the Elks would care for my widow and children.

"You're just the sort of a man," he said, "that we'd like to have in our lodge. I'd enjoy giving you the grip of fellowship."

He was a rotund, good-humoured man with a shining red nose and a husky voice. He grew so much interested in telling me about his lodges that I think (I *think*) he forgot momentarily that he was selling corn-planters, which was certainly to his credit.

As I drove homeward this afternoon I could not help thinking of the Masons, the Oddfellows and the Elks—and curiously not without a sense of depression. I wondered if my friend of the corn-planters had found the pearl of great price that I have been looking for so long. For is not friendliness the thing of all things that is most pleasant in this world? Sometimes it has seemed to me that the faculty of reaching out and touching one's neighbour where he really lives is the greatest of human achievements. And it was with an indescribable depression that I wondered if these Masons and Oddfellows and Elks had in reality caught the Elusive Secret and confined it within the insurmountable and impenetrable walls of their mysteries, secrets, grips, passes, benefits.

"It must, indeed," I said to myself, "be a precious sort of fraternity that they choose to protect so sedulously."

I felt as though life contained something that I was not permitted to live. I recalled how my friend of the corn-planters had wished to give me the grip of the fellowship—only he could not. I was not entitled to it. I knew no grips or passes. I wore no uniform.

"It is a complicated matter, this fellowship," I said to myself.

So I jogged along feeling rather blue, marvelling that those things which often seem so simple should be in reality so difficult.

But on such an afternoon as this no man could possibly remain long depressed. The moment I passed the straggling outskirts of the town and came to the open road, the light and glow of the countryside came in upon me with a newness and sweetness impossible to describe. Looking out across the wide fields I could see the vivid green of the young wheat upon the brown soil; in a distant high pasture the cows had been turned out to the freshening grass; a late pool glistened in the afternoon sunshine. And the crows were calling, and the robins had begun to come: and oh, the moist, cool freshness of the air! In the highest heaven (never so high as at this time of the year) floated a few gauzy clouds: the whole world was busy with spring!

I straightened up in my buggy and drew in a good breath. The mare, half startled, pricked up her ears and began to trot. She, too, felt the spring.

"Here," I said aloud, "is where I belong. I am native to this place; of all these things I am a part."

But presently—how one's mind courses back, like some keen-scented hound, for lost trails—I began to think again of my friend's lodges. And do you know, I had lost every trace of depression. The whole matter lay as clear in my mind, as little complicated, as the countryside which met my eye so openly.

"Why!" I exclaimed to myself, "I need not envy my friend's lodges. I myself belong to the greatest of all fraternal orders. I am a member of the Universal Brotherhood of Men."

It came to me so humorously as I sat there in my buggy that I could not help laughing aloud. And I was so deeply absorbed with the idea that I did not at first see the whiskery old man who was coming my way in a farm wagon. He looked at me curiously. As he passed, giving me half the road, I glanced up at him and called out cheerfully:

"How are you, Brother?"

You should have seen him look—and look—and look. After I had passed I glanced back. He had stopped his team, turned half way around in his high seat and was watching me—for he did not understand.

"Yes, my friend," I said to myself, "I *am* intoxicated—with the wine of spring!"

I reflected upon his astonishment when I addressed him as "Brother." A strange word! He did not recognize it. He actually suspected that he was not my Brother.

So I jogged onward thinking about my fraternity, and I don't know when I have had more joy of an idea. It seemed so explanatory!

"I am glad," I said to myself, "that I am a Member. I am sure the Masons have no such benefits to offer in their lodges as we have in ours. And we do not require money of farmers (who have little to pay). We will accept corn, or hen's eggs, or a sandwich at the door, and as for a cheerful glance of the eye, it is for us the best of minted coin."

(Item: to remember. When a man asks money for any good thing, beware of it. You can get a better for nothing.)

I cannot undertake to tell where the amusing reflections which grew out of my idea would finally have led me if I had not been interrupted. Just as I approached the Patterson farm, near the bridge which crosses the creek, I saw a loaded wagon standing on the slope of the hill ahead. The horses seemed to have been unhooked, for the tongue was down, and a man was on his knees between the front wheels.

Involuntarily I said:

"Another member of my society: and in distress!"

I had a heart at that moment for anything. I felt like some old neighbourly Knight travelling the earth in search of adventure. If there had been a distressed mistress handy at that moment, I feel quite certain I could have died for her—if absolutely necessary.

As I drove alongside, the stocky, stout lad of a farmer in his brown duck coat lined with sheep's wool, came up from between the wheels. His cap was awry, his trousers were muddy at the knees where he had knelt in the moist road, and his face was red and angry.

A true knight, I thought to myself, looks not to the beauty of his lady, but only to her distress.

"What's the matter, Brother?" I asked in the friendliest manner.

"Bolt gone," he said gruffly, "and I got to get to town before nightfall."

"Get in," I said, "and we'll drive back. We shall see it in the road."

So he got in. I drove the mare slowly up the hill and we both leaned out and looked. And presently there in the road the bolt lay. My farmer got out and picked it up.

"It's all right," he said. "I was afraid it was clean busted. I'm obliged to you for the lift."

"Hold on," I said, "get in, I'll take you back."

"Oh, I can walk."

"But I can drive you faster," I said, "and you've got to get the load to town before nightfall."

I could not let him go without taking tribute. No matter what the story books say, I am firmly of the opinion that no gentle knight (who was human) ever parted with the fair lady whose misery he had relieved without exchanging the time of day, or offering her a bun from his dinner pail, or finding out (for instance) if she were maid or married.

My farmer laughed and got in.

"You see," I said, "when a member of my society is in distress I always like to help him out."

He paused; I watched him gradually evolve his reply:

"How did you know I was a Mason?"

"Well, I wasn't *sure.*"

"I only joined last winter," he said. "I like it first-rate. When you're a Mason you find friends everywhere."

I had some excellent remarks that I could have made at this

point, but the distance was short and bolts were irresistibly
uppermost. After helping him to put in the bolt, I said:

"Here's the grip of fellowship."

He returned it with a will, but afterward he said doubtfully:
"I didn't feel the grip."

"Didn't you?" I asked. "Well, Brother, it was all there."

"If ever I can do anything for you," he said, "just you let me
know. Name's Forbes, Spring Brook."

And so he drove away.

"A real Mason," I said to myself, "could not have had any
better advantage of his society at this moment than I. I walked
right into it without a grip or a pass. And benefits have also
been distributed."

As I drove onward I felt as though anything might happen
to me before I got home. I know now exactly how all old
knights, all voyageurs, all crusaders, all poets in new places,
must have felt! I looked out at every turn of the road; and,
finally, after I had grown almost discouraged of encountering
further adventure I saw a man walking in the road ahead of
me. He was much bent over, and carried on his back a bag.

When he heard me coming he stepped out of the road and
stood silent, saving every unnecessary motion, as a weary man

will. He neither looked around nor spoke, but waited for me
to go by. He was weary past expectation. I stopped the mare.

"Get in, Brother," I said; "I am going your way."

He looked at me doubtfully; then, as I moved to one side, he
let his bag roll off his back into his arms. I could see the
swollen veins of his neck; his face had the drawn look of the
man who bears burdens.

"Pretty heavy for your buggy," he remarked.

"Heavier for you," I replied.

So he put the bag in the back of my buggy and stepped in
beside me diffidently.

"Pull up the lap robe," I said, "and be comfortable."

"Well, sir, I'm glad of a lift," he remarked. "A bag of seed
wheat is about all a man wants to carry for four miles."

"Aren't you the man who has taken the old Rucker farm?" I
asked.

"I'm that man."

"I've been intending to drop in and see you," I said.

"Have you?" he asked eagerly.

"Yes," I said. "I live just across the hills from you, and I had
a notion that we ought to be neighbourly—seeing that we belong to the same society."

His face, which had worn a look of set discouragement (he
didn't know beforehand what the Rucker place was like!),
had brightened up, but when I spoke of the society it clouded
again.

"You must be mistaken," he said. "I'm not a Mason."

"No more am I," I said.

"Nor an Oddfellow."

"Nor I."

As I looked at the man I seemed to know all about him. Some
people come to us like that, all at once, opening out to some
unsuspected key. His face bore not a few marks of refinement,
though work and discouragement had done their best to oblit-
erate them; his nose was thin and high, his eye was blue, too
blue, and his chin somehow did not go with the Rucker farm.
I knew! A man who in his time had seen many an open door,

but who had found them all closed when he attempted to enter! If any one ever needed the benefits of my fraternity, he was that man.

"What Society did you think I belonged to?" he asked.

"Well," I said, "when I was in town a man who wanted to sell me a corn-planter asked me if I was a Mason——"

"Did he ask you that, too?" interrupted my companion.

"He did," I said. "He did——" and I reflected not without enthusiasm that I had come away without a corn-planter. "And when I drove out of town I was feeling rather depressed because I wasn't a member of the lodge."

"Were you?" exclaimed my companion. "So was I. I just felt as though I had about reached the last ditch. I haven't any money to pay into lodges and it don't seem's if a man could get acquainted and friendly without."

"Farming is rather lonely work sometimes, isn't it?" I observed.

"You bet it is," he responded. "You've been there yourself, haven't you?"

There may be such a thing as the friendship of prosperity; but surely it cannot be compared with the friendship of adversity. Men, stooping, come close together.

"But when I got to thinking it over," I said, "it suddenly occurred to me that I belonged to the greatest of all fraternities. And I recognized you instantly as a charter member."

He looked around at me expectantly, half laughing. I don't suppose he had so far forgotten his miseries for many a day.

"What's that?" he asked.

"The Universal Brotherhood of Men."

Well, we both laughed—and understood.

After that, what a story he told me!—the story of a misplaced man on an unproductive farm. Is it not marvellous how full people are—all people—of humour, tragedy, passionate human longings, hopes, fears—if only you can unloosen the floodgates! As to my companion, he had been growing bitter and sickly with the pent-up humours of discouragement; all he needed was a listener.

He was so absorbed in his talk that he did not at first realize that we had turned into his own long lane. When he discovered it he exclaimed:

"I didn't mean to bring you out of your way. I can manage the bag all right now."

"Never mind," I said, "I want to get you home, to say nothing of hearing how you came out with your pigs."

As we approached the house, a mournful-looking woman came to the door. My companion sprang out of the buggy as much elated now as he had previously been depressed (for that was the coinage of his temperament), rushed up to his wife and led her down to the gate. She was evidently astonished at his enthusiasm. I suppose she thought he had at length discovered his gold mine!

When I finally turned the mare around, he stopped me, laid his hand on my arm and said in a confidential voice:

"I'm glad we discovered that we belong to the same society."

As I drove away I could not help chuckling when I heard his wife ask suspiciously:

"What society is that?"

I heard no word of his answer: only the note in his voice of eager explanation.

And so I drove homeward in the late twilight, and as I came up the lane, the door of my home opened, the light within gleamed kindly and warmly across the darkened yard: and Harriet was there on the step, waiting.

II

A DAY OF PLEASANT BREAD

THEY HAVE ALL GONE NOW, and the house is very still. For the first time this evening I can hear the familiar sound of the December wind blustering about the house, complaining at closed doorways, asking questions at the shutters; but here in my room, under the green reading lamp, it is warm and still. Although Harriet has closed the doors, covered the coals in the fireplace, and said good-night, the atmosphere still seems to tingle with the electricity of genial humanity.

The parting voice of the Scotch Preacher still booms in my ears:

"This," said he, as he was going out of our door, wrapped like an Arctic highlander in cloaks and tippets, "has been a day of pleasant bread."

One of the very pleasantest I can remember!

I sometimes think we expect too much of Christmas Day. We try to crowd into it the long arrears of kindliness and humanity of the whole year. As for me, I like to take my Christmas a little at a time, all through the year. And thus I drift along into the holidays—let them overtake me unexpectedly—waking up some fine morning and suddenly saying to myself:

"Why, this is Christmas Day!"

How the discovery makes one bound out of his bed! What a new sense of life and adventure it imparts! Almost anything may happen on a day like this—one thinks. I may meet friends I have not seen before in years. Who knows? I may discover that this is a far better and kindlier world than I had ever dreamed it could be.

So I sing out to Harriet as I go down:

"Merry Christmas, Harriet"—and not waiting for her sleepy reply I go down and build the biggest, warmest, friendliest fire of the year. Then I get into my thick coat and mittens and open the back door. All around the sill, deep on the step, and all about the yard lies the drifted snow: it has transformed my wood pile into a grotesque Indian mound, and it frosts the roof of my barn like a wedding cake. I go at it lustily with my wooden shovel, clearing out a pathway to the gate.

Cold, too; one of the coldest mornings we've had—but clear and very still. The sun is just coming up over the hill near Horace's farm. From Horace's chimney the white wood-smoke of an early fire rises straight upward, all golden with sunshine, into the measureless blue of the sky—on its way to heaven, for aught I know. When I reach the gate my blood is racing warmly in my veins. I straighten my back, thrust my shovel into the snow pile, and shout at the top of my voice, for I can no longer contain myself:

"Merry Christmas, Harriet."

Harriet opens the door—just a crack.

"Merry Christmas yourself, you Arctic explorer! Oo—but it's cold!"

And she closes the door.

Upon hearing these riotous sounds the barnyard suddenly awakens. I hear my horse whinnying from the barn, the chickens begin to crow and cackle, and such a grunting and squealing as the pigs set up from behind the straw stack, it would do a man's heart good to hear!

"It's a friendly world," I say to myself, "and full of business."

I plow through the snow to the stable door. I scuff and stamp the snow away and pull it open with difficulty. A cloud of steam arises out of the warmth within. I step inside. My horse

" 'Merry Christmas, Harriet' "

raises his head above the stanchion, looks around at me, and strikes his forefoot on the stable floor—the best greeting he has at his command for a fine Christmas morning. My cow, until now silent, begins to bawl.

I lay my hand on the horse's flank and he steps over in his stall to let me go by. I slap his neck and he lays back his ears playfully. Thus I go out into the passageway and give my horse his oats, throw corn and stalks to the pigs and a handful of grain to Harriet's chickens (it's the only way to stop the cackling!). And thus presently the barnyard is quiet again except for the sound of contented feeding.

Take my word for it, this is one of the pleasant moments of life. I stand and look long at my barnyard family. I observe with satisfaction how plump they are and how well they are bearing the winter. Then I look up at my mountainous straw stack with its capping of snow, and my corn crib with the yellow ears visible through the slats, and my barn with its mow full of hay —all the gatherings of the year, now being expended in growth. I cannot at all explain it, but at such moments the circuit of that dim spiritual battery which each of us conceals within seems to close, and the full current of contentment flows through our lives.

All the morning as I went about my chores I had a peculiar sense of expected pleasure. It seemed certain to me that something unusual and adventurous was about to happen—and if it did not happen offhand, why I was there to make it happen! When I went in to breakfast (do you know the fragrance of broiling bacon when you have worked for an hour before breakfast on a morning of zero weather? If you do not, consider that heaven still has gifts in store for you!)—when I went in to breakfast, I fancied that Harriet looked preoccupied, but I was too busy just then (hot corn muffins) to make an inquiry, and I knew by experience that the best solvent of secrecy is patience.

"David," said Harriet, presently, "the cousins can't come!"

"Can't come!" I exclaimed.

"Why, you act as if you were delighted."

"No—well, yes," I said, "I knew that some extraordinary adventure was about to happen!"

"Adventure! It's a cruel disappointment—I was all ready for them."

"Harriet," I said, "adventure is just what we make it. And aren't we to have the Scotch Preacher and his wife?"

"But I've got such a *good* dinner."

"Well," I said, "there are no two ways about it: it must be eaten! You may depend upon me to do my duty."

"We'll have to send out into the highways and compel them to come in," said Harriet ruefully.

I had several choice observations I should have liked to make upon this problem, but Harriet was plainly not listening; she sat with her eyes fixed reflectively on the coffee-pot. I watched her for a moment, then I remarked:

"There aren't any."

"David," she exclaimed, "how did you know what I was thinking about?"

"I merely wanted to show you," I said, "that my genius is not properly appreciated in my own household. You thought of highways, didn't you? Then you thought of the poor; especially the poor on Christmas day; then of Mrs. Heney, who isn't poor any more, having married John Daniels; and then I said, 'There aren't any.'"

Harriet laughed.

"It has come to a pretty pass," she said, "when there are no poor people to invite to dinner on Christmas day."

"It's a tragedy, I'll admit," I said, "but let's be logical about it."

"I am willing," said Harriet, "to be as logical as you like."

"Then," I said, "having no poor to invite to dinner, we must necessarily try the rich. That's logical, isn't it?"

"Who?" asked Harriet, which is just like a woman. Whenever you get a good healthy argument started with her, she will suddenly short-circuit it, and want to know if you mean Mr. Smith, or Joe Perkins's boys, which I maintain is *not* logical.

"Well, there are the Starkweathers," I said.

"David!"

"They're rich, aren't they?"

"Yes, but you know how they live—what dinners they have—and besides, they probably have a houseful of company."

"Weren't you telling me the other day how many people who were really suffering were too proud to let anyone know about it? Weren't you advising the necessity of getting ac-

quainted with people and finding out—tactfully, of course—you
made a point of tact—what the trouble was?"

"But I was talking of *poor* people."

"Why shouldn't a rule that is good for poor people be equally
as good for rich people? Aren't they proud?"

"Oh, you can argue," observed Harriet.

"And I can act, too," I said. "I am now going over to invite
the Starkweathers. I heard a rumour that their cook has left
them and I expect to find them starving in their parlour. Of
course they'll be very haughty and proud, but I'll be tactful, and
when I go away I'll casually leave a diamond tiara in the front
hall."

"What *is* the matter with you this morning?"

"Christmas," I said.

I can't tell how pleased I was with the enterprise I had in
mind: it suggested all sorts of amusing and surprising develop-
ments. Moreover, I left Harriet, finally, in the breeziest of spirits,
having quite forgotten her disappointment over the non-arrival
of the cousins.

"If you *should* get the Starkweathers——"

" 'In the bright lexicon of youth,' " I observed, " 'there is no
such word as fail.' "

So I set off up the town road. A team or two had already been
that way and had broken a track through the snow. The sun
was now fully up, but the air still tingled with the electricity of
zero weather. And the fields! I have seen the fields of June and
the fields of October, but I think I never saw our countryside,
hills and valleys, tree spaces and brook bottoms, more enchant-
ingly beautiful than it was this morning. Snow everywhere—the
fences half hidden, the bridges clogged, the trees laden: where
the road was hard it squeaked under my feet, and where it was
soft I strode through the drifts. And the air went to one's head
like wine!

So I tramped past the Pattersons'. The old man, a grumpy
old fellow, was going to the barn with a pail on his arm.

"Merry Christmas," I shouted.

He looked around at me wonderingly and did not reply. At

the corners I met the Newton boys so wrapped in tippets that I could see only their eyes and the red ends of their small noses. I passed the Williams's house, where there was a cheerful smoke in the chimney and in the window a green wreath with a lively red bow. And I thought how happy everyone must be on a Christmas morning like this! At the hill bridge who should I meet but the Scotch Preacher himself, God bless him!

"Well, well, David," he exclaimed heartily, "Merry Christmas."

I drew my face down and said solemnly:

"Dr. McAlway, I am on a most serious errand."

"Why, now, what's the matter?" He was all sympathy at once.

"I am out in the highways trying to compel the poor of this neighbourhood to come to our feast."

The Scotch Preacher observed me with a twinkle in his eye.

"David," he said, putting his hand to his mouth as if to speak in my ear, "there is a poor man you will na' have to compel."

"Oh, you don't count," I said. "You're coming anyhow."

Then I told him of the errand with our millionaire friends, into the spirit of which he entered with the greatest zest. He was full of advice and much excited lest I fail to do a thoroughly competent job. For a moment I think he wanted to take the whole thing out of my hands.

"Man, man, it's a lovely thing to do," he exclaimed, "but I ha' me doots—I ha' me doots."

At parting he hesitated a moment, and with a serious face inquired:

"Is it by any chance a goose?"

"It is," I said, "a goose—a big one."

He heaved a sigh of complete satisfaction. "You have comforted my mind," he said, "with the joys of anticipation—a goose, a big goose."

So I left him and went onward toward the Starkweathers'. Presently I saw the great house standing among its wintry trees. There was smoke in the chimney but no other evidence of life. At the gate my spirits, which had been of the best all the morning, began to fail me. Though Harriet and I were well enough

acquainted with the Starkweathers, yet at this late moment on
Christmas morning it did seem rather a hare-brained scheme to
think of inviting them to dinner.

"Never mind," I said, "they'll not be displeased to see me
anyway."

I waited in the reception-room, which was cold and felt damp.
In the parlour beyond I could see the innumerable things of
beauty—furniture, pictures, books, so very, very much of everything—with which the room was filled. I saw it now, as I had

often seen it before, with a peculiar sense of weariness. How all
these things, though beautiful enough in themselves, must clut-
ter up a man's life!

Do you know, the more I look into life, the more things it
seems to me I can successfully lack—and continue to grow happier. How many kinds of food I do not need, nor cooks to cook
them, how much curious clothing nor tailors to make it, how
many books that I never read, and pictures that are not worth
while! The farther I run, the more I feel like casting aside all
such impedimenta—lest I fail to arrive at the far goal of my
endeavour.

I like to think of an old Japanese nobleman I once read about,
who ornamented his house with a single vase at a time, living

with it, absorbing its message of beauty, and when he tired of it, replacing it with another. I wonder if he had the right way, and we, with so many objects to hang on our walls, place on our shelves, drape on our chairs, and spread on our floors, have mistaken our course and placed our hearts upon the multiplicity rather than the quality of our possessions!

Presently Mr. Starkweather appeared in the doorway. He wore a velvet smoking-jacket and slippers; and somehow, for a bright morning like this, he seemed old, and worn, and cold.

"Well, well, friend," he said, "I'm glad to see you."

He said it as though he meant it.

"Come into the library; it's the only room in the whole house that is comfortably warm. You've no idea what a task it is to heat a place like this in really cold weather. No sooner do I find a man who can run my furnace than he goes off and leaves me."

"I can sympathize with you," I said, "we often have trouble at our house with the man who builds the fires."

He looked around at me quizzically.

"He lies too long in bed in the morning," I said.

By this time we had arrived at the library, where a bright fire was burning in the grate. It was a fine big room, with dark oak furnishings and books in cases along one wall, but this morning it had a dishevelled and untidy look. On a little table at one side of the fireplace were the remains of a breakfast; at the other a number of wraps were thrown carelessly upon a chair. As I came in Mrs. Starkweather rose from her place, drawing a silk scarf around her shoulders. She is a robust, rather handsome woman, with many rings on her fingers, and a pair of glasses hanging to a little gold hook on her ample bosom; but this morning she, too, looked worried and old.

"Oh, yes," she said with a rueful laugh, "we're beginning a merry Christmas, as you see. Think of Christmas with no cook in the house!"

I felt as if I had discovered a gold mine. Poor starving millionaires!

But Mrs. Starkweather had not told the whole of her sorrowful story.

"We had a company of friends invited for dinner to-day," she said, "and our cook was ill—or said she was—and had to go. One of the maids went with her. The man who looks after the furnace disappeared on Friday, and the stableman has been drinking. We can't very well leave the place without some one who is responsible in charge of it—and so here we are. Merry Christmas!"

I couldn't help laughing. Poor people!

"You might," I said, "apply for Mrs. Heney's place."

"Who is Mrs. Heney?" asked Mrs. Starkweather.

"You don't mean to say that you never heard of Mrs. Heney!" I exclaimed. "Mrs. Heney, who is now Mrs. 'Penny' Daniels? You've missed one of our greatest celebrities."

With that, of course, I had to tell them about Mrs. Heney, who has for years performed a most important function in this community. Alone and unaided she has been the poor whom we are supposed to have always with us. If it had not been for the devoted faithfulness of Mrs. Heney at Thanksgiving, Christmas and other times of the year, I suppose our Woman's Aid Society and the King's Daughters would have perished miserably of undisturbed turkeys and tufted comforters. For years Mrs. Heney filled the place most acceptably. Curbing the natural outpourings of a rather jovial soul she could upon occasion look as deserving of charity as any person that ever I met. But I pitied the little Heneys: it always comes hard on the children. For weeks after every Thanksgiving and Christmas they always wore a painfully stuffed and suffocated look. I only came to appreciate fully what a self-sacrificing public servant Mrs. Heney really was when I learned that she had taken the desperate alternative of marrying "Penny" Daniels.

"So you think we might possibly aspire to the position?" laughed Mrs. Starkweather.

Upon this I told them of the trouble in our household and asked them to come down and help us enjoy Dr. McAlway and the goose.

When I left, after much more pleasant talk, they both came with me to the door seeming greatly improved in spirits.

"You've given us something to live for, Mr. Grayson," said Mrs. Starkweather.

So I walked homeward in the highest spirits, and an hour or more later who should we see in the top of our upper field but Mr. Starkweather and his wife floundering in the snow. They reached the lane literally covered from top to toe with snow and both of them ruddy with the cold.

"We walked over," said Mrs. Starkweather breathlessly, "and I haven't had so much fun in years."

Mr. Starkweather helped her over the fence. The Scotch Preacher stood on the steps to receive them, and we all went in together.

I can't pretend to describe Harriet's dinner: the gorgeous brown goose, and the apple sauce, and all the other things that best go with it, and the pumpkin pie at the end—the finest, thickest, most delicious pumpkin pie I ever ate in all my life. It melted in one's mouth and brought visions of celestial bliss. And I wish I could have a picture of Harriet presiding. I have never seen her happier, or more in her element. Every time she brought in a new dish or took off a cover it was a sort of miracle. And her coffee—but I must not and dare not elaborate.

And what great talk we had afterward!

I've known the Scotch Preacher for a long time, but I never saw him in quite such a mood of hilarity. He and Mr. Starkweather told stories of their boyhood—and we laughed, and laughed—Mrs. Starkweather the most of all. Seeing her so often in her carriage, or in the dignity of her home, I didn't think she had so much jollity in her. Finally she discovered Harriet's cabinet organ, and nothing would do but she must sing for us.

"None of the new-fangled ones, Clara," cried her husband: "some of the old ones we used to know."

So she sat herself down at the organ and threw her head back and began to sing:

"Believe me, if all those endearing young charms,
Which I gaze on so fondly to-day——,"

Mr. Starkweather jumped up and ran over to the organ and joined in with his deep voice. Harriet and I followed. The Scotch Preacher's wife nodded in time with the music, and presently I saw the tears in her eyes. As for Dr. McAlway, he sat on the edge of his chair with his hands on his knees and wagged his shaggy head, and before we got through he, too, joined in with his big sonorous voice:

> *"Thou wouldst still be adored as this moment thou*
> *art——,"*

Oh, I can't tell here—it grows late and there's work to-morrow—all the things we did and said. They stayed until it was dark, and when Mrs. Starkweather was ready to go, she took both of Harriet's hands in hers and said with great earnestness:

"I haven't had such a good time at Christmas since I was a little girl. I shall never forget it."

And the dear old Scotch Preacher, when Harriet and I had wrapped him up, went out, saying:

"This has been a day of pleasant bread."

It has; it has. I shall not soon forget it. What a lot of kindness and common human nature—childlike simplicity, if you will—there is in people once you get them down together and persuade them that the things they think serious are not serious at all.

III

THE OPEN ROAD

"To make space for wandering it is that the world was made so wide."
—GÖETHE, *Wilhelm Meister.*

I LOVE SOMETIMES to have a day alone—a riotous day. Sometimes I do not care to see even my best friends: but I give myself up to the full enjoyment of the world around me. I go out of my door in the morning—preferably a sunny morning, though any morning will do well enough—and walk straight out into the world. I take with me the burden of no duty or responsibility. I draw in the fresh air, odour-laden from orchard and wood. I look about me as if everything were new—and behold everything *is* new. My barn, my oaks, my fences—I declare I never saw them before. I have no preconceived impressions, or beliefs, or opinions. My lane fence is the end of the known earth. I am a discoverer of new fields among old ones. I see, feel, hear, smell, taste all these wonderful things for the first time. I have no idea what discoveries I shall make!

So I go down the lane, looking up and about me. I cross the town road and climb the fence on the other side. I brush one shoulder among the bushes as I pass: I feel the solid yet easy pressure of the sod. The long blades of the timothy-grass clasp at my legs and let go with reluctance. I break off a twig here and there and taste the tart or bitter sap. I take off my hat and let the warm sun shine on my head. I am an adventurer upon a new earth.

Is it not marvellous how far afield some of us are willing to travel in pursuit of that beauty which we leave behind us at home? We mistake unfamiliarity for beauty; we darken our perceptions with idle foreignness. For want of that ardent inner curiosity which is the only true foundation for the appreciation of beauty—for beauty is inward, not outward—we find ourselves hastening from land to land, gathering mere curious resemblances which, like unassimilated property, possess no power of fecundation. With what pathetic diligence we collect peaks and passes in Switzerland; how we come laden from England with vain cathedrals!

Beauty? What is it but a new way of approach? For wilderness, for foreignness, I have no need to go a mile: I have only to come up through my thicket or cross my field from my own roadside—and behold, a new heaven and a new earth!

Things grow old and stale, not because they are old, but because we cease to see them. Whole vibrant significant worlds around us disappear within the sombre mists of familiarity. Whichever way we look the roads are dull and barren. There is a tree at our gate we have not seen in years: a flower blooms in our door-yard more wonderful than the shining heights of the Alps!

It has seemed to me sometimes as though I could see men hardening before my eyes, drawing in a feeler here, walling up an opening there. Naming things! Objects fall into categories for them and wear little sure channels in the brain. A mountain is a mountain, a tree a tree to them, a field forever a field. Life solidifies itself in words. And finally how everything wearies them and that is old age!

Is it not the prime struggle of life to keep the mind plastic? To see and feel and hear things newly? To accept nothing as settled; to defend the eternal right of the questioner? To reject every conclusion of yesterday before the surer observations of to-day?—is not that the best life we know?

And so to the Open Road! Not many miles from my farm there is a tamarack swamp. The soft dark green of it fills the round bowl of a valley. Around it spread rising forests and fields; fences divide it from the known land. Coming across my fields one day, I saw it there. I felt the habit of avoidance. It is

a custom, well enough in a practical land, to shun such a spot of perplexity; but on that day I was following the Open Road, and it led me straight to the moist dark stillness of the tamaracks. I cannot here tell all the marvels I found in that place. I trod where human foot had never trod before. Cobwebs barred my passage (the bars to most passages when we came to them are only cobwebs), the earth was soft with the thick swamp mosses, and with many an autumn of fallen dead, brown leaves. I crossed the track of a muskrat, I saw the nest of a hawk—and how, how many other things of the wilderness I must not here relate. And I came out of it renewed and refreshed; I know now the feeling of the pioneer and the discoverer. Peary has no more than I; Stanley tells me nothing I have not experienced!

What more than that is the accomplishment of the great inventor, poet, painter? Such cannot abide habit-hedged wildernesses. They follow the Open Road, they see for themselves, and will not accept the paths or the names of the world. And Sight, kept clear, becomes, curiously, Insight. A thousand had seen apples fall before Newton. But Newton was dowered with the spirit of the Open Road!

Sometimes as I walk, seeking to see, hear, feel, everything newly, I devise secret words for the things I see: words that convey to me alone the thought, or impression, or emotion of a peculiar spot. All this, I know, to some will seem the acme of foolish illusion. Indeed, I am not telling of it because it is practical; there is no cash at the end of it. I am reporting it as an experience in life; those who understand will understand. And thus out of my journeys I have words which bring back to me with indescribable poignancy the particular impression of a time or a place. I prize them more highly than almost any other of my possessions, for they come to me seemingly out of the air, and the remembrance of them enables me to recall or live over a past experience with scarcely diminished emotion.

And one of these words—how it brings to me the very mood of a gray October day! A sleepy west wind blowing. The fields are bare, the corn shocks brown, and the long road looks flat and dull. Away in the marsh I hear a single melancholy crow. A heavy day, namelessly sad! Old sorrows flock to one's memory and old regrets. The creeper is red in the swamp and the grass is brown on the hill. It comes to me that I was a boy once——

So to the flat road and away! And turn at the turning and rise with the hill. Will the mood change: will the day? I see a lone man in the top of a pasture crying "Coo-ee, coo-ee." I do not see at first why he cries and then over the hill comes the ewes, a dense gray flock of them, huddling toward me. The yokel behind has a stick in each hand. "Coo-ee, coo-ee," he also cries. And the two men, gathering in, threatening, sidling, advancing slowly, the sheep turning uncertainly this way and that, come at last to the boarded pen.

"That's the idee," says the helper.

"A poor lot," remarks the leader: "such is the farmer's life."

From the roadway they back their frame-decked wagon to the fence and unhook their team. The leader throws off his coat and stands thick and muscular in his blue jeans—a roistering fellow with a red face, thick neck and chapped hands.

"I'll pass 'em up," he says; "that's a man's work. You stand in the wagon and put 'em in."

So he springs into the yard and the sheep huddle close into the corner, here and there raising a timid head, here and there darting aside in a panic.

"Hi there, it's for you," shouts the leader, and thrusts his hands deep in the wool of one of the ewes.

"Come up here, you Southdown with the bare belly," says the man in the wagon.

"That's my old game—wrastling," the leader remarks, struggling with the next ewe. "Stiddy, stiddy, now I got you, up with you, dang you!"

"That's the idee," says the man in the wagon.

So I watch and they pass up the sheep one by one and as I go down the road I hear the leader's thick voice, "Stiddy, stiddy," and the response of the other, "That's the idee." And so on into the gray day!

My Open Road leads not only to beauty, not only to fresh

adventures in outer observation. I believe in the Open Road in religion, in education, in politics: there is nothing really settled, fenced in, nor finally decided upon this earth. Nothing that is not questionable. I do not mean that I would immediately tear down well-built fences or do away with established and beaten roads. By no means. The wisdom of past ages is likely to be wiser than any hasty conclusions of mine. I would not invite any other person to follow my road until I had well proven it a better way toward truth than that which time had established. And yet I would have every man tread the Open Road; I would have him upon occasion question the smuggest institution and look askance upon the most ancient habit. I would have him throw a doubt upon Newton and defy Darwin! I would have him look straight at men and nature with his own eyes. He should acknowledge no common gods unless he proved them gods for himself. The "equality of men" which we worship: is there not a higher inequality? The material progress which we deify: is it real progress? Democracy—is it after all better than monarchy? I would have him question the canons of art, literature, music, morals: so will he continue young and useful!

And yet sometimes I ask myself. What do I travel for? Why all this excitement and eagerness of inquiry? What is it that I go forth to find? Am I better for keeping my roads open than my neighbour is who travels with contentment the paths of ancient habit? I am gnawed by the tooth of unrest—to what end? Often as I travel I ask myself that question and I have never had a convincing answer. I am looking for something I cannot find. My Open Road is open, too, at the end! What is it that drives a man onward, that scourges him with unanswered questions! We only know that we are driven; we do not know who drives. We travel, we inquire, we look, we work—only knowing that these activities satisfy a certain deep and secret demand within us. We have Faith that there is a Reason: and is there not a present Joy in following the Open Road?

> "And O the joy that is never won,
>   But follows and follows the journeying sun."

And at the end of the day the Open Road, if we follow it with wisdom as well as fervour, will bring us safely home again. For after all the Open Road must return to the Beaten Path. The Open Road is for adventure; and adventure is not the food of life, but the spice.

Thus I came back this evening from rioting in my fields. As I walked down the lane I heard the soft tinkle of a cowbell, a certain earthy exhalation, as of work, came out of the bare fields, the duties of my daily life crowded upon me bringing a pleasant calmness of spirit, and I said to myself:

"Lord be praised for that which is common."

And after I had done my chores I came in, hungry, to my supper.

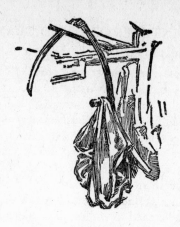

IV

ON BEING WHERE YOU BELONG

Sunday Morning, May 20th.

O<small>N FRIDAY</small> I began planting my corn. For many days previously I went out every morning at sun-up, in the clear, sharp air, and thrust my hand deep down in the soil of the field. I do not know that I followed any learned agricultural rule, but somehow I liked to do it. It has seemed reasonable to me, instead of watching for a phase of the moon (for I do not cultivate the moon), to inquire of the earth itself. For many days I had no response; the soil was of an icy, moist coldness, as of death. "I am not ready yet," it said; "I have not rested my time."

Early in the week we had a day or two of soft sunshine, of fecund warmth, to which the earth lay open, willing, passive. On Thursday morning, though a white frost silvered the harrow ridges, when I thrust my hand into the soil I felt, or seemed to feel, a curious response: a strange answering of life to life. The stone had been rolled from the sepulchre!

And I knew then that the destined time had arrived for my planting. That afternoon I marked out my corn-field, driving

177

the mare to my home-made wooden marker, carefully observant of the straightness of the rows; for a crooked corn-row is a sort of immorality. I brought down my seed corn from the attic, where it had hung waiting all winter, each ear suspended separately by the white, up-turned husks. They were the selected ears of last year's crop, even of size throughout, smooth of kernel, with tips well-covered—the perfect ones chosen among many to perpetuate the highest excellencies of the crop. I carried them to the shed next my barn, and shelled them out in my hand machine: as fine a basket of yellow dent seed as a man ever saw. I have listened to endless discussions as to the relative merits of flint and dent corn. I here cast my vote emphatically for yellow dent: it is the best Nature can do!

I found my seed-bag hanging, dusty, over a rafter in the shed, and Harriet sewed a buckle on the strip that goes around the waist. I cleaned and sharpened my hoe.

"Now," I said to myself, "give me a good day and I am ready to plant."

The sun was just coming up on Friday, looking over the trees into a world of misty and odorous freshness. When I climbed the fence I dropped down in the grass at the far corner of the field. I had looked forward this year with pleasure to the planting of a small field by hand—the adventure of it—after a number of years of horse planting (with Horace's machine) of far larger fields. There is an indescribable satisfaction in answering, "Present!" to the roll-call of Nature: to plant when the earth is ready, to cultivate when the soil begins to bake and harden, to harvest when the grain is fully ripe. It is the chief joy of him who lives close to the soil that he comes, in time, to beat in consonance with the pulse of the earth; its seasons become his seasons; its life his life.

Behold me, then, with a full seed-bag suspended before me, buckled both over the shoulders and around the waist, a shiny hoe in my hand (the scepter of my dominion), a comfortable, rested feeling in every muscle of my body, standing at the end of the first long furrow there in my field on Friday morning—a whole spring day open before me! At that moment I would not have changed my place for the place of any king, prince, or president.

At first I was awkward enough, for it has been a long time since I have done much hand planting; but I soon fell into the rhythmic swing of the sower, the sure, even, accurate step; the turn of the body and the flexing of the wrists as the hoe strikes downward; the deftly hollowed hole; the swing of the hand to the seed-bag; the sure fall of the kernels; the return of the hoe;

the final determining pressure of the soil upon the seed. One falls into it and follows it as he would follow the rhythm of a march.

Even the choice of seed becomes automatic, instinctive. At first there is a conscious counting by the fingers—five seeds:

> *One for the blackbird,*
> *One for the crow,*
> *One for the cutworm,*
> *Two to grow.*

But after a time one ceases to count five, and *feels* five, instinctively rejecting a monstrous six, or returning to complete an inferior four.

I wonder if you know the feel of the fresh, soft soil, as it answers to your steps, giving a little, responding a little (as life always does)—and is there not something endlessly good and pleasant about it? And the movement of the arms and shoulders, falling easily into that action and reaction which yields the most service to the least energy! Scientists tell us that the awkward young eagle has a wider wing-stretch than the old, skilled eagle. So the corn planter, at noon, will do his work with half the expended energy of the early morning: he attains the artistry of motion. And quite beyond and above this physical accomplishment is the ever-present, scarcely conscious sense of reward, repayment, which one experiences as he covers each planting of seeds.

As the sun rose higher the mists stole secretly away, first toward the lower brook-hollows, finally disappearing entirely; the morning coolness passed, the tops of the furrows dried out to a lighter brown, and still I followed the long planting. At each return I refilled my seed-bag, and sometimes I drank from the jug of water which I had hidden in the grass. Often I stood a moment by the fence to look up and around me. Through the clear morning air I could hear the roosters crowing vaingloriously from the barnyard, and the robins were singing, and occasionally from the distant road I heard the rumble of a wagon. I noted the slow kitchen smoke from Horace's chimney, the tip of which I could just see over the hill from the margin of my field—and my own pleasant home among its trees—and my barn—all most satisfying to look upon. Then I returned to the sweat and heat of the open field, and to the steady swing of the sowing.

Joy of life seems to me to arise from a sense of being where one belongs, as I feel right here; of being foursquare with the life we have chosen. All the discontented people I know are trying sedulously to be something they are not, to do something they cannot do. In the advertisements of the country paper I find men angling for money by promising to make women beautiful and men learned or rich—overnight—by inspiring good farmers and carpenters to be poor doctors and lawyers. It is curious, is it not, with what skill we will adapt our sandy land

"Often I stood a moment by the fence"

to potatoes and grow our beans in clay, and with how little wisdom we farm the soils of our own natures. We try to grow poetry where plumbing would thrive grandly!—not knowing that plumbing is as important and honourable and necessary to this earth as poetry.

I understand it perfectly; I too, followed long after false gods. I thought I must rush forth to see the world, I must forthwith become great, rich, famous; and I hurried hither and thither, seeking I knew not what. Consuming my days with the infinite distractions of travel, I missed, as one who attempts two occupations at once, the sure satisfaction of either. Beholding the exteriors of cities and of men, I was deceived with shadows; my life took no hold upon that which is deep and true. Colour I got, and form, and a superficial aptitude in judging by symbols. It was like the study of a science: a hasty review gives one the general rules, but it requires a far profounder insight to know the fertile exceptions.

But as I grow older I remain here on my farm, and wait quietly for the world to pass this way. My oak and I, we wait, and we are satisfied. Here we stand among our clods; our feet are rooted deep within the soil. The wind blows upon us and delights us, the rain falls and refreshes us, the sun dries and sweetens us. We are become calm, slow, strong; so we measure rectitudes and regard essentials, my oak and I.

I would be a hard person to dislodge or uproot from this spot of earth. I belong here; I grow here. I like to think of the old fable of the wrestler of Irassa. For I am veritably that Anteus who was the wrestler of Irassa and drew his strength from the ground. So long as I tread the long furrows of my planting, with my feet upon the earth, I am invincible and unconquerable. Hercules himself, though he comes upon me in the guise of Riches, or Fame, or Power, cannot overthrow me—save as he takes me away from this soil. For at each step my strength is renewed. I forget weariness, old age has no dread for me.

Some there may be who think I talk dreams; they do not know reality. My friend, did it ever occur to you that you are unhappy because you have lost connection with life? Because your feet are not somewhere firm planted upon the soil of reality? Contentment, and indeed usefulness, comes as the infallible result of great acceptances, great humilities—of not trying to make ourselves this or that (to conform to some dramatized version of ourselves), but of surrendering ourselves to the fullness of life—of letting life flow through us. To be used!—that is the sublimest thing we know.

It is a distinguishing mark of greatness that it has a tremendous hold upon real things. I have seen men who seemed to have behind them, or rather within them, whole societies, states, institutions: how they come at us, like Atlas bearing the world! For they act not with their own feebleness, but with a strength as of the Whole of Life. They speak, and the words are theirs, but the voice is the Voice of Mankind.

I don't know what to call it: being right with God or right with life. It is strangely the same thing; and God is not particular as to the name we know him by, so long as we know Him. Musing upon these secret things, I seem to understand what the theologians in their darkness have made so obscure. Is it not just this at-one-ment with life which sweetens and saves us all?

In all these writings I have glorified the life of the soil until I am ashamed. I have loved it because it saved me. The farm for me, I decided long ago, is the only place where I can flow strongly and surely. But to you, my friend, life may present a wholly different aspect, variant necessities. Knowing what I have experienced in the city, I have sometimes wondered at the happy (even serene) faces I have seen in crowded streets. There must be, I admit, those who can flow and be at one with the life, too. And let them handle their money, and make shoes, and sew garments, and write in ledgers—if that completes and contents them. I have no quarrel with any one of them. It is, after all, a big and various world, where men can be happy in many ways.

For every man is a magnet, highly and singularly sensitized. Some draw to them fields and woods and hills, and are drawn in return; and some draw swift streets and the riches which are known to cities. It is not of importance what we draw, but that we really draw. And the greatest tragedy in life, as I see it, is that thousands of men and women never have the opportunity to draw with freedom; but they exist in weariness and labour, and are drawn upon like inanimate objects by those who live in unhappy idleness. They do not farm: they are farmed. But that is a question foreign to present considerations. We may be assured, if we draw freely, like the magnet of steel which gathers its iron filings about it in beautiful and symmetrical forms, that the things which we attract will also become symmetrical and harmonious with our lives.

Thus flowing with life, self-surrendering to life a man becomes indispensable to life, he is absolutely necessary to the conduct of this universe. And it is the feeling of being necessary, of being desired, flowing into a man that produces the satisfaction of contentment. Often and often I think to myself:

These fields have need of me; my horse whinnies when he hears my step; my dog barks a welcome. These, my neighbours, are glad of me. The corn comes up fresh and green to my planting; my buckwheat bears richly. I am indispensable in this place. What is more satisfactory to the human heart than to be needed and to know we are needed? One line in the Book of Chronicles, when I read it, flies up at me out of the printed page as though it were alive, conveying newly the age-old agony of a misplaced man. After relating the short and evil history of Jehoram, King of Judah, the account ends—with the appalling terseness which often crowns the dramatic climaxes of that matchless writing:

"And (he) departed without being desired."

Without being desired! I have wondered if any man was ever cursed with a more terrible epitaph!

And so I planted my corn; and in the evening I felt the dumb weariness of physical toil. Many times in older days I have known the wakeful nerve-weariness of cities. This was not it. It was the weariness which, after supper, seizes upon one's limbs with half-aching numbness. I sat down on my porch with a nameless content. I looked off across the countryside. I saw the evening shadows fall, and the moon come up. And I wanted nothing I had not. And finally sleep swept in resistless waves upon me and I stumbled up to bed—and sank into dreamless slumber.

V

THE STORY OF ANNA

IT IS THE PRIME SECRET of the Open Road (but I may here tell it aloud) that you are to pass nothing, reject nothing, despise nothing upon this earth. As you travel, many things both great and small will come to your attention; you are to regard all with open eyes and a heart of simplicity. Believe that everything belongs somewhere; each thing has its fitting and luminous place within this mosaic of human life. The True Road is not open to those who withdraw the skirts of intolerance or lift the chin of pride. Rejecting the least of those who are called common or unclean, it is (curiously) you yourself that you reject. If you despise that which is ugly you do not know that which is beautiful. For what is beauty but completeness? The roadside beggar belongs here, too; and the idiot boy who wanders idly in the open fields; and the girl who withholds (secretly) the name of the father of her child.

I remember as distinctly as though it happened yesterday the particular evening three years ago when I saw the Scotch Preacher come hurrying up the road toward my house. It was June. I had come out after supper to sit on my porch and look out upon the quiet fields. I remember the grateful cool of the evening air, and the scents rising all about me from garden and roadway and orchard. I was tired after the work of the day and sat with a sort of complete comfort and contentment which comes only to those who work long in the quiet of outdoor places. I remember the thought came to me, as it has come in various forms so many times, that in such a big and beautiful world there should be no room for the fever of unhappiness or discontent.

And then I saw McAlway coming up the road. I knew instantly that something was wrong. His step, usually so de-deliberate, was rapid; there was agitation in every line of his countenance. I walked down through the garden to the gate and met him there. Being somewhat out of breath he did not speak at once. So I said:

"It is not, after all, as bad as you anticipate."

"David," he said, and I think I never heard him speak more seriously, "it is bad enough."

He laid his hand on my arm.

"Can you hitch up your horse and come with me—right away?"

McAlway helped with the buckles and said not a word. In ten minutes, certainly not more, we were driving together down the lane.

"Do you know a family named Williams living on the north road beyond the three corners?" asked the Scotch Preacher.

Instantly a vision of a somewhat dilapidated house, standing not unpicturesquely among ill-kept fields, leaped to my mind.

"Yes," I said; "but I can't remember any of the family except a gingham girl with yellow hair. I used to see her on her way to school."

"A girl!" he said, with a curious note in his voice; "but a woman now."

He paused a moment; then he continued sadly:

"As I grow older it seems a shorter and shorter step between child and child. David, she has a child of her own."

"But I didn't know—she isn't——"

"A woods child," said the Scotch Preacher.

I could not find a word to say. I remember the hush of the evening there in the country road, the soft light fading in the fields. I heard a whippoorwill calling from the distant woods.

"They made it hard for her," said the Scotch Preacher, "especially her older brother. About four o'clock this afternoon she ran away, taking her baby with her. They found a note saying they would never again see her alive. Her mother says she went toward the river."

I touched up the mare. For a few minutes the Scotch Preacher sat silent, thinking. Then he said, with a peculiar tone of kindness in his voice,

"She was a child, just a child. When I talked with her yesterday she was perfectly docile and apparently contented. I cannot imagine her driven to such a deed of desperation. I asked her: 'Why did you do it, Anna?' She answered, 'I don't know: I— I don't know!' Her reply was not defiant or remorseful: it was merely explanatory."

He remained silent again for a long time.

"David," he said finally, "I sometimes think we don't know half as much about human nature as we—we preach. If we did, I think we'd be more careful in our judgments."

He said it slowly, tentatively: I knew it came straight from his heart. It was this spirit, more than the title he bore, far more than the sermons he preached, that made him in reality the minister of our community. He went about thinking that, after all, he didn't know much, and that therefore he must be kind.

As I drove up to the bridge, the Scotch Preacher put one hand on the reins. I stopped the horse on the embankment and we both stepped out.

"She would undoubtedly have come down this road to the river," McAlway said in a low voice.

It was growing dark. When I walked out on the bridge my legs were strangely unsteady; a weight seemed pressing on my breast so that my breath came hard. We looked down into the shallow, placid water: the calm of the evening was upon it; the middle of the stream was like a rumpled glassy ribbon, but the edges, deep-shaded by overhanging trees, were of a mysterious darkness. In all my life I think I never experienced such a degree of silence—of breathless, oppressive silence. It seemed as if, at any instant, it must burst into some fearful excess of sound.

Suddenly we heard a voice—in half-articulate exclamation. I turned, every nerve strained to the uttermost. A figure, seemingly materialized out of darkness and silence, was moving on the bridge.

"Oh!—McAlway," a voice said.

Then I heard the Scotch Preacher in low tones.

"Have you seen Anna Williams?"

"She is at the house," answered the voice.

"Get your horse," said the Scotch Preacher.

I ran back and led the mare across the bridge (how I remember, in that silence, the thunder of her hoofs on the loose boards!). Just at the top of the little hill leading up from the bridge the two men turned in at a gate. I followed quickly and the three of us entered the house together. I remember the musty, warm, shut-in odour of the front room. I heard the faint cry of a child. The room was dim, with a single kerosene lamp, but I saw three women huddled by the stove, in which a new fire was blazing. Two looked up as we entered, with feminine instinct moving aside to hide the form of the third.

"She's all right, as soon as she gets dry," one of them said.

The other woman turned to us half complainingly:

"She ain't said a single word since we got her in here, and she won't let go of the baby for a minute."

"She don't cry," said the other, "but just sits there like a statue."

McAlway stepped forward and said:

"Well—Anna?"

The girl looked up for the first time. The light shone full in her face: a look I shall never forget. Yes, it was the girl I had seen so often, and yet not the girl. It was the same childish face, but all marked upon with inexplicable wan lines of a certain mysterious womanhood. It was childish, but bearing upon it an inexpressible look of half-sad dignity, that stirred a man's heart to its profoundest depths. And there was in it, too, as I have thought since, a something I have seen in the faces of old, wise men: a light (how shall I explain it?) as of experience—of boundless experience. Her hair hung in wavy dishevelment about her head and shoulders, and she clung passionately to the child in her arms.

The Scotch Preacher had said, "Well—Anna?" She looked up and replied:

"They were going to take my baby away."

"Were they!" exclaimed McAlway in his hearty voice. "Well, we'll never permit *that*. Who's got a better right to the baby than you, I'd like to know?"

Without turning her head, the tears came to her eyes and rolled unheeded down her face.

"Yes, sir, Dr. McAlway," the man said, "I was coming across the bridge with the cows when I see her standing there in the water, her skirts all floating around her. She was hugging the baby up to her face and saying over and over, just like this: 'I don't dare! Oh, I don't dare! But I must. I must.' She was sort of singin' the words: 'I don't dare. I don't dare, but I must.' I jumped the railing and run down to the bank of the river. And I says, 'Come right out o' there'; and she turned and come out just as gentle as a child, and I brought her up here to the house."

It seemed perfectly natural at this time that I should take the girl and her child home to Harriet. She would not go back to her own home, though we tried to persuade her, and the Scotch Preacher's wife was visiting in the city, so she could not go there. But after I found myself driving homeward with the girl—while McAlway went over the hill to tell her family—the mood of action passed. It struck me suddenly, "What will Harriet say?" Upon which my heart sank curiously, and refused to resume its natural position.

In the past I had brought her tramps and peddlers and itinerant preachers, all of whom she had taken in with patience—but this, I knew, was different. For a few minutes I wished devoutly I were in Timbuctu or some other far place. And then the absurdity of the situation struck me all at once, and I couldn't help laughing aloud.

"It's a tremendous old world," I said to myself. "Why, anything may happen anywhere!"

The girl stirred, but did not speak. I was afraid I had frightened her.

"Are you cold?" I asked.

"No, sir," she answered faintly.

I could think of nothing whatever to say, so I said it:

"Are you fond of hot corn-meal mush?"

"Yes, sir," very faintly.

"With cream on it—rich yellow cream—and plenty of sugar?"

"Yes, sir."

"Well, I'll bet a nickel that's what we're going to get!"

"Yes, sir."

We drove up the lane and stopped at the yard gate. Harriet opened the door. I led the small dark figure into the warmth and light of the kitchen. She stood helplessly holding the baby tight in her arms—as forlorn and dishevelled a figure as one could well imagine.

"Harriet," I said, "this is Anna Williams."

Harriet gave me her most tremendous look. It seemed to me at that moment that it wasn't my sister Harriet at all that I was facing, but some stranger and much greater person than I had ever known. Every man has, upon occasion, beheld his wife, his sister, his mother even, become suddenly unknown, suddenly commanding, suddenly greater than himself or any other man.

For a woman possesses the occult power of becoming instantly, miraculously, the Accumulated and Personified Customs, Morals and Institutions of the Ages. At this moment, then, I felt myself slowly but surely shrinking and shrivelling up. It is a most uncomfortable sensation to find one's self face to face with Society-at-Large. Under such circumstances I always know what to do. I run. So I clapped my hat on my head, declared that the mare must be unharnessed immediately, and started for the door. Harriet followed. Once outside she closed the door behind her.

"David, *David,* DAVID," she said.

It occurred to me now for the first time (which shows how stupid I am) that Harriet had already heard the story of Anna Williams. And it had gained so much bulk and robustity in travelling, as such stories do in the country, that I have no doubt the poor child seemed a sort of devastating monster of iniquity. How the country scourges those who do not walk the beaten path! In the careless city such a one may escape to unfamiliar streets and consort with unfamiliar people, and still find a way of life, but here in the country the eye of Society never sleeps!

For a moment I was appalled by what I had done. Then I thought of the Harriet I knew so well: the inexhaustible heart of her. With a sudden inspiration I opened the kitchen door and we both looked in. The girl stood motionless just where I left her: an infinitely pathetic figure.

"Harriet," I said, "that girl is hungry—and cold."

Well, it worked. Instantly Harriet ceased to be Society-at-Large and became the Harriet I know, the Harriet of infinite compassion for all weak creatures. When she had gone in I pulled my hat down and went straight for the barn. I guess I know when it's wise to be absent from places.

I unharnessed the mare, and watered and fed her; I climbed up into the loft and put down a rackful of hay; I let the cows out into the pasture and set up the bars. And then I stood by the gate and looked up into the clear June sky. No man, I think, can remain long silent under the stars, with the brooding, mysterious night around about him, without feeling, poignantly, how little he understands anything, how inconsequential his actions are, how feeble his judgments.

And I thought as I stood there how many a man, deep down in his heart, knows to a certainty that he has escaped being an outcast, not because of any real moral strength or resolution of his own, but because Society has bolstered him up, hedged him about with customs and restrictions until he never has had a really good opportunity to transgress. And some do not sin for very lack of courage and originality: they are helplessly good.

How many men in their vanity take to themselves credit for the built-up virtues of men who are dead! There is no cause for surprise when we hear of a "foremost citizen," the "leader in all good works," suddenly gone wrong; not the least cause for surprise. For it was not he that was moral, but Society. Individually he had never been tested, and when the test came he fell. It will give us a large measure of true wisdom if we stop sometimes when we have resisted a temptation and ask ourselves why, at that moment, we did right and not wrong. Was it the deep virtue, the high ideals in our souls, or was it the compulsion of the Society around us? And I think most of us will be astonished to discover what fragile persons we really are—in ourselves.

I stopped for several minutes at the kitchen door before I dared to go in. Then I stamped vigorously on the boards, as if I had come rushing up to the house without a doubt in my mind—

I even whistled—and opened the door jauntily. And had my pains for nothing!

The kitchen was empty, but full of comforting and homelike odours. There was undoubtedly hot mush in the kettle. A few minutes later Harriet came down the stairs. She held up one finger warningly. Her face was transfigured.

"David," she whispered, "the baby's asleep."

So I tiptoed across the room. She tiptoed after me. Then I faced about, and we both stood there on our tiptoes, holding our breath—at least I held mine.

"David," Harriet whispered, "did you see the baby?"

"No," I whispered.

"I think it's the finest baby I ever saw in my life."

When I was a boy, and my great-aunt, who lived for many years in a little room with dormer windows at the top of my father's house, used to tell me stories (the best I ever heard), I was never content with the endings of them. "What happened next?" I remember asking a hundred times; and if I did not ask the question aloud it arose at least in my own mind.

If I were writing fiction I might go on almost indefinitely with the story of Anna; but in real life stories have a curious way of coming to quick fruition, and withering away after having cast the seeds of their immortality.

"Did you see the baby?" Harriet had asked. She said no word about Anna: a BABY had come into the world. Already the present was beginning to draw the charitable curtains of its forgetfulness across this simple drama; already Harriet and Anna and all the rest of us were beginning to look to the "finest baby we ever saw in all our lives."

I might, indeed, go into the character of Anna and the whys and wherefores of her story; but there is curiously little that is strange or unusual about it. It was just Life. A few days with us worked miraculous changes in the girl; like some stray kitten brought in crying from the cold, she curled herself up comfortably there in our home, purring her contentment. She was not in the least a tragic figure: though down deep under

I wish I could here convey the tone of buoyancy with which he said these words. There was a largeness and confidence in them that carried me away. He told me that he was now "working with the experts"—those were his words—and that he would soon begin building a house that would astonish the country. Upon this he turned abruptly away, but came back and with fine courtesy shook my hand.

"You see," he said, "I am a busy man, Mr. Grayson—and a happy man."

So he set off down the road, and as he passed my house he began singing again in his high voice. I walked away with a feeling of wonder, not unmixed with sorrow. It was a strange case!

Gradually I became really acquainted with the bee-man, at first with the exuberant, confident, imaginative, home-going bee-man; far more slowly with the shy, reserved, townward-bound bee-man. It was quite an adventure, my first talk with the shy bee-man. I was driving home; I met him near the lower bridge. I cudgeled my brain to think of some way to get at him. As he passed, I leaned out and said:

"Friend, will you do me a favour? I neglected to stop at the post-office. Would you call and see whether anything has been left for me in the box since the carrier started?"

"Certainly," he said, glancing up at me, but turning his head swiftly aside again.

On his way back he stopped and left me a paper. He told me volubly about the way he would run the post-office if he were "in a place of suitable authority."

"Great things are possible," he said, "to the man of ideas."

At this point began one of the by-plays of my acquaintance with the bee-man. The exuberant bee-man referred disparagingly to the shy bee-man.

"I must have looked pretty seedy and stupid this morning on my way in. I was up half the night; but I feel all right now."

The next time I met the shy bee-man he on his part apologized for the exuberant bee-man—hesitatingly, falteringly, winding up with the words, "I think you will understand." I grasped his hand, and left him with a wan smile on his face. Instinctively

I came to treat the two men in a wholly different manner. With the one I was blustering, hail-fellow-well-met, listening with eagerness to his expansive talk; but to the other I said little, feeling my way slowly to his friendship, for I could not help looking upon him as a pathetic figure. He needed a friend! The exuberant bee-man was sufficient unto himself, glorious in his visions, and I had from him no little entertainment.

I told Harriet about my adventures: they did not meet with her approval. She said I was encouraging a vice.

"Harriet," I said, "go over and see his wife. I wonder what she thinks about it."

"Thinks!" exclaimed Harriet. "What should the wife of a drunkard think?"

But she went over. As soon as she returned I saw that something was wrong, but I asked no questions. During supper she was extraordinarily preoccupied, and it was not until an hour or more afterward that she came into my room.

"David," she said, "I can't understand some things."

"Isn't human nature doing what it ought to?" I asked.

But she was not to be joked with.

"David, that man's wife doesn't seem to be sorry because he

comes home drunken every week or two! I talked with her about it and what do you think she said? She said she knew it was wrong, but she intimated that when he was in that state she loved—liked—him all the better. Is it believable? She said: 'Perhaps you won't understand—it's wrong, I know, but when he comes home that way he seems so full of—life. He—he seems to understand me better then!' She was heartbroken, one could see that, but she would not admit it. I leave it to you, David, what can anyone do with a woman like that? How is the man ever to overcome his habits?"

It is a strange thing, when we ask questions directly of life, how often the answers are unexpected and confusing. Our logic becomes illogical! Our stories won't turn out.

She told much more about her interview: the neat home, the bees in the orchard, the well-kept garden. "When he's sober," she said, "he seems to be a steady, hard worker."

After that I desired more than ever to see deep into the life of the strange bee-man. Why was he what he was?

And at last the time came, as things come to him who desires them faithfully enough. One afternoon not long ago, a fine autumn afternoon, when the trees were glorious on the hills, the Indian summer sun never softer, I was tramping along a wood lane far back of my farm. And at the roadside, near the trunk of an oak tree, sat my friend, the bee-man. He was a picture of despondency, one long hand hanging limp between his knees, his head bowed down. When he saw me he straightened up, looked at me, and settled back again. My heart went out to him, and I sat down beside him.

"Have you ever seen a finer afternoon?" I asked.

He glanced up at the sky.

"Fine?" he answered vaguely, as if it had never occurred to him.

I saw instantly what the matter was; the exuberant bee-man was in process of transformation into the shy bee-man. I don't know exactly how it came about, for such things are difficult to explain, but I led him to talk of himself.

"After it is all over," he said, "of course I am ashamed of myself. You don't know, Mr. Grayson, what it all means. I am ashamed of myself now, and yet I know I shall do it again."

"No," I said, "you will not do it again."

"Yes, I shall. Something inside of me argues: Why should you be sorry? Were you not free for a whole afternoon?"

"Free?" I asked.

"Yes—free. You will not understand. But every day I work, work, work. I have friends, but somehow I can't get to them; I can't even get to my wife. It seems as if a wall hemmed me in, as if I were bound to a rock which I couldn't get away from. I am also afraid. When I am sober I know how to do great things, but I can't do them. After a few glasses—I never take more—I not only know I can do great things, but I feel as though I were really doing them."

"But you never do?"

"No, I never do, but I *feel* that I can. All the bonds break and the wall falls down and I am free. I can really touch people. I feel friendly and neighbourly."

He was talking eagerly now, trying to explain, for the first time in his life, he said, how it was that he did what he did. He told me how beautiful it made the world, where before it was miserable and friendless, how he thought of great things and made great plans, how his home seemed finer and better to him, and his work more noble. The man had a real gift of imagination and spoke with an eagerness and eloquence that stirred me deeply. I was almost on the point of asking him where his magic liquor was to be found! When he finally gave me an opening, I said:

"I think I understand. Many men I know are in some respects drunkards. They all want some way to escape themselves —to be free of their own limitations."

"That's it! That's it!" he exclaimed eagerly.

We sat for a time side by side, saying nothing. I could not help thinking of that line of Virgil referring to quite another sort of intoxication:

"With Voluntary dreams they cheat their minds."

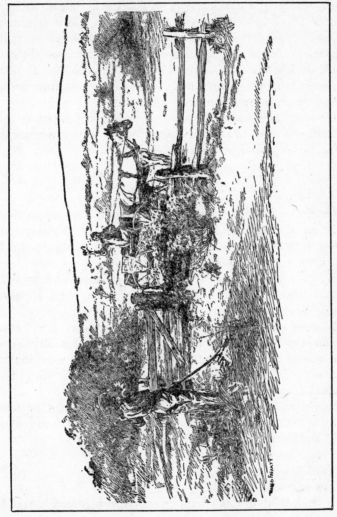

"He usually came in the evening"

Instead of that beautiful unity of thought and action which marks the finest character, here was this poor tragedy of the divided life. When Fate would destroy a man it first separates his forces! It drives him to think one way and act another; it encourages him to seek through outward stimulation—whether drink, or riches, or fame—a deceptive and unworthy satisfaction in place of that true contentment which comes only from unity within. No man can be two men successfully.

So we sat and said nothing. What indeed can any man *say* to another under such circumstances? As Bobbie Burns remarks out of the depths of his own experience:

> "*What's done we partly may compute*
> *But know not what's resisted.*"

I've always felt that the best thing one man can give another is the warm hand of understanding. And yet when I thought of the pathetic, shy bee-man, hemmed in by his sunless walls, I felt that I should also say something. Seeing two men struggling shall I not assist the better? Shall I let the sober one be despoiled by him who is riotous? There are realities, but there are also moralities—if we can keep them properly separated.

"Most of us," I said finally, "are in some respects drunkards. We don't give it so harsh a name, but we are just that. Drunkenness is not a mere matter of intoxicating liquors; it goes deeper —far deeper. Drunkenness is the failure of a man to control his thoughts."

The bee-man sat silent, gazing out before him. I noted the blue veins in the hand that lay on his knee. It came over me with sudden amusement and I said:

"I often get drunk myself."

"You?"

"Yes—dreadfully drunk."

He looked at me and laughed—for the first time! And I laughed, too. Do you know, there's a lot of human nature in people! And when you think you are deep in tragedy, behold, humour lurks just around the corner!

"I used to laugh at it a good deal more than I do now," he

said. "I've been through it all. Sometimes when I go to town I say to myself, 'I will not turn at that corner,' but when I come to the corner, I do turn. Then I say 'I will not go into that bar,' but I do go in. 'I will not order anything to drink,' I say to myself, and then I hear myself talking aloud to the barkeeper just as though I were some other person. 'Give me a glass of rye,' I say, and I stand off looking at myself, very angry and sor-

rowful. But gradually I seem to grow weaker and weaker—or rather stronger and stronger—for my brain begins to become clear, and I see things and feel things I never saw or felt before. I want to sing."

"And you do sing," I said.

"I do, indeed," he responded, laughing, "and it seems to me the most beautiful music in the world."

"Sometimes," I said, "when I'm on *my* kind of spree, I try not so much to empty my mind of the thoughts which bother me, but rather to fill my mind with other, stronger thoughts——"

Before I could finish he had interrupted:

"Haven't I tried that, too? Don't I think of other things? I think of bees—and that leads me to honey, doesn't it? And that makes me think of putting the honey in the wagon and taking it to town. Then, of course, I think how it will sell. Instantly, stronger than you can imagine, I see a dime in my hand. Then it appears on the wet bar. I *smell* the *smell* of the liquor. And there you are!"

We did not talk much more that day. We got up and shook hands and looked each other in the eye. The bee-man turned away, but came back hesitatingly.

"I am glad of this talk, Mr. Grayson. It makes me feel like taking hold again. I have been in hell for years——"

"Of course," I said. "You needed a friend. You and I will come up together."

As I walked toward home that evening I felt a curious warmth of satisfaction in my soul—and I marvelled at the many strange things that are to be found upon this miraculous earth.

I suppose, if I were writing a story, I should stop at this point; but I am dealing in life. And life does not always respond to our impatience with satisfactory moral conclusions. Life is inconclusive: quite open at the end. I had a vision of a new life for my neighbour, the bee-man—and have it yet, for I have not done with him—but——

Last evening, and that is why I have been prompted to write the whole story, my bee-man came again along the road by my farm; my exuberant bee-man. I heard him singing afar off.

He did not see me as he went by, but as I stood looking out at him, it came over me with a sudden sense of largeness and quietude that the sun shone on him as genially as it did on me, and that the leaves did not turn aside from him, nor the birds stop singing when he passed.

"He also belongs here," I said.

And I watched him as he mounted the distant hill, until I could no longer hear the high clear cadences of his song. And it seemed to me that something human, in passing, had touched me.

VII

AN OLD MAID

Oɴᴇ ᴏꜰ ᴍʏ ɴᴇɪɢʜʙᴏᴜʀs whom I never have chanced to mention before in these writings is a certain Old Maid. She lives about two miles from my farm in a small white house set in the midst of a modest, neat garden with well-kept apple trees in the orchard behind it. She lives all alone save for a good-humoured, stupid nephew who does most of the work on the farm—and does it a little unwillingly. Harriet and I had not been here above a week when we first made the acquaintance of Miss Aiken, or rather she made our acquaintance. For she fills the place, most important in a country community, of a sensitive social tentacle—reaching out to touch with sympathy the stranger. Harriet was amused at first by what she considered an almost unwarrantable curiosity, but we soon formed a genuine liking for the little old lady, and since then we have often seen her in her home, and often she has come to ours.

She was here only last night. I considered her as she sat rocking in front of our fire; a picture of wholesome comfort. I have had much to say of contentment. She seems really to live it, although I have found that contentment is easier to discover in the lives of our neighbours than in our own. All her life long she has lived here in this community, a world of small things, one is tempted to say, with a sort of expected and predictable life. I thought last night, as I observed her gently stirring her rocking-chair, how her life must be made up of small, often-repeated events: pancakes, puddings, patchings, who knows what other orderly, habitual, minute affairs? Who knows? Who knows when he looks at you or at me that there is anything in us beyond the humdrummery of this day?

In front of her house are two long, boarded beds of old-fashioned flowers, mignonette and petunias chiefly, and over the small, very white door with its shiny knob, creeps a white clematis vine. Just inside the hall-door you will discover a bright, clean, oval rag rug, which prepares you, as small things lead to greater, for the larger, brighter, cleaner rug of the sitting-room. There on the centre-table you will discover "Snow Bound," by John Greenleaf Whittier; Tupper's Poems; a large embossed Bible; the family plush album; and a book, with a gilt ladder on the cover which leads upward to gilt stars, called the "Path of Life." On the wall are two companion pictures of a rosy fat child, in faded gilt frames, one called "Wide Awake," the other "Fast Asleep." Not far away, in a corner, on the top of the walnut whatnot, is a curious vase filled with pampas plumes; there are sea-shells and a piece of coral on the shelf below. And right in the midst of the room are three very large black rocking-chairs with cushions in every conceivable and available place—including cushions on the arms. Two of them are for you and me, if we should come in to call; the other is for the cat.

When you sit down you can look out between the starchiest of starchy curtains into the yard, where there is an innumerable busy flock of chickens. She keeps chickens, and all the important ones are named. She has one called Martin Luther, another is Josiah Gilbert Holland. Once she came over to our house with a basket, from one end of which were thrust the sturdy red legs of a pullet. She informed us that she had brought us one of Evangeline's daughters.

But I am getting out of the house before I am fairly well into it. The sitting-room expresses Miss Aiken; but not so well, somehow, as the immaculate bedroom beyond, into which, upon one occasion, I was permitted to steal a modest glimpse. It was of an incomparable neatness and order, all hung about—or so it seemed to me—with white starchy things, and ornamented with bright (but inexpensive) nothings. In this wonderful bedroom there is a secret and sacred drawer into which, once in her life, Harriet had a glimpse. It contains the clothes, all gently folded,

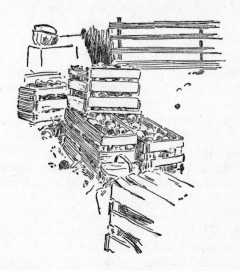

exhaling an odour of lavender, in which our friend will appear when she has closed her eyes to open them no more upon this earth. In such calm readiness she awaits her time.

Upon the bureau in this sacred apartment stands a small rose-wood box, which is locked, into which no one in our neighbour-hood has had so much as a single peep. I should not dare, of course, to speculate upon its contents; perhaps an old letter or two, "a ring and a rose," a ribbon that is more than a ribbon, a picture that is more than art. Who can tell? As I passed that way I fancied I could distinguish a faint, mysterious odour which I associated with the rosewood box: an old-fashioned odour composed of many simples.

On the stand near the head of the bed and close to the candlestick is a Bible—a little, familiar, daily Bible, very different indeed from the portentous and imposing family Bible which reposes on the centre-table in the front room, which is never opened except to record a death. It has been well worn, this small nightly Bible, by much handling. Is there a care or a trouble in this world, here is the sure talisman. She seeks (and finds) the inspired text. Wherever she opens the book she seizes the first words her eyes fall upon as a prophetic message to her. Then she goes forth like some David with his sling, so panoplied with courage that she is daunted by no Goliath of the Philistines. Also she has a worshipfulness of all ministers. Sometimes when the Scotch Preacher comes to tea and remarks that her pudding is good, I firmly believe that she interprets the words into a spiritual message for her.

Besides the drawer, the rosewood box, and the worn Bible, there is a certain Black Cape. Far be it from me to attempt a description, but I can say with some assurance that it also occupies a shrine. It may not be in the inner sanctuary, but it certainly occupies a goodly part of the outer porch of the temple. All this, of course, is figurative, for the cape hangs just inside the closet door on a hanger, with a white cloth over the shoulders to keep off the dust. For the vanities of the world enter even such a sanctuary as this. I wish, indeed, that you could see Miss Aiken wearing her cape on a Sunday in the late fall when she comes to church, her sweet old face shining under her black hat, her old-fashioned silk skirt giving out an audible, not unimpressive sound as she moves down the aisle. With what dignity she steps into her pew! With what care she sits down so that she may not crush the cookies in her ample pocket; with what meek pride—if there is such a thing as meek pride—she looks up at the Scotch Preacher as he stands sturdily in his pulpit announcing the first hymn! And many an eye turning that way to look turns with affection.

Several times Harriet and I have been with her to tea. Like many another genius, she has no conception of her own art in such matters as apple puddings. She herself prefers graham gems, in which she believes there inheres a certain mysterious efficacy. She bakes gems on Monday and has them steamed during the remainder of the week—with tea.

And as a sort of dessert she tells us about the Danas, the Aikens and the Carnahans, who are, in various relationships, her progenitors. We gravitate into the other room, and presently she shows us, in the plush album, the portraits of various cousins, aunts and uncles. And by-and-by Harriet warms up and begins to tell about the Scribners, the MacIntoshes, and the Strayers, who are *our* progenitors.

"The Aikens," says Miss Aiken, "were always like that—downright and outspoken. It is an Aiken trait. No Aiken could ever help blurting out the truth if he knew he were to die for it the next minute."

"That was like the MacIntoshes," Harriet puts in. "Old Grandfather MacIntosh——"

By this time I am settled comfortably in the cushioned rocking-chair to watch the fray. Miss Aiken advances a Dana, Harriet counters with a Strayer. Miss Aiken deploys the Carnahans in open order, upon which Harriet entrenches herself with the heroic Scribners and lets fly a MacIntosh who was a general in the colonial army. Surprised, but not defeated, Miss Aiken withdraws in good order, covering her retreat with two *Mayflower* ancestors, the existence of whom she establishes with a blue cup and an ancient silver spoon. No one knows the joy of fighting relatives until he has watched such a battle, following the complete comfort of a good supper.

If any one is sick in the community Miss Aiken hears instantly of it by a sort of wireless telegraphy, or telepathy which would astonish a mystery-loving East Indian. She appears with her little basket, which has two brown flaps for covers opening from the middle and with a spring in them somewhere so that they fly shut with a snap. Out of this she takes a bowl of chicken broth, a jar of ambrosial jelly, a cake of delectable honey and a bottle of celestial raspberry shrub. If the patient will only eat, he will immediately rise up and walk. Or if he dies, it is a pleasant sort of death. I have myself thought on several occasions of being taken with a brief fit of sickness.

In telling all these things about Miss Aiken, which seem to describe her, I have told only the commonplace, the expected or predictable details. Often and often I pause when I see an interesting man or woman and ask myself: "How, after all, does this person live?" For we all know it is not chiefly by the clothes we wear or the house we occupy or the friends we touch. There is something deeper, more secret, which furnishes the real motive and character of our lives. What a triumph, then, is every fine old man! To have come out of a long life with a spirit still sunny, is not that an heroic accomplishment?

Of the real life of our friend I know only one thing; but that thing is precious to me, for it gives me a glimpse of the far dim Alps that rise out of the Plains of Contentment. It is nothing very definite—such things never are; and yet I like to think of it when I see her treading the useful round of her simple life. As I said, she has lived here in this neighbourhood—oh, sixty years. The country knew her father before her. Out of that past, through the dimming eyes of some of the old inhabitants, I have had glimpses of the sprightly girlhood which our friend must have enjoyed. There is even a confused story of a wooer (how people try to account for every old maid!)—a long time

ago—who came and went away again. No one remembers much
about him—such things are not important, of course, after so
many years——

But I must get to *the* thing I treasure. One day Harriet called
at the little house. It was in summer and the door stood open;
she presumed on the privilege of friendship and walked straight
in. There she saw, sitting at the table, her head on her arm in a
curious girlish abandon unlike the prim Miss Aiken we knew
so well, our Old Maid. When she heard Harriet's step she
started up with breath quickly indrawn. There were tears in her
eyes. Something in her hand she concealed in the folds of her
skirt then impulsively—unlike her, too—she threw an arm
around Harriet and buried her face on Harriet's shoulder. In response to Harriet's question she said:

"Oh, an old, old trouble. No *new* trouble."

That was all there was to it. All the new troubles were the
troubles of other people. You may say this isn't much of a clue;
well it isn't, and yet I like to have it in mind. It gives me somehow the *other* woman who is not expected or predictable or
commonplace. I seem to understand our Old Maid the better;
and when I think of her bustling, inquisitive, helpful, gentle
ways and the shine of her white soul, I'm sure I don't know
what we should do without her in this community.

VIII

A ROADSIDE PROPHET

Fʀᴏᴍ ᴍʏ ᴜᴘᴘᴇʀ ꜰɪᴇʟᴅ, when I look across the countryside, I can see in the distance a short stretch of the gray town road. It winds out of a little wood, crosses a knoll, and loses itself again beyond the trees of an old orchard. I love that spot in my upper field, and the view of the road beyond. When I am at work there I have only to look up to see the world go by—part of it going down to the town, and part of it coming up again. And I never see a traveller on the hill, especially if he be afoot, without feeling that if I met him I should like him, and that whatever he had to say I should like to hear.

At first I could not make out what the man was doing. Most of the travellers I see from my field are like the people I commonly meet—so intent upon their destination that they take no joy of the road they travel. They do not even see me here in the fields; and if they did, they would probably think me a slow and unprofitable person. I have nothing that they can carry away and store up in barns, or reduce to percentages, or calculate as profit and loss; they do not perceive what a wonderful place this is; they do not know that here, too, we gather a crop of contentment.

But apparently this man was the pattern of a loiterer. I saw him stop on the knoll and look widely about him. Then he stooped down as though searching for something, then moved slowly forward for a few steps. Just at that point in the road lies a great smooth boulder which road-makers long since dead had rolled out upon the wayside. Here to my astonishment I saw him kneel upon the ground. He had something in one hand with which he seemed intently occupied. After a time he stood up, and retreating a few steps down the road, he scanned the boulder narrowly.

"This," I said to myself, "may be something for me."

So I crossed the fence and walked down the neighbouring field. It was an Indian summer day with hazy hillsides, and still sunshine, and slumbering brown fields—the sort of a day I love. I leaped the little brook in the valley and strode hastily up the opposite slope. I cannot describe what a sense I had of new worlds to be found here in old fields. So I came to the fence on the other side and looked over. My man was kneeling again at the rock. I was scarcely twenty paces from him, but so earnestly was he engaged that he never once saw me. I had a good look at him. He was a small, thin man with straight gray hair; above his collar I could see the weather-brown wrinkles of his neck. His coat was of black, of a noticeably neat appearance, and I observed, as a further evidence of fastidiousness rare upon the Road, that he was saving his trousers by kneeling on a bit of carpet. What he could be doing there so intently by the roadside I could not imagine. So I climbed the fence, making some little intentional noise as I did so. He arose immediately. Then I saw at his side on the ground two small tin cans, and in his hands a pair of paint brushes. As he stepped aside I saw the words he had been painting on the boulder:

GOD IS LOVE

A meek figure, indeed, he looked, and when he saw me advancing he said, with a deference that was almost timidity:

"Good morning, sir."

"Good morning, brother," I returned heartily.

His face brightened perceptibly.

"Don't stop on my account," I said; "finish off your work."

He knelt again on his bit of carpet and proceeded busily with his brushes. I stood and watched him. The lettering was somewhat crude, but he had the swift deftness of long practice.

"How long," I inquired, "have you been at this sort of work?"

"Ten years," he replied, looking up at me with a pale smile.

"Off and on for ten years. Winters I work at my trade—I am a journeyman painter—but when spring comes, and again in the fall, I follow the road."

He paused a moment and then said, dropping his voice, in words of the utmost seriousness:

"I live by the Word."

"By the Word?" I asked.

"Yes, by the Word," and putting down his brushes he took from an inner pocket a small package of papers, one of which he handed to me. It bore at the top this sentence in large type:

"Is not my word like fire, saith the Lord: and like a hammer that breaketh the rock in pieces?"

I stood and looked at him a moment. I suppose no one man is stranger than any other, but at that moment it seemed to me I had never met a more curious person. And I was consumed with a desire to know why he was what he was.

"Do you always paint the same sign?" I asked.

"Oh, no," he answered. "I have a feeling about what I should paint. When I came up the road here this morning I stopped a minute, and it all seemed so calm and nice"—he swept his arm in the direction of the fields—"that I says to myself, 'I will paint "God is Love."'"

"An appropriate text," I said, "for this very spot."

He seemed much gratified.

"Oh, you can follow your feelings!" he exclaimed. "Sometimes near towns I can't paint anything but 'Hell yawns,' and 'Prepare to meet thy God.' I don't like 'em as well as 'God is Love,' but it seems like I had to paint 'em. Now, when I was in Arizona——"

He paused a moment, wiping his brushes.

"When I was in Arizona," he was saying, "mostly I painted 'Repent ye.' It seemed like I couldn't paint anything else, and in some places I felt moved to put 'Repent ye' twice on the same rock."

I began to ask him questions about Arizona, but I soon found how little he, too, had taken toll of the road he travelled: for he seemed to have brought back memories only of the texts he painted and the fact that in some places good stones were scarce, and that he had to carry extra turpentine to thin his paint, the weather being dry. I don't know that he is a lone representative of this trait. I have known farmers who, in travelling, saw only plows and butter-tubs and corn-cribs, and preachers who, looking across such autumn fields as these would carry away only a musty text or two. I pity some of those who expect to go to heaven: they will find so little to surprise them in the golden streets.

But I persevered with my painter, and it was not long before we were talking with the greatest friendliness. Having now finished his work, he shook out his bit of carpet, screwed the tops on his paint cans, wrapped up his brushes, and disposed of them all with the deftness of long experience in his small black bag. Then he stood up and looked critically at his work.

"It's all right," I said; "a great many people coming this way in the next hundred years will see it."

"That's what I want," he said eagerly; "that's what I want. Most people never hear the Word at all."

He paused a moment and then continued:

"It's a curious thing, Mister—perhaps you've noticed it yourself—that the best things of all in the world people won't have as a gift."

"I've noticed it," I said.

"It's strange, isn't it?" he again remarked.

"Very strange," I said.

"I don't know's I can blame them," he continued. "I was that way myself for a good many years: all around me gold and diamonds and precious jewels, and me never once seeing them. All I had to do was to stoop and take them—but I didn't do it."

I saw that I had met a philosopher, and I decided that I would stop and wrestle with him and not let him go without his story—something like Jacob, wasn't it, with the angel?

"Do you do all this without payment?"

He looked at me in an injured way.

"Who'd pay me?" he asked. "Mostly people think me a sort of fool. Oh, I know, but I don't mind. I live by the Word. No, nobody pays me: I am paying myself."

By this time he was ready to start. So I said, "Friend, I'm going your way, and I'll walk with you."

So we set off together down the hill.

"You see, sir," he said, "when a man has got the best thing in the world, and finds it's free, he naturally wants to let other people know about it."

He walked with the unmistakable step of those who knew the long road—an easy, swinging, steady step—carrying his small black bag. So I gradually drew him out, and when I had his whole story it was as simple and common, but as wonderful, as daylight: as fundamental as a tree or a rock.

"You see, Mister," he said, "I was a wild sort when I was young. The drink, and worse. I hear folks say sometimes that if they'd known what was right they'd have done it. But I think that conscience never stops ringing little bells in the back of a man's head; and that if he doesn't do what is right, it's because he *wants* to do what is wrong. He thinks it's more amusing and interesting. I went through all that, Mister, and plenty more besides. I got pretty nearly as low as a man ever gets. Oh, I was down and out: no home, no family, not a friend that wanted to see me. If you never got down that low, Mister, you don't know what it is. You are just as much dead as if you were in your grave. I'm telling you.

"I thought there was no help for me, and I don't know's I wanted to be helped. I said to myself, 'You're just naturally born

weak and it isn't your fault.' It makes a lot of men easier in their minds to lay up their troubles to the way they are born. I made all sorts of excuses for myself, but all the time I knew I was wrong; a man can't fool himself.

"So it went along for years. I got married and we had a little girl."

He paused for a long moment.

"I thought *that* was going to help me. I thought the world and all of that little girl——" He paused again.

"Well, *she* died. Then I broke my wife's heart and went on down to hell. When a man lets go that way he kills everything he loves and everything that loves him. He's on the road to loneliness and despair, that man. I'm telling you.

"One day, ten years ago this fall, I was going along the main street in Quinceyville. I was near the end of my rope. Not even money enough to buy drink with, and yet I was then more'n half drunk. I happened to look up on the end of that stone wall near the bridge—were you ever there, Mister?—and I saw the words 'God is Love' painted there. It somehow hit me hard. I couldn't anyways get it out of my mind. 'God is Love.' Well, says I to myself, if God is Love, he's the only one that *is* Love for a chap like me. And there's no one else big enough to save me—I says. So I stopped right there in the street, and you may believe it or explain it anyhow you like, Mister, but it seemed to me a kind of light came all around me, and I said, solemn-like, 'I will try God.' "

He stopped a moment. We were walking down the hill: all about us on either side spread the quiet fields. In the high air above a few lacy clouds were drifting eastward. Upon this story of tragic human life crept in pleasantly the calm of the country-side.

"And I did try Him," my companion was saying, "and I found that the words on the wall were true. They were true back there and they've been true ever since. When I began to be decent again and got back my health and my job, I figured that I owed a lot to God. I wa'n't no orator, and no writer and I had no money to give, 'but,' says I to myself, 'I'm a painter. I'll help God with paint.' So here I am a-travelling up and down the roads and mostly painting 'God is Love,' but sometimes 'Repent ye' and 'Hell yawns.' I don't know much about religion— but I do know that His Word is like a fire, and that a man can live by it, and if once a man has it he has everything else he wants."

He paused: I looked around at him again. His face was set steadily ahead—a plain face showing the marks of his hard earlier life, and yet marked with a sort of high beauty.

"The trouble with people who are unhappy, Mister," he said, "is that they won't try God."

I could not answer my companion. There seemed, indeed, nothing more to be said. All my own speculative incomings and outgoings—how futile they seemed compared with this!

Near the foot of the hill there is a little bridge. It is a pleasant, quiet spot. My companion stopped and put down his bag.

"What do you think," said he, "I should paint here?"

"Well," I said, "you know better than I do. What would *you* paint?"

He looked around at me and then smiled as though he had a quiet little joke with himself.

"When in doubt," he said, "I always paint 'God is Love.' I'm sure of that. Of course 'Hell yawns' and 'Repent ye' have to be painted—near towns—but I much rather paint 'God is Love.'"

I left him kneeling there on the bridge, the bit of carpet under his knees, his two little cans at his side. Half way up the hill I turned to look back. He lifted his hand with the paint brush in it, and I waved mine in return. I have never seen him since, though it will be a long, long time before the sign of him disappears from our roadsides.

At the top of the hill, near the painted boulder, I climbed the fence, pausing a moment on the top rail to look off across the hazy countryside, warm with the still sweetness of autumn. In the distance, above the crown of a little hill, I could see the roof of my own home—and the barn near it—and the cows feeding quietly in the pastures.

IX

THE GUNSMITH

Harriet and I had the first intimation of what we have since called the "gunsmith problem" about ten days ago. It came to us, as was to be expected, from that accomplished spreader of burdens, the Scotch Preacher. When he came in to call on us that evening after supper I could see that he had something important on his mind; but I let him get to it in his own way.

"David," he said finally, "Carlstrom, the gunsmith, is going home to Sweden."

"At last!" I exclaimed.

Dr. McAlway paused a moment and then said hesitatingly: "He *says* he is going."

Harriet laughed. "Then it's all decided," she said; "he isn't going."

"No," said the Scotch Preacher, "it's not decided—yet."

"Dr. McAlway hasn't made up his mind," I said, "whether Carlstrom is to go or not."

But the Scotch Preacher was in no mood for joking.

"David," he said, "did you ever know anything about the homesickness of the foreigner?"

He paused a moment and then continued, nodding his great shaggy head:

"Man, man, how my old mither greeted for Scotland! I mind how a sprig of heather would bring the tears to her eyes; and for twenty years I dared not whistle 'Bonnie Doon' or 'Charlie Is My Darling' lest it break her heart. 'Tis a pain you've not had, I'm thinking, Davy."

"We all know the longing for old places and old times," I said.

"No, no, David, it's more than that. It's the wanting and the longing to see the hills of your own land, and the town where you were born, and the street where you played, and the house——"

He paused, "Ah, well, it's hard for those who have it."

"But I haven't heard Carlstrom refer to Sweden for years," I said. "Is it homesickness, or just old age?"

"There ye have it, Davy; the nail right on the head!" exclaimed the Scotch Preacher. "Is it homesickness, or is he just old and tired?"

With that we fell to talking about Carlstrom, the gunsmith. I have known him pretty nearly ever since I came here, now more than ten years ago—and liked him well, too—but it seemed, as Dr. McAlway talked that evening, as though we were making the acquaintance of quite a new and wonderful person. How dull we all are! How we need such an artist as the Scotch Preacher to mould heroes out of the common human clay around us! It takes a sort of greatness to recognize greatness.

In an hour's time the Scotch Preacher had both Harriet and me much excited, and the upshot of the whole matter was that I promised to call on Carlstrom the next day when I went to town.

I scarcely needed the prompting of the Scotch Preacher, for Carlstrom's gunshop has for years been one of the most interesting places in town for me. I went to it now with a new understanding.

Afar off I began to listen for Carlstrom's hammer, and presently I heard the familiar sounds. There were two or three mellow strokes, and I knew that Carlstrom was making the sparks fly from the red iron. Then the hammer rang, and I knew he was striking down on the cold steel of the anvil. It is a pleasant sound to hear.

Carlstrom's shop is just around the corner from the main street. You may know it by a great weather-beaten wooden gun

fastened over the doorway, pointing in the daytime at the sky, and in the night at the stars. A stranger passing that way might wonder at the great gun and possibly say to himself:

"A gunshop! How can a man make a living mending guns in such a peaceful community!"

Such a remark merely shows that he doesn't know Carlstrom, nor the shop, nor *us*.

I tied my horse at the corner and went down to the shop with a peculiar new interest. I saw as if for the first time the old wheels which have stood weathering so long at one end of the building. I saw under the shed at the other end the wonderful assortment of old iron pipes, kettles, tires, a pump or two, many parts of farm machinery, a broken water wheel, and I don't know what other flotsam of thirty years of diligent mending of the iron works of an entire community. All this, you may say—the disorder of old iron, the cinders which cover part of the yard but do not keep out the tangle of goldenrod and catnip and boneset which at this time of the year grows thick along the neighbouring fences—all this, you say, makes no inviting picture. You are wrong. Where honest work is, there is always that which invites the eye.

I know of few things more inviting than to step up to the wide-open doors and look into the shop. The floor, half of hard worn boards, half of cinders, the smoky rafters of the roof, the confusion of implements on the benches, the guns in the corners—how all of these things form the subdued background for the flaming forge and the square chimney above it.

At one side of the forge you will see the great dusty bellows and you will hear its stertorous breathing. In front stands the old brown anvil set upon a gnarly maple block. A long sweep made of peeled hickory wood controls the bellows, and as you look in upon this lively and pleasant scene you will see that the grimy hand of Carlstrom himself is upon the hickory sweep. As he draws it down and lets it up again with the peculiar rhythmic swing of long experience—heaping up his fire with a little iron paddle held in the other hand—he hums to himself in a high curious old voice, no words at all, just a tune of contented employment in consonance with the breathing of the bellows and the mounting flames of the forge.

As I stood for a moment in the doorway the other day before Carlstrom saw me, I wished I could picture my friend as the typical blacksmith with the brawny arms, the big chest, the deep voice and all that. But as I looked at him newly, the Scotch Preacher's words still in my ears, he seemed, with his stooping shoulders, his gray beard not very well kept, and his thin gray hair, more than ordinarily small and old.

I remember as distinctly as though it were yesterday the first time Carlstrom really impressed himself upon me. It was in my early blind days at the farm. I had gone to him with a part of a horse-rake which I had broken on one of my stony hills.

"Can you mend it?" I asked.

If I had known him better I should never have asked such a question. I saw, indeed, at the time that I had not said the right thing; but how could I know then that Carlstrom never let any broken thing escape him? A watch, or a gun, or a locomotive—they are all alike to him, if they are broken. I believe he would agree to patch the wrecked chariot of Phaëthon!

A week later I came back to the shop.

"Come in, come in," he said when he saw me.

He turned from his forge, set his hands on his hips and looked at me a moment with feigned seriousness.

"So!" he said. "You have come for your job?"

He softened the "j" in job; his whole speech, indeed, had the engaging inflection of the Scandinavian tongue overlaid upon the English words.

"So," he said, and went to his bench with a quick step and an air of almost childish eagerness. He handed me the parts of my hay-rake without a word. I looked them over carefully.

"I can't see where you mended them," I said.

You should have seen his face brighten with pleasure! He allowed me to admire the work in silence for a moment and then he had it out of my hand, as if I couldn't be trusted with anything so important, and he explained how he had done it. A special tool for his lathe had been found necessary in order to do my work properly. This he had made at his forge, and I suppose it had taken him twice as long to make the special tool as it had to mend the parts of my rake; but when I would have paid him for it he would take nothing save for the mending itself. Nor was this a mere rebuke to a doubter. It had delighted him to do a difficult thing, to show the really great skill he had. Indeed, I think our friendship began right there and was based upon the favour I did in bringing him a job that I thought he couldn't do!

When he saw me the other day in the door of his shop he seemed greatly pleased.

"Come in, come in," he said.

"What is this I hear," I said, "about your going back to Sweden?"

"For forty years," he said, "I've been homesick for Sweden. Now I'm an old man and I'm going home."

"But, Carlstrom," I said, "we can't get along without you. Who's going to keep us mended up?"

"You have Charles Baxter," he said, smiling.

For years there had been a quiet sort of rivalry between Carlstrom and Baxter, though Baxter is in the country and works chiefly in wood.

"But Baxter can't mend a gun or a hay-rake, or a pump, to save his life," I said. "You know that."

The old man seemed greatly pleased: he had the simple vanity which is the right of the true workman. But for answer he merely shook his head.

"I have been here forty years," he said, "and all the time I have been homesick for Sweden."

I found that several men of the town had been in to see Carlstrom and talked with him of his plans, and even while I was there two other friends came in. The old man was delighted with the interest shown. After I left him I went down the street. It seemed as though everybody had heard of Carlstrom's plans, and here and there I felt that the secret hand of the Scotch Preacher had been at work. At the store where I usually trade the merchant talked about it, and the postmaster when I went in for my mail, and the clerk at the drug store, and the harness-maker. I had known a good deal about Carlstrom in the past, for one learns much of his neighbours in ten years, but it seemed to me that day as though his history stood out as something separate and new and impressive.

When he first came here forty years ago I suppose Carlstrom was not unlike most of the foreigners who immigrate to our shores, fired with faith in a free country. He was poor—as poor as a man could possibly be. For several years he worked on a farm—hard work, for which, owing to his frail physique, he was not well fitted. But he saved money constantly, and after a time he was able to come to town and open a little shop. He made nearly all of his tools with his own hands, he built his own chimney and forge, he even whittled out the wooden gun which stands for a sign over the door of his shop. He had learned his trade in the careful old-country way. Not only could he mend a gun, but he could make one outright, even to the barrel and the wooden stock. In all the years I have known him he has always had on hand some such work—once I remember, a pistol —which he was turning out at odd times for the very satisfaction it gave him. He could not sell one of his hand-made guns for half as much as it cost him, nor does he seem to want to sell them, preferring rather to have them stand in the corner of his shop where he can look at them. His is the incorruptible spirit of the artist!

What a tremendous power there is in work. Carlstrom worked. He was up early in the morning to work, and he worked in the evening as long as daylight lasted, and once I found him in his shop in the evening, bending low over his bench with a kerosene lamp in front of him. He was humming his inevitable tune and smoothing off with a fine file the nice curves of a rifle trigger. When he had trouble—and what a lot of it he has had in his time!—he worked; and when he was happy he worked all the harder. All the leisurely ones of the town drifted by, all the children and the fools, and often rested in the doorway of his shop. He made them all welcome: he talked with them, but he never stopped working. Clang, clang, would go his anvil, whish, whish, would respond his bellows, creak, creak, would go the hickory sweep—he was helping the world go round!

All this time, though he had sickness in his family, though his wife died, and then his children one after another until only one now remains, he worked and he saved. He bought a lot and built a house to rent; then he built another house; then he bought the land where his shop stands and rebuilt the shop itself. It was an epic of homely work. He took part in the work of the church and on election days he changed his coat, and went to the town hall to vote.

In the years since I have known the old gunsmith and something of the town where he works, I have seen young men, born Americans, with every opportunity and encouragement of a free country, growing up there and going to waste. One day I heard one of them, sitting in front of a store, grumbling about the foreigners who were coming in and taking up the land. The

"The children . . . often rested in the doorway of his shop"

young man thought it should be prevented by law. I said nothing; but I listened and heard from the distance the steady clang, clang, of Carlstrom's hammer upon the anvil.

Ketchell, the store-keeper, told me how Carlstrom had longed and planned and saved to be able to go back once more to the old home he had left. Again and again he had got almost enough money ahead to start, and then there would be an interest payment due, or a death in the family, and the money would all go to the banker, the doctor, or the undertaker.

"Of recent years," said Ketchell, "we thought he'd given up the idea. His friends are all here now, and if he went back, he certainly would be disappointed."

A sort of serenity seemed, indeed, to come upon him: his family lie on the quiet hill, old things and old times have grown distant, and upon that anvil of his before the glowing forge he has beaten out for himself a real place in this community. He has beaten out the respect of a whole town; and from the crude human nature with which he started he has fashioned himself wisdom, and peace of mind, and the ripe humour which sees that God is in his world. There are men I know who read many books, hoping to learn how to be happy; let me commend them to Carlstrom, the gunsmith.

I have often reflected upon the incalculable influence of one man upon a community. The town is better for having stood often looking into the fire of Carlstrom's forge, and seeing his hammer strike. I don't know how many times I have heard men repeat observations gathered in Carlstrom's shop. Only the other day I heard the village school teacher say, when I asked him why he always seemed so merry and had so little fault to find with the world.

"Why," he replied, "as Carlstrom, the gunsmith says, 'when I feel like finding fault I always begin with myself and then I never get any farther.'"

Another of Carlstrom's sayings is current in the country.

"It's a good thing," he says, "when a man knows what he pretends to know."

The more I circulated among my friends, the more I heard of

Carlstrom. It is odd that I should have gone all these years knowing Carlstrom, and yet never consciously until last week setting him in his rightful place among the men I know. It makes me wonder what other great souls about me are thus concealing themselves in the guise of familiarity. This stooped gray neighbour of mine whom I have seen so often working in his field that he has almost become a part of the landscape—who can tell what heroisms may be locked away from my vision under his old brown hat?

On Wednesday night Carlstrom was at Dr. McAlway's house —with Charles Baxter, my neighbour Horace, and several others. And I had still another view of him.

I think there is always something that surprises one in finding a familiar figure in a wholly new environment. I was so accustomed to the Carlstrom of the gunshop that I could not at once reconcile myself to the Carlstrom of Dr. McAlway's sitting room. And, indeed, there was a striking change in his appearance. He came dressed in the quaint black coat which he wears at funerals. His hair was brushed straight back from his broad, smooth forehead and his mild blue eyes were bright behind an especially shiny pair of steel-bowed spectacles. He looked more like some old-fashioned college professor than he did like a smith.

The old gunsmith had that pride of humility which is about the best pride in this world. He was perfectly at home at the Scotch Preacher's hearth. Indeed, he radiated a sort of beaming good will; he had a native desire to make everything pleasant. I did not realize before what a fund of humour the old man had. The Scotch Preacher rallied him on the number of houses he now owns, and suggested that he ought to get a wife to keep at least one of them for him. Carlstrom looked around with a twinkle in his eye.

"When I was a poor man," he said, "and carried boxes from Ketchell's store to help build my first shop, I used to wish I had a wheelbarrow. Now I have four. When I had no house to keep my family in, I used to wish that I had one. Now I have four. I have thought sometimes I would like a wife—but I have not dared to wish for one."

The old gunsmith laughed noiselessly, and then from habit, I suppose, began to hum as he does in his shop—stopping instantly, however, when he realized what he was doing.

During the evening the Scotch Preacher got me to one side and said:

"David, we can't let the old man go."

"No, sir," I said, "we can't."

"All he needs, Davy, is cheering up. It's a cold world sometimes to the old."

I suppose the Scotch Preacher was saying the same thing to all the other men of the company.

When we were preparing to go, Dr. McAlway turned to Carlstrom and said:

"How is it, Carlstrom, that you have come to hold such a place in this community? How is it that you have got ahead so rapidly."

The old man leaned forward, beaming through his spectacles, and said eagerly:

"It ist America; it ist America."

"No, Carlstrom, no—it is not all America. It is Carlstrom, too. You work, Carlstrom, and you save."

Every day since Wednesday there has been a steady pressure on Carlstrom; not so much said in words, but people stopping in at the shop and passing a good word. But up to Monday morning the gunsmith went forward steadily with his preparations to leave. On Sunday I saw the Scotch Preacher and found him perplexed as to what to do. I don't know yet positively, that he had a hand in it, though I suspect it, but on Monday afternoon Charles Baxter went by my house on his way to town with a broken saw in his buggy. Such is the perversity of rival artists that I don't think Charles Baxter had ever been to Carlstrom with any work. But this morning when I went to town and stopped at Carlstrom's shop I found the gunsmith humming louder than ever.

"Well, Carlstrom, when are we to say good-bye?" I asked.

"I'm not going," he said, and taking me by the sleeve he led me over to his bench and showed me a saw he had mended. Now, a broken saw is one of the high tests of the genius of the mender. To put the pieces together so that the blade will be perfectly smooth, so that the teeth match accurately, is an art which few workmen of to-day would even attempt.

"Charles Baxter brought it in," answered the old gunsmith, unable to conceal his delight. "He thought I couldn't mend it!"

To the true artist there is nothing to equal the approbation of a rival. It was Charles Baxter, I am convinced, who was the deciding factor. Carlstrom couldn't leave with one of Baxter's saws unmended! But back of it all, I know, is the hand and the heart of the Scotch Preacher.

The more I think of it the more I think that our gunsmith possesses many of the qualities of true greatness. He has the serenity, and the humour, and the humility of greatness. He has a real faith in God. He works, he accepts what comes. He thinks there is no more honourable calling than that of gunsmith, and that the town he lives in is the best of all towns, and the people he knows the best people.

Yes, it *is* greatness.

X

THE MOWING

"Now I see the secret of the making of the best persons,
It is to grow in the open air and to eat and sleep with
the earth."

THIS is a well earned Sunday morning. My chores were all done long ago, and I am sitting down here after a late and leisurely breakfast with that luxurious feeling of irresponsible restfulness and comfort which comes only upon a clean, still Sunday morning like this—after a week of hard work—a clean Sunday morning, with clean clothes, and a clean chin, and clean thoughts, and the June airs stirring the clean white curtains at my windows. From across the hills I can hear very faintly the drowsy sounds of early church bells, never indeed to be heard here except on a morning of surpassing tranquillity. And in the barnyard back of the house Harriet's hens are cackling triumphantly: they are impiously unobservant of the Sabbath day.

I turned out my mare for a run in the pasture. She has rolled herself again and again in the warm earth and shaken herself after each roll with an equine delight most pleasant to see. Now, from time to time, I can hear her gossipy whickerings as she calls across the fields to my neighbour Horace's young bay colts.

When I first woke up this morning I said to myself:

"Well, nothing happened yesterday."

Then I lay quiet for some time—it being Sunday morning —and I turned over in my mind all that I had heard or seen or felt or thought about in that one day. And presently I said aloud to myself:

"Why, nearly everything happened yesterday."

And the more I thought of it the more interesting, the more wonderful, the more explanatory of high things, appeared the common doings of that June Saturday. I had walked among unusual events—and had not known the wonder of them! I had eyes, but I did not see—and ears, but I heard not. It may be, it *may* be, that the Future Life of which we have had such confusing but wistful prophecies is only the reliving with a full understanding, of this marvellous Life that we now know. To a full understanding this day, this moment even—here in this quiet room—would contain enough to crowd an eternity. Oh, we are children yet—playing with things much too large for us—much too full of meaning.

Yesterday I cut my field of early clover. I should have been at it a full week earlier if it had not been for the frequent and sousing spring showers. Already half the blossoms of the clover had turned brown and were shrivelling away into inconspicuous seediness. The leaves underneath on the lower parts of the stems were curling up and fading; many of them had already dropped away. There is a tide also in the affairs of clover and if a farmer would profit by his crop, it must be taken at its flood.

I began to watch the skies with some anxiety, and on Thursday I was delighted to see the weather become clearer, and a warm dry wind spring up from the southwest. On Friday there was not so much as a cloud of the size of a man's hand to be seen anywhere in the sky, not one, and the sun with lively diligence had begun to make up for the listlessness of the past week. It was hot and dry enough to suit the most exacting hay-maker.

Encouraged by these favourable symptoms I sent word to Dick Sheridan (by one of Horace's men) to come over bright and early on Saturday morning. My field is only a small one and so rough and uneven that I had concluded with Dick's help to cut it by hand. I thought that on a pinch it could all be done in one day.

"Harriet," I said, "we'll cut the clover to-morrow."

"That's fortunate," said Harriet, "I'd already arranged to have Ann Spencer in to help me."

Yesterday morning, then, I got out earlier than usual. It was a perfect June morning, one of the brightest and clearest I think I ever saw. The mists had not yet risen from the hollows of my lower fields, and all the earth was fresh with dew and sweet with the mingled odours of growing things. No hour of the whole day is more perfect than this.

I walked out along the edge of the orchard and climbed the fence of the field beyond. As I stooped over I could smell the heavy sweet odour of the clover blossoms. I could see the billowy green sweep of the glistening leaves. I lifted up a mass of the tangled stems and laid the palm of my hand on the earth under-neath. It was neither too wet nor too dry.

"We shall have good cutting to-day," I said to myself.

So I stood up and looked with a satisfaction impossible to describe across the acres of my small domain, marking where in the low spots the crop seemed heaviest, where it was lodged and tangled by the wind and the rain, and where in the higher spaces it grew scarce thick enough to cover the sad baldness of the knolls. How much more we get out of life than we deserve!

So I walked along the edge of the field to the orchard gate, which I opened wide.

"Here," I said, "is where we will begin."

So I turned back to the barn. I had not reached the other side of the orchard when who should I see but Dick Sheridan himself, coming in at the lane gate. He had an old, coarse-woven straw hat stuck resplendently on the back of his head. He was carrying his scythe jauntily over his shoulder and whistling "Good-bye, Susan" at the top of his capacity.

Dick Sheridan is a cheerful young fellow with a thin brown face and (milky) blue eyes. He has an enormous Adam's apple which has an odd way of moving up and down when he talks—and one large tooth out in front. His body is like a bundle of

wires, as thin and muscular and enduring as that of a broncho pony. He can work all day long and then go down to the lodge-hall at the Crossing and dance half the night. You should really see him when he dances! He can jump straight up and click his heels twice together before he comes down again! On such occasions he is marvellously clad, as befits the gallant that he really is, but this morning he wore a faded shirt and one of his suspender cords behind was fastened with a nail instead of a button. His socks are sometimes pale blue and sometimes lavender and commonly, therefore, he turns up his trouser legs so that these vanities may not be wholly lost upon a dull world. His full name is Richard Tecumseh Sheridan, but every one calls him Dick. A good, cheerful fellow, Dick, and a hard worker. I like him.

"Hello, Dick," I shouted.

"Hello yourself, Mr. Grayson," he replied.

He hung his scythe in the branches of a pear tree and we both turned into the barnyard to get the chores out of the way. I wanted to delay cutting as long as I could—until the dew on the clover should begin—at least—to disappear.

By half-past-seven we were ready for work. We rolled back our sleeves, stood our scythes on end and gave them a final lively stoning. You could hear the brisk sound of the ringing metal pealing through the still morning air.

"It's a great day for haying," I said.

"A dang good one," responded the laconic Dick, wetting his thumb to feel the edge of his scythe.

I cannot convey with any mere pen upon any mere paper the feeling of jauntiness I had at that moment, as of conquest and fresh adventure, as of great things to be done in a great world! You may say if you like that this exhilaration was due to good health and the exuberance of youth. But it was more than that—far more. I cannot well express it, but it seemed as though at that moment Dick and I were stepping out into some vast current of human activity: as though we had the universe itself behind us, and the warm regard and approval of all men.

I stuck my whetstone in my hip-pocket, bent forward and cut the first short sharp swath in the clover. I swept the mass of tangled green stems into the open space just outside the gate. Three or four more strokes and Dick stopped whistling suddenly, spat on his hands and with a lively "Here she goes!" came swinging in behind me. The clover-cutting had begun.

At first I thought the heat would be utterly unendurable, and, then, with dripping face and wet shoulders, I forgot all about it. Oh, there is something incomparable about such work—the long steady pull of willing and healthy muscles, the mind undisturbed by any disquieting thought, the feeling of attainment through vigorous effort! It was a steady swing and swish, swish and swing! When Dick led I have a picture of him in my mind's eye—his wiry thin legs, one heel lifted at each step and held rigid for a single instant, a glimpse of pale blue socks above his rusty shoes and three inches of whetstone sticking from his tight hip-pocket. It was good to have him there whether he led or followed.

At each return to the orchard end of the field we looked for and found a gray stone jug in the grass. I had brought it up with me filled with cool water from the pump. Dick had a way of swinging it up with one hand, resting it in his shoulder, turning his head just so and letting the water gurgle into his throat. I have never been able myself to reach this refinement in the art of drinking from a jug.

And oh! the good feel of a straightened back after two long swathes in the boiling sun! We would stand a moment in the shade, whetting our scythes, not saying much, but glad to be there together. Then we would go at it again with renewed energy. It is a great thing to have a working companion. Many times that day Dick and I looked aside at each other with a curious sense of friendliness—that sense of friendliness which grows out of common rivalries, common difficulties and a common weariness. We did not talk much: and that little of trivial matters.

"Jim Brewster's mare had a colt on Wednesday."

"This'll go three tons to the acre, or I'll eat my shirt."

Dick was always about to eat his shirt if some particular prophecy of his did not materialize.

"Dang it all," says Dick, "the moon's drawin' water."

"Something is undoubtedly drawing it," said I, wiping my dripping face.

A meadow lark sprang up with a song in the adjoining field, a few heavy old bumble-bees droned in the clover as we cut it, and once a frightened rabbit ran out, darting swiftly under the orchard fence.

So the long forenoon slipped away. At times it seemed endless, and yet we were surprised when we heard the bell from the house (what a sound it was!) and we left our cutting in the middle of the field, nor waited for another stroke.

"Hungry, Dick?" I asked.

"Hungry!" exclaimed Dick with all the eloquence of a lengthy oration crowded into one word.

So we drifted through the orchard, and it was good to see the house with smoke in the kitchen chimney, and the shade of the big maple where it rested upon the porch. And not far from the maple we could see our friendly pump with the moist boards of the well-cover in front of it. I cannot tell you how good it looked as we came in from the hot, dry fields.

"After you," says Dick.

I gave my sleeves another roll upward and unbuttoned and turned in the moist collar of my shirt. Then I stooped over and put my head under the pump spout.

"Pump, Dick," said I.

And Dick pumped.

"Harder, Dick," said I in a strangled voice.

And Dick pumped still harder, and presently I came up gasping with my head and hair dripping with the cool water. Then I pumped for Dick.

"Gee, but that's good," says Dick.

Harriet came out with clean towels, and we dried ourselves, and talked together in low voices. And feeling a delicious sense of coolness we sat down for a moment in the shade of the maple and rested our arms on our knees. From the kitchen, as we sat there, we could hear the engaging sounds of preparation, and busy voices, and the tinkling of dishes, and agreeable odours! Ah, friend and brother, there may not be better moments in life than this!

So we sat resting, thinking of nothing; and presently we heard the screen door click and Ann Spencer's motherly voice:

"Come in now, Mr. Grayson, and get your dinner."

Harriet had set the table on the east porch, where it was cool and shady. Dick and I sat down opposite each other and between us there was a great brown bowl of moist brown beans with crispy strips of pork on top, and a good steam rising from its depths; and a small mountain of baked potatoes, each a little broken to show the snowy white interior; and two towers of such new bread as no one on this earth (or in any other planet so far as I know) but Harriet can make. And before we had even begun our dinner in came the ample Ann Spencer, quaking with hospitality, and bearing a platter—let me here speak of it with the bated breath of a proper respect, for I cannot even now think of it without a sort of inner thrill—bearing a platter of her most famous fried chicken. Harriet had sacrificed the promising careers of two young roosters upon the altar of this important occasion. I may say in passing that Ann Spencer is more celebrated in our neighbourhood by virtue of her genius at frying chicken, than Aristotle or Solomon or Socrates, or indeed all the big-wigs of the past rolled into one.

So we fell to with a silent but none the less fervid enthusiasm. Harriet hovered about us, in and out of the kitchen, and poured the tea and the buttermilk, and Ann Spencer upon every possible occasion passed the chicken.

"More chicken, Mr. Grayson?" she would inquire in a tone of voice that made your mouth water.

"More chicken, Dick?" I'd ask.

"More chicken, Mr. Grayson," he would respond—and thus we kept up a tenuous, but pleasant little joke between us.

Just outside the porch in a thicket of lilacs a catbird sang to us while we ate, and my dog lay in the shade with his nose on his paws and one eye open just enough to show any stray flies that he was not to be trifled with—and far away to the North and East one could catch glimpses—if he had eyes for such things—of the wide-stretching pleasantness of our country-side.

I soon saw that something mysterious was going on in the kitchen. Harriet would look significantly at Ann Spencer and Ann Spencer, who could scarcely contain her overflowing smiles, would look significantly at Harriet. As for me, I sat there with perfect confidence in myself—in my ultimate capacity, as it were. Whatever happened, I was ready for it!

And the great surprise came at last: a SHORT-CAKE: a great, big, red, juicy, buttery, sugary short-cake, with rasp-berries heaped up all over it. When It came in—and I am speaking of it in that personal way because it radiated such an effulgence that I cannot now remember whether it was Harriet or Ann Spencer who brought it in—when It came in, Dick, who pretends to be abashed upon such occasions, gave one swift glance upward and then emitted a long, low, expressive whistle. When Beethoven found himself throbbing with undescribable emotions he composed a sonata; when Keats felt odd things stirring within him he wrote an ode to an urn, but my friend Dick, quite as evidently on fire with his emotions, merely whistled—and then looked around evidently embarrassed lest

he should have infringed upon the proprieties of that occasion.

"Harriet," I said, "you and Ann Spencer are benefactors of the human race."

"Go 'way now," said Ann Spencer, shaking all over with pleasure, "and eat your short-cake."

And after dinner how pleasant it was to stretch at full length for a few minutes on the grass in the shade of the maple tree and look up through the dusky thick shadows of the leaves. If ever a man feels the blissfulness of complete content it is at such a moment—every muscle in the body deliciously resting, and a peculiar exhilaration animating the mind to quiet thoughts. I have heard talk of the hard work of the hay-fields, but I never yet knew a healthy man who did not recall many moments of exquisite pleasure connected with the hardest and the hottest work.

I think sometimes that the nearer a man can place himself in the full current of natural things the happier he is. If he can become a part of the Universal Process and know that he is a part, that is happiness. All day yesterday I had that deep quiet feeling that I was somehow not working for myself, not because I was covetous for money, nor driven by fear, not surely for fame, but somehow that I was a necessary element in the processes of the earth. I was a primal force! I was the indispensable Harvester. Without me the earth could not revolve!

Oh, friend, there are spiritual values here, too. For how can a man know God without yielding himself fully to the processes of God?

I *lived* yesterday. I played my part. I took my place. And all hard things grew simple, and all crooked things seemed straight, and all roads were open and clear before me. Many times that day I paused and looked up from my work knowing that I had something to be happy for.

At one o'clock Dick and I lagged our way unwillingly out to work again—rusty of muscles, with a feeling that the heat would now surely be unendurable and the work impossibly hard. The scythes were oddly heavy and hot to the touch, and the stones seemed hardly to make a sound in the heavy noon air. The cows had sought the shady pasture edges, the birds were still, all the air shook with heat. Only man must toil!

"It's danged hot," said Dick conclusively.

How reluctantly we began the work and how difficult it seemed compared with the task of the morning! In half an hour, however, the reluctance passed away and we were swinging as steadily as we did at any time in the forenoon. But we said less— if that were possible—and made every ounce of energy count. I shall not here attempt to chronicle all the events of the afternoon, how we finished the mowing of the field and how we went over it swiftly and raked the long windrows into cocks, or how, as the evening began to fall, we turned at last wearily toward the house. The day's work was done.

Dick had stopped whistling long before the middle of the afternoon, but now as he shouldered his scythe he struck up "My Fairy Fay" with some marks of his earlier enthusiasm.

"Well, Dick," said I, "we've had a good day's work together."

"You bet," said Dick.

And I watched him as he went down the lane with a pleasant friendly feeling of companionship. We had done great things together.

I wonder if you ever felt the joy of utter physical weariness: not exhaustion, but weariness. I wonder if you have ever sat down, as I did last night, and felt as though you would like to remain just there always—without stirring a single muscle, without speaking, without thinking even!

Such a moment is not painful, but quite the reverse—it is supremely pleasant. So I sat for a time last evening on my porch. The cool, still night had fallen sweetly after the burning heat of the day. I heard all the familiar sounds of the night. A whippoorwill began to whistle in the distant thicket. Harriet came out quietly—I could see the white of her gown—and sat near me. I heard the occasional sleepy tinkle of a cowbell, and the crickets were calling. A star or two came out in the perfect dark blue of the sky. The deep, sweet, restful night was on. I don't know that I said it aloud—such things need not be said aloud—but as I turned almost numbly into the house, stumbling on my way to bed, my whole being seemed to cry out: "Thank God, thank God."

XI

AN OLD MAN

To-DAY I saw Uncle Richard Summers walking in the town road: and cannot get him out of my mind. I think I never knew any one who wears so plainly the garment of Detached Old Age as he. One would not now think of calling him a farmer, any more than one would think of calling him a doctor, a lawyer, or a justice of the peace. No one would think now of calling him "Squire Summers," though he bore that name with no small credit many years ago. He is no longer known as hardworking, or able, or grasping, or rich, or wicked: he is just Old. Everything seems to have been stripped away from Uncle Richard except age.

How well I remember the first time Uncle Richard Summers impressed himself upon my mind. It was after the funeral of his old wife, now several years ago. I saw him standing at the open grave with his broad-brimmed felt hat held at his breast. His head was bowed and his thin, soft, white hair stirred in the warm breeze. I wondered at his quietude. After fifty years or more together his nearest companion and friend had gone, and he did not weep aloud. Afterward I was again impressed with the same fortitude or quietude. I saw him walking down the long drive to the main road with all the friends of our neighbourhood about him—and the trees rising full and calm on one side, and the still greenery of the cemetery stretching away on the other. Half way down the drive he turned aside to the fence and all unconscious of the halted procession, he picked a handful of the large leaves of the wild grape. It was a hot day; he took off his hat, and put the cool leaves in the crown of it and rejoined the procession. It did not seem to me to be the mere forgetfulness of old age, nor yet callousness to his own great sorrow. It was rather an instinctive return to the immeasurable continuity of the trivial things of life—the trivial necessary things which so often carry us over the greatest tragedies.

I talked with the Scotch Preacher afterward about the incident. He said that he, too, marvelling at the old man's calmness, had referred to it in his presence. Uncle Richard turned to him and said slowly:

"I am an old man, and I have learned one thing. I have learned to accept life."

Since that day I have seen Uncle Richard Summers many times walking on the country roads with his cane. He always looks around at me and slowly nods his head, but rarely says anything. At his age what is there to say that has not already been said?

His trousers appear a size too large for him, his hat sets too far down, his hands are long and thin upon the head of his cane. But his face is tranquil. He has come a long way; there have been times of tempest and keen winds, there have been wild hills in his road, and rocky places, and threatening voices in the air. All that is past now: and his face is tranquil.

I think we younger people do not often realize how keenly dependent we are upon our contemporaries in age. We get little understanding and sympathy either above or below them.

Much of the world is a little misty to us, a little out of focus. Uncle Richard Summers' contemporaries have nearly all gone —mostly long ago: one of the last, his old wife. At his home— I have been there often to see his son—he sits in a large rocking-chair with a cushion in it, and a comfortable high back to lean upon. No one else ventures to sit in his chair, even when he is not there. It is not far from the window; and when he sits down he can lean his cane against the wall where he can easily reach it again.

There is a turmoil of youth and life always about him; of fevered incomings and excited outgoings, of work and laughter and tears and joy and anger. He watches it all, for his mind is still clear, but he does not take sides. He accepts everything, refuses nothing; or, if you like, he refuses everything, accepts nothing.

He once owned the house where he now lives, with the great barns behind it and the fertile acres spreading far on every hand. From his chair he can look out through a small window, and see the sun on the quiet fields. He once went out swiftly and strongly, he worked hotly, he came in wearied to sleep.

Now he lives in a small room—and that is more than is really necessary—and when he walks out he does not inquire who owns the land where he treads. He lets the hot world go by, and waits with patience the logic of events.

Often as I have passed him in the road, I have wondered, as I have been wondering to-day, how he must look out upon us all, upon our excited comings and goings, our immense concern over the immeasurably trivial. I have wondered, not without a pang, and a resolution, whether I shall ever reach the point where I can let this eager and fascinating world go by without taking toll of it!

XII

THE CELEBRITY

N<small>OT FOR MANY WEEKS</small> have I had a more interesting, more illuminating, and when all is told, a more amusing experience, than I had this afternoon. Since this afternoon the world has seemed a more satisfactory place to live in, and my own home here, the most satisfactory, the most central place in all the world. I have come to the conclusion that anything may happen here!

We have had a celebrity in our small midst, and the hills, as the Psalmist might say, have lifted up their heads, and the trees have clapped their hands together. He came here last Tuesday evening and spoke at the School House. I was not there myself; if I had been, I should not, perhaps, have had the adventure which has made this day so livable, nor met the Celebrity face to face.

Let me here set down a close secret regarding celebrities: *They cannot survive without common people like you and me.*

It follows that if we do not pursue a celebrity, sooner or later he will pursue us. He must; it is the law of his being. So I wait here very comfortably on my farm, and as I work in my fields I glance up casually from time to time to see if any celebrities are by chance coming up the town road to seek me out. Oh, we are crusty people, we farmers! Sooner or later they all come this way, all the warriors and the poets, all the philosophers and the prophets and the politicians. If they do not, indeed, get time to come before they are dead, we have full assurance that they will straggle along afterward clad neatly in sheepskin, or more gorgeously in green buckram with gilt lettering. Whatever the airs of pompous importance they may assume as they come, back of it all we farmers can see the look of wistful eagerness in their eyes. They know well enough that they must give us something which we in our commonness regard as valuable enough to exchange for a bushel of our potatoes, or a sack of our white onions. No poem that we can enjoy, no speech that tickles us, no prophecy that thrills us— neither dinner nor immortality for them! And we are hardheaded Yankees at our bargainings; many a puffed-up celebrity loses his puffiness at our doors!

This afternoon, as I came out on my porch after dinner, feeling content with myself and all the world, I saw a man driving our way in a one-horse top-buggy. In the country it is our custom first to identify the horse, and that gives us a sure clue to the identification of the driver. This horse plainly did not belong in our neighbourhood and plainly as it drew nearer, it bore the unmistakable marks of the town livery. Therefore, the driver, in all probability, was a stranger in these parts. What strangers were in town who would wish to drive this way? The man who occupied the buggy was large and slow-looking; he wore a black, broad-brimmed felt hat and a black coat, a man evidently of some presence. And he drove slowly and awkwardly; not an agent plainly. Thus the logic of the country bore fruitage.

"Harriet," I said, calling through the open doorway, "I think the Honourable Arthur Caldwell is coming here."

"Mercy me!" exclaimed Harriet, appearing in the doorway, and as quickly disappearing. I did not see her, of course, but I knew instinctively that she was slipping off her apron, moving our most celebrated rocking-chair two inches nearer the door, and whisking a few invisible particles of dust from the centre

table. Every time any one of importance comes our way, or is distantly likely to come our way, Harriet resolves herself into an amiable whirlwind of good order, subsiding into placidity at the first sound of a step on the porch.

As for me I remain in my shirt sleeves, sitting on my porch resting a moment after my dinner. No sir, I will positively not go in and get my coat. I am an American citizen, at home in my house with the sceptre of my dominion—my favourite daily newspaper—in my hand. Let all kings, queens, and other potentates approach!

And besides, though I am really much afraid that the Honourable Arthur Caldwell will not stop at my gate but will pass on towards Horace's, I am nursing a somewhat light opinion of Mr. Caldwell. When he spoke at the School House on Tuesday, I did not go to hear him, nor was my opinion greatly changed by what I learned afterward of the meeting. I take both of our weekly county papers. This is necessary. I add the news of both together, divide by two to strike a fair average, and then ask Horace, or Charles Baxter, or the Scotch Preacher what really happened. The Republican county paper said of the meeting:

"The Honourable Arthur Caldwell, member of Congress, who is seeking a reëlection, was accorded a most enthusiastic reception by a large and sympathetic audience of the citizens of Blandford township on Tuesday evening."

Strangely enough the Democratic paper, observing exactly the same historic events, took this jaundiced view of the matter:

"Arty Caldwell, Republican boss of the Sixth District, who is out mending his political fences, spellbound a handful of his henchmen at the School House near Blandford Crossing on Tuesday evening."

And here was Mr. Caldwell himself, Member of Congress, Leader of the Sixth District, Favourably Mentioned for Governor, drawing up at my gate, deliberately descending from his buggy, with dignity stopping to take the tie-rein from under the seat, carefully tying his horse to my hitching-post.

I confess I could not help feeling a thrill of excitement. Here was a veritable Celebrity come to my house to explain himself! I would not have it known, of course, outside of our select circle of friends, but I confess that although I am a pretty independent person (when I talk) in reality there are few things in this world I would rather see than a new person coming up the walk to my door. We cannot, of course, let the celebrities know it, lest they grow intolerable in their toploftiness, but if they must have us, we cannot well get along without them—without the colour and variety which they lend to a gray world. I have spent many a precious moment alone in my fields looking up the road (with what wistful casualness!) for some new Socrates or Mark Twain, and I have not been wholly disappointed when I have had to content myself with the Travelling Evangelist or the Syrian Woman who comes this way monthly bearing her pack of cheap suspenders and blue bandana handkerchiefs.

"Good afternoon, Mr. Grayson," said the Honourable Mr. Caldwell, taking off his large hat and pausing with one foot on my step.

"Good afternoon, sir," I responded, "won't you come up?"

He sat down in the chair opposite me with a certain measured and altogether impressive dignity. I cannot say that he was exactly condescending in his manners, yet he made me feel that it was no small honour to have so considerable a person sitting there on the porch with me. At the same time he was outwardly not without a sort of patient deference which was evidently calculated to put me at my ease. Oh, he had all the arts of the schooled politician! He knew to the last shading just the attitude that he as a great man, a leader in Congress, a dominant force in his party, a possible candidate for Governor (and yet always a seeker for the votes of the people!), must observe in approaching a free farmer—like me—sitting at ease in his shirt-sleeves on his own porch, taking a moment's rest after dinner. It was a perfect thing to see!

He had evidently heard, what was not altogether true, that I was a questioner of authority, a disturber of the political peace, and that (concretely) I was opposing him for reëlection. And it was as plain as a pike-staff that he was here to lay down the political law to me. He would do it smilingly and patiently, but firmly. He would use all the leverage of his place, his power, his personal appearance, to crush the presumptuous uprising against his authority.

I confess my spirits rose at the thought. What in this world is more enthralling than the meeting of an unknown adversary upon the open field, and jousting him a tourney. I felt like some modern Robin Hood facing the panoplied authority of the King's man.

And what a place and time it was for a combat—in the quietude of the summer afternoon, no sound anywhere breaking the still warmth and sweetness except the buzzing of bees in the clematis at the end of the porch—and all about the green countryside, woods and fields and old fences—and the brown road leading its venturesome way across a distant hill toward the town.

After explaining who he was—I told him I had recognized him on sight—we opened with a volley of small shot. We peppered one another with harmless comments on the weather and the state of the crops. He advanced cabbages and I countered with sugar-beets. I am quite aware that there are good tacticians who deprecate the use of skirmish lines and the desultory fire of the musketry of small talk. They would advance in grim silence and open at once with the crushing fire of their biggest guns.

But such fighting is not for me. I should lose half the joy of the battle, and kill off my adversary before I had begun to like him! It wouldn't do, it wouldn't do at all.

"It's a warm day," observes my opponent, and I take a sure measure of his fighting form. I rather like the look of his eye.

"I never saw the corn ripening better," I observe, and let him feel a little of the cunning of the arrangement of my forces.

There is much in the tone of the voice, the cut of the words, the turn of a phrase. I can be your servant with a "Yes sir," or your master with a "No sir."

Thus we warm up to one another—a little at a time—we mass our forces, each sees the white of his adversary's eyes. I can even see my opponent—with some joy—trotting up his reserves, having found the opposition stronger than he at first supposed.

"I hear," said Mr. Caldwell, finally, with a smile intended to be disarming, "that you are opposing my reëlection."

Boom! the cannon's opening roar!

"Well," I replied, also smiling, and not to be outdone in the directness of my thrust, "I have told a few of my friends that I thought Mr. Gaylord would represent us better in Congress than you have done."

Boom! the fight is on!

"You are a Republican, aren't you, Mr. Grayson?"

It was the inevitable next stroke. When he found that I was a doubtful follower of him personally, he marshalled the Authority of the Institution which he represented.

"I have voted the Republican ticket," I said, "but I confess that recently I have not been able to distinguish Republicans from Democrats—and I've had my doubts," said I, "whether there is any real Republican party left to vote with."

I cannot well describe the expression on his face, nor indeed, now that the battle was on, horsemen, footmen, and big guns, shall I attempt to chronicle every stroke and counter-stroke of that great conflict.

This much is certain: there was something universal and primal about the battle waged this quiet afternoon on my porch between Mr. Caldwell and me; it was the primal struggle between the leader and the follower; between the representative and the represented. And it is a never-ending conflict. When the leader gains a small advantage the pendulum of civilization swings toward aristocracy; and when the follower, beginning to think, beginning to struggle, gains a small advantage, then the pendulum inclines toward democracy.

And always, and always, the leaders tend to forget that they are only servants, and would be masters. "The unending audacity of elected persons!" And always, and always, there must be a following bold enough to prick the pretensions of the leaders and keep them in their places!

Thus, through the long still afternoon, the battle waged upon my porch. Harriet came out and met the Honourable Mr. Caldwell, and sat and listened, and presently went in again, without having got half a dozen words into the conversation. And the bees buzzed, and in the meadows the cows began to come out of the shade to feed in the open land.

Gradually, Mr. Caldwell put off his air of condescension; he put off his appeal to party authority; he even stopped arguing the tariff and the railroad question. Gradually, he ceased to be the great man, Favourably Mentioned for Governor, and came down on the ground with me. He moved his chair up

"He moved his chair closer to mine"

closer to mine; he put his hand on my knee. For the first time I began to see what manner of man he was: to find out how much real fight he had in him.

"You don't understand," he said, "what it means to be down there at Washington in a time like this. Things clear to you are not clear when you have to meet men in the committees and on the floor of the house who have a contrary view from yours and hold to it just as tenaciously as you do to your views."

Well, sir, he gave me quite a new impression of what a Congressman's job was like, of what difficulties and dissensions he had to meet at home, and what compromises he had to accept when he reached Washington.

"Do you know," I said to him, with some enthusiasm, "I am more than ever convinced that farming is good enough for me."

He threw back his head and laughed uproariously, and then moved up still closer.

"The trouble with you, Mr. Grayson," he said, "is that you are looking for a giant intellect to represent you at Washington."

"Yes," I said, "I'm afraid I am."

"Well," he returned, "they don't happen along every day. I'd like to see the House of Representatives full of Washingtons and Jeffersons and Websters and Roosevelts. But there's a Lincoln only once in a century."

He paused and then added with a sort of wry smile:

"And any quantity of Caldwells!"

That took me! I liked him for it. It was so explanatory. The armour of political artifice, the symbols of political power, had now all dropped away from him, and we sat there together, two plain and friendly human beings, arriving through stress and struggle at a common understanding. He was not a great leader, not a statesman at all, but plainly a man of determination, with a fair measure of intelligence and sincerity. He had a human desire to stay in Congress, for the life evidently pleased him, and while he would never be crucified as a prophet, I felt—what I had not felt before in regard to him—that he was sincerely anxious to serve the best interests of his constituents. Added to these qualities he was a man who was loyal to his friends; and not ungenerous to his enemies.

Up to this time he had done most of the talking; but now, having reached a common basis, I leaned forward with some eagerness.

"You won't mind," I said, "if I give you my view—my common country view of the political situation. I am sure I don't under-

stand, and I don't think my neighbours here understand, much about the tariff or the trusts or the railroad question—in detail. We get general impressions—and stick to them like grim death —for we know somehow that we are right. Generally speaking, we here in the country work for what we get——"

"And sometimes put the big apples at the top of the barrel," nodded Mr. Caldwell.

"And sometimes put too much salt on top of the butter," I added—"all that, but on the whole we get only what we earn by the hard daily work of ploughing and planting and reaping: You admit that."

"I admit it," said Mr. Caldwell.

"And we've got the impression that a good many of the men

down in New York and Boston, and elsewhere, through the advantages which the tariff laws, and other laws, are giving them, are getting more than they earn—a lot more. And we feel that laws must be passed which will prevent all that."

"Now, I believe that, too," said Mr. Caldwell very earnestly.

"Then we belong to the same party," I said. "I don't know what the name of it is yet, but we both belong to it."

Mr. Caldwell laughed.

"And I'll appoint you," I said, "my agent in Washington to work out the changes in the laws."

"Well, I'll accept the appointment," said Mr. Caldwell— continuing very earnestly, "if you'll trust to my honesty and not expect too much of me all at once."

With that we both sat back in our chairs and looked at each other and laughed with the greatest good humour and common understanding.

"And now," said I, rising quickly, "let's go and get a drink of buttermilk."

So we walked around the house arm in arm and stopped in the shade of the oak tree which stands near the spring-house. Harriet came out in the whitest of white dresses, carrying a tray with the glasses, and I opened the door of the spring-house, and felt the cool air on my face and smelt the good smell of butter and milk and cottage cheese, and I passed the cool pitcher to Harriet. And so we drank together there in the shade and talked and laughed.

I walked down with Mr. Caldwell to the gate. He took my arm and said to me:

"I'm glad I came out here and had this talk. I feel as though I understand my job better for it."

"Let's organize a new party," I said, "let's begin with two members, you and I, and have only one plank in the platform."

He smiled.

"You'd have to crowd a good deal into that one plank," he said.

"Not at all," I responded.

"What would you have it?"

"I'd have it in one sentence," I said, "and something like this: We believe in the passage of legislation which shall prevent any man taking from the common store any more than he actually earns."

Mr. Caldwell threw up his arms.

"Mr. Grayson," he said, "you're an outrageous idealist."

"Mr. Caldwell," I said, "you'll say one of these days that I'm a practical politician."

"Well, Harriet," I said, "he's got my vote."

"Well, David," said Harriet, "that's what he came for."

"It's an interesting world, Harriet," I said.

"It is, indeed," said Harriet.

As we stood on the porch we could see at the top of the hill, where the town road crosses it, the slow moving buggy, and through the open curtain at the back the heavy form of our Congressman with his slouch hat set firmly on his big head.

"We may be fooled, Harriet," I observed, "on dogmas and doctrines and platforms—but if we cannot trust human nature in the long run, what hope is there? It's men we must work with, Harriet."

"And women," said Harriet.

"And women, of course," said I.

XIII

ON FRIENDSHIP

COME NOW to the last of these Adventures in Friendship. As I go out—I hope not for long—I wish you might follow me to the door, and then as we continue to talk quietly, I may beguile you, all unconsciously, to the top of the steps, or even find you at my side when we reach the gate at the end of the lane. I wish you might hate to let me go, as I myself hate to go!— And when I reach the top of the hill (if you wait long enough) you will see me turn and wave my hand; and you will know that I am still relishing the joy of our meeting, and that I part unwillingly.

Not long ago, a friend of mine wrote a letter asking me an absurdly difficult question—difficult because so direct and simple.

"What is friendship, anyway?" queried this philosophical correspondent.

The truth is, the question came to me with a shock, as something quite new. For I have spent so much time thinking of my friends that I have scarcely ever stopped to reflect upon the abstract quality of friendship. My attention being thus called to the subject, I fell to thinking of it the other night as I sat by the fire, Harriet not far away rocking and sewing, and my dog sleeping on the rug near me (his tail stirring whenever I made a motion to leave my place). And whether I would or no my friends came trooping into my mind. I thought of our neighbour Horace, the dryly practical and sufficient farmer, and of our much loved Scotch Preacher; I thought of the Shy Bee-man and

of his boisterous double, the Bold Bee-man; I thought of the Old Maid, and how she talks, for all the world like a rabbit running in a furrow (all on the same line until you startle her out, when she slips quickly into the next furrow and goes on running as ardently as before). And I thought of John Starkweather, our rich man; and of the life of the girl Anna. And it was good to think of them all living around me, not far away, connected with me through darkness and space by a certain mysterious human cord. (Oh, there are mysteries still left upon this scientific earth!) As I sat there by the fire I told them over one by one, remembering with warmth or amusement or concern this or that characteristic thing about each of them. It was the next best thing to hearing the tramp of feet on my porch, to seeing the door fly open (letting in a gust of the fresh cool air!), to crying a hearty greeting, to drawing up an easy chair to the open fire, to watching with eagerness while my friend unwraps (exclaiming all the while of the state of the weather: "Cold, Grayson, mighty cold!") and finally sits down beside me, not too far away.

The truth is,—my philosophical correspondent—I cannot formulate any theory of friendship which will cover all the conditions. I know a few things that friendship is not, and a few things that it is, but when I come to generalize upon the abstract quality I am quite at a loss for adequate language.

Friendship, it seems to me, is like happiness. She flies pursuit, she is shy, and wild, and timid, and will be best wooed by indirection. Quite unexpectedly, sometimes, as we pass in the open road, she puts her hand in ours, like a child. Friendship is neither a formality nor a mode: it is rather a life. Many and many a time I have seen Charles Baxter at work in his carpentry-shop—just working, or talking in his quiet voice, or looking around occasionally through his steel-bowed spectacles, and I have had the feeling that I should like to go over and sit on the bench near him. He literally talks me over! I even want to touch him!

It is not the substance of what we say to one another that makes us friends, nor yet the manner of saying it, nor is it what you do or I do, nor is it what I give you, or you give me, nor is it because we chance to belong to the same church, or society or party that makes us friendly. Nor is it because we entertain the same views or respond to the same emotions. All these things may serve to bring us nearer together but no one of them can of itself kindle the divine fire of friendship. A friend is one with whom we are fond of being when no business is afoot nor any entertainment contemplated. A man may well be silent with a friend. "I do not need to ask the wounded person how he feels," says the poet, "I myself became the wounded person."

Not all people come to friendship in the same way. Some possess a veritable genius for intimacy and will be making a dozen friends where I make one. Our Scotch Preacher is such a person. I never knew any man with a gift of intimacy so persuasive as his. He is so simple and direct that he cuts through

the stoniest reserve and strikes at once upon those personal
things which with all of us are so far more real than any outward
interest. "Good-morning, friend," I have heard him say to a
total stranger, and within half an hour they had their heads
together and were talking of things which make men cry. It is
an extraordinary gift.

As for me, I confess it to be a selfish interest or curiosity
which causes me to stop almost any man by the way, and to

take something of what he has—because it pleases me to do so.
I try to pay in coin as good as I get, but I recognize it as a law-
less procedure. For the coin I give (being such as I myself
secretly make) is for them sometimes only spurious metal, while
what I get is for me the very treasure of the Indies. For a lift in
my wagon, a drink at the door, a flying word across my fences,
I have taken argosies of minted wealth!

Especially do I enjoy all travelling people. I wait for them
(how eagerly) here on my farm. I watch the world drift by in
daily tides upon the road, flowing outward in the morning
toward the town, and as surely at evening drifting back again. I
look out with a pleasure impossible to convey upon those who

come this way from the town: the Syrian woman going by in the gray town road, with her bright-coloured head-dress, and her oil-cloth pack; and the Old-ironman with his dusty wagon, jangling his little bells, and the cheerful weazened Herb-doctor in his faded hat, and the Signman with his mouth full of nails—how they are all marked upon by the town, all dusted with the rosy bloom of human experience. How often in fancy I have pursued them down the valley and watched them until they drifted out of sight beyond the hill! Or how often I have stopped them or they (too willingly) have stopped me—and we have fenced and parried with fine bold words.

If you should ever come by my farm—you, whoever you are—take care lest I board you, hoist my pirate flag, and sail you away to the Enchanted Isle where I make my rendezvous.

It is not short of miraculous how, with cultivation, one's capacity for friendship increases. Once I myself had scarcely room in my heart for a single friend, who am now so wealthy in friendships. It is a phenomenon worthy of consideration by all hardened disbelievers in that which is miraculous upon this earth that when a man's heart really opens to a friend he finds there room for two. And when he takes in the second, behold the skies lift, and the earth grows wider, and he finds there room for two more!

In a curious passage (which I understand no longer darkly) old mystical Swedenborg tells of his wonderment that the world of spirits (which he says he visited so familiarly) should not soon become too small for all the swelling hosts of its ethereal inhabitants, and was confronted with the discovery that the more angels there were, the more heaven to hold them!

So let it be with our friendships!

BOOK III

THE FRIENDLY ROAD

I

I LEAVE MY FARM

*"Is it so small a thing
To have enjoyed the sun,
To have lived light in spring?"*

It is eight o'clock of a sunny spring morning. I have been on the road for almost three hours. At five I left the town of Holt, before six I had crossed the railroad at a place called Martin's Landing, and an hour ago, at seven, I could see in the distance the spires of Nortontown. And all the morning as I came tramping along the fine country roads with my pack-strap resting warmly on my shoulder, and a song in my throat—just nameless words to a nameless tune—and all the birds singing, and all the brooks bright under their little bridges, I knew that I must soon step aside and put down, if I could, some faint impression of the feeling of this time and place. I cannot hope to convey any adequate sense of it all—of the feeling of lightness, strength, clearness, I have as I sit here under this maple tree—but I am going to write as long as ever I am happy at it, and when I am no longer happy at it, why, here at my very hand lies the pleasant

267

country road, stretching away toward newer hills and richer scenes.

Until to-day I have not really been quite clear in my own mind as to the step I have taken. My sober friend, have you ever tried to do anything that the world at large considers not quite sensible, not quite sane? Try it! It is easier to commit a thundering crime. A friend of mine delights in walking to town bareheaded, and I fully believe the neighbourhood is more disquieted thereby than it would be if my friend came home drunken or failed to pay his debts.

Here I am then, a farmer, forty miles from home in planting time, taking his ease under a maple tree and writing in a little book held on his knee! Is not that the height of absurdity? Of all my friends the Scotch Preacher was the only one who seemed to understand why it was that I must go away for a time. Oh, I am a sinful and revolutionary person!

When I left home last week, if you could have had a truthful picture of me—for is there not a photography so delicate that it will catch the dim thought-shapes which attend upon our lives?—if you could have had such a truthful picture of me, you would have seen, besides a farmer named Grayson with a gray bag hanging from his shoulder, a strange company following close upon his steps. Among this crew you would have made out easily:

Two fine cows.

Four Berkshire pigs.

One team of gray horses, the old mare a little lame in her right foreleg.

About fifty hens, four cockerels, and a number of ducks and geese.

More than this—I shall offer no explanation in these writings of any miracles that may appear—you would have seen an entirely respectable old farmhouse bumping and hobbling along as best it might in the rear. And in the doorway, Harriet Grayson, in her immaculate white apron, with the veritable look in her eyes which she wears when I am not comporting myself with quite the proper decorum.

Oh, they would not let me go! How they all followed clamoring after me. My thoughts coursed backward faster than ever I could run away. If you could have heard that motley crew of the barnyard as I did—the hens all cackling, the ducks quacking, the pigs grunting, and the old mare neighing and stamping, you would have thought it a miracle that I escaped at all.

So often we think in a superior and lordly manner of our possessions, when, as a matter of fact, we do not really possess them, they possess us. For ten years I have been the humble servant, attending upon the commonest daily needs of sundry hens, ducks, geese, pigs, bees, and of a fussy and exacting old gray mare. And the habit of servitude, I find, has worn deep scars upon me. I am almost like the life prisoner who finds the door of his cell suddenly open, and fears to escape. Why, I had almost become *all* farmer.

On the first morning after I left home I awoke as usual about five o'clock with the irresistible feeling that I must do the milking. So well disciplined had I become in my servitude that I instinctively thrust my leg out of bed—but pulled it quickly back in again, turned over, drew a long, luxurious breath, and said to myself:

"Avaunt cows! Get thee behind me, swine! Shoo, hens!"

Instantly the clatter of mastery to which I had responded so quickly for so many years grew perceptibly fainter, the hens cackled less domineeringly, the pigs squealed less insistently, and as for the strutting cockerel, that lordly and despotic bird stopped fairly in the middle of a crow, and his voice gurgled away in a spasm of astonishment. As for the old farmhouse, it grew so dim I could scarcely see it at all! Having thus published abroad my Declaration of Independence, nailed my defiance to the door, and otherwise established myself as a free person, I turned over in my bed and took another delicious nap.

Do you know, friend, we can be free of many things that dominate our lives by merely crying out a rebellious "Avaunt!"

But in spite of this bold beginning, I assure you it required several days to break the habit of cows and hens. The second morning I awakened again at five o'clock, but my leg did not make for the side of the bed; the third morning I was only partially awakened, and on the fourth morning I slept like a millionaire (or at least I slept as a millionaire is supposed to sleep!) until the clock struck seven.

For some days after I left home—and I walked out as casually that morning as though I were going to the barn—I scarcely thought or tried to think of anything but the Road. Such an unrestrained sense of liberty, such an exaltation of freedom, I have not known since I was a lad. When I came to my farm from the city many years ago it was as one bound, as one who had lost out in the world's battle and was seeking to get hold again somewhere upon the realities of life. I have related elsewhere how I thus came creeping like one sore wounded from the field of battle, and how, among our hills, in the hard, steady labour in the soil of the fields, with new and simple friends around me, I found a sort of rebirth or resurrection. I that was worn out, bankrupt both physically and morally, learned to live again. I have achieved something of high happiness in these years, something I know of pure contentment; and I have learned two or three deep and simple things about life: I have learned that happiness is not to be had for the seeking, but comes quietly to him who pauses at his difficult task and looks upward. I have learned that friendship is very simple, and, more than all else, I have learned the lesson of being quiet, of looking out across the meadows and hills, and of trusting a little in God.

And now, for the moment, I am regaining another of the joys of youth—that of the sense of perfect freedom. I made no plans when I left home, I scarcely chose the direction in which I was to travel, but drifted out, as a boy might, into the great busy world. Oh, I have dreamed of that! It seems almost as though, after ten years, I might again really touch the highest joys of adventure!

So I took the Road as it came, as a man takes a woman, for better or worse—I took the Road, and the farms along it, and the sleepy little villages, and the streams from the hillsides— all with high enjoyment. They were good coin in my purse! And when I had passed the narrow horizon of my acquaintanceship, and reached country new to me, it seemed as though every sense I had began to awaken. I must have grown dull, unconsciously, in the last years there on my farm. I cannot describe the eagerness of discovery I felt at climbing each new hill, nor the long breath I took at the top of it as I surveyed new stretches of pleasant countryside.

Assuredly this is one of the royal moments of all the year—fine, cool, sparkling spring weather. I think I never saw the meadows richer and greener—and the lilacs are still blooming, and the catbirds and orioles are here. The oaks are not yet in full leaf, but the maples have nearly reached their full mantle of verdure—they are very beautiful and charming to see.

It is curious how at this moment of the year all the world seems astir. I suppose there is no moment in any of the seasons when the whole army of agriculture, regulars and reserves, is so fully drafted for service in the fields. And all the doors and windows, both in the little villages and on the farms, stand wide open to the sunshine, and all the women and girls are busy in the yards and gardens. Such a fine, active, gossipy, adventurous world as it is at this moment of the year!

It is the time, too, when all sorts of travelling people are afoot. People who have been mewed up in the cities for the winter now take to the open road—all the peddlers and agents and umbrella-menders, all the nursery salesmen and fertilizer agents, all the tramps and scientists and poets—all abroad in the wide sunny roads. They, too, know well this hospitable moment of the spring; they, too, know that doors and hearts are open and that even into dull lives creeps a bit of the spirit of adventure. Why, a farmer will buy a corn planter, feed a tramp, or listen to a poet twice as easily at this time of year as at any other!

For several days I found myself so fully occupied with the bustling life of the Road that I scarcely spoke to a living soul, but strode straight ahead. The spring has been late and cold: most of the corn and some of the potatoes are not yet in, and the tobacco lands are still bare and brown. Occasionally I

stopped to watch some ploughman in the fields: I saw with a
curious, deep satisfaction how the moist furrows, freshly turned,
glistened in the warm sunshine. There seemed to be something right and fit about it, as well as human and beautiful. Or
at evening I would stop to watch a ploughman driving homeward across his new brown fields, raising a cloud of fine dust
from the fast drying furrow crests. The low sun shining through
the dust and glorifying it, the weary-stepping horses, the man
all sombre-coloured like the earth itself and knit into the scene
as though a part of it, made a picture exquisitely fine to see.

And what a joy I had also of the lilacs blooming in many a
dooryard, the odour often trailing after me for a long distance
in the road, and of the pungent scent at evening in the cool
hollows of burning brush heaps and the smell of barnyards as I
went by—not unpleasant, not offensive—and above all, the deep,
earthy, moist odour of new-ploughed fields.

And then, at evening, to hear the sound of voices from the
dooryards as I pass quite unseen; no words, but just pleasant,
quiet intonations of human voices, borne through the still air,
or the low sounds of cattle in the barnyards, quieting down for
the night, and often, if near a village, the distant, slumbrous
sound of a church bell, or even the rumble of a train—how good
all these sounds are! They have all come to me again this week
with renewed freshness and impressiveness. I am living deep
again!

It was not, indeed, until last Wednesday that I began to get
my fill, temporarily, of the outward satisfaction of the Road—
the primeval takings of the senses—the mere joys of seeing,
hearing, smelling, touching. But on that day I began to wake
up; I began to have a desire to know something of all the
strange and interesting people who are working in their fields,
or standing invitingly in their doorways, or so busily afoot in
the country roads. Let me add, also, for this is one of the most
important parts of my present experience, that this new desire
was far from being wholly esoteric. I had also begun to have
cravings which would not in the least be satisfied by landscapes
or dulled by the sights and sounds of the road. A whiff here and

there from a doorway at mealtime had made me long for my own home, for the sight of Harriet calling from the steps:

"Dinner, David."

But I had covenanted with myself long before starting that I would literally "live light in spring." It was the one and

"Such a fine, gossipy world"

primary condition I made with myself—and made with serious purpose—and when I came away I had only enough money in my pocket and sandwiches in my pack to see me through the first three or four days. Any man may brutally pay his way any-where, but it is quite another thing to be accepted by your human-kind not as a paid lodger but as a friend. Always, it seems to me, I have wanted to submit myself, and indeed submit the stranger, to that test. Moreover, how can any man look for true adventure in life if he always knows to a certainty where his next meal is coming from? In a world so completely domi nated by goods, by things, by possessions, and smothered by security, what fine adventure is left to a man of spirit save the adventure of poverty?

I do not mean by this the adventure of involuntary poverty, for I maintain that involuntary poverty, like involuntary riches, is a credit to no man. It is only as we dominate life that we really live. What I mean here, if I may so express it, is an adventure in achieved poverty. In the lives of such true men as Francis of Assisi and Tolstoi, that which draws the world to them in secret sympathy is not that they lived lives of poverty, but rather, having riches at their hands, or for the very asking, that they chose poverty as the better way of life.

As for me, I do not in the least pretend to have accepted the final logic of an achieved poverty. I have merely abolished temporarily from my life a few hens and cows, a comfortable old farmhouse, and certain other emoluments and hereditaments—but remain the slave of sundry cloth upon my back and sundry articles in my gray bag—including a fat pocket volume or so, and a tin whistle. Let them pass now. To-morrow I may wish to attempt life with still less. I might survive without my battered copy of "Montaigne" or even submit to existence without that sense of distant companionship symbolized by a postage-stamp, and as for trousers——

In this deceptive world, how difficult of attainment is perfection!

No, I expect I shall continue for a long time to owe the worm his silk, the beast his hide, the sheep his wool, and the cat his perfume! What I am seeking is something as simple and as quiet as the trees or the hills—just to look out around me at the pleasant countryside, to enjoy a little of this passing show, to meet (and to help a little if I may) a few human beings, and thus to get more nearly into the sweet kernel of human life. My friend, you may or may not think this a worthy object; if you do not, stop here, go no further with me; but if you do, why, we'll exchange great words on the road; we'll look up at the sky together, we'll see and hear the finest things in this world! We'll enjoy the sun! We'll live light in spring!

Until last Tuesday, then, I was carried easily and comfortably onward by the corn, the eggs, and the honey of my past labours, and before Wednesday noon I began to experience in certain vital centres recognizable symptoms of a variety of discomfort anciently familiar to man. And it was all the sharper because I did not know how or where I could assuage it. In all my life, in spite of various ups and downs in a fat world, I don't think I was ever before genuinely hungry. Oh, I've been hungry in a reasonable, civilized way, but I have always known where in an hour or so I could get all I wanted to eat—a condition accountable, in this world, I am convinced, for no end of stupidity. But to be both physically and, let us say, psychologically hungry, and not to know where or how to get anything to eat, adds something to the zest of life.

By noon on Wednesday, then, I was reduced quite to a point of necessity. But where was I to begin, and how? I know from long experience the suspicion with which the ordinary farmer meets the Man of the Road—the man who appears to wish to enjoy the fruits of the earth without working for them with his hands. It is a distrust deep-seated and ages old. Nor can the Man of the Road ever quite understand the Man of the Fields. And here was I, for so long the stationary Man of the Fields, essaying the rôle of the Man of the Road. I experienced a sudden sense of the enlivenment of the faculties: I must now depend upon wit or cunning or human nature to win my way, not upon mere skill of the hand or strength in the bent back. Whereas in my former life, when I was assailed by a Man of the Road, whether tramp or peddler or poet, I had only to stand stock-still within my fences and say nothing—though indeed I never could do that, being far too much interested in every one who came my way—and the invader was soon repelled. There is nothing so resistant as the dull security of possession: the stolidity of ownership!

Many times that day I stopped by a field side or at the end of a lane, or at a house-gate, and considered the possibilities of making an attack. Oh, I measured the houses and barns I saw with a new eye! The kind of country I had known so long and familiarly became a new and foreign land, full of strange possibilities. I spied out the men in the fields and did not fail, also, to see what I could of the commissary department of each farmstead as I passed. I walked for miles looking thus for a favourable opening—and with a sensation of embarrassment at once disagreeable and pleasurable. As the afternoon began to deepen I saw that I must absolutely do something: a whole day tramping in the open air without a bite to eat is an irresistible argument.

Presently I saw from the road a farmer and his son planting potatoes in a sloping field. There was no house at all in view. At the bars stood a light wagon half filled with bags and seed potatoes, and the horse which had drawn it stood quietly, not far off, tied to the fence. The man and the boy, each with a basket on his arm, were at the farther end of the field, dropping potatoes. I stood quietly watching them. They stepped quickly and kept their eyes on the furrows: good workers. I liked the looks of them. I liked also the straight, clean furrows; I liked the appearance of the horse.

"I will stop here," I said to myself.

I cannot at all convey the sense of high adventure I had as I stood there. Though I had not the slightest idea of what I should do or say, yet I was determined upon the attack.

Neither father nor son saw me until they had nearly reached the end of the field.

"Step lively, Ben," I heard the man say with some impatience; "we've got to finish this field to-day."

"I *am* steppin' lively, dad," responded the boy, "but it's awful hot. We can't possibly finish to-day. It's too much."

"We've got to get through here to-day," the man replied grimly; "we're already two weeks late."

I know just how the man felt; for I knew well the difficulty a farmer has in getting help in planting time. The spring waits for no man. My heart went out to the man and boy struggling there in the heat of their sloping field. For this is the real warfare of the common life.

"Why," I said to myself with a curious lift of the heart, "they have need of a fellow just like me."

At that moment the boy saw me and, missing a step in the rhythm of the planting, the father also looked up and saw me. But neither said a word until the furrows were finished, and the planters came to refill their baskets.

"Fine afternoon," I said, sparring for an opening.

"Fine," responded the man rather shortly, glancing up from his work. I recalled the scores of times I had been exactly in his place, and had glanced up to see the stranger in the road.

"Got another basket handy?" I asked.

"There is one somewhere around here," he answered not too cordially. The boy said nothing at all, but eyed me with absorbing interest. The gloomy look had already gone from his face.

I slipped my gray bag from my shoulder, took off my coat, and put them both down inside the fence. Then I found the basket and began to fill it from one of the bags. Both man and boy looked up at me questioningly. I enjoyed the situation immensely.

"I heard you say to your son," I said, "that you'd have to hurry in order to get in your potatoes to-day. I can see that for myself. Let me take a hand for a row or two."

The unmistakable shrewd look of the bargainer came suddenly into the man's face, but when I went about my business without hesitation or questioning, he said nothing at all. As for the boy, the change in his countenance was marvellous to see. Something new and astonishing had come into the world. Oh, I know what a thing it is to be a boy and have to work in trouting time!

"How near are you planting, Ben?" I asked.

"About fourteen inches."

So we began in fine spirits. I was delighted with the favourable beginning of my enterprise; there is nothing which so draws men together as their employment at a common task.

Ben was a lad some fifteen years old—very stout and stocky, with a fine open countenance and a frank blue eye—all boy. His nose was as freckled as the belly of a trout. The whole situation, including the prospect of help in finishing a tiresome job, pleased him hugely. He stole a glimpse from time to time at me and then at his father. Finally he said:

"Say, you'll have to step lively to keep up with dad."

"I'll show you," I said, "how we used to drop potatoes when I was a boy."

And with that I began to step ahead more quickly and make the pieces fairly fly.

"We old fellows," I said to the father, "must give these young sprouts a lesson once in a while."

"You will, will you?" responded the boy, and instantly began to drop the potatoes at a prodigious speed. The father followed with more dignity, but with evident amusement, and so we all came with a rush to the end of the row.

"I guess that beats the record across *this* field!" remarked the lad, puffing and wiping his forehead. "Say, but you're a good one!"

It gave me a peculiar thrill of pleasure; there is nothing more pleasing than the frank admiration of a boy.

We paused a moment and I said to the man:

"This looks like fine potato land."

"The' ain't any better in these parts," he replied with some pride in his voice.

And so we went at the planting again: and as we planted we had great talk of seed potatoes and the advantages and disadvantages of mechanical planters, of cultivating and spraying, and all the lore of prices and profits. Once we stopped at the lower end of the field to get a drink from a jug of water set in the shade of a fence corner, and once we set the horse in the thills and moved the seed farther up the field. And tired and hungry as I felt I really enjoyed the work; I really enjoyed talking with this busy father and son, and I wondered what their home life was like and what were their real ambitions and hopes. Thus the sun sank lower and lower, the long shadows began to creep into the valleys, and we came finally toward the end of the field. Suddenly the boy Ben cried out:

"There's Sis!"

I glanced up and saw standing near the gateway a slim, bright girl of about twelve in a fresh gingham dress.

"We're coming!" roared Ben, exultantly.

While we were hitching up the horse, the man said to me: "You'll come down with us and have some supper."

"Indeed I will," I replied, trying not to make my response too eager.

"Did mother make gingerbread to-day?" I heard the boy whisper audibly.

"Sh-h—" replied the girl; "who is that man?"

"*I* don't know"—with a great accent of mystery—"and dad don't know. Did mother make gingerbread?'

"Sh-h—he'll hear you."

"Gee! but he can plant potatoes. He dropped down on us out of a clear sky."

"What is he?" she asked. "A tramp?"

"Nope, not a tramp. He works. But, Sis, did mother make gingerbread?"

So we all got into the light wagon and drove briskly out along the shady country road. The evening was coming on, and the air was full of the scent of blossoms. We turned finally into a lane and thus came promptly, for the horse was as eager as we, to the capacious farmyard. A motherly woman came out from the house, spoke to her son, and nodded pleasantly to me. There was no especial introduction. I said merely, "My name is Grayson," and I was accepted without a word.

I waited to help the man, whose name I had now learned—it was Stanley—with his horse and wagon, and then we came up to the house. Near the back door there was a pump, with a bench and basin set just within a little cleanly swept, open shed. Rolling back my collar and baring my arms I washed myself in the cool water, dashing it over my head until I gasped, and then stepping back, breathless and refreshed, I found the slim girl, Mary, at my elbow with a clean soft towel. As I stood wiping quietly I could smell the ambrosial odours from the kitchen. In all my life I never enjoyed a moment more than that, I think.

"Come in now," said the motherly Mrs. Stanley.

So we filed into the roomy kitchen, where an older girl, called Kate, was flying about placing steaming dishes upon the table. There was also an older son, who had been at the farm chores. It was altogether a fine, vigorous, independent American family. So we all sat down and drew up our chairs. Then we paused a moment, and the father, bowing his head, said in a low voice:

"For all Thy good gifts, Lord, we thank Thee. Preserve us and keep us through another night."

I suppose it was a very ordinary farm meal, but it seems to me I never tasted a better one. The huge piles of new baked bread, the sweet farm butter, already delicious with the flavour of new grass, the bacon and eggs, the potatoes, the rhubarb sauce, the great plates of new, hot gingerbread and, at the last, the custard pie—a great wedge of it, with fresh cheese. After the first ravenous appetite of hardworking men was satisfied, there came to be a good deal of lively conversation. The girls had some joke between them which Ben was trying in vain to fathom. The older son told how much milk a certain Alderney cow had given, and Mr. Stanley, quite changed now as he sat at his own table from the rather grim farmer of the afternoon, revealed a capacity for a husky sort of fun, joking Ben about his potato-planting and telling in a lively way of his race with me. As for Mrs. Stanley, she sat smiling behind her tall coffee pot, radiating good cheer and hospitality. They asked me no questions at all, and I was so hungry and tired that I volunteered no information.

After supper we went out for half or three quarters of an hour to do some final chores, and Mr. Stanley and I stopped in the cattle yard and looked over the cows, and talked learnedly about the pigs, and I admired his spring calves to his heart's content, for they really were a fine lot. When we came in again the lamps had been lighted in the sitting-room and the older daughter was at the telephone exchanging the news of the day with some neighbour—and with great laughter and enjoyment. Occasionally she would turn and repeat some bit of gossip to the family, and Mrs. Stanley would exclaim:

"Do tell!"

"Can't we have a bit of music to-night?" inquired Mr. Stanley.

Instantly Ben and the slim girl, Mary, made a wild dive for the front room—the parlour—and came out with a first-rate phonograph which they placed on the table.

"Something lively now," said Mr. Stanley.

So they put on a rollicking negro song called "My Georgia Belle," which, besides the tuneful voices, introduced a steamboat whistle and a musical clangour of bells. When it wound up with a bang, Mr. Stanley took his big comfortable pipe out of his mouth and cried out:

"Fine, fine!"

We had further music of the same sort and with one record the older daughter, Kate, broke into the song with a full, strong though uncultivated voice—which pleased us all very much indeed.

Presently Mrs. Stanley, who was sitting under the lamp with a basket of socks to mend, began to nod.

"Mother's giving the signal," said the older son.

"No, no, I'm not a bit sleepy," exclaimed Mrs. Stanley.

But with further joking and laughing the family began to move about. The older daughter gave me a hand lamp and showed me the way upstairs to a little room at the end of the house.

"I think," she said with pleasant dignity, "you will find everything you need."

I cannot tell with what solid pleasure I rolled into bed or how soundly and sweetly I slept.

This was the first day of my real adventures.

II

I WHISTLE

WHEN I WAS A BOY I learned after many discouragements to play on a tin whistle. There was a wandering old fellow in our town who would sit for hours on the shady side of a certain ancient hotel-barn, and with his little whistle to his lips, and gently swaying his head to his tune and tapping one foot in the gravel, he would produce the most wonderful and beguiling melodies. His favourite selections were very lively; he played, I remember, "Old Dan Tucker," and "Money Musk," and the tune of a rollicking old song, now no doubt long forgotten, called "Wait for the Wagon." I can see him yet, with his jolly eyes half closed, his lips puckered around the whistle, and his fingers curiously and stiffly poised over the stops. I am sure I shall never forget the thrill which his music gave to the heart of a certain barefoot boy.

At length, by means I have long since forgotten, I secured a tin whistle exactly like Old Tom Madison's and began diligently to practise such tunes as I knew. I am quite sure now that I must have made a nuisance of myself, for it soon appeared to be the set purpose of every member of the family to break up my efforts. Whenever my father saw me with the whistle to my lips, he would instantly set me at some useful work (oh, he was an adept in discovering useful work to do—for a boy!). And at the very sight of my stern aunt I would instantly secrete my whistle in my blouse and fly for the garret or cellar, like a cat caught in the cream. Such are the early tribulations of musical genius!

At last I discovered a remote spot on a beam in the hay-barn where, lighted by a ray of sunlight which came through a crack in the eaves and pointed a dusty golden finger into that hay-scented interior, I practised rapturously and to my heart's content upon my tin whistle. I learned "Money Musk" until I could play it in Old Tom Madison's best style—even to the last nod and final foot-tap. I turned a certain church hymn called "Yield Not to Temptation" into something quite inspiriting, and I played "Marching Through Georgia" until all the "happy hills of hay" were to the fervid eye of a boy's imagination full of tramping soldiers. Oh, I shall never forget the joys of those hours in the hay-barn, nor the music of that secret tin whistle! I can hear yet the crooning of the pigeons in the eaves, and the slatey sound of their wings as they flew across the open spaces in the great barn; I can smell yet the odour of the hay.

But with years, and the city, and the shame of youth, I put aside and almost forgot the art of whistling. When I was preparing for the present pilgrimage, however, it came to me with a sudden thrill of pleasure that nothing in the wide world now prevented me from getting a whistle and seeing whether I had forgotten my early cunning. At the very first good-sized town I came to I was delighted to find at a little candy and toy shop just the sort of whistle I wanted, at the extravagant price of ten cents. I bought it and put it in the bottom of my knapsack.

"Am I not old enough now," I said to myself, "to be as youthful as I choose?"

Isn't it the strangest thing in the world how long it takes us to learn to accept the joys of simple pleasures?—and some of us never learn at all. "Boo!" says the neighbourhood, and we are instantly frightened into doing a thousand unnecessary and unpleasant things, or prevented from doing a thousand beguiling things.

For the first few days I was on the road I thought often with pleasure of the whistle lying there in my bag, but it was not until after I left the Stanleys' that I felt exactly in the mood to try it.

The fact is, my adventures on the Stanley farm had left me in a very cheerful frame of mind. They convinced me that some of the great things I had expected of my pilgrimage were realizable possibilities. Why, I had walked right into the heart of as fine a family as I have seen these many days.

I remained with them the entire day following the potato-planting. We were out at five o'clock in the morning, and after helping with the chores, and eating a prodigious breakfast, we went again to the potato-field, and part of the time I helped plant a few remaining rows, and part of the time I drove a team attached to a wing-plow to cover the planting of the previous day.

In the afternoon a slashing spring rain set in, and Mr. Stanley, who was a fore-handed worker, found a job for all of us in the barn. Ben, the younger son, and I sharpened mower-blades and a scythe or so, Ben turning the grindstone and I holding the blades and telling him stories into the bargain. Mr. Stanley and his stout older son overhauled the work-harness and tinkered the corn-planter. The doors at both ends of the barn stood wide open, and through one of them, framed like a picture, we could see the scudding floods descend upon the meadows, and through the other, across a fine stretch of open country, we could see all the roads glistening and the tree-tops moving under the rain.

"Fine, fine!" exclaimed Mr. Stanley, looking out from time to time, "we got in our potatoes just in the nick of time."

After supper that evening I told them of my plan to leave them on the following morning.

"Don't do that," said Mrs. Stanley heartily; "stay on with us."

"Yes," said Mr. Stanley, "we're short-handed, and I'd be glad to have a man like you all summer. There ain't any one around here will pay a good man more'n I will, nor treat 'im better."

"I'm sure of it, Mr. Stanley," I said, "but I can't stay with you."

At that the tide of curiosity which I had seen rising ever since I came began to break through. Oh, I know how difficult it is to let the wanderer get by without taking toll of him! There are not so many people here in the country that we can afford to neglect them. And as I had nothing in the world to conceal, and, indeed, loved nothing better than the give and take of getting acquainted, we were soon at it in good earnest.

But it was not enough to tell them that my name was David Grayson and where my farm was located, and how many acres there were, and how much stock I had, and what I raised. The great particular "Why?"—as I knew it would be—concerned my strange presence on the road at this season of the year and the

reason why I should turn in by chance, as I had done, to help at their planting. If a man is stationary, it seems quite impossible for him to imagine why any one should care to wander; and as for the wanderer it is inconceivable to him how any one can remain permanently at home.

We were all sitting comfortably around the table in the living-room. The lamps were lighted, and Mr. Stanley, in slippers, was smoking his pipe and Mrs. Stanley was darning socks over a mending-gourd, and the two young Stanleys were whispering and giggling about some matter of supreme consequence to youth. The windows were open, and we could smell the sweet scent of the lilacs from the yard and hear the drumming of the rain as it fell on the roof of the porch.

"It's easy to explain," I said. "The fact is, it got to the point on my farm that I wasn't quite sure whether I owned it or it owned me. And I made up my mind I'd get away for a while from my own horses and cattle and see what the world was like. I wanted to see how people lived up here, and what they are thinking about, and how they do their farming."

As I talked of my plans and of the duty one had, as I saw it, to be a good broad man as well as a good farmer, I grew more and more interested and enthusiastic. Mr. Stanley took his pipe slowly from his mouth, held it poised until it finally went out, and sat looking at me with a rapt expression. I never had a better audience. Finally, Mr. Stanley said very earnestly:

"And you have felt that way, too?"

"Why, father!" exclaimed Mrs. Stanley, in astonishment.

Mr. Stanley hastily put his pipe back into his mouth and confusedly searched in his pockets for a match; but I knew I had struck down deep into a common experience. Here was this brisk and prosperous farmer having his dreams too—dreams that even his wife did not know!

So I continued my talk with even greater fervour. I don't think that the boy Ben understood all that I said, for I was dealing with experiences common mostly to older men, but he somehow seemed to get the spirit of it, for quite unconsciously he began to hitch his chair toward me, then he laid his hand on my chair-arm and finally and quite simply he rested his arm against mine and looked at me with all his eyes. I keep learning that there is nothing which reaches men's hearts like talking straight out the convictions and emotions of your innermost soul. Those who hear you may not agree with you, or they may not understand you fully, but something incalculable, something vital, passes. And as for a boy or girl it is one of the sorriest of mistakes to talk down to them; almost always your lad of fifteen thinks more simply, more fundamentally, than you do; and what he accepts as good coin is not facts or precepts, but feelings and convictions—*life*. And why shouldn't we speak out?

"I long ago decided," I said, "to try to be fully what I am and not to be anything or anybody else."

"That's right, that's right!" exclaimed Mr. Stanley, nodding his head vigorously.

"It's about the oldest wisdom there is," I said, and with that I thought of the volume I carried in my pocket, and straightway I pulled it out and after a moment's search found the passage I wanted.

"Listen," I said, "to what this old Roman philosopher said"— and I held the book up to the lamp and read aloud:

" 'You can be invincible if you enter into no contest in which it is not in your power to conquer. Take care, then, when you observe a man honoured before others or possessed of great power, or highly esteemed for any reason, not to suppose him happy and be not carried away by the appearance. For if the nature of the good is in our power, neither envy nor jealousy will have a place in us. But you yourself will not wish to be a general or a senator or consul, but a free man, and there is only one way to do this, to care not for the things which are not in our power.' "

"That," said Mr. Stanley triumphantly, "is exactly what I've always said, but I didn't know it was in any book. I always said I didn't want to be a senator or a legislator, or any other sort of office-holder. It's good enough for me right here on this farm."

At that moment I glanced down into Ben's shining eyes.

"But I want to be a senator or—something—when I grow up," he said eagerly.

At this the older brother, who was sitting not far off, broke into a laugh, and the boy, who for a moment had been drawn out of his reserve, shrank back again and coloured to the hair.

"Well, Ben," said I, putting my hand on his knee, "don't you let anything stop you. I'll back you up; I'll vote for you."

After breakfast the next morning Mr. Stanley drew me aside and said:

"Now I want to pay you for your help yesterday and the day before."

"No," I said. "I've had more than value received. You've taken me in like a friend and brother. I've enjoyed it."

So Mrs. Stanley half filled my knapsack with the finest

luncheon I've seen in many a day, and thus, with as pleasant a farewell as if I'd been a near relative, I set off up the country road. I was a little distressed in parting to see nothing of the boy Ben, for I had formed a genuine liking for him, but upon reaching a clump of trees which hid the house from the road I saw him standing in the moist grass of a fence corner.

"I want to say good-bye," he said in the gruff voice of embarrassment.

"Ben," I said, "I missed you, and I'd have hated to go off without seeing you again. Walk a bit with me."

So we walked side by side, talking quietly, and when at last I shook his hand I said:

"Ben, don't you ever be afraid of acting up to the very best thoughts you have in your heart."

He said nothing for a moment, and then: "Gee! I'm sorry you're goin' away!"

"Gee!" I responded, "I'm sorry, too!"

With that we both laughed, but when I reached the top of the hill, and looked back, I saw him still standing there bare-footed in the road looking after me. I waved my hand and he waved his: and I saw him no more.

No country, after all, produces any better crop than its inhabitants. And as I travelled onward I liked to think of these brave, temperate, industrious, God-friendly American people. I have no fear of the country while so many of them are still to be found upon the farms and in the towns of this land.

So I tramped onward full of cheerfulness. The rain had ceased, but all the world was moist and very green and still. I walked for more than two hours with the greatest pleasure. About ten o'clock in the morning I stopped near a brook to drink and rest, for I was warm and tired. And it was then that I bethought me of the little tin pipe in my knapsack, and straightway I got it out, and, sitting down at the foot of a tree near the brook, I put it to my lips and felt for the stops with unaccustomed fingers. At first I made the saddest sort of work of it, and was not a little disappointed, indeed, with the sound of the whistle itself. It was nothing to my memory of it! It seemed thin and tinny.

"What are you doing, neighbour?"

However, I persevered at it, and soon produced a recognizable imitation of Tom Madison's "Old Dan Tucker." My success quite pleased me, and I became so absorbed that I quite lost account of the time and place. There was no one to hear me save a bluejay which for an hour or more kept me company. He sat on a twig just across the brook, cocking his head at me, and saucily wagging his tail. Occasionally he would dart away among the trees crying shrilly; but his curiosity would always get the better of him and back he would come again to try to solve the mystery of this rival whistling, which I'm sure was as shrill and as harsh as his own.

Presently, quite to my astonishment, I saw a man standing near the brookside not a dozen paces away from me. How long he had been there I don't know, for I had heard nothing of his coming. Beyond him in the town road I could see the head of his horse and the top of his buggy. I said not a word, but continued with my practising. Why shouldn't I? But it gave me quite a thrill for the moment; and at once I began to think of the possibilities of the situation. What a thing it was to have so many unexpected and interesting situations developing! So I nodded my head and tapped my foot, and blew into my whistle all the more energetically. I knew my visitor could not possibly keep away. And he could not; presently he came nearer and said:

"What are you doing, neighbour?"

I continued a moment with my playing, but commanded him with my eye. Oh, I assure you I assumed all the airs of a virtuoso. When I had finished my tune I removed my whistle deliberately and wiped my lips.

"Why, enjoying myself," I replied with greatest good humour. "What are you doing?"

"Why," he said, "watching you enjoy yourself. I heard you playing as I passed in the road, and couldn't imagine what it could be."

I told him I thought it might still be difficult, having heard me near at hand, to imagine what it could be—and thus, tossing the ball of good-humoured repartee back and forth, we walked down to the road together. He had a quiet old horse and a curious top buggy with the unmistakable box of an agent or peddler built on behind.

"My name," he said, "is Canfield. I fight dust."

"And mine," I said, "is Grayson. I whistle."

I discovered that he was an agent for brushes, and he opened his box and showed me the greatest assortment of big and little brushes: bristle brushes, broom brushes, yarn brushes, wire brushes, brushes for man and brushes for beast, brushes of every conceivable size and shape that ever I saw in all my life. He had out one of his especial pets—he called it his "leader"—and feeling it familiarly in his hand he instinctively began the jargon of well-handled and voice-worn phrases which went with that particular brush. It was just as though some one had touched a button and had started him going. It was amazing to me that any one in the world should be so much interested in mere brushes—until he actually began to make me feel that brushes were as interesting as anything else!

What a strange, little, dried-up old fellow he was, with his balls of muttonchop side-whiskers, his thick eyebrows, and his lively blue eyes!—a man evidently not readily turned aside by rebuffs. He had already shown that his wit as a talker had been sharpened by long and varied contact with a world of reluctant purchasers. I was really curious to know more of him, so I said finally:

"See here, Mr. Canfield, it's just noon. Why not sit down here with me and have a bit of luncheon?"

"Why not?" he responded with alacrity. "As the fellow said, why not?"

He unhitched his horse, gave him a drink from the brook, and then tethered him where he could nip the roadside grass. I opened my bag and explored the wonders of Mrs. Stanley's luncheon. I cannot describe the absolutely carefree feeling I had. Always at home, when I would have liked to stop at the roadside with a stranger, I felt the nudge of a conscience troubled with cows and corn, but here I could stop where I liked, or go on when I liked, and talk with whom I pleased, as long as I pleased.

So we sat there, the brush-peddler and I, under the trees, and ate Mrs. Stanley's fine luncheon, drank the clear water from the brook, and talked great talk. Compared with Mr. Canfield I was a babe at wandering—and equally at talking. Was there any business he had not been in, or any place in the country he had

not visited? He had sold everything from fly-paper to threshing-machines, he had picked up a large working knowledge of the weaknesses of human nature, and had arrived at the age of sixty-six with just enough available cash to pay the manufacturer for a new supply of brushes. In strict confidence, I drew certain conclusions from the colour of his nose! He had once had a family, but dropped them somewhere along the road. Most of our brisk neighbours would have put him down as a failure—an old man, and nothing laid by! But I wonder—I wonder—— One thing I am coming to learn in this world, and that is to let people haggle along with their lives as I haggle along with mine.

We both made tremendous inroads on the luncheon, and I presume we might have sat there talking all the afternoon if I had not suddenly bethought myself with a not unpleasant thrill that my resting-place for the night was still gloriously un-decided.

"Friend," I said, "I've got to be up and going. I haven't so much as a penny in my pocket, and I've got to find a place to sleep."

The effect of this remark upon Mr. Canfield was magical. He threw up both his hands and cried out:

"You're that way, are you?"—as though for the first time he really understood. We were at last on common ground.

"Partner," said he, "you needn't tell me nothin' about it. I've been right there myself."

At once he began to bustle about with great enthusiasm. He was for taking complete charge of me, and I think, if I had permitted it, would instantly have made a brush-agent of me. At least he would have carried me along with him in his buggy; but when he suggested it I felt very much, I think, as some old monk must have felt who had taken a vow to do some particular thing in some particular way. With great difficulty I convinced him finally that my way was different from his—though he was regally impartial as to what road he took next—and, finally, with some reluctance, he started to climb into his buggy.

A thought, however, struck him suddenly, and he stepped down again, ran around to the box at the back of his buggy, opened it with a mysterious and smiling look at me, and took out a small broom-brush with which he instantly began brushing off my coat and trousers—in the liveliest and most exuberant way. When he had finished this occupation, he quickly handed the brush to me.

"A token of esteem," he said, "from a fellow traveller."

I tried in vain to thank him, but he held up his hand, scrambled quickly into his buggy, and was for driving off instantly, but paused and beckoned me toward him. When I approached the buggy, he took hold of one of the lapels of my coat, bent over, and said with the utmost seriousness:

"No man ought to take the road without a brush. A good broom-brush is the world's greatest civilizer. Are you looking seedy or dusty?—why, this here brush will instantly make you a respectable citizen. Take my word for it, friend, never go into any strange house without stoppin' and brushin' off. It's money in your purse! You can get along without dinner sometimes, or even without a shirt, but without a brush—never! There's nothin' in the world so necessary to rich *an'* poor, old *an'* young as a good brush!"

And with a final burst of enthusiasm the brush-peddler drove off up the hill. I stood watching him and when he looked around I waved the brush high over my head in token of a grateful farewell.

It was a good, serviceable, friendly brush. I carried it throughout my wanderings; and as I sit here writing in my study, at this moment, I can see it hanging on a hook at the side of my fireplace.

III

THE HOUSE BY THE SIDE OF THE ROAD

Eᴠᴇʀʏ ᴏɴᴇ," remarks Tristram Shandy, "will speak of the fair as his own market has gone in it."

It came near being a sorry fair for me on the afternoon following my parting with the amiable brush-peddler. The plain fact is, my success at the Stanleys', and the easy manner in which I had fallen in with Mr. Canfield, gave me so much confidence in myself as a sort of Master of the Road that I proceeded with altogether too much assurance.

I am firmly convinced that the prime quality to be cultivated by the pilgrim is humility of spirit; he must be willing to accept Adventure in whatever garb she chooses to present herself. He must be able to see the shining form of the unusual through the dull garments of the normal.

The fact is, I walked that afternoon with my head in air and passed many a pleasant farmstead where men were working in the fields, and many an open doorway, and a mill or two, and a town—always looking for some Great Adventure.

Somewhere upon this road, I thought to myself, I shall fall in with a Great Person, or become a part of a Great Incident. I recalled with keen pleasure the experience of that young Spanish student of whom Carlyle writes in one of his volumes, who, riding out from Madrid one day, came unexpectedly upon the greatest man in the world. This great man, of whom Carlyle observes (I have looked up the passage since I came home), "a kindlier, meeker, or braver heart has seldom looked upon the sky in this world," had ridden out from the city for the last time in his life "to take one other look at the azure firmament and green mosaic pavements and the strange carpentry and arras work of this noble palace of a world."

As the old story has it, the young student "came pricking on hastily, complaining that they went at such a pace as gave him little chance of keeping up with them. One of the party made answer that the blame lay with the horse of Don Miguel de Cervantes, whose trot was of the speediest. He had hardly pronounced the name when the student dismounted and, touching the hem of Cervantes' left sleeve, said, 'Yes, yes, it is indeed the maimed perfection, the all-famous, the delightful writer, the joy and darling of the Muses! You are that brave Miguel.'"

It may seem absurd to some in this cool and calculating twentieth century that any one should indulge in such vain imaginings as I have described—and yet, why not? All things are as we see them. I once heard a man—a modern man, living to-day—tell with a hush in his voice, and a peculiar light in his eye, how, walking in the outskirts of an unromantic town in New Jersey, he came suddenly upon a vigorous, bearded, rather rough-looking man swinging his stick as he walked, and stopping often at the roadside and often looking up at the sky. I shall never forget the curious thrill in his voice as he said:

"And *that* was Walt Whitman."

And thus quite absurdly intoxicated by the possibilities of the road, I let the big, full afternoon slip by—I let slip the rich possibilities of half a hundred farms and scores of travelling people —and as evening began to fall I came to a stretch of wilder country with wooded hills and a dashing stream by the roadside. It was a fine and beautiful country—to look at—but the farms, and with them the chances of dinner, and a friendly place to sleep, grew momentarily scarcer. Upon the hills here and there, indeed, were to be seen the pretentious summer homes of rich dwellers from the cities, but I looked upon them with no great hopefulness.

"Of all places in the world," I said to myself, "surely none could be more unfriendly to a man like me."

But I amused myself with conjectures as to what might happen (until the adventure seemed almost worth trying) if a dusty

man with a bag on his back should appear at the door of one of those well-groomed establishments. It came to me, indeed, with a sudden deep sense of understanding, that I should probably find there, as everywhere else, just men and women. And with that I fell into a sort of Socratic dialogue with myself:

ME: Having decided that the people in these houses are, after all, merely men and women, what is the best way of reaching them?

MYSELF: Undoubtedly by giving them something they want and have not.

ME: But these are rich people from the city; what can they want that they have not?

MYSELF: Believe me, of all people in the world those who want the most are those who have the most. These people are also consumed with desires.

ME: And what, pray, do you suppose they desire?

MYSELF: They want what they have not got; they want the un-attainable: they want chiefly the rarest and most precious of all things—a little mystery in their lives.

"That's it!" I said aloud; "that's it! Mystery—the things of the spirit, the things above ordinary living—is not that the essential thing for which the world is sighing, and groaning, and longing —consciously, or unconsciously?"

I have always believed that men in their innermost souls de-sire the highest, bravest, finest things they can hear, or see, or feel in all the world. Tell a man how he can increase his income and he will be grateful to you and soon forget you; but show him the highest, most mysterious things in his own soul and give him the word which will convince him that the finest things are really attainable, and he will love and follow you always.

I now began to look with much excitement to a visit at one of the houses on the hill, but to my disappointment I found the next two that I approached still closed up, for the spring was not yet far enough advanced to attract the owners to the coun-try. I walked rapidly onward through the gathering twilight, but with increasing uneasiness as to the prospects for the night, and thus came suddenly upon the scene of an odd adventure.

From some distance I had seen a veritable palace set high among the trees and overlooking a wonderful green valley— and, drawing nearer, I saw evidences of well-kept roadways and a visible effort to make invisible the attempt to preserve the wild beauty of the place. I saw, or thought I saw, people on the wide veranda, and I was sure I heard the snort of a climbing motor-car, but I had scarcely decided to make my way up to the house when I came, at the turning of the country road, upon a bit of open land laid out neatly as a garden, near the edge of which, nestling among the trees, stood a small cottage. It seemed somehow to belong to the great estate above it, and I concluded, at the first glance, that it was the home of some caretaker or gardener.

It was a charming place to see, and especially the plantation of trees and shrubs. My eye fell instantly upon a fine magnolia—

rare in this country—which had not yet cast all its blossoms, and I paused for a moment to look at it more closely. I myself have tried to raise magnolias near my house, and I know how difficult it is.

As I approached nearer to the cottage I could see a man and woman sitting upon the porch in the twilight and swaying back and forth in rocking-chairs. I fancied—it may have been only a fancy—that when I first saw them their hands were clasped as they rocked side by side.

It was indeed a charming little cottage. Crimson ramblers, giving promise of the bloom that was yet to come, climbed over one end of the porch, and there were fine dark-leaved lilac-bushes near the doorway: oh, a pleasant, friendly, quiet place!

I opened the front gate and walked straight in, as though I had at last reached my destination. I cannot give any idea of the lift of the heart which which I entered upon this new adventure. Without the slightest premeditation and not knowing what I should say or do, I realized that everything depended upon a few sentences spoken within the next minute or two. Believe me, this experience, to a man who does not know where his next meal is coming from, nor where he is to spend the night, is well worth having. It is a marvellous sharpener of the faculties.

I knew, of course, just how these quiet people of the cottage would ordinarily regard an intruder whose bag and clothing must infallibly class him as a follower of the road. And so many followers of the road are—well——

As I came nearer, the man and woman stopped rocking, but said nothing. An old dog that had been sleeping on the top step rose slowly and stood there.

"As I passed your garden," I said, grasping desperately for a way of approach, "I saw your beautiful specimen of the magnolia tree—the one still in blossom. I myself have tried to grow magnolias—but with small success—and I'm making bold to inquire what variety you are so successful with."

It was a shot in the air—but I knew from what I had seen that they must be enthusiastic gardeners. The man glanced around at the magnolia with evident pride, and was about to answer when the woman rose and with a pleasant, quiet cordiality said:

"Won't you step up and have a chair?"

I swung my bag from my shoulder and took the proffered seat. As I did so I saw on the table just behind me a number of magazines and books—books of unusual sizes and shapes, indicating that they were not mere summer novels.

"They like books!" I said to myself with a sudden rise of spirits.

"I have tried magnolias, too," said the man, "but this is the only one that has been really successful. It is a Chinese white magnolia."

"The one Downing describes?" I asked.

This was also a random shot, but I conjectured that if they loved both books and gardens they would know Downing—the Bible of the gardener. And if they did, why, we belonged to the same church.

"The very same," exclaimed the woman; "it was Downing's enthusiasm for the Chinese magnolia which led us first to try it."

With that, like true disciples, we fell into great talk of Downing, at first all in praise of him, and later—for may not the faithful be permitted latitude in their comments so long as it is all within the cloister?—we indulged in a bit of higher criticism.

"It won't do," said the man, "to follow too slavishly every detail of practice as recommended by Downing. We have learned a good many things since the forties."

"The fact is," I said, "no literal-minded man should be trusted with Downing."

"Any more than with the Holy Scriptures," exclaimed the woman.

"Exactly!" I responded with the greatest enthusiasm; "exactly! We go to him for inspiration, for fundamental teachings, for the great literature and poetry of the art. Do you remember," I asked, "that passage in which Downing quotes from some old Chinaman upon the true secret of the pleasures of a garden——?"

"Do we?" exclaimed the man, jumping up instantly; "do we? Just let me get the book——"

With that he went into the house and came back immediately bringing a lamp in one hand—for it had grown pretty dark—and a familiar, portly, blue-bound book in the other. While he was gone the woman said:

"You have touched Mr. Vedder in his weakest spot."

"I know of no combination in this world," said I, "so certain to produce a happy heart as good books and a farm or garden."

Mr. Vedder, having returned, slipped on his spectacles, sat forward on the edge of his rocking-chair, and opened the book with pious hands.

"I'll find it," he said. "I can put my finger right on it."

"You'll find it," said Mrs. Vedder, "in the chapter on 'Hedges.'"

"You are wrong, my dear," he responded, "it is in 'Mistakes of Citizens in Country Life.'"

He turned the leaves eagerly.

"No," he said, "here it is in 'Rural Taste.' Let me read you the passage, Mr. ——"

"Grayson."

"—Mr. Grayson. The Chinaman's name was Lieu-tscheu. 'What is it,' asks this old Chinaman, 'that we seek in the pleasure of a garden? It has always been agreed that these plantations should make men amends for living at a distance from what would be their more congenial and agreeable dwelling-place—in the midst of nature, free and unrestrained.'"

"That's it," I exclaimed, "and the old Chinaman was right! A garden excuses civilization."

"It's what brought us here," said Mrs. Vedder.

With that we fell into the liveliest discussion of gardening and farming and country life in all their phases, resolving that while there were bugs and blights, and droughts and floods, yet upon the whole there was no life so completely satisfying as life in which one may watch daily the unfolding of natural life.

A hundred things we talked about freely that had often risen dimly in my own mind almost to the point—but not quite—of spilling over into articulate form. The marvellous thing about good conversation is that it brings to birth so many half-realized thoughts of our own—besides sowing the seed of innumerable other thought-plants. How they enjoyed their garden, those two, and not only the garden itself, but all the lore and poetry of gardening!

We had been talking thus an hour or more when, quite unexpectedly, I had what was certainly one of the most amusing adventures of my whole life. I can scarcely think of it now without a thrill of pleasure. I have had pay for my work in many ways, but never such a reward as this.

"By the way," said Mr. Vedder, "we have recently come across a book which is full of the spirit of the garden as we have long known it, although the author is not treating directly of gardens, but of farming and of human nature."

"It is really all one subject," I interrupted.

"Certainly," said Mr. Vedder, "but many gardeners are nothing but gardeners. Well, the book to which I refer is called 'Adventures in Contentment,' and is by—— Why, by a man of your own name!"

With that Mr. Vedder reached for a book—a familiar-looking book—on the table, but Mrs. Vedder looked at me. I give you my word, my heart turned entirely over, and in a most remarkable way righted itself again; and I saw Roman candles and Fourth of July rockets in front of my eyes. Never in all my experience was I so completely bowled over. I felt like a small boy who has been caught in the pantry with one hand in the jam-pot—and plenty of jam on his nose. And like that small boy I enjoyed the jam, but did not like being caught at it.

Mr. Vedder had no sooner got the book in his hand than I saw Mrs. Vedder rising as though she had seen a spectre, and pointing dramatically at me, she exclaimed:

"You are David Grayson!"

I can say truthfully now that I know how the prisoner at the bar must feel when the judge, leaning over his desk, looks at him sternly and says:

"I declare you guilty of the offence as charged, and sentence you——" and so on, and so on.

Mr. Vedder stiffened up, and I can see him yet looking at me through his glasses. I must have looked as foolishly guilty as any man ever looked, for Mr. Vedder said promptly:

"Let me take you by the hand, sir. We know you, and have known you for a long time."

I shall not attempt to relate the conversation which followed, nor tell of the keen joy I had in it—after the first cold plunge. We found that we had a thousand common interests and enthusiasms. I had to tell them of my farm, and why I had left it temporarily, and of the experiences on the road. No sooner had I related what had befallen me at the Stanleys' than Mrs. Vedder disappeared into the house and came out again presently with a tray loaded with cold meat, bread, a pitcher of fine milk, and other good things.

"I shall not offer any excuses," said I, "I'm hungry," and with that I laid in, Mr. Vedder helping with the milk, and all three of us talking as fast as ever we could.

It was nearly midnight when at last Mr. Vedder led the way to the immaculate little bedroom where I spent the night.

The next morning I awoke early and, quietly dressing, slipped down to the garden and walked about among the trees and the shrubs and the flower-beds. The sun was just coming up over the hill, the air was full of the fresh odours of morning, and the orioles and cat-birds were singing.

In the back of the garden I found a charming rustic arbour with seats around a little table. And here I sat down to listen to the morning concert, and I saw, cut or carved upon the table, this verse, which so pleased me that I copied it in my book:

> *A garden is a lovesome thing, God wot!*
> *Rose plot,*
> *Fringed pool,*
> *Ferned grot—*
> *The veriest school of peace; and yet the fool*
> *Contends that God is not—*
> *Not God! in gardens? when the even is cool?*
> *Nay, but I have a sign,*
> *'Tis very sure God walks in mine.*

I looked about after copying this verse, and said aloud:

"I like this garden: I like these Vedders."

And with that I had a moment of wild enthusiasm.

"I will come," I said, "and buy a little garden next them, and bring Harriet, and we will live here always. What's a farm compared with a friend?"

But with that I thought of the Scotch preacher, and of Horace, and Mr. and Mrs. Starkweather, and I knew I could never leave the friends at home.

"It's astonishing how many fine people there are in this world," I said aloud; "one can't escape them!"

"Good morning, David Grayson," I heard some one saying, and glancing up I saw Mrs. Vedder at the doorway. "Are you hungry?"

"I am always hungry," I said.

Mr. Vedder came out and linking his arm in mine and pointing out various spireas and Japanese barberries, of which he was very proud, we walked into the house together.

I did not think of it especially at the time—Harriet says I never see anything really worth while, by which she means dishes, dresses, doilies, and such like—but as I remembered afterward the table that Mrs. Vedder set was wonderfully dainty —dainty not merely with flowers (with which it was loaded), but with the quality of the china and silver. It was plainly the table of no ordinary gardener or caretaker—but this conclusion did not come to me until afterward, for as I remember it, we were in a deep discussion of fertilizers.

Mrs. Vedder cooked and served breakfast herself, and did it with a skill almost equal to Harriet's—so skilfully that the talk went on and we never once heard the machinery of service.

After breakfast we all went out into the garden, Mrs. Vedder in an old straw hat and a big apron, and Mr. Vedder in a pair of old brown overalls. Two men had appeared from somewhere, and were digging in the vegetable garden. After giving them certain directions Mr. Vedder and I both found five-tined forks and went into the rose garden and began turning over the rich

"Glancing up, I saw Mrs. Vedder at the doorway"

soil, while Mrs. Vedder, with pruning-shears, kept near us, cutting out the dead wood.

It was one of the charming forenoons of my life. This pleasant work, spiced with the most interesting conversation and interrupted by a hundred little excursions into other parts of the garden, to see this or that wonder of vegetation, brought us to dinner-time before we fairly knew it.

About the middle of the afternoon I made the next discovery. I heard first the choking cough of a big motor-car in the country road, and a moment later it stopped at our gate. I thought I saw the Vedders exchanging significant glances. A number of merry young people tumbled out, and an especially pretty girl of about twenty came running through the garden.

"Mother," she exclaimed, "you *must* come with us!"

"I can't, I can't," said Mrs. Vedder, "the roses *must* be pruned —and see! The azaleas are coming into bloom."

With that she presented me to her daughter.

And, then, shortly, for it could no longer be concealed, I learned that Mr. and Mrs. Vedder were not the caretakers but the owners of the estate and of the great house I had seen on the hill. That evening, with an air almost of apology, they explained to me how it all came about.

"We first came out here," said Mrs. Vedder, "nearly twenty years ago, and built the big house on the hill. But the more we came to know of country life the more we wanted to get down into it. We found it impossible up there—so many unnecessary things to see to and care for—and we couldn't—we didn't see——"

"The fact is," Mr. Vedder put in, "we were losing touch with each other."

"There is nothing like a big house," said Mrs. Vedder, "to separate a man and his wife."

"So we came down here," said Mr. Vedder, "built this little cottage, and have developed this garden mostly with our own hands. We would have sold the big place long ago if it hadn't been for our friends. They like it."

"I have never heard a more truly romantic story," said I.

And it *was* romantic: these fine people escaping from too many possessions, too much property, to the peace and quietude of a garden where they could be lovers again.

"It seems, sometimes," said Mrs. Vedder, "that I never really believed in God until we came down here——"

"I saw the verse on the table in your arbour," said I.

"And it is true," said Mr. Vedder. "We got a long, long way from God for many years: here we seem to get back to Him."

I had fully intended to take the road again that afternoon, but how could any one leave such people as those? We talked again late that night, but the next morning, at the leisurely Sunday breakfast, I set my hour of departure with all the firmness I could command. I left them, indeed, before ten o'clock that forenoon. I shall never forget the parting. They walked with me to the top of the hill, and there we stopped and looked back. We could see the cottage half hidden among the trees, and the little opening that the precious garden made. For a time we stood there quite silent.

"Do you remember," I said presently, "that character in Homer who was a friend of men and lived in a house by the side of the road? I shall always think of you as friends of men —you took in a dusty traveller. And I shall never forget your house by the side of the road."

"The House by the Side of the Road—you have christened it anew, David Grayson," exclaimed Mrs. Vedder.

And so we parted like old friends, and I left them to return to their garden, where " 'tis very sure God walks."

IV

I AM A SPECTATOR OF A MIGHTY BATTLE, IN WHICH CHRISTIAN AGAIN MEETS APOLLYON

It is one of the prime joys of the long road that no two days are ever remotely alike—no two hours even; and sometimes a day that begins calmly will end with the most stirring events.

It was thus, indeed, with that perfect spring Sunday when I left my friends, the Vedders, and turned my face again to the open country. It began as quietly as any Sabbath morning of my life, but what an end it had! I would have travelled a thousand miles for the adventures which a bounteous road that day spilled carelessly into my willing hands.

I can give no adequate reason why it should be so, but there are Sunday mornings in the spring—at least in our country—which seem to put on, like a Sabbath garment, an atmosphere of divine quietude. Warm, soft, clear, but, above all, immeasurably serene.

Such was that Sunday morning; and I was no sooner well afoot than I yielded to the ingratiating mood of the day. Usually I am an active walker, loving the sense of quick motion and the stir it imparts to both body and mind, but that morning I found

308

myself loitering, looking widely about me, and enjoying the lesser and quieter aspects of nature. It was a fine wooded country in which I found myself, and I soon struck off the beaten road and took to the forest and the fields. In places the ground was almost covered with meadow-rue, like green shadows on the hillsides, not yet in seed, but richly umbrageous. In the long green grass of the meadows shone the yellow star-flowers, and the sweet-flags were blooming along the marshy edges of the ponds. The violets had disappeared, but they were succeeded by wild geraniums and rank-growing vetches.

I remember that I kept thinking from time to time, all the forenoon, as my mind went back swiftly and warmly to the two fine friends from whom I had so recently parted:

How the Vedders would enjoy this! Or, I must tell the Vedders that. And two or three times I found myself in animated conversations with them in which I generously supplied all three parts. It may be true for some natures, as Leonardo said, that "if you are alone you belong wholly to yourself; if you have a companion, you belong only half to yourself"; but it is certainly not so with me. With me friendship never divides: it multiplies. A friend always makes me more than I am, better than I am, bigger than I am. We two make four, or fifteen, or forty.

Well, I loitered through the fields and woods for a long time that Sunday forenoon, not knowing in the least that Chance held me close by the hand and was leading me onward to great events. I knew, of course, that I had yet to find a place for the night, and that this might be difficult on Sunday, and yet I spent that forenoon as a man spends his immortal youth—with a glorious disregard for the future.

Some time after noon—for the sun was high and the day was growing much warmer—I turned from the road, climbed an inviting little hill, and chose a spot in an old meadow in the shade of an apple tree, and there I lay down on the grass and looked up into the dusky shadows of the branches above me. I could feel the soft airs on my face; I could hear the buzzing of bees in the meadow flowers, and by turning my head just a little I could see the slow fleecy clouds, high up, drifting across the perfect blue of the sky. And the scent of the fields in spring!—he who has known it, even once, may indeed die happy.

Men worship God in various ways: it seemed to me that Sabbath morning, as I lay quietly there in the warm silence of midday, that I was truly worshipping God. That Sunday morning everything about me seemed somehow to be a miracle—a miracle gratefully accepted and explainable only by the presence of God. There was another strange, deep feeling which I had that morning, which I have had a few other times in my life at the rare heights of experience—I hesitate always when I try to put down the deep, deep things of the human heart—a feeling immeasurably real, that if I should turn my head quickly, I should indeed *see* that Immanent Presence. . . .

One of the few birds I know that sings through the long midday is the vireo. The vireo sings when otherwise the woods are still. You do not see him; you cannot find him; but you know he is there. And his singing is wild, and shy, and mystical. Often it haunts you like the memory of some former happiness. That day I heard the vireo singing. . . .

I don't know how long I lay there under the tree in the meadow, but presently I heard, from no great distance, the sound of a church-bell. It was ringing for the afternoon service which among the farmers of this part of the country often takes the place, in summer, of both morning and evening services.

"I believe I'll go," I said, thinking first of all, I confess, of the interesting people I might meet there.

But when I sat up and looked about me the desire faded, and rummaging in my bag I came across my tin whistle. Immediately I began practising a tune called "Sweet Afton," which I had learned when a boy; and, as I played, my mood changed swiftly, and I began to smile at myself as a tragically serious person, and to think of pat phrases with which to characterize the execrableness of my attempts upon the tin whistle. I should have liked some one near to joke with.

Long ago I made a motto about boys: Look for a boy any-

where. Never be surprised when you shake a cherry tree if a boy
drops out of it; never be disturbed when you think yourself in
complete solitude if you discover a boy peering out at you from
a fence corner.

I had not been playing long before I saw two boys looking at
me from out of a thicket by the roadside; and a moment later
two others appeared.

Instantly I switched into "Marching Through Georgia," and
began to nod my head and tap my toe in the liveliest fashion.
Presently one boy climbed up on the fence, then another, then a
third. I continued to play. The fourth boy, a little chap, ven-
tured to climb up on the fence.

They were bright-faced, tow-headed lads, all in Sunday
clothes.

"It's hard luck," said I, taking my whistle from my lips, "to
have to wear shoes and stockings on a warm Sunday like this."

"You bet it is!" said the bold leader.

"In that case," said I, "I will play 'Yankee Doodle.'"

I played. All the boys, including the little chap, came up
around me, and two of them sat down quite familiarly on the
grass. I never had a more devoted audience. I don't know what
interesting event might have happened next, for the bold leader,
who stood nearest, was becoming dangerously inflated with
questions—I don't know what might have happened had we
not been interrupted by the appearance of a Spectre in Black.
It appeared before us there in the broad daylight in the middle
of a sunny afternoon while we were playing "Yankee Doodle."
First I saw the top of a black hat rising over the rim of the hill.
This was followed quickly by a black tie, a long black coat,
black trousers, and, finally, black shoes. I admit I was shaken,
but being a person of iron nerve in facing such phenomena I
continued to play "Yankee Doodle." In spite of this counter-
attraction, toward which all four boys turned uneasy glances, I
held my audience. The Black Spectre, with a black book under
its arm, drew nearer. Still I continued to play and nod my head
and tap my toe. I felt like some modern Pied Piper piping away

the children of these modern hills—piping them away from older people who could not understand them.

I could see an accusing look on the Spectre's face. I don't know what put it into my head, and I had no sooner said it than I was sorry for my levity, but the figure with the sad garments there in the matchless and triumphant spring day affected me with a curious sharp impatience. Had any one the right to look out so dolefully upon such a day and such a scene of simple happiness as this? So I took my whistle from my lips and asked:

"Is God dead?"

I shall never forget the indescribable look of horror and astonishment that swept over the young man's face.

"What do you mean, sir?" he asked with an air of stern authority which surprised me. His calling for the moment lifted him above himself: it was the Church which spoke.

I was on my feet in an instant, regretting the pain I had given him; and yet it seemed worth while now, having made my inadvertent remark, to show him frankly what lay in my mind. Such things sometimes help men.

"I meant no offence, sir," I said, "and I apologize for my flummery, but when I saw you coming up the hill, looking so gloomy and disconsolate on this bright day, as though you disapproved of God's world, the question slipped out before I knew it."

My words evidently struck deep down into some disturbed inner consciousness, for he asked—and his words seemed to slip out before he thought:

"Is *that* the way I impressed you?"

I found my heart going out strongly toward him. "Here," I thought to myself, "is a man in trouble."

I took a good long look at him. He was still a young man, though worn-looking—and sad, as I now saw it, rather than gloomy—with the sensitive lips and the unworldly look one sees sometimes in the faces of saints. His black coat was immaculately neat, but the worn button-covers and the shiny lapels told their own eloquent story. Oh, it seemed to me I knew him as well as if every incident of his life were written plainly upon his

high, pale forehead! I have lived long in a country neighbourhood, and I knew him—poor flagellant of the rural church—
I knew how he groaned under the sins of a community too comfortably willing to cast all its burdens on the Lord, or on the
Lord's accredited local representative. I inferred also the usual
large family and the low salary (scandalously unpaid) and the
frequent moves from place to place.

Unconsciously heaving a sigh the young man turned partly
aside and said to me in a low, gentle voice:

"You are detaining my boys from church."

"I am very sorry," I said, "and I will detain them no longer,"
and with that I put aside my whistle, took up my bag and
moved down the hill with them.

"The fact is," I said, "when I heard your bell I thought of
going to church myself."

"Did you?" he asked eagerly. "Did you?"

I could see that my proposal of going to church had instantly
affected his spirits. Then he hesitated abruptly with a sidelong
glance at my bag and rusty clothing. I could see exactly what
was passing in his mind.

"No," I said, smiling, as though answering a spoken question, "I am not exactly what you would call a tramp."

He flushed.

"I didn't mean—I *want* you to come. That's what a church is for. If I thought——"

But he did not tell me what he thought; and, though he walked quietly at my side, he was evidently deeply disturbed. Something of his discouragement I sensed even then, and I don't think I was ever sorrier for a man in my life than I was for him at that moment. Talk about the sufferings of sinners! I wonder if they are to be compared with the trials of the saints?

So we approached the little white church, and caused, I am certain, a tremendous sensation. Nowhere does the unpredictable, the unusual, excite such confusion as in that settled institution—the church.

I left my bag in the vestibule, where I have no doubt it was the object of much inquiring and suspicious scrutiny, and took my place in a convenient pew. It was a small church with an odd air of domesticity, and the proportion of old ladies and children in the audience was pathetically large. As a ruddy, vigorous, out-of-door person, with the dust of life upon him, I felt distinctly out of place.

I could pick out easily the Deacon, the Old Lady Who Brought Flowers, the President of the Sewing Circle, and, above all, the Chief Pharisee, sitting in his high place. The Chief Pharisee—his name I learned was Nash, Mr. J. H. Nash (I did not know then that I was soon to make his acquaintance)—the Chief Pharisee looked as hard as nails, a middle-aged man with stiff white chin-whiskers, small, round, sharp eyes, and a pugnacious jaw.

"That man," said I to myself, "runs this church," and instantly I found myself looking upon him as a sort of personification of the troubles I had seen in the minister's eyes.

I shall not attempt to describe the service in detail. There was a discouraging droop and quaver in the singing, and the mournful-looking deacon who passed the collection-plate seemed inured to disappointment. The prayer had in it a note of despairing appeal which fell like a cold hand upon one's living soul. It gave one the impression that this was indeed a miserable, dark, despairing world, which deserved to be wrathfully destroyed, and that this miserable world was full of equally miserable, broken, sinful, sickly people.

The sermon was a little better, for somewhere hidden within him this pale young man had a spark of the divine fire, but it was so dampened by the atmosphere of the church that it never rose above a pale luminosity.

I found the service indescribably depressing. I had an impulse to rise up and cry out—almost anything to shock these people into opening their eyes upon real life. Indeed, though I hesitate about setting it down here, I was filled for some time with the liveliest imaginings of the following serio-comic enterprise:

I would step up the aisle, take my place in front of the Chief Pharisee, wag my finger under his nose, and tell him a thing or two about the condition of the church.

"The only live thing here," I would tell him, "is the spark in that pale minister's soul; and you're doing your best to smother that."

And I fully made up my mind that when he answered back in his chief-pharisaical way I would gently but firmly remove him from his seat, shake him vigorously two or three times (men's souls have often been saved with less!), deposit him flat in the aisle, and—yes—stand on him while I elucidated the situation to the audience at large. While I confined this amusing and interesting project to the humours of the imagination I am still convinced that something of the sort would have helped enormously in clearing up the religious and moral atmosphere of the place.

I had a wonderful sensation of relief when at last I stepped out again into the clear afternoon sunshine and got a reviving glimpse of the smiling green hills and the quiet fields and the sincere trees—and felt the welcome of the friendly road.

I would have made straight for the hills, but the thought of that pale minister held me back, and I waited quietly there under the trees till he came out. He was plainly looking for me, and asked me to wait and walk along with him, at which his four boys, whose acquaintance I had made under such thrilling cir-cumstances earlier in the day, seemed highly delighted, and waited with me under the tree and told me a hundred important things about a certain calf, a pig, a kite, and other things at home.

Arriving at the minister's gate, I was invited in with a whole-heartedness that was altogether charming. The minister's wife, a faded-looking woman who had once possessed a delicate sort of prettiness, was waiting for us on the steps with a fine chubby baby on her arm—number five.

The home was much the sort of place I had imagined—a small house undesirably located (but cheap!), with a few straggling acres of garden and meadow upon which the minister and his boys were trying with inexperienced hands to piece out their inadequate living. At the very first glimpse of the garden I wanted to throw off my coat and go at it.

And yet—and yet—what a wonderful thing love is! There was, after all, something incalculable, something pervasively beautiful about this poor household. The moment the minister stepped inside his own door he became a different and livelier person. Something boyish crept into his manner, and a new look came into the eyes of his faded wife that made her almost pretty again. And the fat, comfortable baby rolled and gurgled about on the floor as happily as though there had been two nurses and a governess to look after him. As for the four boys, I have never seen healthier or happier ones.

I sat with them at their Sunday-evening luncheon. As the minister bowed his head to say grace I felt him clasp my hand on one side while the oldest boy clasped my hand on the other, and thus, linked together, and accepting the stranger utterly, the family looked up to God.

There was a fine, modest gayety about the meal. In front of Mrs. Minister stood a very large yellow bowl filled with what she called rusk—a preparation unfamiliar to me, made by browning and crushing the crusts of bread and then rolling them down into a coarse meal. A bowl of this, with sweet, rich, yellow milk (for they kept their own cow), made one of the most appetizing dishes that ever I ate. It was downright good: it gave one the unalloyed aroma of the sweet new milk and the satisfying taste of the crisp bread.

Nor have I ever enjoyed a more perfect hospitality. I have been in many a richer home where there was not a hundredth part of the true gentility—the gentility of unapologizing simplicity and kindness.

And after it was over and cleared away—the minister himself donning a long apron and helping his wife—and the chubby baby put to bed, we all sat around the table in the gathering twilight.

I think men perish sometimes from sheer untalked talk. For lack of a creative listener they gradually fill up with unexpressed emotion. Presently this emotion begins to ferment, and finally—bang!—they blow up, burst, disappear in thin air. In all that community I suppose there was no one but the little faded wife to whom the minister dared open his heart, and I think he found me a godsend. All I really did was to look from one to the other and put in here and there an inciting comment or ask an understanding question. After he had told me his situation and the difficulties which confronted him and his small church, he exclaimed suddenly:

"A minister should by rights be a leader not only inside of his church, but outside of it in the community."

"You are right," I exclaimed with great earnestness; "you are right."

And with that I told him of our own Scotch preacher and how he led and moulded our community; and as I talked I could see him actually growing, unfolding, under my eyes.

"Why," said I, "you not only ought to be the moral leader of this community, but you are!"

"That's what I tell him," exclaimed his wife.

"But he persists in thinking, doesn't he, that he is a poor sinner?"

"He thinks it too much," she laughed.

"Yes, yes," he said, as much to himself as to us, "a minister ought to be a fighter!"

It was beautiful, the boyish flush which now came into his face and the light that came into his eyes. I should never have identified him with the Black Spectre of the afternoon.

"Why," said I, "you *are* a fighter; you're fighting the greatest battle in the world to-day—the only real battle—the battle for the spiritual view of life."

Oh, I knew exactly what was the trouble with his religion—at least the religion which, under the pressure of that church, he felt obliged to preach! It was the old, groaning, denying, resisting religion. It was the sort of religion which sets a man apart and assures him that the entire universe in the guise of the Powers of Darkness is leagued against him. What he needed was a reviving draught of the new faith which affirms, accepts, rejoices, which feels the universe triumphantly behind it. And so whenever the minister told me what he ought to be—for he too sensed the new impulse—I merely told him he was just that. He needed only this little encouragement to unfold.

"Yes," said he again, "I am the real moral leader here."

At this I saw Mrs. Minister nodding her head vigorously.

"It's you," she said, "and not Mr. Nash, who should lead this community."

How a woman loves concrete applications! She is your only true pragmatist. If a philosophy will not work, says she, why bother with it?

The minister rose quickly from his chair, threw back his head, and strode quickly up and down the room.

"You are right," said he; "and I *will* lead it. I'll have my farmers' meetings as I planned."

It may have been the effect of the lamplight, but it seemed to me that little Mrs. Minister, as she glanced up at him, looked actually pretty.

The minister continued to stride up and down the room with his chin in the air.

"Mr. Nash," said she in a low voice to me, "is always trying to hold him down and keep him back. My husband *wants* to do the great things"——wistfully.

"By every right," the minister was repeating quite oblivious of our presence, "I should lead this people."

"He sees the weakness of the church," she continued, "as well as any one, and he wants to start some vigorous community work—have agriculture meetings and boys' clubs, and lots of things like that—but Mr. Nash says it is no part of a minister's work: that it cheapens religion. He says that when a parson— Mr. Nash always calls him parson, and I just *loathe* that name— has preached, and prayed, and visited the sick, that's enough for *him*."

At this very moment a step sounded upon the walk, and an instant later a figure appeared in the doorway.

"Why, Mr. Nash," exclaimed little Mrs. Minister, exhibiting that astonishing gift of swift recovery which is the possession of even the simplest women, "come right in."

It was some seconds before the minister could come down from the heights and greet Mr. Nash. As for me, I was never more interested in my life.

"Now," said I to myself, "we shall see Christian meet Apollyon."

As soon as Mrs. Minister lighted the lamp I was introduced to the great man. He looked at me sharply with his small, round eyes, and said:

"Oh, you are the—the man who was in church this afternoon."

I admitted it, and he looked around at the minister with an accusing expression. He evidently did not approve of me, nor could I wholly blame him, for I knew well how he, as a rich farmer, must look upon a rusty man of the road like me. I should have liked dearly to cross swords with him myself, but greater events were imminent.

In no time at all the discussion, which had evidently been broken off at some previous meeting, concerning the proposed farmers' assembly at the church, had taken on a really lively tone. Mr. Nash was evidently in the somewhat irritable mood with which important people may sometimes indulge themselves, for he bit off his words in a way that was calculated to make any but an unusually meek and saintly man exceedingly uncomfortable. But the minister, with the fine, high humility of those whose passion is for great or true things, was quite oblivious to the harsh words. Borne along by an irresistible enthusiasm, he told in glowing terms what his plan would mean to the community, how the people needed a new social and civic spirit —a "neighbourhood religious feeling" he called it. And as he talked his face flushed and his eyes shone with the pure fire of a great purpose. But I could see that all this enthusiasm impressed the practical Mr. Nash as mere moonshine. He grew more and more uneasy. Finally he brought his hand down with a resounding thwack upon his knee, and said in a high, cutting voice:

"I don't believe in any such newfangled nonsense. It ain't none of a parson's business what the community does. You're hired, ain't you, an' paid to run the church? That's the end of it. We ain't goin' to have any mixin' of religion an' farmin' in *this* neighbourhood."

My eyes were on the pale man of God. I felt as though a human soul were being weighed in the balance. What would he do now? What was he worth *really* as a man as well as a minister?

He paused a moment with downcast eyes. I saw little Mrs. Minister glance at him—once—wistfully. He rose from his place, drew himself up to his full height—I shall not soon forget the look on his face—and uttered these amazing words:

"Martha, bring the ginger-jar."

Mrs. Minister, without a word, went to a little cupboard on the farther side of the room and took down a brown earthenware jar, which she brought over and placed on the table, Mr. Nash following her movements with astonished eyes. No one spoke.

The minister took the jar in his hands as he might the communion-cup just before saying the prayer of the sacrament.

"Mr. Nash," said he in a loud voice, "I've decided to hold that farmers' meeting."

Before Mr. Nash could reply the minister seated himself and was pouring out the contents of the jar upon the table—a clatter of dimes, nickels, pennies, a few quarters and half dollars, and a very few bills.

"He turned, reached for his hat, and then went out of the door into the darkness"

"Martha, just how much money is there here?"

"Twenty-four dollars and sixteen cents."

The minister put his hand into his pocket and, after counting out certain coins, said:

"Here's one dollar and eighty-four cents more. That makes twenty-six dollars. Now, Mr. Nash, you're the largest contributor to my salary in this neighbourhood. You gave twenty-six dollars last year—fifty cents a week. It is a generous contribution, but I cannot take it any longer. It is fortunate that my wife has saved up this money to buy a sewing-machine, so that we can pay back your contribution in full."

He paused; no one of us spoke a word.

"Mr. Nash," he continued, and his face was good to see, "I am the minister here. I am convinced that what the community needs is more of a religious and social spirit, and I am going about getting it in the way the Lord leads me."

At this I saw Mrs. Minister look up at her husband with such a light in her eyes as any man might well barter his life for— I could not keep my own eyes from the pure beauty of it.

I knew too what this defiance meant. It meant that this little family was placing its all upon the altar—even the pitiful coins for which they had skimped and saved for months for a particular purpose. Talk of the heroism of the men who charged with Pickett at Gettysburg! Here was a courage higher and whiter than that; here was a courage that dared to fight alone.

As for Mr. Nash, the face of that Chief Pharisee was a study. Nothing is so paralyzing to a rich man as to find suddenly that his money will no longer command him any advantage. Like all hard-shelled, practical people, Mr. Nash could only dominate in a world which recognized the same material supremacy that he recognized. Any one who insisted upon flying was lost to Mr. Nash.

The minister pushed the little pile of coins toward him.

"Take it, Mr. Nash," said he.

At that Mr. Nash rose hastily.

"I will not," he said gruffly.

He paused, and looked at the minister with a strange expression in his small round eyes—was it anger, or was it fear, or could it have been admiration?

"If you want to waste your time on fiddlin' farmers' meetings —a man that knows as little of farmin' as you do—why, go ahead for all o' me. But don't count me in."

He turned, reached for his hat, and then went out of the door into the darkness.

For a moment we all sat perfectly silent, then the minister rose, and said solemnly:

"Martha, let's sing something."

Martha crossed the room to the cottage organ and seated herself on the stool.

"What shall we sing?" said she.

"Something with fight in it, Martha," he responded; "something with plenty of fight in it."

So we sang "Onward, Christian Soldiers, Marching as to War," and followed that up with:

> *Awake, my soul, stretch every nerve*
> *And press with vigour on;*
> *A heavenly race demands thy zeal*
> *And an immortal crown.*

When we had finished, and as Martha rose from her seat, the minister impulsively put his hands on her shoulders, and said:

"Martha, this is the greatest night of my life."

He took a turn up and down the room, and then with an exultant boyish laugh said:

"We'll go to town to-morrow and pick out that sewing-machine!"

I remained with them that night and part of the following day, taking a hand with them in the garden, but of the events of that day I shall speak in another chapter.

V

I PLAY THE PART OF A SPECTACLE-PEDDLER

Y<small>ESTERDAY</small> was exactly the sort of a day I love best—a spicy, unexpected, amusing day—a day crowned with a droll adventure.

I cannot at all account for it, but it seems to me I take the road each morning with a livelier mind and keener curiosity. If you were to watch me narrowly these days you would see that I am slowly shedding my years. I suspect that some one of the clear hill streams from which I have been drinking (lying prone on my face) was in reality the fountain of eternal youth. I shall not go back to see.

It seems to me, when I feel like this, that in every least thing upon the roadside, or upon the hill, lurks the stuff of adventure. What a world it is! A mile south of here I shall find all that Stanley found in the jungles of Africa; a mile north I am Perry at the Pole!

You there, brown-clad farmer on the tall seat of your wagon, driving townward with a red heifer for sale, I can show you that life—your life—is not all a gray smudge, as you think it is, but crammed, packed, loaded with miraculous things. I can show you wonders past belief in your own soul. I can easily convince you that you are in reality a poet, a hero, a true lover, a saint.

It is because we are not humble enough in the presence of the divine daily fact that adventure knocks so rarely at our door. A thousand times I have had to learn this truth (what lesson so hard to learn as the lesson of humility!) and I suppose I shall have to learn it a thousand times more. This very day, straining my eyes to see the distant wonders of the mountains, I nearly missed a miracle by the roadside.

Soon after leaving the minister and his family—I worked with them in their garden with great delight most of the forenoon—I came, within a mile, to the wide white turnpike—the Great Road.

Now, I usually prefer the little roads, the little, unexpected, curving, leisurely country roads. The sharp hills, the pleasant deep valleys, the bridges not too well kept, the verdure deep grown along old fences, the houses opening hospitably at the very roadside, all these things I love. They come to me with the same sort of charm and flavour, only vastly magnified, which I find often in the essays of the older writers—those leisurely old fellows who took time to write, *really* write. The important thing to me about a road, as about life and literature, is not that it goes anywhere, but that it is livable while it goes. For if I were to arrive—and who knows that I ever shall arrive?—I think I should be no happier than I am here.

Thus I have commonly avoided the Great White Road—the broad, smooth turnpike—rock-bottomed and rolled by a beneficent State—without so much as a loitering curve to whet one's curiosity, nor a thank-you-ma'am to laugh over, nor a sinful hill to test your endurance—not so much as a dreamy valley! It pursues its hard, unshaded, practical way directly from some particular place to some other particular place—and from time to time a motor-car shoots in at one end of it and out at the other, leaving its dust to settle upon quiet travellers like me.

Thus to-day when I came to the turnpike I was at first for

making straight across it and taking to the hills beyond, but at that very moment a motor-car whirled past me as I stood there, and a girl with a merry face waved her hand at me. I lifted my hat in return, and as I watched them out of sight I felt a curious new sense of warmth and friendliness in the Great Road.

"These are just people, too," I said aloud—"and maybe they really like it!"

And with that I began laughing at myself, and at the whole big, amazing, interesting world. Here was I pitying them for their benighted state, and there were they, no doubt, pitying me for mine!

And with that pleasant and satisfactory thought in my mind and a song in my throat I swung into the Great Road.

"It doesn't matter in the least," said I to myself, "whether a man takes hold of life by the great road or the little ones so long as he takes hold."

And oh, it was a wonderful day! A day with movement in it; a day that flowed! In every field the farmers were at work, the cattle fed widely in the meadows, and the Great Road itself was alive with a hundred varied sorts of activity. Light winds stirred the tree-tops and rippled in the new grass; and from the thickets I heard the blackbirds crying. Everything animate and inanimate, that morning, seemed to have its own clear voice and to cry out at me for my interest, or curiosity, or sympathy. Under such circumstances it could not have been long—nor was it long —before I came plump upon the first of a series of odd adventures.

A great many people, I know, abominate the roadside sign. It seems to them a desecration of nature, the intrusion of rude commercialism upon the perfection of natural beauty. But not I. I have no such feeling. Oh, the signs in themselves are often rude and unbeautiful, and I never wished my own barn or fences to sing the praises of swamproot or sarsaparilla—and yet there is something wonderfully human about these painted and pasted vociferations of the roadside signs; and I don't know why they are less "natural" in their way than a house or barn or a planted field of corn. They also tell us about life. How eagerly they cry out at us, "Buy me, buy me!" What enthusiasm they have in their own concerns, what boundless faith in themselves! How they speak of the enormous energy, activity, resourcefulness of human kind!

Indeed, I like all kinds of signs. The autocratic warnings of the road, the musts and the must-nots of traffic, I observe in passing; and I often stand long at the crossings and look up at the finger-posts, and consider my limitless wealth as a traveller. By this road I may, at my own pleasure, reach the Great City; by that—who knows?—the far wonders of Cathay. And I respond always to the appeal which the devoted pilgrim paints on the rocks at the roadside: "Repent ye, for the kingdom of God is at hand," and though I am certain that the kingdom of God is already here, I stop always and repent—just a little—knowing that there is always room for it. At the entrance of the little towns, also, or in the squares of the villages, I stop often to read the signs of taxes assessed, or of political meetings; I see the evidences of homes broken up in the notices of auction sales, and of families bereaved in the dry and formal publications of the probate court. I pause, too, before the signs of amusements flaming red and yellow on the barns (boys, the circus is coming to town!), and I pause also, but no longer, to read the silent signs carved in stone in the little cemeteries as I pass. Symbols, you say? Why, they're the very stuff of life. If you cannot see life here in the wide road, you will never see it at all.

Well, I saw a sign yesterday at the roadside that I never saw anywhere before. It was not a large sign—indeed rather inconspicuous—consisting of a single word rather crudely painted in black (as by an amateur) upon a white board. It was nailed to a tree where those in swift passing cars could not avoid seeing it:

REST

I cannot describe the odd sense of enlivenment, of pleasure I had when I saw this new sign.

"Rest!" I exclaimed aloud. "Indeed I will," and I sat down on a stone not far away.

"Rest!"

What a sign for this very spot! Here in the midst of the haste and hurry of the Great Road a quiet voice was saying, "Rest." Some one with imagination, I thought, evidently put that up; some quietist offering this mild protest against the breathless progress of the age. How often I have felt the same way myself —as though I were being swept onward through life faster than I could well enjoy it. For nature passes the dishes far more rapidly than we can help ourselves.

Or perhaps, thought I, eagerly speculating, this may be only some cunning advertiser with rest for sale (in these days even rest has its price), thus piquing the curiosity of the traveller for the disclosure which he will make a mile or so farther on. Or else some humourist wasting his wit upon the Fraternity of the Road, too willing (like me, perhaps) to accept his ironical advice. But it would be well worth while, should I find him, to see him chuckle behind his hand.

So I sat there, very much interested, for a long time, even framing a rather amusing picture in my own mind of the sort of person who painted these signs, deciding finally that he must be a zealot rather than a trader or humourist. (Confidentially, I could not make a picture of him in which he was not endowed with plentiful long hair!) As I walked onward again, I decided that in any guise I should like to see him, and I enjoyed thinking what I should say if I met him. A mile farther up the road I saw another sign exactly like the first.

"Here he is again," I said exultantly, and that sign being somewhat nearer the ground I was able to examine it carefully front and back, but it bore no evidence of its origin.

In the next few miles I saw two other signs with nothing on them but the single word "Rest."

Now this excellent admonition—like much of the excellent admonition in this world—affected me perversely: it made me more restless than ever. I felt that I could not rest properly until I found out who wanted me to rest, and why. It opened indeed a limitless vista for new adventure.

Presently, away ahead of me in the road, I saw a man standing near a one-horse wagon. He seemed to be engaged in some activity near the roadside, but I could not tell exactly what. As I hastened nearer I discovered that he was a short, strongly built, sun-bronzed man in working-clothes—and with the shortest of short hair. I saw him take a shovel from the wagon and begin digging. He was the road-worker.

I asked the road-worker if he had seen the curious signs. He looked up at me with a broad smile (he had good-humoured, very bright blue eyes).

"Yes," he said, "but they ain't for me."

"Then you don't follow the advice they give?"

"Not with a section like mine," said he, and he straightened up and looked first one way of the road and then the other. "I have from Grabow Brook, but not the bridge, to the top o'

Sullivan Hill, and all the culverts between, though two of 'em are by rights bridges. And I claim that's a job for any full-grown man."

He began shovelling again in the road as if to prove how busy he was. There had been a small landslide from an open cut on one side and a mass of gravel and small boulders lay scattered on the smooth macadam. I watched him for a moment. I love to watch the motions of vigorous men at work, the easy play of the muscles, the swing of the shoulders, the vigour of stoutly planted legs. He evidently considered the conversation closed, and I, as—well, as a dusty man of the road—easily dismissed. (You have no idea, until you try it, what a weight of prejudice the man of the road has to surmount before he is accepted on easy terms by the ordinary members of the human race.)

A few other well-intentioned observations on my part having elicited nothing but monosyllabic replies, I put my bag down by the roadside and, going up to the wagon, got out a shovel, and without a word took my place at the other end of the landslide and began to shovel for all I was worth.

I said not a word to the husky road-worker and pretended not to look at him, but I saw him well enough out of the corner of my eye. He was evidently astonished and interested, as I knew he would be: it was something entirely new on the road. He didn't quite know whether to be angry, or amused, or sociable. I caught him looking over at me several times, but I offered no response; then he cleared his throat and said:

"Where you from?"

I answered with a monosyllable which I knew he could not quite catch. Silence again for some time, during which I shovelled valiantly and with great inward amusement. Oh, there is nothing like cracking a hard human nut! I decided at that moment to have him invite me to supper.

Finally, when I showed no signs of stopping my work, he himself paused and leaned on his shovel. I kept right on.

"Say, partner," said he, finally, "did *you* read those signs as you come up the road?"

"Yes," I said, "but they weren't for me, either. My section's a long one, too."

"Say, you ain't a road-worker, are you?" he asked eagerly.

"Yes," said I, with a sudden inspiration, "that's exactly what I am—a road-worker."

"Put her there, then, partner," he said, with a broad smile on his bronzed face.

He and I struck hands, rested on our shovels (like old hands at it), and looked with understanding into each other's eyes. We both knew the trade and the tricks of the trade; all bars were down between us. The fact is, we had both seen and profited by the peculiar signs at the roadside.

"Where's your section?" he asked easily.

"Well," I responded after considering the question, "I have a very long and hard section. It begins at a place called Prosy Common—do you know it?—and reaches to the top of Clear Hill. There are several bad spots on the way, I can tell you."

"Don't know it," said the husky road-worker; " 'tain't round here, is it? In the town of Sheldon, maybe?"

Just at this moment, perhaps fortunately, for there is nothing so difficult to satisfy as the appetite of people for specific information, a motor-car whizzed past, the driver holding up his hand in greeting, and the road-worker and I responding in accord with the etiquette of the Great Road.

"There he goes in the ruts again," said the husky road-worker. "Why is it, I'd like to know, that every one wants to run in the same *i*-dentical track when they've got the whole wide road before 'em?"

"That's what has long puzzled me, too," I said. "Why *will* people continue to run in ruts?"

"It don't seem to do no good to put up signs," said the road-worker.

"Very little indeed," said I. "The fact is, people have got to be bumped out of most of the ruts they get into."

"You're right," said he enthusiastically, and his voice dropped

A motor-car whizzed past. "There he goes in the ruts
again," said the husky road-worker

into the tone of one speaking to a member of the inner guild, "I know how to get 'em."

"How?" I asked in an equally mysterious voice.

"I put a stone or two in the ruts!"

"Do you?" I exclaimed. "I've done that very thing myself—many a time! Just place a good hard true—I mean stone, with a bit of common dust sprinkled over it, in the middle of the rut, and they'll look out for *that* rut for some time to come."

"Ain't it gorgeous," said the husky road-worker, chuckling joyfully, "to see 'em bump?"

"It is," said I—"gorgeous."

After that, shovelling part of the time in a leisurely way, and part of the time responding to the urgent request of the signs by the roadside (it pays to advertise!), the husky road-worker and I discussed many great and important subjects, all, however, curiously related to roads. Working all day long with his old horse, removing obstructions, draining out the culverts, filling ruts and holes with new stone, and repairing the damage of rain and storm, the road-worker was filled with a world of practical information covering roads and road-making. And having learned that I was of the same calling we exchanged views with the greatest enthusiasm. It was astonishing to see how nearly in agreement we were as to what constituted an ideal road.

"Almost everything," said he, "depends on depth. If you get a good solid foundation, the' ain't anything that can break up your road."

"Exactly what I have discovered," I responded. "Get down to bedrock and do an honest job of building."

"And don't have too many sharp turns."

"No," said I, "long, leisurely curves are best—all through life. You have observed that nearly all the accidents on the road are due to sharp turnings."

"Right you are!" he exclaimed.

"A man who tries to turn too sharply on his way nearly always skids."

"Or else turns turtle in the ditch."

But it was not until we reached the subject of oiling that we mounted to the real summit of enthusiastic agreement. Of all things on the road, or above the road, or in the waters under the road, there is nothing that the road-worker dislikes more than oil.

"It's all right," said he, "to use oil for surfacin' and to keep down the dust. You don't need much and it ain't messy. But sometimes when you see oil pumped on a road, you know that either the contractor has been jobbin', or else the road's worn out and ought to be rebuilt."

"That's exactly what I've found," said I. "Let a road become almost impassable with ruts and rocks and dust, and immediately some man says, 'Oh, it's all right—put on a little oil——' "

"That's what our supervisor is always sayin'," said the road-worker.

"Yes," I responded, "it usually is the supervisor. He lives by it. He wants to smooth over the defects, he wants to lay the dust that every passerby kicks up, he tries to smear over the truth regarding conditions with messy and ill-smelling oil. Above everything, he doesn't want the road dug up and rebuilt—says it will interfere with traffic, injure business, and even set people to talking about changing the route entirely! Oh, haven't I seen it in religion, where they are doing their best to oil up roads that are entirely worn out—and as for politics, is not the cry of the party-roadster and the harmony-oilers abroad in the land?"

In the excited interest with which this idea now bore me along I had entirely forgotten the existence of my companion, and as I now glanced at him I saw him standing with a curious look of astonishment and suspicion on his face. I saw that I had unintentionally gone a little too far. So I said abruptly:

"Partner, let's get a drink. I'm thirsty."

He followed me, I thought a bit reluctantly, to a little brook not far up the road where we had been once before. As we were drinking, silently, I looked at the stout young fellow standing there, and I thought to myself:

What a good, straightforward young fellow he is anyway, and how thoroughly he knows his job. I thought how well he was equipped with unilluminated knowledge, and it came to me whimsically, that here was a fine bit of road-mending for me to do.

Most people have sight, but few have insight; and as I looked into the clear blue eyes of my friend I had a sudden swift inspiration, and before I could repent of it I had said to him in the most serious voice that I could command:

"Friend, I am in reality a spectacle-peddler——"

His glance shifted uncomfortably to my gray bag.

"And I want to sell you a pair of spectacles," I said. "I see that you are nearly blind."

"Me blind!"

It would be utterly impossible to describe the expression on his face. His hand went involuntarily to his eyes, and he glanced quickly, somewhat fearfully, about.

"Yes, nearly blind," said I. "I saw it when I first met you. You don't know it yourself yet, but I can assure you it is a bad case."

I paused, and shook my head slowly. If I had not been so much in earnest, I think I should have been tempted to laugh outright. I had begun my talk with him half jestingly, with the amusing idea of breaking through his shell, but I now found myself tremendously engrossed, and desiring nothing in the world (at that moment) so much as to make him see what I saw. I felt as though I held a live human soul in my hand.

"Say, partner," said the road-worker, "are you sure you aren't——" He tapped his forehead and began to edge away.

I did not answer his question at all, but continued, with my eyes fixed on him:

"It is a peculiar sort of blindness. Apparently, as you look about, you see everything there is to see, but as a matter of fact you see nothing in the world but this road——"

"It's time that I was seein' it again then," said he, making as if to turn back to work, but remaining with a disturbed expression on his countenance.

"The spectacles I have to sell," said I, "are powerful magnifiers"—he glanced again at the gray bag. "When you put them on you will see a thousand wonderful things besides the road——"

"Then you ain't a road-worker after all!" he said, evidently trying to be bluff and outright with me.

Now your substantial, sober, practical American will stand only about so much verbal foolery; and there is nothing in the world that makes him more uncomfortable—yes, downright mad!—than to feel that he is being played with. I could see that I had nearly reached the limit with him, and that if I held him now it must be by driving the truth straight home. So I stepped over toward him and said very earnestly:

"My friend, don't think I am merely joking you. I was never more in earnest in all my life. When I told you I was a road-worker I meant it, but I had in mind the mending of other kinds of roads than this."

I laid my hand on his arm, and explained to him as directly and simply as English words could do it, how, when he had spoken of oil for his roads, I thought of another sort of oil for another sort of roads, and when he spoke of curves in his roads I was thinking of curves in the roads I dealt with, and I explained to him what my roads were. I have never seen a man more intensely interested: he neither moved nor took his eyes from my face.

"And when I spoke of selling you a pair of spectacles," said I, "it was only a way of telling you how much I wanted to make you see my kinds of roads as well as your own."

I paused, wondering if, after all, he could be made to see. I know now how the surgeon must feel at the crucial moment of his accomplished operation. Will the patient live or die?

The road-worker drew a long breath as he came out from under the anesthetic.

"I guess, partner," said he, "you're trying to put a stone or two in my ruts!"

I had him!

"Exactly," I exclaimed eagerly.

We both paused. He was the first to speak—with some embarrassment:

"Say, you're just like a preacher I used to know when I was a kid. He was always sayin' things that meant something else, and when you found out what he was drivin' at you always felt kind of queer in your insides."

I laughed.

"It's a mighty good sign," I said, "when a man begins to feel queer in the insides. It shows that something is happening to him."

With that we walked back to the road, feeling very close and friendly—and began shovelling again, not saying much. After quite a time, when we had nearly cleaned up the landslide, I heard the husky road-worker chuckling to himself; finally, straightening up, he said:

"Say, there's more things in a road than ever I dreamt of."

"I see," said I, "that the new spectacles are a good fit."

The road-worker laughed long and loud.

"You're a good one, all right," he said. "I see what *you* mean. I catch your point."

"And now that you've got them on," said I, "and they are serving you so well, I'm not going to sell them to you at all. I'm going to present them to you—for I haven't seen anybody in a long time that I've enjoyed meeting more than I have you."

We nurse a fiction that people love to cover up their feelings; but I have learned that if the feeling is real and deep they love far better to find a way to uncover it.

"Same here," said the road-worker simply, but with a world of genuine feeling in his voice.

Well, when it came time to stop work the road-worker insisted that I get in and go home with him.

"I want you to see my wife and kids," said he.

The upshot of it was that I not only remained for supper—and a good supper it was—but I spent the night in his little home, close at the side of the road near the foot of a fine hill. And from time to time all night long, it seemed to me, I could hear the rush of cars going by in the smooth road outside, and sometimes their lights flashed in at my window, and sometimes I heard them sound their brassy horns.

I wish I could tell more of what I saw there, of the garden back of the house, and of all the road-worker and his wife told me of their simple history—but the road calls!

When I set forth early this morning the road-worker followed me out to the smooth macadam (his wife standing in the doorway with her hands rolled in her apron) and said to me, a bit shyly:

"I'll be more sort o'—sort o' interested in roads since I've seen you."

"I'll be along again some of these days," said I, laughing, "and I'll stop in and show you my new stock of spectacles. Maybe I can sell you another pair!"

"Maybe you kin," and he smiled a broad, understanding smile.

Nothing brings men together like having a joke in common.

So I walked off down the road—in the best of spirits—ready for the events of another day.

It will surely be a great adventure, one of these days, to come this way again—and to visit the Stanleys, and the Vedders, and the Minister, and drop in and sell another pair of specs to the Road-worker. It seems to me I have a wonderfully rosy future ahead of me!

P.S.—I have not yet found out who painted the curious signs; but I am not as uneasy about it as I was. I have seen two more of them already this morning—and find they exert quite a psychological influence.

VI

AN EXPERIMENT IN HUMAN NATURE

In the early morning after I left the husky road-mender (wearing his new spectacles), I remained steadfastly on the Great Road or near it. It was a prime spring day, just a little hazy, as though promising rain, but soft and warm.

"They will be working in the garden at home," I thought, "and there will be worlds of rhubarb and asparagus." Then I remembered how the morning sunshine would look on the little vine-clad back porch (reaching halfway up the weathered door) of my own house among the hills.

It was the first time since my pilgrimage began that I had thought with any emotion of my farm—or of Harriet.

And then the road claimed me again, and I began to look out for some further explanation of the curious sign, the single word "Rest," which had interested me so keenly on the preceding day. It may seem absurd to some who read these lines—some practical people!—but I cannot convey the pleasure I had in the very elusiveness and mystery of the sign, nor how I wished I might at the next turn come upon the poet himself. I decided that no one but a poet could have contented himself with a lyric in one word, unless it might have been a humourist, to whom sometimes a single small word is more blessed than all the verbal riches of Webster himself. For it is nothing short of genius that uses one word when twenty will say the same thing!

Or, would he, after all, turn out to be only a more than ordinarily alluring advertiser? I confess my heart went into my throat that morning, when I first saw the sign, lest it read:

> REST aurant 2 miles east

nor should I have been surprised if it had.

I caught a vicarious glimpse of the sign-man to-day, through the eyes of a young farmer. Yes, he s'posed he'd seen him, he said; wore a slouch hat, couldn't tell whether he was young or old. Drove into the bushes (just daown there beyond the brook) and, standin' on the seat of his buggy, nailed something to a tree. A day or two later—the dull wonder of mankind!—the young farmer, passing that way to town, had seen the odd sign "Rest" on the tree: he s'posed the fellow put it there.

"What does it mean?"

"Well, naow, I hadn't thought," said the young farmer.

"Did the fellow by any chance have long hair?"

"Well, naow, I didn't notice," said he.

"Are you sure he wore a slouch hat?"

"Ye-es—or it may a-been straw," replied the observant young farmer.

So I tramped that morning; and as I tramped I let my mind go out warmly to the people living all about on the farms or in the hills. It is pleasant at times to feel life, as it were, in general terms; no specific Mr. Smith or concrete Mr. Jones, but just human life. I love to think of people all around going out busily in the morning to their work and returning at night, weary, to rest. I like to think of them growing up, growing old, loving, achieving, sinning, failing—in short, living.

In such a live-minded mood as this it often happens that the most ordinary things appear charged with new significance. I suppose I had seen a thousand rural-mail boxes along country roads before that day, but I had seen them as the young farmer saw the sign-man. They were mere inert objects of iron and wood.

But as I tramped, thinking of the people in the hills, I came quite unexpectedly upon a sandy by-road that came out through

a thicket of scrub oaks and hazel-brush like some shy country-man, to join the turnpike. As I stood looking into it—for it seemed peculiarly inviting—I saw at the entrance a familiar group of rural-mail boxes. And I saw them not as dead things, but for the moment—the illusion was over-powering—they were living, eager hands outstretched to the passing throng. I could feel, hear, see the farmers up there in the hills reaching out to me, to all the world, for a thousand inexpressible things, for more life, more companionship, more comforts, more money.

It occurred to me at that moment, whimsically and yet some-how seriously, that I might respond to the appeal of the shy country road and the outstretched hands. At first I did not think of anything I could do—save to go up and eat dinner with one of the hill farmers, which might not be an unmixed bless-ing!—and then it came to me.

"I will write a letter!"

Straightway and with the liveliest amusement I began to formulate in my mind what I should say:

DEAR FRIEND: You do not know me. I am a passerby in the road. My name is David Grayson. You do not know me, and it may seem odd to you to receive a letter from an entire stranger. But I am something of a farmer myself, and as I went by I could not help thinking of you and of your family and your farm. The fact is, I should like to look you up, and talk with you about many things. I myself cultivate a number of curious fields, and raise many kinds of crops——

At this interesting point my inspiration suddenly collapsed, for I had a vision, at once amusing and disconcerting, of my hill farmer (and his practical wife!) receiving such a letter (along with the country paper, a circular advertising a cure for catarrh, and the most recent catalogue of the largest mail-order house in creation). I could see them standing there in their doorway, the man with his coat off, doubtfully scratching his head as he read my letter, the woman wiping her hands on her apron and looking over his shoulder, and a youngster squeezing between the two and demanding, "What is it, Paw?"

I found myself wondering how they would receive such an unusual letter, what they would take it to mean. And in spite of all I could do, I could imagine no expression on their faces save one of incredulity and suspicion. I could fairly see the shrewd, worldly wise look come into the farmer's face; I could hear him say:

"Ha, guess he thinks we ain't cut our eye-teeth!" And he would instantly begin speculating as to whether this was a new scheme for selling him second-rate nursery stock, or the smooth introduction of another sewing-machine agent.

Strange world, strange world! Sometimes it seems to me that the hardest thing of all to believe in is simple friendship. Is it not a comment upon our civilization that it is so often easier to believe that a man is a friend-for-profit, or even a cheat, than that he is frankly a well-wisher of his neighbours?

These reflections put such a damper upon my enthusiasm that I was on the point of taking again to the road, when it came to me powerfully: Why not try the experiment? Why not?

"Friendship," I said aloud, "is the greatest thing in the world. There is no door it will not unlock, no problem it will not solve. It is, after all, the only real thing in this world."

The sound of my own voice brought me suddenly to myself, and I found that I was standing there in the middle of the public road, one clenched fist absurdly raised in air, delivering an oration to a congregation of rural-mail boxes!

And yet, in spite of the humorous aspects of the idea, it still appeared to me that such an experiment would not only fit in with the true object of my journeying, but that it might be full of amusing and interesting adventures. Straightway I got my notebook out of my bag and, sitting down near the roadside, wrote my letter. I wrote it as though my life depended upon it, with the intent of making some one household there in the hills feel at least a little wave of warmth and sympathy from the great world that was passing in the road below. I tried to prove the validity of a kindly thought with no selling device attached to it; I tried to make it such a word of frank companionship as I myself, working in my own fields, would like to receive.

Among the letter-boxes in the group was one that stood a little detached and behind the others, as though shrinking from such prosperous company. It was made of unpainted wood, with leather hinges, and looked shabby in comparison with the jaunty red, green, and gray paint of some of the other boxes (with their cocky little metallic flags upraised). It bore the good American name of Clark—T. N. Clark—and it seemed to me that I could tell something of the Clarks by the box at the crossing.

"I think they need a friendly word," I said to myself.

So I wrote the name T. N. Clark on my envelope and put the letter in his box.

It was with a sense of joyous adventure that I now turned aside into the sandy road and climbed the hill. My mind busied itself with thinking how I should carry out my experiment, how I should approach these Clarks, and how and what they were. A thousand ways I pictured to myself the receipt of the letter: it would at least be something new for them, something just a little disturbing, and I was curious to see whether it might open the rift of wonder wide enough to let me slip into their lives.

I have often wondered why it is that men should be so fearful of new ventures in social relationships, when I have found them so fertile, so enjoyable. Most of us fear (actually fear) people who differ from ourselves, either up or down the scale. Your Edison pries fearlessly into the most intimate secrets of matter; your Marconi employs the mysterious properties of the "jellied ether," but let a man seek to experiment with the laws of that singular electricity which connects you and me (though you be a millionaire and I a ditch-digger), and we think him a wild visionary, an academic person. I think sometimes that the science of humanity to-day is in about the state of darkness that the natural sciences were when Linnæus and Cuvier and Lamarck began groping for the great laws of natural unity. Most of the human race is still groaning under the belief that each of us is a special and unrelated creation, just as men for ages saw no relationships between the fowls of the air, the beasts of the field, and the fish of the sea. But, thank God, we are beginning to learn that unity is as much a law of life as selfish struggle, and love a more vital force than avarice or lust of power or place. A Wandering Carpenter knew it, and taught it, twenty centuries ago.

"The next house beyond the ridge," said the toothless old woman, pointing with a long finger, "is the Clarks'. You can't miss it," and I thought she looked at me oddly.

I had been walking briskly for some three miles, and it was with keen expectation that I now mounted the ridge and saw the farm for which I was looking, lying there in the valley before me. It was altogether a wild and beautiful bit of country— stunted cedars on the knolls of the rolling hills, a brook trailing its way among alders and willows down a long valley, and shaggy old fields smiling in the sun. As I came nearer I could see

346 ADVENTURES OF DAVID GRAYSON

that the only disharmony in the valley was the work (or idleness) of men. A broken mowing-machine stood in the field
where it had been left the summer before, rusty and forlorn,
and dead weeds marked the edges of a field wherein the spring
ploughing was now only half done. The whole farmstead, indeed, looked tired. As for the house and barn, they had reached
that final stage of decay in which the best thing that could be
said of them was that they were picturesque. Everything was as
different from the farm of the energetic and joyous Stanleys,
whose work I had shared only a few days before, as anything
that could be imagined.

Now, my usual way of getting into step with people is simplicity itself. I take off my coat and go to work with them and
the first thing I know we have become first-rate friends. One
doesn't dream of the possibilities of companionship in labour
until he has tried it.

But how shall one get into step with a man who is not stepping?

On the porch of the farmhouse, there in the mid-afternoon, a
man sat idly; and children were at play in the yard. I went in at
the gate, not knowing in the least what I should say or do, but
determined to get hold of the problem somewhere. As I approached the step, I swung my bag from my shoulder.

"Don't want to buy nothin'," said the man.

"Well," said I, "that is fortunate, for I have nothing to sell.
But you've got something I want."

He looked at me dully.

"What's that?"

"A drink of water."

Scarcely moving his head, he called to a shy older girl who
had just appeared in the doorway.

"Mandy, bring a dipper of water."

As I stood there the children gathered curiously around me,
and the man continued to sit in his chair, saying absolutely
nothing, a picture of dull discouragement.

"How they need something to stir them up," I thought.

When I had emptied the dipper, I sat down on the top step

THOMAS FOGARTY

"As I stood there the children gathered curiously
around me"

of the porch, and, without saying a word to the man, placed my
bag beside me and began to open it. The shy girl paused, dipper
in hand, the children stood on tiptoe, and even the man showed
signs of curiosity. With studied deliberation I took out two
books I had with me and put them on the porch; then I proceeded to rummage for a long time in the bottom of the bag as
though I could not find what I wanted. Every eye was glued
upon me, and I even heard the step of Mrs. Clark as she came
to the doorway, but I did not look up or speak. Finally I pulled
out my tin whistle and, leaning back against the porch column,
placed it to my lips, and began playing in Tom Madison's best
style (eyes half closed, one toe tapping to the music, head
nodding, fingers lifted high from the stops), I began playing

"Money Musk," and "Old Dan Tucker." Oh, I put vim into it, I can tell you! And bad as my playing was, I had from the start an absorption of attention from my audience that Paderewski himself might have envied. I wound up with a lively trill in the high notes and took my whistle from my lips with a hearty laugh, for the whole thing had been downright good fun, the playing itself, the make-believe which went with it, the surprise and interest in the children's faces, the slow-breaking smile of the little girl with the dipper.

"I'll warrant you, madam," I said to the woman who now stood frankly in the doorway with her hands wrapped in her apron, "you haven't heard those tunes since you were a girl and danced to 'em."

"You're right," she responded heartily.

"I'll give you another jolly one," I said, and, replacing my whistle, I began with even greater zest to play "Yankee Doodle."

When I had gone through it half a dozen times with such added variations and trills as I could command, and had two of the children hopping about in the yard, and the forlorn man tapping his toe to the tune, and a smile on the face of the forlorn woman, I wound up with a rush, and then, as if I could hold myself in no longer (and I couldn't either!), I suddenly burst out:

> *Yankee doodle dandy!*
> *Yankee doodle dandy!*
> *Mind the music and the step,*
> *And with the girls be handy.*

It may seem surprising, but I think I can understand why it was—when I looked up at the woman in the doorway there were tears in her eyes!

"Do you know 'John Brown's Body'?" eagerly inquired the little girl with the dipper, and then, as if she had done something quite bold and improper, she blushed and edged toward the doorway.

"How does it go?" I asked, and one of the bold lads in the yard instantly puckered his lips to show me, and immediately they were all trying it.

"Here goes," said I, and for the next few minutes, and in my very best style, I hung Jeff Davis on the sour apple-tree, and I sent the soul of John Brown marching onward with an altogether unnecessary number of hallelujahs.

I think sometimes that people—whole families of 'em—literally perish for want of a good, hearty, whole-souled, mouth-opening, throat-stretching, side-aching laugh. They begin to think themselves the abused of creation, they begin to advise with their livers and to hate their neighbours, and the whole world becomes a miserable dark blue place quite unfit for human habitation. Well, all this is often only the result of a neglect to exercise properly those muscles of the body (and of the soul) which have to do with honest laughter.

I've never supposed I was an especially amusing person, but before I got through with it I had the Clark family well loosened up with laughter, although I wasn't quite sure some of the time whether Mrs. Clark was laughing or crying. I had them all laughing and talking, asking questions and answering them as though I were an old and valued neighbour.

Isn't it odd how unconvinced we often are by the crises in the lives of other people? They seem to us trivial or unimportant; but the fact is, the crises in the life of a boy, for example, or of a poor man, are as commanding as the crises in the life of the greatest statesman or millionaire, for they involve equally the whole personality, the entire prospects.

The Clark family, I soon learned, had lost its pig. A trivial matter, you say? I wonder if anything is ever trivial. A year of poor crops, sickness, low prices, discouragement—and, at the end of it, on top of it all, the cherished pig had died!

From all accounts (and the man on the porch quite lost his apathy in telling me about it) it must have been a pig of re-markable virtues and attainments, a paragon of pigs—in whom had been bound up the many possibilities of new shoes for the children, a hat for the lady, a new pair of overalls for the gentleman, and I know not what other kindred luxuries. I do not think, indeed, I ever had the portrait of a pig drawn for me with quite such ardent enthusiasm of detail, and the more questions I asked the more eager the story, until finally it became necessary for me to go to the barn, the cattle-pen, the pig-pen and the chicken-house, that I might visualize more clearly the scene of the tragedy. The whole family trooped after us like a classic chorus, but Mr. Clark himself kept the centre of the stage.

How plainly I could read upon the face of the land the story of this hill farmer and his meagre existence—his ill-directed effort to wring a poor living for his family from these upland fields, his poverty, and, above all, his evident lack of knowledge of his own calling. Added to these things, and perhaps the most depressing of all his difficulties, was the utter loneliness of the task, the feeling that it mattered little to any one whether the Clark family worked or not, or indeed whether they lived or died. A perfectly good American family was here being wasted, with the precious land they lived on, because no one had taken the trouble to make them feel that they were a part of this Great American Job.

As we went back to the house, a freckled-nosed neighbour's boy came in at the gate.

"A letter for you, Mr. Clark," said he. "I brought it up with our mail."

"A letter!" exclaimed Mrs. Clark.

"A letter!" echoed at least three of the children in unison.

"Probably a dun from Brewster," said Mr. Clark discouragingly.

I felt a curious sensation about the heart, and an eagerness of interest I have rarely experienced. I had no idea what a mere letter—a mere unopened unread letter—would mean to a family like this.

"It has no stamp on it!" exclaimed the older girl.

Mrs. Clark turned it over wonderingly in her hands. Mr. Clark hastily put on a pair of steel-bowed spectacles.

"Let me see it," he said, and when he also had inspected it minutely he solemnly tore open the envelope and drew forth my letter.

I assure you I never awaited the reading of any writing of mine with such breathless interest. How would they take it? Would they catch the meaning that I meant to convey? And would they suspect me of having written it?

Mr. Clark sat on the porch and read the letter slowly through to the end, turned the sheet over and examined it carefully, and then began reading it again to himself, Mrs. Clark leaning over his shoulder.

"What does it mean?" asked Mr. Clark.

"It's too good to be true," said Mrs. Clark with a sigh.

I don't know how long the discussion might have continued—probably for days or weeks—had not the older girl, now flushed of face and rather pretty, looked at me and said breathlessly (she was as sharp as a briar):

"You wrote it."

I stood the battery of all their eyes for a moment, smiling and rather excited.

"Yes," I said earnestly, "I wrote it, and I mean every word of it."

I had anticipated some shock of suspicion and inquiry, but to my surprise it was accepted as simply as a neighbourly good morning. I suppose the mystery of it was eclipsed by my astonishing presence there upon the scene with my tin whistle.

At any rate, it was a changed, eager, interested family which now occupied the porch of that dilapidated farmhouse. And immediately we fell into a lively discussion of crops and farming, and indeed the whole farm question, in which I found both the man and his wife singularly acute—sharpened upon the stone of hard experience.

Indeed, I found right here, as I have many times found among our American farmers, an intelligence (a literacy growing out of what I believe to be improper education) which was better able to discuss the problems of rural life than to grapple with and solve them. A dull, illiterate Polish farmer, I have found, will sometimes succeed much better at the job of life than his American neighbour.

Talk with almost any man for half an hour, and you will find that his conversation, like an old-fashioned song, has a regularly recurrent chorus. I soon discovered Mr. Clark's chorus.

"Now, if only I had a little cash," he sang, or, "If I had a few dollars, I could do so and so."

Why, he was as helplessly dependent upon money as any soft-handed millionairess. He considered himself poor and helpless because he lacked dollars, whereas people are really poor and helpless only when they lack courage and faith.

We were so much absorbed in our talk that I was greatly surprised to hear Mrs. Clark's voice at the doorway.

"Won't you come in to supper?"

After we had eaten, there was a great demand for more of my tin whistle (oh, I know how Caruso must feel!), and I played over every blessed tune I knew, and some I didn't, four or five times, and after that we told stories and cracked jokes in a way that must have been utterly astonishing in that household. After the children had been, yes, driven to bed, Mr. Clark seemed about to drop back into his lamentations over his condition (which I have no doubt had come to give him a sort of pleasure), but I turned to Mrs. Clark, whom I had come to respect very highly, and began to talk about the little garden she had started, which was about the most enterprising thing about the place.

"Isn't it one of the finest things in this world," said I, "to go out into a good garden in the summer days and bring in loaded baskets filled with beets and cabbages and potatoes, just for the gathering?"

I knew from the expression on Mrs. Clark's face that I had touched a sounding note.

"Opening the green corn a little at the top to see if it is ready and then stripping it off and tearing away the moist white husks——"

"And picking tomatoes?" said Mrs. Clark.

"And knuckling the watermelons to see if they are ripe? Oh, I tell you there are thousands of people in this country who'd like to be able to pick their dinner in the garden!"

"It's fine!" said Mrs. Clark with amused enthusiasm, "but I like best to hear the hens cackling in the barnyard in the morning after they've laid, and to go and bring in the eggs."

"Just like a daily present!" I said.

"Ye-es," responded the soundly practical Mrs. Clark, thinking, no doubt, that there were other aspects of the garden and chicken problem.

"I'll tell you another thing I like about a farmer's life," said I, "that's the smell in the house in the summer when there are preserves, or sweet pickles, or jam, or whatever it is, simmering on the stove. No matter where you are, up in the garret or down cellar, it's cinnamon, and allspice, and cloves, and every sort of sugary odour. Now, that gets me where I live!"

"It *is* good!" said Mrs. Clark with a laugh that could certainly be called nothing if not girlish.

All this time I had been keeping one eye on Mr. Clark. It was amusing to see him struggling against a cheerful view of life. He now broke into the conversation.

"Well, but——" he began.

Instantly I headed him off.

"And think," said I, "of living a life in which you are beholden to no man. It's a free life, the farmer's life. No one can discharge you because you are sick, or tired, or old, or because you are a Democrat or a Baptist!"

"Well, but——"

"And think of having to pay no rent, nor of having to live upstairs in a tenement!"

"Well, but——"

"Or getting run over by a street-car, or having the children play in the gutters."

"I never did like to think of what my children would do if we went to town," said Mrs. Clark.

"I guess not!" I exclaimed.

The fact is, most people don't think half enough of themselves and of their jobs; but before we went to bed that night I had the forlorn T. N. Clark talking about the virtues of his farm in quite a surprising way.

I even saw him eying me two or three times with a shrewd

look in his eyes (your American is an irrepressible trader) as though I might possibly be some would-be purchaser in disguise.

(I shall write some time a dissertation on the advantages of wearing shabby clothing.)

The farm really had many good points. One of them was a shaggy old orchard of good and thriving but utterly neglected apple-trees.

"Man alive," I said, when we went out to see it in the morning, "you've got a gold mine here!" And I told him how in our

neighbourhood we were renovating the old orchards, pruning them back, spraying, and bringing them into bearing again.

He had never, since he owned the place, had a salable crop of fruit. When we came in to breakfast I quite stirred the practical Mrs. Clark with my enthusiasm, and she promised at once to send for a bulletin on apple-tree renovation, published by the state experiment station. I am sure I was no more earnest in my advice than the conditions warranted.

After breakfast we went into the field, and I suggested that instead of ploughing any more land—for the season was already late—we get out all the accumulations of rotted manure from around the barn and strew it on the land already ploughed and harrow it in.

"A good job on a little piece of land," I said, "is far more profitable than a poor job on a big piece of land."

Without more ado we got his old team hitched up and began loading and hauling out the manure, and spent all day long at it. Indeed, such was the height of enthusiasm which T. N. Clark now reached (for his was a temperament that must either soar in the clouds or grovel in the mire), that he did not wish to stop when Mrs. Clark called us in to supper. In that one day his crop of corn, in perspective, overflowed his crib, he could not find boxes and barrels for his apples, his shed would not hold all his tobacco, and his barn was already being enlarged to accommodate a couple more cows! He was also keeping bees and growing ginseng.

But it was fine, that evening, to see Mrs. Clark's face, the renewed hope and courage in it. I thought as I looked at her (for she was the strong and steady one in that house):

"If you can keep the enthusiasm up, if you can make that husband of yours grow corn, and cows, and apples as you raise chickens and make garden, there is victory yet in this valley."

That night it rained, but in spite of the moist earth we spent almost all the following day hard at work in the field, and all the time talking over ways and means for the future, but the next morning, early, I swung my bag on my back and left them.

I shall not attempt to describe the friendliness of our parting. Mrs. Clark followed me wistfully to the gate.

"I can't tell you——" she began, with the tears starting in her eyes.

"Then don't try——" said I, smiling.

And so I swung off down the country road, without looking back.

VII

THE UNDISCOVERED COUNTRY

In some strange deep way there is no experience of my whole pilgrimage that I look back upon with so much wistful affection as I do upon the events of the day—the day and the wonderful night—which followed my long visit with the forlorn Clark family upon their hill farm. At first I hesitated about including an account of it here because it contains so little of what may be called thrilling or amusing incident.

"They want only the lively stories of my adventures," I said to myself, and I was at the point of pushing my notes to the edge of the table where (had I let go) they would have fallen into the convenient oblivion of the waste-basket. But something held me back.

"No," said I, "I'll tell it; if it meant so much to me, it may mean something to the friends who are following these lines."

For, after all, it is not what goes on outside of a man, the clash and clatter of superficial events, that arouses our deepest interest, but what goes on inside. Consider then that in this narrative I shall open a little door in my heart and let you look in, if you care to, upon the experiences of a day and a night in which I was supremely happy.

If you had chanced to be passing, that crisp spring morning, you would have seen a traveller on foot with a gray bag on his shoulder, swinging along the country road; and you might have been astonished to see him lift his hat at you and wish you a good morning. You might have turned to look back at him, as you passed, and found him turning also to look back at you—and wishing he might know you. But you would not have known what he was chanting under his breath as he tramped (how little we know of a man by the shabby coat he wears), nor how keenly he was enjoying the light airs and the warm sunshine of that fine spring morning.

After leaving the hill farm he had walked five miles up the valley, had crossed the ridge at a place called the Little Notch, where all the world lay stretched before him like the open palm of his hand, and had come thus to the boundaries of the Undis-covered Country. He had been for days troubled with the deep problems of other people, and it seemed to him this morning as though a great stone had been rolled from the door of his heart, and that he was entering upon a new world—a wonderful, high, free world. And, as he tramped, certain lines of a stanza long ago caught up in his memory from some forgotten page came up to his lips, and these were the words (you did not know as you passed) that he was chanting under his breath as he tramped, for they seem charged with the spirit of the hour:

> *I've bartered my sheets for a starlit bed;*
> *I've traded my meat for a crust of bread;*
> *I've changed my book for a sapling cane,*
> *And I'm off to the end of the world again.*

In the Undiscovered Country that morning it was wonderful how fresh the spring woods were, and how the birds sang in the trees, and how the brook sparkled and murmured at the road-side. The recent rain had washed the atmosphere until it was as clear and sparkling and heady as new wine, and the footing was firm and hard. As one tramped he could scarcely keep from singing or shouting aloud for the very joy of the day.

"I think," I said to myself, "I've never been in a better coun-try," and it did not seem to me I cared to know where the gray road ran, nor how far away the blue hills were.

"It is wonderful enough anywhere here," I said.

And presently I turned from the road and climbed a gently sloping hillside among oak and chestnut trees. The earth was well carpeted for my feet, and here and there upon the hillside, where the sun came through the green roof of foliage, were warm splashes of yellow light, and here and there, on shadier slopes, the new ferns were spread upon the earth like some lacy coverlet. I finally sat down at the foot of a tree where through a rift in the foliage in the valley below I could catch a glimpse in the distance of the meadows and the misty blue hills. I was glad to rest, just rest, for the two previous days of hard labour, the labour and the tramping, had wearied me, and I sat for a long time quietly looking about me, scarcely thinking at all, but seeing, hearing, smelling—feeling the spring morning, and the woods, and the hills, and the patch of sky I could see.

For a long, long time I sat thus, but finally my mind began to flow again, and I thought how fine it would be if I had some good friend there with me to enjoy the perfect surroundings—some friend who would understand. And I thought of the Vedders with whom I had so recently spent a wonderful day; and I wished that they might be with me; there were so many things to be said—to be left unsaid. Upon this it occurred to me, suddenly, whimsically, and I exclaimed aloud:

"Why, I'll just call them up."

Half turning to the trunk of the tree where I sat, I placed one hand to my ear and the other to my lips and said:

"Hello, Central, give me Mr. Vedder."

I waited a moment, smiling a little at my own absurdity and yet quite captivated by the enterprise.

"Is this Mr. Vedder? Oh, Mrs. Vedder! Well, this is David Grayson." . . .

"Yes, the very same. A bad penny, a rolling stone." . . .

"Yes. I want you both to come here as quickly as you can. I have the most important news for you. The mountain laurels are blooming, and the wild strawberries are setting their fruit. Yes, yes, and in the fields—all around here, to-day—there are wonderful white patches of daisies, and from where I sit I can see an old meadow as yellow as gold with buttercups. And the bobolinks are hovering over the low spots. Oh, but it is fine here—and we are not together!" . . .

"No; I cannot give exact directions. But take the Long Road and turn at the turning by the tulip-tree, and you will find me at home. Come right in without knocking."

I hung up the receiver. For a single instant it had seemed almost true, and indeed I believe—I wonder——

Some day, I thought, just a bit sadly, for I shall probably not be here then—some day, we shall be able to call our friends through space and time. Some day we shall discover that marvellously simple coherer by which we may better utilize the mysterious ether of love.

For a time I was sad with thoughts of the unaccomplished future, and then I reflected that if I could not call up the Vedders so informally I could at least write down a few paragraphs which would give them some faint impression of that time and place. But I had no sooner taken out my note-book and put down a sentence or two than I stuck fast. How foolish and feeble written words are anyway! With what glib facility they describe, but how inadequately they convey. A thousand times I have thought to myself, "If only I could *write!*"

Not being able to write I turned, as I have so often turned before, to some good old book, trusting that I might find in the writing of another man what I lacked in my own. I took out my battered copy of Montaigne and, opening it at random, as I love to do, came, as luck would have it, upon a chapter devoted to coaches, in which there is much curious (and worthless) information, darkened with Latin quotations. This reading had an unexpected effect upon me.

I could not seem to keep my mind down upon the printed page; it kept bounding away at the sight of the distant hills, at the sound of a woodpecker on a dead stub which stood near me, and at the thousand and one faint rustlings, creepings, murmurings, tappings, which animate the mystery of the forest. How dull indeed appeared the printed page in comparison with the book of life, how shut-in its atmosphere, how tinkling and distant the sound of its voices. Suddenly I shut my book with a snap.

"Musty coaches and Latin quotations!" I exclaimed. "Montaigne's no writer for the open air. He belongs at a study fire on a quiet evening!"

I had anticipated, when I started out, many a pleasant hour by the roadside or in the woods with my books, but this was almost the first opportunity I had found for reading (as it was

almost the last), so full was the present world of stirring events. As for poor old Montaigne, I have been out of harmony with him ever since, nor have I wanted him in the intimate case at my elbow.

After a long time in the forest, and the sun having reached the high heavens, I gathered up my pack and set forth again along the slope of the hills—not hurrying, just drifting and enjoying every sight and sound. And thus walking I came in sight, through the trees, of a glistening pool of water and made my way straight toward it.

A more charming spot I have rarely seen. In some former time an old mill had stood at the foot of the little valley, and a ruinous stone dam still held the water in a deep, quiet pond between two round hills. Above it a brook ran down through the woods, and below, with a pleasant musical sound, the water dripped over the mossy stone lips of the dam and fell into the rocky pool below. Nature had long ago healed the wounds of men; she had half covered the ruined mill with verdure, had softened the stone walls of the dam with mosses and lichens, and had crept down the steep hillside and was now leaning so far out over the pool that she could see her reflection in the quiet water.

Near the upper end of the pond I found a clear white sand-bank, where no doubt a thousand fishermen had stood, half hidden by the willows, to cast for trout in the pool below. I intended merely to drink and moisten my face, but as I knelt by the pool and saw my reflection in the clear water I wanted something more than that! In a moment I had thrown aside my bag and clothes and found myself wading naked into the water.

It was cold! I stood a moment there in the sunny air, the great world open around me, shuddering, for I dreaded the plunge—and then with a run, a shout and a splash I took the deep water. Oh, but it was fine! With long, deep strokes I carried myself fairly to the middle of the pond. The first chill was succeeded by a tingling glow, and I can convey no idea whatever of the glorious sense of exhilaration I had. I swam with the broad front stroke, I swam on my side, head half submerged, with a deep under stroke, and I rolled over on my back and swam with the water lapping my chin. Thus I came to the end of the pool near the old dam, touched my feet on the bottom, gave a primeval whoop, and dove back into the water again. I have rarely experienced keener physical joy. After swimming thus boisterously for a time, I quieted down to long, leisurely strokes, conscious of the water playing across my shoulders and singing at my ears, and finally, reaching the centre of the pond, I turned over on my back and, paddling lazily, watched the slow procession of light clouds across the sunlit openings of the trees above me. Away up in the sky I could see a hawk slowly swimming about (in his element as I was in mine), and nearer at hand, indeed fairly in the thicket about the pond, I could hear a wood-thrush singing.

And so, shaking the water out of my hair and swimming with long and leisurely strokes, I returned to the sand-bank, and there, standing in a spot of warm sunshine, I dried myself with the towel from my bag. And I said to myself:

"Surely it is good to be alive at a time like this!"

Slowly I drew on my clothes, idling there in the sand, and afterward I found an inviting spot in an old meadow where I threw myself down on the grass under an apple-tree and looked up into the shadowy places in the foliage above me. I felt a delicious sense of physical well-being, and I was pleasantly tired.

So I lay there—and the next thing I knew, I turned over, feeling cold and stiff, and opened my eyes upon the dusky shadows of late evening. I had been sleeping for hours!

The next few minutes (or was it an hour, or eternity?), I recall as containing some of the most exciting and, when all is said, amusing incidents in my whole life. And I got quite a new glimpse of that sometimes bumptious person known as David Grayson.

The first sensation I had was one of complete panic. What was I to do? Where was I to go?

Hastily seizing my bag—and before I was half awake—I started rapidly across the meadow, in my excitement tripping and falling several times in the first hundred yards. In daylight I have no doubt that I should easily have seen a gateway or at least an opening from the old meadow, but in the fast-gathering darkness it seemed to me that the open field was surrounded on every side by impenetrable forests. Absurd as it may seem, for no one knows what his mind will do at such a moment, I recalled vividly a passage from Stanley's story of his search for Livingstone, in which he relates how he escaped from a difficult place in the jungle by KEEPING STRAIGHT AHEAD.

I print these words in capitals because they seemed written that night upon the sky. *Keeping straight ahead,* I entered the forest on one side of the meadow (with quite a heroic sense of adventure), but scraped my shin on a fallen log and ran into a tree with bark on it that felt like a gigantic currycomb —and stopped!

Up to this point I think I was still partly asleep. Now, however, I waked up.

"All you need," said I to myself in my most matter-of-fact tone, "is a little cool sense. Be quiet now and reason it out."

So I stood there for some moments reasoning it out, with the result that I turned back and found the meadow again.

"What a fool I've been!" I said. "Isn't it perfectly plain that I should have gone down to the pond, crossed over the inlet, and reached the road by the way I came?"

Having thus settled my problem, and congratulating myself on my perspicacity, I started straight for the mill-pond, but to my utter amazement, in the few short hours while I had been asleep, that entire body of water had evaporated, the dam had disappeared, and the stream had dried up. I must certainly present the facts in this remarkable case to some learned society.

I then decided to return to the old apple-tree where I had slept, which now seemed quite like home, but, strange to relate, the apple-tree had also completely vanished from the enchanted meadow. At that I began to suspect that in coming out of the forest I had somehow got into another and somewhat similar old field. I have never had a more confused or eerie sensation; not fear, but a sort of helplessness in which for an instant I actually began to doubt whether it was really I myself, David Grayson, who stood there in the dark meadow, or whether I was the victim of a peculiarly bad dream. I suppose many other people have had these sensations under similar conditions, but they were new to me.

I turned slowly around and looked for a light; I think I never wanted so much to see some sign of human habitation as I did at that moment.

What a coddled world we live in, truly. That being out after dark in a meadow should so disturb the very centre of our being! In all my life, indeed, and I suppose the same is true of ninety-nine out of a hundred of the people in America to-day, I had never before found myself where nothing stood between nature and me, where I had no place to sleep, no shelter for the night—nor any prospect of finding one. I was infinitely less resourceful at that moment than a rabbit, or a partridge, or a gray squirrel.

Presently I sat down on the ground where I had been standing, with a vague fear (absurd to look back upon!) that it, too, in some manner might slip away from under me. And as I sat there I began to have familiar gnawings at the pit of my stomach, and I remembered that, save for a couple of Mrs. Clark's doughnuts eaten while I was sitting on the hillside ages ago, I had had nothing since my early breakfast.

With this thought of my predicament—and the glimpse I had of myself "hungry and homeless"—the humour of the whole situation suddenly came over me, and, beginning with a chuckle, I wound up, as my mind dwelt upon my recent adventures, with a long, loud, hearty laugh.

As I laughed—and what a roar it made in that darkness!—I got up on my feet and looked up at the sky. One bright star shone out over the woods, and in the high heavens I could see dimly the white path of the Milky Way. And all at once I seemed again to be in command of myself and of the world. I felt a sudden lift and thrill of the spirits, a warm sense that this too was part of the great adventure—the Thing Itself.

"This is the light," I said looking up again at the sky and the single bright star, "which is set for me to-night. I will make my bed by it."

I can hope to make no one understand (unless he understands already) with what joy of adventure I now crept through the meadow toward the wood. It was an unknown, unexplored world I was in, and I, the fortunate discoverer, had here to shift for himself, make his home under the stars! Marquette on the wild shores of the Mississippi, or Stanley in Africa, had no joy that I did not know at that moment.

I crept along the meadow and came at last to the wood. Here

I chose a somewhat sheltered spot at the foot of a large tree— and yet a spot not so obscured that I could not look out over the open spaces of the meadow and see the sky. Here, groping in the darkness, like some primitive creature, I raked together a pile of leaves with my fingers, and found dead twigs and branches of trees; but in that moist forest (where the rain had fallen only the day before) my efforts to kindle a fire were unavailing. Upon this, I considered using some pages from my notebook, but another alternative suggested itself:

"Why not Montaigne?"

With that I groped for the familiar volume, and with a curious sensation of satisfaction I tore out a handful of pages from the back.

"Better Montaigne than Grayson," I said, with a chuckle. It was amazing how Montaigne sparkled and crackled when he was well lighted.

"There goes a bundle of quotations from Vergil," I said, "and there's his observations on the eating of fish. There are more uses than one for the classics."

So I ripped out a good part of another chapter, and thus, by coaxing, got my fire to going. It was not difficult after that to find enough fuel to make it blaze up warmly.

I opened my bag and took out the remnants of the luncheon which Mrs. Clark had given me that morning; and I was surprised and delighted to find, among other things, a small bottle of coffee. This suggested all sorts of pleasing possibilities and, the spirit of invention being now awakened, I got out my tin cup, split a sapling stick so that I could fit it into the handle, and set the cup, full of coffee, on the coals at the edge of the fire. It was soon heated, and although I spilled some of it in getting it off, and although it was well spiced with ashes, I enjoyed it, with Mrs. Clark's doughnuts and sandwiches (some of which I toasted with a sapling fork) as thoroughly, I think, as ever I enjoyed any meal.

How little we know—we who dread life—how much there is in life!

My activities around the fire had warmed me to the bone,

and after I was well through with my meal I gathered a plentiful supply of wood and placed it near at hand, I got out my waterproof cape and put it on, and, finally piling more sticks on the fire, I sat down comfortably at the foot of the tree.

I wish I could convey the mystery and the beauty of that night. Did you ever sit by a campfire and watch the flames dance, and the sparks fly upward into the cool dark air? Did you ever see the fitful light among the tree-depths, at one moment opening vast shadowy vistas into the forest, at the next dying downward and leaving it all in sombre mystery? It came to me that night with the wonderful vividness of a fresh experience.

And what a friendly and companionable thing a campfire is! How generous and outright it is! It plays for you when you wish it to be lively, and it glows for you when you wish to be reflective.

After a while, for I did not feel in the least sleepy, I stepped out of the woods to the edge of the pasture. All around me lay the dark and silent earth, and above the blue bowl of the sky, all glorious with the blaze of a million worlds. Sometimes I have been oppressed by this spectacle of utter space, of infinite distance, of forces too great for me to grasp or understand, but that night it came upon me with fresh wonder and power, and with a sense of great humility, that I belonged here too, that I was a part of it all—and would not be neglected or forgotten. It seemed to me I never had a moment of greater faith than that.

And so, with a sense of satisfaction and peace, I returned to my fire. As I sat there I could hear the curious noises of the woods, the little droppings, cracklings, rustlings which seemed to make all the world alive. I even fancied I could see small bright eyes looking out at my fire, and once or twice I was almost sure I heard voices—whispering—whispering—perhaps the voices of the woods.

Occasionally I added, with some amusement, a few dry pages of Montaigne to the fire, and watched the cheerful blaze that followed.

"No," said I, "Montaigne is not for the open spaces and the

stars. Without a roof over his head Montaigne would—well, die of sneezing!"

So I sat all night long there by the tree. Occasionally I dropped into a light sleep, and then, as my fire died down, I grew chilly and awakened, to build up the fire and doze again. I saw the first faint gray streaks of dawn above the trees, I saw the pink glow in the east before the sunrise, and I watched the sun himself rise upon a new day——

When I walked out into the meadow by daylight and looked about me curiously, I saw, not forty rods away, the back of a barn.

"Be you the fellow that was daown in my cowpastur' all night?" asked the sturdy farmer.

"I'm that fellow," I said.

"Why didn't you come right up to the house?"

"Well——" I said, and then paused.

"Well . . ." said I.

VIII
THE HEDGE

STRANGE, strange, how small the big world is!

"Why didn't you come right into the house?" the sturdy farmer had asked me when I came out of the meadow where I had spent the night under the stars.

"Well," I said, turning the question as adroitly as I could, "I'll make it up by going into the house now."

So I went with him into his fine, comfortable house.

"This is my wife," said he.

A woman stood there facing me. "Oh!" she exclaimed, "Mr. Grayson!"

I recalled swiftly a child—a child she seemed then—with braids down her back, whom I had known when I first came to my farm. She had grown up, married, and had borne three children, while I had been looking the other way for a minute or two. She had not been in our neighbourhood for several years.

"And how is your sister and Doctor McAlway?"

Well, we had quite a wonderful visit, and she made breakfast for me, asking questions and talking eagerly as I ate.

"We've just had news that old Mr. Toombs is dead."

"Dead!" I exclaimed, dropping my fork; "old Nathan Toombs!"

"Yes, he was my uncle. Did you know him?"

"I knew Nathan Toombs," I said.

I spent two days there with the Ransomes, for they would not hear of my leaving, and half of our spare time, I think, was spent in discussing Nathan Toombs. I was not able to get him out of my mind for days, for his death was one of those events which prove so much and leave so much unproven.

I can recall vividly my astonishment at the first evidence I ever had of the strange old man or of his work. It was not very long after I came to my farm to live. I had taken to spending my spare evenings—the long evenings of summer—in exploring the country roads for miles around, getting acquainted with each farmstead, each bit of grove and meadow and marsh, making my best bow to each unfamiliar hill, and taking everywhere that toll of pleasure which comes of quiet discovery.

One evening, having walked farther than usual, I came quite suddenly around a turn in the road and saw stretching away before me an extraordinary sight.

I feel that I am conveying no adequate impression of what I beheld by giving it any such prim and decorous name as—a Hedge. It was a menagerie, a living, green menagerie! I had no sooner seen it than I began puzzling my brain as to whether one of the curious ornaments into which the upper part of the hedge had been clipped and trimmed was made to represent the head of a horse, or a camel, or an Egyptian sphinx.

The hedge was of arbor vitæ and as high as a man's waist. At more or less regular intervals the trees in it had been allowed to grow much taller and had been wonderfully pruned into the similitude of towers, pinacles, bells, and many other strange designs. Here and there the hedge held up a spindling umbrella of greenery, sometimes a double umbrella—a little one above the big one—and over the gateway at the centre, as a sort of final triumph, rose a grandiose arch of interlaced branches upon which the artist had outdone himself in marvels of ornamentation.

I shall never forget the sensation of delight I had over this discovery, or of how I walked, tiptoe, along the road in front, studying each of the marvellous adornments. How eagerly, too,

I looked over at the house beyond—a rather bare, bleak house set on a slight knoll or elevation and guarded at one corner by a dark spruce tree. At some distance behind I saw a number of huge barns, a cattle yard and a silo—all the evidences of prosperity—with well-nurtured fields, now yellowing with the summer crops, spreading pleasantly away on every hand.

It was nearly dark before I left that bit of roadside, and I shall never forget the eerie impression I had as I turned back to take a final look at the hedge, the strange, grotesque aspect it presented there in the half light with the bare, lonely house rising from the knoll behind.

It was not until some weeks later that I met the owner of the wonderful hedge. By that time, however, having learned of my interest, I found the whole countryside alive with stories about it and about Old Nathan Toombs, its owner. It was as though I had struck the rock of refreshment in a weary land.

I remember distinctly how puzzled I was by the stories I heard. The neighbourhood portrait—and ours is really a friendly neighbourhood—was by no means flattering. Old Toombs was apparently of that type of hard-shelled, grasping, self-reliant, old-fashioned farmer not unfamiliar to many country neighbourhoods. He had come of tough old American stock and he was a worker, a saver, and thus he had grown rich, the richest farmer in the whole neighbourhood. He was a regular individualistic American.

"A dour man," said the Scotch Preacher, "but just—you must admit that he is just."

There was no man living about whom the Scotch Preacher could not find something good to say.

"Yes, just," replied Horace, skeptically, "but hard—hard, and as mean as pusley."

This portrait was true enough in itself, for I knew just the sort of an aggressive, undoubtedly irritable old fellow it pictured, but somehow, try as I would, I could not see any such old fellow wasting his moneyed hours clipping bells, umbrellas, and camel's heads on his ornamental greenery. It left just that

incongruity which is at once the lure, the humour, and the perplexity of human life. Instead of satisfying my curiosity I was
more anxious than ever to see Old Toombs with my own eyes.

But the weeks passed and somehow I did not meet him. He
was a lonely, unneighbourly old fellow. He had apparently
come to fit into the community without ever really becoming a
part of it. His neighbours accepted him as they accepted a hard
hill in the town road. From time to time he would foreclose a

mortgage where he had loaned money to some less thrifty
farmer, or he would extend his acres by purchase, hard cash
down, or he would build a bigger barn. When any of these
things happened the community would crowd over a little, as it
were, to give him more room. It is a curious thing, and tragic,
too, when you come to think of it, how the world lets alone
those people who appear to want to be let alone. "I can live to
myself," says the unneighbourly one. "Well, live to yourself,
then," cheerfully responds the world, and it goes about its more
or less amusing affairs and lets the unneighbourly one cut himself off.

So our small community had let Old Toombs go his way with
all his money, his acres, his hedge, and his reputation for being
a just man.

Not meeting him, therefore, in the familiar and friendly life of the neighbourhood, I took to walking out toward his farm, looking freshly at the wonderful hedge and musing upon that most fascinating of all subjects—how men come to be what they are. And at last I was rewarded.

One day I had scarcely reached the end of the hedge when I saw Old Toombs himself moving toward me down the country road. Though I had never seen him before, I was at no loss to identify him. The first and vital impression he gave me, if I can compress it into a single word, was, I think, force—force. He came stubbing down the country road with a brown hickory stick in his hand, which at every step he set vigorously into the soft earth. Though not tall, he gave the impression of being enormously strong. He was thick, solid, firm—thick through the body, thick through the thighs; and his shoulders —what shoulders they were!—round like a maple log; and his great head with its thatching of coarse iron-gray hair, though thrust slightly forward, seemed set immovably upon them.

He presented such a forbidding appearance that I was of two minds about addressing him. Dour he was indeed! Nor shall I ever forget how he looked when I spoke to him. He stopped short there in the road. On his big square nose he wore a pair of curious spring-bowed glasses with black rims. For a moment he looked at me through these glasses, raising his chin a little, and then, deliberately wrinkling his nose, they fell off and dangled at the length of the faded cord by which they were hung. There was something almost uncanny about this peculiar habit of his and of the way in which, afterward, he looked at me from under his bushy gray brows. This was in truth the very man of the neighbourhood portrait.

"I am a new settler here," I said, "and I've been interested in looking at your wonderful hedge."

The old man's eyes rested upon me a moment with a mingled look of suspicion and hostility.

"So you've heard o' me," he said in a high-pitched voice, "and you've heard o' my hedge."

Again he paused and looked me over.

"Well," he said, with an indescribably harsh, cackling laugh,

"I warrant you've heard nothing good o' me down there. I'm a skinflint, ain't I? I'm a hard citizen, ain't I? I grind the faces o' the poor, don't I?"

At first his words were marked by a sort of bitter humour, but as he continued to speak his voice rose higher and higher until it was positively menacing.

There were just two things I could do—haul down the flag and retreat ingloriously, or face the music. With a sudden sense of rising spirits—for such things do not often happen to a man in a quiet country road—I paused a moment, looking him squarely in the eye.

"Yes," I said, with great deliberation, "you've given me just about the neighbourhood picture of yourself as I have had it. They do say you are a skinflint, yes, and a hard man. They say that you are rich and friendless; they say that while you are a just man, you do not know mercy. These are terrible things to say of any man if they are true."

I paused. The old man looked for a moment as though he were going to strike me with his stick, but he neither stirred nor spoke. It was evidently a wholly new experience for him.

"Yes," I said, "you are not popular in this community, but what do you suppose I care about that? I'm interested in your hedge. What I'm curious to know—and I might as well tell you frankly—is how such a man as you are reputed to be could grow such an extraordinary hedge. You must have been at it a very long time."

I was surprised at the effect of my words. The old man turned partly aside and looked for a moment along the proud and flaunting embattlements of the green marvel before us. Then he said in a moderate voice:

"It's a putty good hedge, a putty good hedge."

"I've got him," I thought exultantly. "I've got him!"

"How long ago did you start it?" I pursued my advantage eagerly.

"Thirty-two years come spring," said he.

"Thirty-two years!" I repeated; "you've been at it a long time."

With that I plied him with questions in the liveliest manner, and in five minutes I had the gruff old fellow stumping along at my side and pointing out the various notable features of his wonderful creation. His suppressed excitement was quite wonderful to see. He would point his hickory stick with a poking motion, and, when he looked up, instead of throwing back his big, rough head, he bent at the hips, thus imparting an impression of astonishing solidity.

"It took me all o' ten years to get that bell right," he said, and, "Take a look at that arch: now what is your opinion o' that?"

Once, in the midst of our conversation, he checked himself abruptly and looked around at me with a sudden dark expression of suspicion. I saw exactly what lay in his mind, but I continued my questioning as though I perceived no change in him. It was only momentary, however, and he was soon as much interested as before. He talked as though he had not had such an opportunity before in years—and I doubt whether he had. It was plain to see that if any one ever loved anything in this world, Old Toombs loved that hedge of his. Think of it, indeed! He had lived with it, nurtured it, clipped it, groomed it—for thirty-two years.

So we walked down the sloping field within the hedge, and it seemed as though one of the deep mysteries of human nature was opening there before me. What strange things men set their hearts upon!

Thus, presently, we came nearly to the farther end of the hedge. Here the old man stopped and turned around, facing me.

"Do you see that valley?" he asked. "Do you see that slopin' valley up through my meadow?"

His voice rose suddenly to a sort of high-pitched violence.

"That passel o' hounds up there," he said, "want to build a road down my valley."

He drew his breath fiercely.

"They want to build a road through my land. They want to ruin my farm—they want to cut down my hedge. I'll fight 'em. I'll fight 'em. I'll show 'em yet!"

It was appalling. His face grew purple, his eyes narrowed to pin points and grew red and angry—like the eyes of an infuriated boar. His hands shook. Suddenly he turned upon me, poising his stick in his hand, and said violently.

"And who are you? Who are you? Are you one of these surveyor fellows?"

"My name," I answered as quietly as I could, "is Grayson. I live on the old Mather farm. I am not in the least interested in any of your road troubles."

He looked at me a moment more, and then seemed to shake himself or shudder, his eyes dropped away and he began walking toward his house. He had taken only a few steps, however, before he turned, and, without looking at me, asked if I would like to see the tools he used for trimming his hedge. When I hesitated, for I was decidedly uncomfortable, he came up to me and laid his hand awkwardly on my arm.

"You'll see something, I warrant, you never see before."

It was so evident that he regretted his outbreak that I followed him, and he showed me an odd double ladder set on low wheels which he said he used in trimming the higher parts of his hedge.

"It's my own invention," he said with pride.

"And that"—he pointed as we came out of the tool shed—"is my house—a good house. I planned it all myself. I never needed to take lessons of any carpenter I ever see. And there's my barns. What do you think o' my barns? Ever see any bigger ones? They ain't any bigger in this country than Old Toombs's barns. They don't like Old Toombs, but they ain't any of 'em can ekal his barns!"

He followed me down to the roadside now quite loquacious. Even after I had thanked him and started to go he called after me. When I stopped he came forward hesitatingly—and I had the impressions, suddenly, and for the first time, that he was an old man. It may have been the result of his sudden fierce explosion of anger, but his hand shook, his face was pale, and he seemed somehow broken.

"You—you like my hedge?" he asked.

"It is certainly a wonderful hedge," I said. "I never have seen anything like it."

"The' *ain't* nothing like it," he responded, quickly. "The' ain't nothing like it anywhere."

In the twilight as I passed onward I saw the lonely figure of the old man moving with his hickory stick up the pathway to his lonely house. The poor rich old man!

"He thinks he can live wholly to himself," I said aloud.

I thought, as I tramped homeward, of our friendly and kindly community, of how we often come together of an evening with skylarking and laughter, of how we weep with one another, of how we join in making better roads and better schools, and in building up the Scotch Preacher's friendly little church. And in all these things Old Toombs has never had a part. He is not even missed.

As a matter of fact, I reflected, and this is a strange, deep thing, no man is in reality more dependent upon the community which he despises and holds at arm's length than this same Old Nathan Toombs. Everything he has, everything he does, gives evidence of it. And I don't mean this in any mere material sense, though of course his wealth and his farm would mean no more than the stones in his hills to him if he did not have us here around him. Without our work, our buying, our selling, our governing, his dollars would be dust. But we are still more necessary to him in other ways: the unfriendly man is usually the one who demands most from his neighbours. Thus, if he have not people's love or confidence, then he will smite them until they fear him, or admire him, or hate him. Oh, no man, however he may try, can hold himself aloof!

I came home deeply stirred from my visit with Old Toombs and lost no time in making further inquiries. I learned, speedily, that there was indeed something in the old man's dread of a road being built through his farm. The case was already in the courts. His farm was a very old one and extensive, and of recent years a large settlement of small farmers had been developing the rougher lands in the upper part of the township, called the

Swan Hill district. Their only way to reach the railroad was by
a rocky, winding road among the hills, while their natural outlet
was down a gently sloping valley through Old Toombs's farm.
They were now so numerous and politically important that they
had stirred up the town authorities. A proposition had been
made to Old Toombs for a right-of-way; they argued with him
that it was a good thing for the whole country, that it would
enhance the values of his own upper lands, and that they
would pay him far more for a right-of-way than the land
was actually worth, but he had spurned them—I can imagine
with what vehemence.

"Let' em drive round," he said. "Didn't they know what they'd
hev to do when they settled up there? What a passel o' curs!
They can keep off o' my land, or I'll have the law on 'em."

And thus the matter came to the courts with the town attempting to condemn the land for a road through Old Toombs's
farm.

"What can we do?" asked the Scotch Preacher, who was
deeply distressed by the bitterness of feeling displayed. "There
is no getting to the man. He will listen to no one."

At one time I thought of going over and talking with Old
Toombs myself, for it seemed that I had been able to get nearer
to him than any one had in a long time. But I dreaded it. I
kept dallying—for what, indeed, could I have said to him? If he
had been suspicious of me before, how much more hostile he
might be when I expressed an interest in his difficulties. As to
reaching the Swan Hill settlers, they were now aroused to an
implacable state of bitterness; and they had the people of the
whole community with them, for no one liked Old Toombs.

Thus while I hesitated time passed and my next meeting with
Old Toombs, instead of being premeditated, came about quite
unexpectedly. I was walking in the town road late one afternoon when I heard a wagon rattling behind me, and then, quite
suddenly, a shouted, "Whoa!"

Looking around, I saw Old Toombs, his great solid figure
mounted high on the wagon seat, the reins held fast in the
fingers of one hand. I was struck by the strange expression in

his face—a sort of grim exaltation. As I stepped aside he burst out in a loud, shrill, cackling laugh:

"He-he-he—he-he-he——"

I was too astonished to speak at once. Ordinarily when I meet any one in the town road it is in my heart to cry out to him, "Good morning, friend," or, "How are you, brother?" but I had no such prompting that day.

"Git in, Grayson," he said; "git in, git in."

I climbed up beside him, and he slapped me on the knee with another burst of shrill laughter.

"They thought they had the old man," he said, starting up his horses. "They thought there weren't no law left in Israel. I showed 'em.'

I cannot convey the bitter triumphancy of his voice.

"You mean the road case?" I asked.

"Road case!" he exploded, "they wan't no road case; they didn't have no road case. I beat 'em. I says to 'em, 'What right hev any o' you on my property? Go round with you,' I says. Oh, I beat 'em. If they'd had their way, they'd 'a' cut through my hedge—the hounds!"

When he set me down at my door I had said hardly a word. There seemed nothing that could be said. I remember I stood for some time watching the old man as he rode away, his wagon jolting in the country road, his stout figure perched firmly in the seat. I went in with a sense of heaviness at the heart.

"Harriet," I said, "there are some things in this world beyond human remedy."

Two evenings later I was surprised to see the Scotch Preacher drive up to my gate and hastily tie his horse.

"David," said he, "there's bad business afoot. A lot of the young fellows in Swan Hill are planning a raid on Old Toombs's hedge. They are coming down to-night."

I got my hat and jumped in with him. We drove up the hilly road and out around Old Toombs's farm and thus came, near sundown, to the settlement. I had no conception of the bitterness that the lawsuit had engendered.

"Where once you start men hating one another," said the Scotch Preacher, "there's utterly no end of it."

I have seen our Scotch Preacher in many difficult places, but never have I seen him rise to greater heights than he did that night. It is not in his preaching that Doctor McAlway excels, but what a power he is among men! He was like some stern old giant, standing there and holding up the portals of civilization. I saw men melt under his words like wax; I saw wild young fellows subdued into quietude; I saw unwise old men set to thinking.

"Man, man," he'd say, lapsing in his earnestness into the broad Scotch accent of his youth, "you canna' mean plunder, and destruction, and riot! You canna! Not in this neighbourhood!"

"What about Old Toombs?" shouted one of the boys.

I never shall forget how Doctor McAlway drew himself up, nor the majesty that looked from his eye.

"Old Toombs!" he said in a voice that thrilled one to the bone, "Old Toombs! Have you no faith, that you stand in the place of Almighty God and measure punishments?"

Before we left it was past midnight and we drove home, almost silent, in the darkness.

"Doctor McAlway," I said, "if Old Toombs could know the history of this night it might change his point of view."

"I doot it," said the Scotch Preacher. "I doot it."

The night passed serenely; the morning saw Old Toombs's hedge standing as gorgeous as ever. The community had again stepped aside and let Old Toombs have his way: they had let him alone, with all his great barns, his wide acres and his wonderful hedge. He probably never even knew what had threatened him that night, nor how the forces of religion, of social order, of neighbourliness in the community which he despised had, after all, held him safe. There is a supreme faith among common people—it is, indeed, the very taproot of democracy—that although the unfriendly one may persist long in his power and arrogance, there is a moving Force which commands events.

I suppose if I were writing a mere story I should tell how Old Toombs was miraculously softened at the age of sixty-eight years, and came into new relationships with his neighbours, or else I should relate how the mills of God, grinding slowly, had crushed the recalcitrant human atom into dust.

Either of these results conceivably might have happened— all things are possible—and being ingeniously related would somehow have answered a need in the human soul that the logic of events be constantly and conclusively demonstrated in the lives of individual men and women.

But as a matter of fact, neither of these things did happen in this quiet community of ours. There exists, assuredly, a logic of events, oh, a terrible, irresistible logic of events, but it is careless of the span of any one man's life. We would like to have each man enjoy the sweets of his own virtues and suffer the lash of his own misdeeds—but it rarely so happens in life. No, it is the community which lives or dies, is regenerated or marred by the deeds of men.

So Old Toombs continued to live. So he continued to buy more land, raise more cattle, collect more interest, and the wonderful hedge continued to flaunt its marvels still more notably upon the country road. To what end? Who knows? Who knows?

I saw him afterward from time to time, tried to maintain

some sort of friendly relations with him; but it seemed as the years passed that he grew ever lonelier and more bitter, and not only more friendless, but seemingly more incapable of friendliness. In times past I have seen what men call tragedies —I saw once a perfect young man die in his strength—but it seems to me I never knew anything more tragic than the life and death of Old Toombs. If it cannot be said of a man when he dies that either his nation, his state, his neighbourhood, his family, or at least his wife or child, is better for his having lived, what *can* be said for him?

Old Toombs is dead. Like Jehoram, King of Judah, of whom it is terribly said in the Book of Chronicles, "he departed without being desired."

Of this story of Nathan Toombs we talked much and long and there in the Ransome home. I was with them, as I said, about two days—kept inside most of the time by a driving spring rain which filled the valley with a pale gray mist and turned all the country roads into running streams. One morning, the weather having cleared, I swung my bag to my shoulder, and with much warmth of parting I set my face again to the free road and the open country.

IX

THE MAN POSSESSED

I suppose I was predestined (and likewise foreordained) to reach the city sooner or later. My fate in that respect was settled for me when I placed my trust in the vagrant road. I thought for a time that I was more than a match for the Road, but I soon learned that the Road was more than a match for me. Sly? There's no name for it. Alluring, lovable, mysterious—as the heart of a woman. Many a time I've followed the Road where it led through innocent meadows or climbed leisurely hill slopes only to find that it had crept around slyly and led me before I knew it into the back door of some busy town.

Mostly in this country the towns squat low in the valleys, they lie in wait by the rivers, and often I scarcely know of their presence until I am so close upon them that I can smell the breath of their heated nostrils and hear their low growlings and grumblings.

My fear of these lesser towns has never been profound. I have even been bold enough, when I came across one of them, to hasten straight through as though assured that Cerberus was securely chained; but I found, after a time, what I might indeed have guessed, that the Road also led irresistibly to the lair of the Old Monster himself, the He-one of the species, where he lies upon the plain, lolling under his soiled gray blanket of smoke.

It is wonderful to be safe at home again, to watch the tender, reddish brown shoots of the Virginia creeper reaching in at my study window, to see the green of my own quiet fields, to hear the peaceful clucking of the hens in the sunny dooryard—and Harriet humming at her work in the kitchen.

When I left the Ransomes that fine spring morning, I had not the slightest presentiment of what the world held in store for me. After being a prisoner of the weather for so long, I took to the Road with fresh joy. All the fields were of a misty greenness and there were pools still shining in the road, but the air was deliciously clear, clean, and soft. I came through the hill country for three or four miles, even running down some of the steeper places for the very joy the motion gave me, the feel of the air on my face.

Thus I came finally to the Great Road, and stood for a moment looking first this way, then that.

"Where now?" I asked aloud.

With an amusing sense of the possibilities that lay open before me, I closed my eyes, turned slowly around several times and then stopped. When I opened my eyes I was facing nearly southward: and that way I set out, not knowing in the least what Fortune had presided at that turning. If I had gone the other way——

I walked vigorously for two or three hours, meeting or passing many interesting people upon the busy road. Automobiles there were in plenty, and loaded wagons, and jolly families off for town, and a herdsman driving sheep, and small boys on their way to school with their dinner pails, and a gypsy wagon with lean, led horses following behind, and even a Jewish peddler with a crinkly black beard, whom I was on the very point of stopping.

"I should like sometime to know a Jew," I said to myself.

As I travelled, feeling like one who possesses hidden riches, I came quite without warning upon the beginning of my great adventure. I had been looking for a certain thing all the morning, first on one side of the road, then the other, and finally I was rewarded. There it was, nailed high upon a tree, the curious, familiar sign:

REST

I stopped instantly. It seemed like an old friend.

"Well," said I. "I'm not at all tired, but I want to be agreeable."

With that I sat down on a convenient stone, took off my hat, wiped my forehead, and looked about me with satisfaction, for it was a pleasant country.

I had not been sitting there above two minutes when my eyes fell upon one of the oddest specimens of humanity (I thought then) that ever I saw. He had been standing near the roadside, just under the tree upon which I had seen the sign, "Rest." My heart dotted and carried one.

"The sign man himself!" I exclaimed.

I arose instantly and walked down the road toward him.

"A man has only to stop anywhere here," I said exultantly, "and things happen."

The stranger's appearance was indeed extraordinary. He seemed at first glimpse to be about twice as large around the hips as he was at the shoulders, but this I soon discovered to be due to no natural avoirdupois but to the prodigious number of soiled newspapers and magazines with which the low-hanging pockets of his overcoat were stuffed. For he was still wearing an old shabby overcoat—though the weather was warm and bright—and on his head was an odd and outlandish hat. It was of fur, flat at the top, flat as a pie tin, with the moth-eaten ear-laps turned up at the sides and looking exactly like small furry ears. These, with the round steel spectacles which he wore—

the only distinctive feature of his countenance—gave him an indescribably droll appearance.

"A fox!" I thought.

Then I looked at him more closely.

"No," said I, "an owl, an owl!"

The stranger stepped out into the road and evidently awaited my approach. My first vivid impression of his face—I remember it afterward shining with a strange inward illumination—was not favourable. It was a deep-lined, scarred, worn-looking face, insignificant if not indeed ugly in its features, and yet, even at the first glance, revealing something inexplainable—incalculable——

"Good day, friend," I said heartily.

Without replying to my greeting, he asked:

"Is this the road to Kilburn?"—with a faint flavour of foreignness in his words.

"I think it is," I replied, and I noticed as he lifted his hand to thank me that one finger was missing and that the hand itself was cruelly twisted and scarred.

The stranger instantly set off up the Road without giving me much more attention than he would have given any other sign-post. I stood a moment looking after him—the wings of his overcoat beating about his legs and the small furry ears on his cap wagging gently.

"There," said I aloud, "is a man who is actually going somewhere."

So many men in this world are going nowhere in particular that when one comes along—even though he be amusing and insignificant—who is really (and passionately) going somewhere, what a stir he communicates to a dull world! We catch sparks of electricity from the very friction of his passage.

It was so with this odd stranger. Though at one moment I could not help smiling at him, at the next I was following him.

"It may be," said I to myself, "that this is really the sign man!"

I felt like Captain Kidd under full sail to capture a treasure ship; and as I approached, I was much agitated as to the best method of grappling and boarding. I finally decided, being a lover of bold methods, to let go my largest gun first—for moral effect.

"So," said I, as I ran alongside, "you are the man who puts up the signs."

He stopped and looked at me.

"What signs?"

"Why the sign 'Rest' along this road."

He paused for some seconds with a perplexed expression on his face.

"Then you are not the sign man," I said.

"No," he replied, "I ain't any sign man."

I was not a little disappointed, but having made my attack, I determined to see if there was any treasure aboard—which, I suppose, should be the procedure of any well-regulated pirate.

"I'm going this way myself," I said, "and if you have no objections——"

He stood looking at me curiously, indeed suspiciously, through his round spectacles.

"Have you got the passport?" he asked finally.

"The passport!" I exclaimed, mystified in my turn.

"Yes," said he, "the passport. Let me see your hand."

When I held out my hand he looked at it closely for a moment, and then took it with a quick warm pressure in one of his, and gave it a little shake, in a way not quite American.

"You are one of us," said he, "you work."

I thought at first that it was a bit of pleasantry, and I was about to return it in kind when I saw plainly in his face a look of solemn intent.

"So," he said, "we shall travel like comrades."

He thrust his scarred hand through my arm, and we walked up the road side by side, his bulging pockets beating first against his legs and then against mine, quite impartially.

"I think," said the stranger, "that we shall be arrested at Kilburn."

"We shall!" I exclaimed with something, I admit, of a shock.

"Yes," he said, "but it is all in the day's work."

"How is that?"

He stopped in the road and faced me. Throwing back his overcoat he pointed to a small red button on his coat lapel.

"They don't want me in Kilburn," said he, "the mill men are strikin' there, and the bosses have got armed men on every corner. Oh, the capitalists are watchin' for me, all right."

I cannot convey the strange excitement I felt. It seemed as though these words suddenly opened a whole new world around me—a world I had heard about for years, but never entered. And the tone in which he had used the word "capitalist!" I had almost to glance around to make sure that there were no ravening capitalists hiding behind the trees.

"So you are a Socialist," I said.

"Yes," he answered. "I'm one of those dangerous persons."

First and last I have read much of Socialism, and thought about it, too, from the quiet angle of my farm among the hills, but this was the first time I had ever had a live Socialist on my arm. I could not have been more surprised if the stranger had said, "Yes, I am Theodore Roosevelt."

One of the discoveries we keep making all our life long (provided we remain humble) is the humorous discovery of the ordinariness of the extraordinary. Here was this disrupter of society, this man of the red flag—here he was with his mild spectacled eyes and his furry ears wagging as he walked. It was unbelievable!—and the sun shining on him quite as impartially as it shone on me.

Coming at last to a pleasant bit of woodland, where a stream ran under the roadway, I said:

"Stranger, let's sit down and have a bite of luncheon."

He began to expostulate, said he was expected in Kilburn.

"Oh, I've plenty for two," I said, "and I can say, at least, that I am a firm believer in coöperation."

Without more urging he followed me into the woods, where we sat down comfortably under a tree.

Now, when I take a fine thick sandwich out of my bag, I always feel like making it a polite bow, and before I bite into a big brown doughnut, I am tempted to say, "By your leave, madam," and as for MINCE PIE—Beau Brummel himself could not outdo me in respectful consideration. But Bill Hahn neither saw, nor smelled, nor, I think, tasted Mrs. Ransome's cookery. As soon as we sat down he began talking. From time to time he would reach out for another sandwich or doughnut or pickle (without knowing in the least which he was getting), and when that was gone some reflex impulse caused him to reach out for some more. When the last crumb of our luncheon had disappeared Bill Hahn still reached out. His hand groped absently about, and coming in contact with no more doughnuts or pickles he withdrew it—and did not know, I think, that the meal was finished. (Confidentially, I have speculated on what might have happened if the supply had been unlimited!)

But that was Bill Hahn. Once started on his talk, he never thought of food or clothing or shelter; but his eyes glowed, his face lighted up with a strange effulgence, and he quite lost himself upon the tide of his own oratory. I saw him afterward by a flare-light at the centre of a great crowd of men and women —but that is getting ahead of my story.

His talk bristled with such words as "capitalism," "proletariat," "class-consciousness"—and he spoke with fluency of "economic determinism" and "syndicalism." It was quite wonderful! And from time to time, he would bring in a smashing quotation from Aristotle, Napoleon, Karl Marx, or Eugene V. Debs, giving them all equal values, and he cited statistics!—oh, marvellous statistics, that never were on sea or land.

Once he was so swept away by his own eloquence that he sprang to his feet and, raising one hand high above his head (quite unconscious that he was holding up a dill pickle), he worked through one of his most thrilling periods.

Yes, I laughed, and yet there was so brave a simplicity about this odd, absurd little man that what I laughed at was only his outward appearance (and that he himself had no care for), and all the time I felt a growing respect and admiration for him. He was not only sincere, but he was genuinely simple—a much higher virtue, as Fenelon says. For while sincere people do not aim at appearing anything but what they are, they are always in fear of passing for something they are not. They are forever thinking about themselves, weighing all their words and thoughts and dwelling upon what they have done, in the fear of having done too much or too little, whereas simplicity, as Fenelon says, is an uprightness of soul which has ceased wholly to dwell upon itself or its actions. Thus there are plenty of sincere folk in the world but few who are simple.

Well, the longer he talked, the less interested I was in what he said and the more fascinated I became in what he was. I felt a wistful interest in him: and I wanted to know what way he took to purge himself of himself. I think if I had been in that group, nineteen hundred years ago, which surrounded the beggar who was born blind, but whose anointed eyes now looked out upon the glories of the world, I should have been among the questioners:

"What did he to thee? How opened he thine eyes?"

I tried ineffectually several times to break the swift current of his oratory and finally succeeded (when he paused a moment to finish off a bite of pie crust).

"You must have seen some hard experiences in your life," I said.

"That I have," responded Bill Hahn, "the capitalistic sys-tem——"

"Did you ever work in the mills yourself?" I interrupted hastily.

"Boy and man," said Bill Hahn, "I worked in that hell for thirty-two years—The class-conscious proletariat have only to exert themselves——"

"And your wife, did she work too—and your sons and daughters?"

A spasm of pain crossed his face.

"My daughter?" he said. "They killed her in the mills."

It was appalling—the dead level of the tone in which he uttered those words—the monotone of an emotion long ago burned out, and yet leaving frightful scars.

"My friend!" I exclaimed, and I could not help laying my hand on his arm.

I had the feeling I often have with troubled children—an in-describable pity that they have had to pass through the valley of the shadow, and I not there to take them by the hand.

"And was this—your daughter—what brought you to your present belief?"

"No," said he, "oh, no. I was a Socialist, as you might say, from youth up. That is, I called myself a Socialist, but, comrade, I've learned this here truth: that it ain't of so much importance that you possess a belief, as that the belief possess you. Do you understand?"

"I think," said I, "that I understand."

Well, he told me his story, mostly in a curious, dull, detached way—as though he were speaking of some third person in whom he felt only a brotherly interest, but from time to time some incident or observation would flame up out of the narrative, like the opening of the door of a molten pit—so that the glare hurt one!—and then the story would die back again into quiet narrative.

Like most working people he had never lived in the twentieth century at all. He was still in the feudal age, and his whole life had been a blind and ceaseless struggle for the bare necessaries of life, broken from time to time by fierce irregular wars called strikes. He had never known anything of a real self-governing commonwealth, and such progress as he and his kind had made was never the result of their citizenship, of their powers as voters, but grew out of the explosive and ragged upheavals of their own half-organized societies and unions.

It was against the "black people" he said that he was first on strike back in the early nineties. He told me all about it, how he had been working in the mills pretty comfortably—he was young and strong then, with a fine growing family and a small home of his own.

"It was as pretty a place as you would want to see," he said; "we grew cabbages and onions and turnips—everything grew fine!—in the garden behind the house."

And then the "black people" began to come in, little by little at first, and then by the carload. By the "black people" he meant the people from Southern Europe, he called them "hordes"— "hordes and hordes of 'em"—Italians mostly, and they began getting into the mills and underbidding for the jobs, so that wages slowly went down and at the same time the machines were speeded up. It seems that many of these "black people" were single men or vigorous young married people with only themselves to support, while the old American workers were men with families and little homes to pay for, and plenty of old grandfathers and grandmothers, to say nothing of babies, depending upon them.

"There wasn't a living for a decent family left," he said.

So they struck—and he told me in his dull monotone of the long bitterness of that strike, the empty cupboards, the approach of winter with no coal for the stoves and no warm clothing for the children. He told me that many of the old workers began to leave the town (some bound for the larger cities, some for the Far West).

"But," said he with a sudden outburst of emotion, "I couldn't leave. I had the woman and the children!"

And presently the strike collapsed, and the workers rushed helter skelter back to the mills to get their old jobs. "Begging like whipped dogs," he said bitterly.

Many of them found their places taken by the eager "black people," and many had to go to work at lower wages in poorer places—punished for the fight they had made.

But he got along somehow, he said—"the woman was a good manager"—until one day he had the misfortune to get his hand caught in the machinery. It was a place which should have been protected with guards, but was not. He was laid up for several weeks, and the company, claiming that the accident was due to his own stupidity and carelessness, refused even to pay his wages while he was idle. Well, the family had to live somehow, and the woman and the daughter—"she was a little thing," he said, "and frail"—the woman and the daughter went into the mill. But even with this new source of income they began to fall behind. Money which should have gone toward making the last payments on their home (already long delayed by the strike) had now to go to the doctor and the grocer.

"We had to live," said Bill Hahn.

Again and again he used this same phrase, "We had to live!" as a sort of bedrock explanation for all the woes of life.

After a time, with one finger gone and a frightfully scarred hand—he held it up for me to see—he went back into the mill.

"But it kept getting worse and worse," said he, "and finally I couldn't stand it any longer."

He and a group of friends got together secretly and tried to organize a union, tried to get the workmen together to improve their own condition; but in some way ("they had spies everywhere," he said) the manager learned of the attempt and one morning when he reported at the mill he was handed a slip asking him to call for his wages, that his help was no longer required.

"I'd been with that one company for twenty years and four months," he said bitterly, "I'd helped in my small way to build it up, make it a big concern payin' 28 per cent. dividends every year; I'd given part of my right hand in doin' it—and they threw me out like an old shoe."

He said he would have pulled up and gone away, but he still had the little home and the garden, and his wife and daughter were still at work, so he hung on grimly, trying to get some other job. "But what good is a man for any other sort of work," he said, "when he has been trained to the mills for thirty-two years!"

It was not very long after that when the "great strike" began —indeed, it grew out of the organization which he had tried to launch—and Bill Hahn threw himself into it with all his strength. He was one of the leaders. I shall not attempt to repeat here his description of the bitter struggle, the coming of the soldiery, the street riots, the long lists of arrests ("some," said he, "got into jail on purpose, so that they could at least have enough to eat!"), the late meetings of strikers, the wild turmoil and excitement.

Of all this he told me, and then he stopped suddenly, and after a long pause he said in a low voice:

"Comrade, did ye ever see your wife and your sickly daughter and your kids sufferin' for bread to eat?"

He paused again with a hard, dry sob in his voice.

"Did ye ever see that?"

"No," said I, very humbly, "I have never seen anything like that."

He turned on me suddenly, and I shall never forget the look on his face, nor the blaze in his eyes:

"Then what can you know about working-men!"

What could I answer?

A moment passed and then he said, as if a little remorseful at having turned thus upon me:

"Comrade, I tell you, the iron entered my soul—them days."

It seems that the leaders of the strike were mostly old employees like Bill Hahn, and the company had conceived the idea that if these men could be eliminated the organization would collapse, and the strikers be forced back to work. One day Bill Hahn found that proceedings had been started to turn him out of his home, upon which he had not been able to keep up his payments, and at the same time the merchant, of whom he had been a respected customer for years, refused to give him any further credit.

"But we lived somehow," he said, "we lived and we fought."

It was then that he began to see clearly what it all meant. He said he made a great discovery: that the "black people" against whom they had struck in 1894 were not to blame!

"I tell you," said he, "we found when we got started that them black people—we used to call 'em dagoes—were just workin' people like us—and in hell with us. They were good soldiers, them Eyetalians and Poles and Syrians, they fought with us to the end."

I shall not soon forget the intensely dramatic but perfectly simple way in which he told me how he came, as he said, "to see the true light." Holding up his maimed right hand (that trembled a little), he pointed one finger upward.

"I seen the big hand in the sky," he said, "I seen it as clear as daylight."

He said he saw at last what Socialism meant.

One day he went home from a strikers' meeting—one of the last, for the men were worn out with their long struggle. It was a bitter cold day, and he was completely discouraged. When he reached his own street he saw a pile of household goods on the sidewalk in front of his home. He saw his wife there wringing her hands and crying. He said he could not take a step further, but sat down on a neighbour's porch and looked and looked. "It was curious," he said, "but the only thing I could see or think about was our old family clock which they had stuck on top of the pile, half tipped over. It looked odd and I wanted to set it up straight. It was the clock we bought when we were married, and we'd had it about twenty years on the mantel in the livin'-room. It was a good clock," he said.

He paused and then smiled a little.

"I never had figured it out why I should have been able to think of nothing but that clock," he said, "but so it was."

When he got home, he found his frail daughter just coming out of the empty house, "coughing as though she was dyin'." Something, he said, seemed to stop inside of him. Those were his words: "Something seemed to stop inside 'o me."

He turned away without saying a word, walked back to strike headquarters, borrowed a revolver from a friend, and started out along the main road which led into the better part of the town.

"Did you ever hear o' Robert Winter?" he asked.

"No," said I.

"Well, Robert Winter was the biggest gun of 'em all. He owned the mills there, and the largest store and the newspaper —he pretty nearly owned the town."

He told me much more about Robert Winter which betrayed still a curious sort of feudal admiration for him, and for his great place and power; but I need not dwell on it here. He told me how he climbed in through a hemlock hedge (for the stone gateway was guarded) and walked through the snow toward the great house.

"An' all the time I seemed to be seein' my daughter Margy right there before my eyes coughing as though she was dyin'."

It was just nightfall and all the windows were alight. He crept up to a clump of bushes under a window and waited there a moment while he drew out and cocked his revolver. Then he slowly reached upward until his head cleared the sill and he could look into the room. "A big, warm room," he described it.

"Comrade," said he, "I had murder in my heart that night."

So he stood there looking in with the revolver ready cocked in his hand.

"And what do you think I seen there?" he asked.

"I cannot guess," I said.

"Well," said Bill Hahn, "I seen the great Robert Winter that we had been fighting for five long months—and he was down on his hands and knees on the carpet—and he had his little daughter on his back—and he was creepin' about with her—an' she was laughin'."

Bill Hahn paused.

"I had a bead on him," he said finally, "but I couldn't do it— I just couldn't do it."

He came away all weak and trembling and cold, and, "Comrade," he said, "I was cryin' like a baby, and didn't know why."

The next day the strike collapsed and there was the familiar stampede for work—but Bill Hahn did not go back. He knew it would be useless. A week later his frail daughter died and was buried in the pauper's field.

"She was as truly killed," he said, "as though someone had fired a bullet at her through a window."

"And what did you do after that?" I asked, when he had paused for a long time with his chin on his breast.

"Well," said he, "I did a lot of thinking them days, and I says to myself: 'This thing is wrong, and I will go out and stop it—I will go out and stop it.'"

As he uttered these words, I looked at him curiously—his absurd flat fur hat with the moth-eaten ears, the old bulging overcoat, the round spectacles, the scarred, insignificant face—he seemed somehow transformed, a person elevated above himself, the tool of some vast incalculable force.

I shall never forget the phrase he used to describe his own feelings when he had reached this astonishing decision to go out and stop the wrongs of the world. He said he "began to feel all clean inside."

"I see it didn't matter what become o' me, and I began to feel all clean inside."

It seemed, he explained, as though something big and strong had got hold of him, and he began to be happy.

"Since then," he said in a low voice, "I've been happier than I ever was before in all my life. I ain't got any family, nor any home—rightly speakin'—nor any money, but, comrade, you see here in front of you, a happy man."

When he had finished his story we sat quiet for some time.

"Well," said he, finally, "I must be goin'. The committee will wonder what's become o' me."

I followed him out to the road. There I put my hand on his shoulder, and said:

"Bill Hahn, you are a better man than I am."

He smiled, a beautiful smile, and we walked off together down the road.

I wish I had gone on with him at that time into the city, but somehow I could not do it. I stopped near the top of the hill where one can see in the distance that smoky huddle of buildings which is known as Kilburn, and though he urged me, I turned aside and sat down in the edge of a meadow. There were many things I wanted to think about, to get clear in my mind.

As I sat looking out toward that great city, I saw three men walking in the white road. As I watched them, I could see them coming quickly, eagerly. Presently they threw up their hands and evidently began to shout, though I could not hear what they said. At that moment I saw my friend Bill Hahn running in the road, his coat skirts flapping heavily about his legs. When they met they almost fell into one another's arms.

I suppose it was so that the early Christians, those who hid in the Roman catacombs, were wont to greet one another.

So I sat thinking.

"A man," I said to myself, "who can regard himself as a function, not an end of creation, has arrived."

After a time I got up and walked down the hill—some strange force carrying me onward—and came thus to the city of Kilburn.

X

I AM CAUGHT UP INTO LIFE

I CAN SCARCELY CONVEY in written words the whirling emotions I felt when I entered the city of Kilburn. Every sight, every sound, recalled vividly and painfully the unhappy years I had once spent in another and greater city. Every mingled odour of the streets—and there is nothing that will so surely re-create (for me) the inner emotion of a time or place as a remembered odour—brought back to me the incidents of that immemorial existence.

For a time, I confess it frankly here, I felt afraid. More than once I stopped short in the street where I was walking, and considered turning about and making again for the open country. Some there may be who will feel that I am exaggerating my sensations and impressions, but they do not know of my memories of a former life, nor of how, many years ago, I left the city quite defeated, glad indeed that I was escaping, and thinking (as I have related elsewhere) that I should never again set foot upon a paved street. These things went deep with me. Only the other day, when a friend asked me how old I was,

I responded instantly—our unpremeditated words are usually truest—with the date of my arrival at this farm.

"Then you are only ten years old!" he exclaimed with a laugh, thinking I was joking.

"Well," I said, "I am counting only the years worth living."

No; I existed, but I never really lived until I was reborn, that wonderful summer, here among these hills.

I said I felt afraid in the streets of Kilburn, but it was no physical fear. Who could be safer in the city than the man who has not a penny in his pockets? It was rather a strange, deep, spiritual shrinking. There seemed something so irresistible about this life of the city, so utterly overpowering. I had a sense of being smaller than I had previously felt myself, that in some way my personality, all that was strong or interesting or original about me, was being smudged over, rubbed out. In the country I had in some measure come to command life, but here, it seemed to me, life was commanding me and crushing me down. It is a difficult thing to describe: I never felt just that way before.

I stopped at last on the main street of Kilburn in the very heart of the town. I stopped because it seemed necessary to me, like a man in a flood, to touch bottom, to get hold upon something immovable and stable. It was just at that hour of evening when the stores and shops are pouring forth their rivulets of humanity to join the vast flood of the streets. I stepped quickly aside into a niche near the corner of an immense building of brick and steel and glass, and there I stood with my back to the wall, and I watched the restless, whirling, torrential tide of the streets. I felt again, as I had not felt it before in years, the mysterious urge of the city—the sense of unending, overpowering movement.

There was another strange, indeed uncanny, sensation that began to creep over me as I stood there. Though hundreds upon hundreds of men and women were passing me every minute, not one of them seemed to see me. Most of them did not even look in my direction, and those who did turn their eyes toward me seemed to glance through me to the building behind. I wonder if this is at all a common experience, or whether I was unduly sensitive that day, unduly wrought up? I began to feel like one clad in garments of invisibility. I could see, but was not seen. I could feel, but was not felt. In the country there are few who would not stop to speak to me, or at least appraise me with their eyes; but here I was a wraith, a ghost—not a palpable human being at all. For a moment I felt unutterably lonely.

It is this way with me. When I have reached the very depths of any serious situation or tragic emotion, something within me seems at last to stop—how shall I describe it?—and I rebound suddenly and see the world, as it were, double—see that my condition instead of being serious or tragic is in reality amusing —and I usually came out of it with an utterly absurd or whimsical idea. It was so upon this occasion. I think it was the image of my robust self as a wraith that did it.

"After all," I said aloud taking a firm hold on the good hard flesh of one of my legs, "this is positively David Grayson."

I looked out again into that tide of faces—interesting, tired, passive, smiling, sad, but above all, preoccupied faces.

"No one," I thought, "seems to know that David Grayson has come to town."

I had the sudden, almost irresistible notion of climbing up a step near me, holding up one hand, and crying out:

"Here I am, my friends. I am David Grayson. I am real and solid and opaque; I have plenty of red blood running in my veins. I assure you that I am a person well worth knowing."

I should really have enjoyed some such outlandish enterprise, and I am not at all sure yet that it would not have brought me adventures and made me friends worth while. We fail far more often by under-daring than by over-daring.

But this imaginary object had the result, at least, of giving me a new grip on things. I began to look out upon the amazing spectacle before me in a different mood. It was exactly like some enormous anthill into which an idle traveller had thrust his cane. Everywhere the ants were running out of their tunnels and burrows, many carrying burdens and giving one strangely the impression that while they were intensely alive and active, not more than half of them had any clear idea of where they were going. And serious, deadly serious, in their haste! I felt a strong inclination to stop a few of them and say:

"Friends, cheer up. It isn't half as bad as you think it is. Cheer up!"

After a time the severity of the human flood began to abate, and here and there at the bottom of that gulch of a street, which had begun to fill with soft, bluish-gray shadows, the evening lights appeared. The air had grown cooler; in the distance around a corner I heard a street organ break suddenly and joyously into the lively strains of "The Wearin' o' the Green."

I stepped out into the street with quite a new feeling of adventure. And as if to testify that I was now a visible person a sharp-eyed newsboy discovered me—the first human being in Kilburn who had actually seen me—and came up with a paper in his hand.

"*Herald,* boss?"

I was interested in the shrewd, world-wise, humorous look in the urchin's eyes.

"No," I began, with the full intent of bantering him into some sort of acquaintance; but he evidently measured my purchasing capacity quite accurately, for he turned like a flash to another customer.

"*Herald,* boss?"

"You'll have to step lively, David Grayson," I said to myself, "if you get aboard in this city."

A slouchy negro with a cigarette in his fingers glanced at me in passing and then, hesitating, turned quickly toward me.

"Got a match, boss?"

I gave him a match.

"Thank you, boss," and he passed on down the street.

"I seem to be 'boss' around here," I said.

This contact, slight as it was, gave me a feeling of warmth, removed a little the sensation of aloofness I had felt, and I strolled slowly down the street, looking in at the gay windows, now ablaze with lights, and watching the really wonderful procession of vehicles of all shapes and sizes that rattled by on the pavement. Even at that hour of the day I think there were more of them in one minute than I see in a whole month at my farm.

It's a great thing to wear shabby clothes and an old hat. Some of the best things I have ever known, like these experiences of the streets, have resulted from coming up to life from under-neath; of being taken for less than I am rather than for more than I am.

I did not always believe in this doctrine. For many years—the years before I was rightly born into this alluring world—I tried quite the opposite course. I was constantly attempting to come down to life from above. Instead of being content to carry through life a sufficiently wonderful being named David Grayson I tried desperately to set up and support a sort of dummy creature which, so clad, so housed, so fed, should appear to be what I thought David Grayson ought to appear in the eyes of the world. Oh, I spent quite a lifetime trying to satisfy other people!

Once I remember staying at home, in bed, reading "Huckle-berry Finn," while I sent my trousers out to be mended.

Well, that dummy Grayson perished in a cornfield. His empty coat served well for a scarecrow. A wisp of straw stuck out through a hole in his finest hat.

And I—the man within—I escaped, and have been out freely upon the great adventure of life.

If a shabby coat (and I speak here also symbolically, not forgetful of spiritual significances) lets you into the adventurous world of those who are poor it does not on the other hand rob you of any true friendship among those who are rich or mighty. I say true friendship, for unless a man who is rich and mighty is able to see through my shabby coat (as I see through his fine one), I shall gain nothing by knowing him.

I've permitted myself all this digression—left myself walking alone there in the streets of Kilburn while I philosophized upon the ways and means of life—not without design, for I could have had no such experiences as I did have in Kilburn if I had worn a better coat or carried upon me the evidences of security in life.

I think I have already remarked upon the extraordinary enlivenment of wits which comes to the man who has been without a meal or so and does not know when or where he is again to break his fast. Try it, friend, and see! It was already getting along in the evening, and I knew or supposed I knew no one in Kilburn save only Bill Hahn, Socialist, who was little better off than I was.

In this emergency my mind began to work swiftly. A score of fascinating plans for getting my supper and a bed to sleep in flashed through my mind.

"Why," said I, "when I come to think of it, I'm comparatively rich. I'll warrant there are plenty of places in Kilburn, and good ones, too, where I could barter a chapter of Montaigne and a little good conversation for a first-rate supper, and I've no doubt that I could whistle up a bed almost anywhere!"

I thought of a little motto I often repeat to myself:

To know life, begin anywhere!

There were several people on the streets of Kilburn that night who don't know yet how very near they were to being boarded by a somewhat shabby looking farmer who would have offered them, let us say, a notable musical production called "Old Dan Tucker," exquisitely performed on a tin whistle, in exchange for a good honest supper.

There was one man in particular—a fine, pompous citizen who came down the street swinging his cane and looking as though the universe was a sort of Christmas turkey, lying all brown and sizzling before him ready to be carved—a fine pompous citizen who never realized how nearly Fate with a battered volume of Montaigne in one hand and a tin whistle in the other— came to pouncing upon him that evening! And I am firmly convinced that if I had attacked him with the Great Particular Word he would have carved me off a juicy slice of the white breast meat.

"I'm getting hungry," I said; "I must find Bill Hahn!"

I had turned down a side street, and seeing there in front of a building a number of lounging men with two or three cabs or carriages standing nearby in the street I walked up to them. It was a livery barn.

Now I like all sorts of out-of-door people: I seem to be related to them through horses and cattle and cold winds and sunshine. I like them and understand them, and they seem to like me and understand me. So I walked up to the group of jolly drivers and stablemen intending to ask my directions. The talking died out and they all turned to look at me. I suppose I was not altogether a familiar type there in the city streets. My bag, especially, seemed to set me apart as a curious person.

"Friends," I said, "I am a farmer——"

They all broke out laughing; they seemed to know it already! I was just a little taken aback, but I laughed, too, knowing that there was a way of getting at them if only I could find it.

"It may surprise you," I said, "but this is the first time in some dozen years that I've been in a big city like this."

"You nadn't 'ave told us, partner!" said one of them, evidently the wit of the group, in a rich Irish brogue.

"Well," I responded, laughing with the rest of them, "you've been living right here all the time, and don't realize how amusing and curious the city looks to me. Why, I feel as though I had been away sleeping for twenty years, like Rip Van Winkle. When I left the city there was scarcely an automobile to be seen anywhere—and now look at them snorting through the streets. I counted twenty-two passing that corner up there in five minutes by the clock."

This was a fortunate remark, for I found instantly that the invasion of the automobile was a matter of tremendous import to such Knights of Bucephalus as these.

At first the wit interrupted me with amusing remarks, as wits will, but I soon had him as quiet as the others. For I have found the things that chiefly interest people are the things they already know about—provided you show them that these common things are still mysterious, still miraculous, as indeed they are.

After a time some one pushed me a stable stool and I sat down among them, and we had quite a conversation, which finally developed into an amusing comparison (I wish I had room to repeat it here) between the city and the country. I told them something about my farm, how much I enjoyed it, and what a wonderful free life one had in the country. In this I was really taking an unfair advantage of them, for I was trading on the fact that every man, down deep in his heart, has more or less of an instinct to get back to the soil—at least all outdoor men have. And when I described the simplest things about my barn, and the cattle and pigs, and the bees—and the good things we have to eat—I had every one of them leaning forward and hanging on my words.

Harriet sometimes laughs at me for the way I celebrate farm life. She says all my apples are the size of Hubbard squashes, my eggs all double-yolked, and my cornfields tropical jungles. Practical Harriet! My apples may not *all* be the size of Hubbard squashes, but they are good, sizable apples, and as for flavour— all the spices of Arcady——! And I believe, I *know,* from my own experience that these fields and hills are capable of healing men's souls. And when I see people wandering around a lonesome city like Kilburn, with never a soft bit of soil to put their heels into, nor a green thing to cultivate, nor any corn or apples or honey to harvest, I feel—well, that they are wasting their time.

(It's a fact, Harriet!)

Indeed, I had the most curious experience with my friend the wit—his name I soon learned was Healy—a jolly, round, red-nosed, outdoor chap with fists that looked like small-sized hams, and a rich, warm Irish voice. At first he was inclined to use me as the ready butt of his lively mind, but presently he became so much interested in what I was saying that he sat squarely in front of me with both his jolly eyes and his smiling mouth wide open.

"If ever you pass my way," I said to him, "just drop in and I'll give you a dinner of baked beans"—and I smacked—"and home made bread"—and I smacked again—"and pumpkin pie"—and I smacked a third time—"that will make your mouth water."

All this smacking and the description of baked beans and pumpkin pie had an odd counter effect upon *me;* for I suddenly recalled my own tragic state. So I jumped up quickly and asked directions for getting down to the mill neighbourhood, where I hoped to find Bill Hahn. My friend Healy instantly volunteered the information.

"And now," I said, "I want to ask a small favour of you. I'm looking for a friend, and I'd like to leave my bag here for the night."

"Sure, sure," said the Irishman heartily. "Put it there in the office—on top o' the desk. It'll be all right."

So I put it in the office and was about to say good-bye, when my friend said to me:

"Come in, partner, and have a drink before you go"—and he pointed to a nearby saloon.

"Thank you," I answered heartily, for I knew it was as fine a bit of hospitality as he could offer me, "thank you, but I must find my friend before it gets too late."

"Aw, come on now," he cried, taking my arm. "Sure you'll be better off for a bit o' warmth inside."

I had hard work to get away from them, and I am as sure as can be that they would have found supper and a bed for me if they had known I needed either.

"Come agin," Healy shouted after me, "we're glad to see a farmer any toime."

My way led me quickly out of the well-groomed and glittering main streets of the town. I passed first through several blocks of quiet residences, and then came to a street near the river which was garishly lighted, and crowded with small, poor shops and stores, with a saloon on nearly every corner. I passed a huge, dark, silent box of a mill, and I saw what I never saw before in a city, armed men guarding the streets.

Although it was growing late—it was after nine o'clock—crowds of people were still parading the streets, and there was something intangibly restless, something tense, in the very atmosphere of the neighbourhood. It was very plain that I had reached the strike district. I was about to make some further inquiries for the headquarters of the mill men or for Bill Hahn personally, when I saw, not far ahead of me, a black crowd of people reaching out into the street. Drawing nearer I saw that an open space or block between two rows of houses was literally black with human beings, and in the centre on a raised platform, under a gasolene flare, I beheld my friend of the road, Bill Hahn. The overcoat and the hat with the furry ears had disappeared, and the little man stood there, bare-headed, before that great audience.

My experience in the world is limited, but I have never heard anything like that speech for sheer power. It was as unruly and powerful and resistless as life itself. It was not like any other speech I ever heard, for it was no mere giving out by the orator of ideas and thoughts and feelings of his own. It seemed rather —how shall I describe it?—as though the speaker was looking into the very hearts of that vast gathering of poor men and poor women and merely telling them what they themselves felt, but could not tell. And I shall never forget the breathless hush of the people or the quality of their responses to the orator's words. It was as though they said, "Yes, yes"—with a feeling of vast relief—"Yes, yes—at last our own hopes and fears and desires are being uttered—yes, yes."

As for the orator himself, he held up one maimed hand and leaned over the edge of the platform, and his undistinguished face glowed with the white light of a great passion within. The man had utterly forgotten himself.

I confess, among those eager working people, clad in their poor garments, I confess I was profoundly moved. Faith is not so bounteous a commodity in this world that we can afford to treat even its unfamiliar manifestations with contempt. And when a movement is hot with life, when it stirs common men to their depths, look out! look out!

Up to that time I had never known much of the practical workings of Socialism; and the main contention of its philosophy has never accorded wholly with my experience in life.

But the Socialism of to-day is no mere intellectual abstraction —as it was, perhaps, in the days of Brook Farm. It is a mode of action. Men whose view of life is perfectly balanced rarely soil themselves with the dusk of battle. The heat necessary to produce social conflict (and social progress—who knows?) is generated by a supreme faith that certain principles are universal in their application when in reality they are only local or temporary.

Thus while one may not accept the philosophy of Socialism as a final explanation of human life, he may yet look upon Socialism in action as a powerful method of stimulating human progress. The world has been lagging behind in its sense of brotherhood, and we now have the Socialists knit together in a fighting friendship as fierce and narrow in its motives as Calvinism, pricking us to reform, asking the cogent question:

"Are we not all brothers?"

Oh, we are going a long way with these Socialists, we are going to discover a new world of social relationships—and then, and *then,* like a mighty wave, will flow in upon us a renewed and more wonderful sense of the worth of the individual human soul. A new individualism, bringing with it, perhaps, some faint realization of our dreams of a race of Supermen, lies just be-

yond! Its prophets, girded with rude garments and feeding
upon the wild honey of poverty, are already crying in the
wilderness.

I think I could have remained there at the Socialist meeting
all night long: there was something about it that brought a hard,
dry twist to my throat. But after a time my friend Bill Hahn,
evidently quite worn out, yielded his place to another and far
less clairvoyant speaker, and the crowd, among whom I now
discovered quite a number of policemen, began to thin out.

I made my way forward and saw Bill Hahn and several other
men just leaving the platform. I stepped up to him, but it was
not until I called him by name (I knew how absent minded he
was!) that he recognized me.

"Well, well," he said; "you came after all!"

He seized me by both arms and introduced me to several of
his companions as "Brother Grayson." They all shook hands
with me warmly.

Although he was perspiring, Bill put on his overcoat and the
old fur hat with the ears, and as he now took my arm I could
feel one of his bulging pockets beating against my leg. I had not
the slightest idea where they were going, but Bill held me by
the arm and presently we came, a block or so distant, to a dark,
narrow stairway leading up from the street. I recall the stumbling sound of steps on the wooden boards, a laugh or two, the
high voice of a woman asserting and denying. Feeling our way
along the wall, we came to the top and went into a long, low,
rather dimly lighted room set about with tables and chairs—a
sort of restaurant. A number of men and a few women had
already gathered there. Among them my eyes instantly singled
out a huge, rough-looking man who stood at the centre of an
animated group. He had thick, shaggy hair, and one side of his
face over the cheekbone was of a dull blue-black and raked and
scarred, where it had been burned in a powder blast. He had
been a miner. His gray eyes, which had a surprisingly youthful
and even humorous expression, looked out from under coarse,
thick, gray brows. A very remarkable face and figure he pre-

sented. I soon learned that he was R—— D——, the leader of whom I had often heard, and heard no good thing. He was quite a different type from Bill Hahn: he was the man of authority, the organizer, the diplomat—as Bill was the prophet, preaching a holy war.

How wonderful human nature is! Only a short time before I had been thrilled by the intensity of the passion of the throng, but here the mood suddenly changed to one of friendly gayety. Fully a third of those present were women, some of them plainly from the mills and some of them curiously different—women from other walks in life who had thrown themselves heart and soul into the strike. Without ceremony but with much laughing and joking, they found their places around the tables. A cook who appeared in a dim doorway was greeted with a shout, to which he responded with a wide smile, waving the long spoon which he held in his hand.

I shall not attempt to give any complete description of the gathering or of what they said or did. I think I could devote a dozen pages to the single man who was placed next to me. I was interested in him from the outset. The first thing that struck me about him was an air of neatness, even fastidiousness, about his person—though he wore no stiff collar, only a soft woollen shirt without a necktie. He had the long, sensitive, beautiful hands of an artist, but his face was thin and marked with the pallor peculiar to the indoor worker. I soon learned that he was a weaver in the mills, an Englishman by birth, and we had not talked two minutes before I found that, while he had never had any education in the schools, he had been a gluttonous reader of books— all kinds of books—and, what is more, had thought about them and was ready with vigorous (and narrow) opinions about this author or that. And he knew more about economics and sociology, I firmly believe, than half the college professors. A truly remarkable man.

It was an Italian restaurant, and I remember how, in my hunger, I assailed the generous dishes of boiled meat and spaghetti. A red wine was served in large bottles which circulated rapidly around the table, and almost immediately the room began to fill with tobacco smoke. Every one seemed to be talking and laughing at once, in the liveliest spirit of good fellowship. They joked from table to table, and sometimes the whole room would quiet down while some one told a joke, which invariably wound up with a roar of laughter.

"Why," I said, "these people have a whole life, a whole society, of their own!"

In the midst of this jollity the clear voice of a girl rang out with the first lines of a song. Instantly the room was hushed:

> *Arise, ye prisoners of starvation,*
> *Arise, ye wretched of the earth,*
> *For justice thunders condemnation*
> *A better world's in birth.*

These were the words she sang, and when the clear, sweet voice died down the whole company, as though by a common impulse, arose from their chairs, and joined in a great swelling chorus:

> *It is the final conflict,*
> *Let each stand in his place,*
> *The Brotherhood of Man*
> *Shall be the human race.*

It was beyond belief, to me, the spirit with which these words were sung. In no sense with jollity—all that seemed to have been dropped when they came to their feet—but with an unmistakable fervour of faith. Some of the things I had thought and dreamed about secretly among the hills of my farm all these years, dreamed about as being something far off and as unrealizable as the millennium, were here being sung abroad with jaunty faith by these weavers of Kilburn, these weavers and workers whom I had schooled myself to regard with a sort of distant pity.

Hardly had the company sat down again, with a renewal of the flow of jolly conversation when I heard a rapping on one of the tables. I saw the great form of R—— D—— slowly rising.

"Brothers and sisters," he said, "a word of caution. The authorities will lose no chance of putting us in the wrong. Above all we must comport ourselves here and in the strike with great care. We are fighting a great battle, bigger than we are——"

At this instant the door from the dark hallway suddenly opened and a man in a policeman's uniform stepped in. There fell an instant's dead silence—an explosive silence. Every person there seemed to be petrified in the position in which his attention was attracted. Every eye was fixed on the figure at the door. For an instant no one said a word; then I heard a woman's shrill voice, like a rifle-shot:

"Assassin!"

I cannot imagine what might have happened next, for the feeling in the room, as in the city itself, was at the tensest, had not the leader suddenly brought the goblet which he held in his hand down with a bang upon the table.

"As I was saying," he continued in a steady, clear voice, "we are fighting to-day the greatest of battles, and we cannot permit trivial incidents, or personal bitterness, or small persecutions, to turn us from the great work we have in hand. However our opponents may comport themselves, we must be calm, steady, sure, patient, for we know that our cause is just and will prevail."

"You're right," shouted a voice back in the room.

Instantly the tension relaxed, conversation started again and every one turned away from the policeman at the door. In a few minutes, he disappeared without having said a word.

There was no regular speaking, and about midnight the party began to break up. I leaned over and said to my friend Bill Hahn:

"Can you find me a place to sleep to-night?"

"Certainly I can," he said heartily.

There was to be a brief conference of the leaders after the sup-per, and most of those present soon departed. I went down the long, dark stairway and out into the almost deserted street. Looking up between the buildings I could see the clear blue sky and the stars. And I walked slowly up and down awaiting my friend and trying, vainly, to calm my whirling emotions.

He came at last and I went with him. That night I slept scarcely at all, but lay looking up into the darkness. And it seemed as though, as I lay there, listening, that I could hear the city moving in its restless sleep, and sighing as with heavy pain. All night long I lay there thinking.

XI

I GRAPPLE WITH THE CITY

I HAVE LAUGHED HEARTILY many times since I came home to think of the Figure of Tragedy I felt myself that morning in the city of Kilburn. I had not slept well, had not slept at all, I think, and the experiences and emotions of the previous night still lay heavy upon me. Not before in many years had I felt such a depression of the spirits.

It was all so different from the thing I love! Not so much as a spear of grass or a leafy tree to comfort the eye, or a bird to sing; no quiet hills, no sight of the sun coming up in the morning over dewy fields, no sound of cattle in the lane, no cheerful cackling of fowls, nor buzzing of bees! That morning, I remember, when I first went out into those squalid streets and saw everywhere the evidences of poverty, dirt, and ignorance—and the sweet, clean country not two miles away—the thought of my own home among the hills (with Harriet there in the doorway) came upon me with incredible longing.

"I must go home; I must go home!" I caught myself saying aloud.

I remember how glad I was when I found that my friend Bill Hahn and other leaders of the strike were to be engaged in conferences during the forenoon, for I wanted to be alone, to try to get a few things straightened out in my mind.

But I soon found that a city is a poor place for reflection or contemplation. It bombards one with an infinite variety of new impressions and new adventures; and I could not escape the impression made by crowded houses, and ill-smelling streets, and dirty sidewalks, and swarming human beings. For a time the burden of these things rested upon my breast like a leaden weight; they all seemed so utterly wrong to me, so unnecessary, so unjust! I sometimes think of religion as only a high sense of good order; and it seemed to me that morning as though the very existence of this disorderly mill district was a challenge to religion, and an offence to the Orderer of an Orderly Universe. I don't know how such conditions may affect other people, but for a time I felt a sharp sense of impatience—yes, anger—with it all. I had an impulse to take off my coat then and there and go at the job of setting things to rights. Oh, I never was more serious in my life: I was quite prepared to change the entire scheme of things to my way of thinking whether the people who lived there liked it or not. It seemed to me for a few glorious moments that I had only to tell them of the wonders in our country, the pleasant, quiet roads, the comfortable farmhouses, the fertile fields, and the wooded hills—and, poof! all this crowded poverty would dissolve and disappear, and they would all come to the country and be as happy as I was.

I remember how, once in my life, I wasted untold energy trying to make over my dearest friends. There was Harriet, for example, dear, serious, practical Harriet. I used to be fretted by the way she was forever trying to clip my wing feathers—I suppose to keep me close to the quiet and friendly and unadventurous roost! We come by such a long, long road, sometimes, to the acceptance of our nearest friends for exactly what they are. Because we are so fond of them we try to make them over to suit some curious ideal of perfection of our own—until one day we suddenly laugh aloud at our own absurdity (knowing that they are probably trying as hard to reconstruct us as we are to reconstruct them!) and thereafter we try no more to change them, we just love 'em and enjoy 'em!

Some such psychological process went on in my consciousness that morning. As I walked briskly through the streets I began to look out more broadly around me. It was really a perfect spring morning, the air crisp, fresh, and sunny, and the streets full of life and activity. I looked into the faces of the people I met, and it began to strike me that most of them seemed oblivious of the fact that they should, by good rights, be looking downcast and dispirited. They had cheered their approval the night before when the speakers had told them how miserable they were (even acknowledging that they were slaves), and yet here they were this morning looking positively good-humoured, cheerful, some of them even gay. I warrant if I had stepped up to one of them that morning and intimated that he was a slave he would have—well, I should have had serious trouble with him! There was a degree of sociability in those back streets, a visiting from window to window, gossipy gatherings in front areaways, a sort of pavement domesticity, that I had never seen before. Being a lover myself of such friendly intercourse I could actually feel the human warmth of that neighbourhood.

A group of brightly clad girl strikers gathered on a corner were chatting and laughing, and children in plenty ran and shouted at their play in the street. I saw a group of them dancing merrily around an Italian hand-organ man who was filling the air with jolly music. I recall what a sinking sensation I had at the pit of my reformer's stomach when it suddenly occurred to me that these people, some of them, anyway, might actually *like* this crowded, sociable neighbourhood! "They might even *hate* the country," I exclaimed.

It is surely one of the fundamental humours of life to see absurdly serious little human beings (like D. G. for example) trying to stand in the place of the Almighty. We are so confoundedly infallible in our judgments, so sure of what is good for our neighbour, so eager to force upon him our particular doctors or our particular remedies; we are so willing to put our childish fingers into the machinery of creation—and we howl so lustily when we get them pinched!

"Why!" I exclaimed, for it came to me like a new discovery, "it's exactly the same here as it is in the country! I haven't got to make over the universe: I've only got to do my own small job, and to look up often at the trees and the hills and the sky and be friendly with all men."

I cannot express the sense of comfort, and of trust, which this reflection brought me. I recall stopping just then at the corner of a small green city square, for I had now reached the better part of the city, and of seeing with keen pleasure the green of the grass and the bright colour of a bed of flowers, and two or three clean nursemaids with clean baby cabs, and a flock of pigeons pluming themselves near a stone fountain, and an old tired horse sleeping in the sun with his nose buried in a feed bag.

"Why," I said, "all this, too, is beautiful!"

So I continued my walk with quite a new feeling in my heart, prepared again for any adventure life might have to offer me.

I supposed I knew no living soul in Kilburn but Bill the Socialist. What was my astonishment and pleasure, then, in one

of the business streets to discover a familiar face and figure. A
man was just stepping from an automobile to the sidewalk. For
an instant, in that unusual environment, I could not place him,
then I stepped up quickly and said:

"Well, well, Friend Vedder."

He looked around with astonishment at the man in the shabby
clothes—but it was only for an instant.

"David Grayson!" he exclaimed, "and how did *you* get into
the city?"

"Walked," I said.

"But I thought you were an incurable and irreproachable
countryman! Why are you here?"

"Love o' life," I said; "love o' life."

"Where are you stopping?"

I waved my hand.

"Where the road leaves me," I said. "Last night I left my bag
with some good friends I made in front of a livery stable and I
spent the night in the mill district with a Socialist named Bill
Hahn."

"Bill Hahn!" The effect upon Mr. Vedder was magical.

"Why, yes," I said, "and a remarkable man he is, too."

I discovered immediately that my friend was quite as much
interested in the strike as Bill Hahn, but on the other side. He
was, indeed, one of the directors of the greatest mill in Kilburn
—the very one which I had seen the night before surrounded by
armed sentinels. It was thrilling to me, this knowledge, for it
seemed to plump me down at once in the middle of things—and
soon, indeed, brought me nearer to the brink of great events
than ever I was before in all my days.

I could see that Mr. Vedder considered Bill Hahn as a sort of
devouring monster, a wholly incendiary and dangerous person.
So terrible, indeed, was the warning he gave me (considering
me, I suppose an unsophisticated person) that I couldn't help
laughing outright.

"I assure you——" he began, apparently much offended.

But I interrupted him.

"I'm sorry I laughed," I said, "but as you were talking about

Bill Hahn, I couldn't help thinking of him as I first saw him."
And I gave Mr. Vedder as lively a description as I could of the
little man with his bulging coat tails, his furry ears, his odd
round spectacles. He was greatly interested in what I said and
began to ask many questions. I told him with all the earnestness
I could command of Bill's history and of his conversion to his
present beliefs. I found that Mr. Vedder had known Robert
Winter very well indeed, and was amazed at the incident which
I narrated of Bill Hahn's attempt upon his life.

I have always believed that if men could be made to understand one another they would necessarily be friendly, so I did
my best to explain Bill Hahn to Mr. Vedder.

"I'm tremendously interested in what you say," he said, "and
we must have more talk about it."

He told me that he had now to put in an appearance at his
office, and wanted me to go with him; but upon my objection he
pressed me to take luncheon with him a little later, an invitation which I accepted with real pleasure.

"We haven't had a word about gardens," he said, "and there
are no end of things that Mrs. Vedder and I found that we
wanted to talk with you about after you had left us."

"Well," I said, much delighted, "let's have a regular old-
fashioned country talk."

So we parted for the time being, and I set off in the highest
spirits to see something more of Kilburn.

A city, after all, is a very wonderful place. One thing, I recall,
impressed me powerfully that morning—the way in which every
one was working, apparently without any common agreement
or any common purpose, and yet with a high sort of understanding. The first hearing of a difficult piece of music (to an
uncultivated ear like mine) often yields nothing but a confused
sense of unrelated motives, but later and deeper hearings reveal
the harmony which ran so clear in the master's soul.

Something of this sort happened to me in looking out upon
the life of that great city of Kilburn. All about on the streets,
in the buildings, under ground and above ground, men were
walking, running, creeping, crawling, climbing, lifting, digging,

driving, buying, selling, sweating, swearing, praying, loving, hating, struggling, failing, sinning, repenting—all working and living according to a vast harmony, which sometimes we can catch clearly and sometimes miss entirely. I think, that morning, for a time, I heard the true music of the spheres, the stars singing together.

Mr. Vedder took me to a quiet restaurant where we had a snug alcove all to ourselves. I shall remember it always as one of the truly pleasant experiences of my pilgrimage.

I could see that my friend was sorely troubled, that the strike rested heavy upon him, and so I led the conversation to the hills and the roads and the fields we both love so much. I plied him with a thousand questions about his garden. I told him in the liveliest way of my adventures after leaving his home, how I had telephoned him from the hills, how I had taken a swim in the mill-pond, and especially how I had lost myself in the old cow-pasture, with an account of all my absurd and laughable adventures and emotions.

Well, before we had finished our luncheon I had every line ironed from the brow of that poor plagued rich man, I had brought jolly crinkles to the corners of his eyes, and once or twice I had him chuckling down deep inside (where chuckles are truly effective). Talk about cheering up the poor: I think the rich are usually far more in need of it!

But I couldn't keep the conversation in these delightful channels. Evidently the strike and all that it meant lay heavy upon Mr. Vedder's consciousness, for he pushed back his coffee and began talking about it, almost in a tone of apology. He told me how kind he had tried to make the mill management in its dealings with its men.

"I would not speak of it save in explanation of our true attitude of helpfulness; but we have really given our men many advantages"—and he told me of the reading-room the company had established, of the visiting nurse they had employed, and of several other excellent enterprises, which gave only another proof of what I knew already of Mr. Vedder's sincere kindness of heart.

"But," he said, "we find they don't appreciate what we try to do for them."

I laughed outright.

"Why," I exclaimed, "you are having the same trouble I have had!"

"How's that?" he inquired, I thought a little sharply. Men don't like to have their seriousness trifled with.

"No longer ago than this morning," I said, "I had exactly that idea of giving them advantages; but I found that the difficulty lies not with the ability to give, but with the inability or unwillingness to take. You see I have a great deal of surplus wealth myself——"

Mr. Vedder's eyes flickered up at me.

"Yes," I said. "I've got immense accumulations of the wealth of the ages—ingots of Emerson and Whitman, for example, gems of Voltaire, and I can't tell what other superfluous coinage!" (And I waved my hand in the most grandiloquent manner.) "I've also quite a store of knowledge of corn and calves and cucumbers, and I've a boundless domain of exceedingly valuable landscapes. I am prepared to give bountifully of all these varied riches (for I shall still have plenty remaining), but the fact is that this generation of vipers doesn't appreciate what I am trying to do for them. I'm really getting frightened, lest they permit me to perish from undistributed riches!"

Mr. Vedder was still smiling.

"Oh," I said, warming up to my idea, "I'm a regular multimillionaire. I've got so much wealth that I'm afraid I shall not be as fortunate as jolly Andy Carnegie, for I don't see how I can possibly die poor!"

"Why not found a university or so?" asked Mr. Vedder.

"Well, I had thought of that. It's a good idea. Let's join our forces and establish a university where truly serious people can take courses in laughter."

"Fine idea!" exclaimed Mr. Vedder; "but wouldn't it require an enormous endowment to accommodate all the applicants? You must remember that this is a very benighted and illiterate world, laughingly speaking."

"It is, indeed," I said, "but you must remember that many people, for a long time, will be too serious to apply. I wonder sometimes if any one ever learns to laugh—*really* laugh—much before he is forty."

"But," said Mr. Vedder anxiously, "do you think such an institution would be accepted by the proletariat of the serious-minded?"

"Ah, that's the trouble," said I, "that's the trouble. The proletariat doesn't appreciate what we are trying to do for them! They don't want your reading-rooms nor my Emerson and cucumbers. The seat of the difficulty seems to be that what seems wealth to us isn't necessarily wealth for the other fellow."

I cannot tell with what delight we fenced our way through this foolery (which was not all foolery, either). I never met a man more quickly responsive than Mr. Vedder. But he now paused for some moments, evidently ruminating.

"Well, David," he said seriously, "what are we going to do about this obstreperous other fellow?"

"Why not try the experiment," I suggested, "of giving him what he considers wealth, instead of what you consider wealth?"

"But what does he consider wealth?"

"Equality," said I.

Mr. Vedder threw up his hand.

"So you're a Socialist, too!"

"That," I said, "is another story."

"Well, supposing we did or could give him this equality you speak of—what would become of us? What would we get out of it?"

"Why, equality, too!" I said.

Mr. Vedder threw up his hands with a gesture of mock resignation.

"Come," said he, "let's get down out of Utopia!"

We had some further good-humoured fencing and then returned to the inevitable problem of the strike. While we were discussing the meeting of the night before which, I learned, had been luridly reported in the morning papers, Mr. Vedder suddenly turned to me and asked earnestly:

"Are you really a Socialist?"

"Well," said I, "I'm sure of one thing. I'm not *all* Socialist. Bill Hahn believes with his whole soul (and his faith has made him a remarkable man) that if only another class of people—his class—could come into the control of material property, that all the ills that man is heir to would be speedily cured. But I wonder if when men own property collectively—as they are going to one of these days—they will quarrel and hate one another any less than they do now. It is not the ownership of material property that interests me so much as the independence of it. When I started out from my farm on this pilgrimage it seemed to me the most blessed thing in the world to get away from property and possession."

"What are you then, anyway?" asked Mr. Vedder, smiling.

"Well, I've thought of a name I would like to have applied to me sometimes," I said. "You see I'm tremendously fond of this world exactly as it is now. Mr. Vedder, it's a wonderful and beautiful place! I've never seen a better one. I confess I could not possibly live in the rarefied atmosphere of a final solution. I want to live right here and now for all I'm worth. The other day a man asked me what I thought was the best time of life. 'Why,' I answered without a thought, 'Now.' It has always seemed to me that if a man can't make a go of it, yes, and be happy at this moment, he can't be at the next moment. But most of all, it seems to me, I want to get close to people, to look into their hearts, and be friendly with them. Mr. Vedder, do you know what I'd like to be called?"

"I cannot imagine," said he.

"Well, I'd like to be called an Introducer. My friend, Mr. Blacksmith, let me introduce you to my friend, Mr. Plutocrat. I could almost swear that you were brothers, so near alike are you! You'll find each other wonderfully interesting once you get over the awkwardness of the introduction. And, Mr. White Man, let me present you particularly to my good friend, Mr. Negro. You will see if you sit down to it that this curious colour of the face is only skin deep."

"It's a good name!" said Mr. Vedder, laughing.

"It's a wonderful name," said I, "and it's about the biggest and finest work in the world—to know human beings just as they are, and to make them acquainted with one another just as they are. Why, it's the foundation of all the democracy there is, or ever will be. Sometimes I think that friendliness is the only achievement of life worth while—and unfriendliness the only tragedy."

I have since felt ashamed of myself when I thought how I lectured my unprotected host that day at luncheon; but it seemed to boil out of me irresistibly. The experiences of the past two days had stirred me to the very depths, and it seemed to me I must explain to somebody how it all impressed me—and to whom better than to my good friend Vedder?

As we were leaving the table an idea flashed across my mind which seemed, at first, so wonderful that it quite turned me dizzy.

"See here, Mr. Vedder," I exclaimed, "let me follow my occupation practically. I know Bill Hahn and I know you. Let me introduce you. If you could only get together, if you could only understand what good fellows you both are, it might go far toward solving these difficulties."

I had some trouble persuading him, but finally he consented, said he wanted to leave no stone unturned, and that he would meet Bill Hahn and some of the other leaders, if proper arrangements could be made.

I left him, therefore, in excitement, feeling that I was at the point of playing a part in a very great event. "Once get these men together," I thought, "and they *must* come to an understanding."

So I rushed out to the mill district, saying to myself over and over (I have smiled about it since!): "We'll settle this strike: we'll settle this strike: we'll settle this strike." After some searching I found my friend Bill in the little room over a saloon that served as strike headquarters. A dozen or more of the leaders were there, faintly distinguishable through clouds of tobacco smoke. Among them sat the great R—— D——, his burly figure looming up at one end of the table, and his strong, rough, iron-jawed face turning first toward this speaker and then toward that. The discussion, which had evidently been lively, died down soon after I appeared at the door, and Bill Hahn came out to me and we sat down together in the adjoining room. Here I broke eagerly into an account of the happenings of the day, described my chance meeting with Mr. Vedder—who was well known to Bill by reputation—and finally asked him squarely whether he would meet him. I think my enthusiasm quite carried him away.

"Sure, I will," said Bill Hahn heartily.

"When and where?" I asked, "and will any of the other men join you?"

Bill was all enthusiasm at once, for that was the essence of his temperament, but he said that he must first refer it to the committee. I waited, in a tense state of impatience, for what seemed to me a very long time; but finally the door opened and Bill Hahn came out bringing R—— D—— himself with him. We all sat down together, and R—— D—— began to ask questions (he was evidently suspicious as to who and what I was); but I think, after I talked with them for some time that I made them see the possibilities and the importance of such a meeting. I was greatly impressed with R—— D——, the calmness and steadiness of the man, his evident shrewdness. "A real general," I said to myself. "I should like to know him better."

After a long talk they returned to the other room, closing the door behind them, and I waited again, still more impatiently.

It seems rather absurd now, but at that moment I felt firmly convinced that I was on the way to the permanent settlement of a struggle which had occupied the best brains of Kilburn for many weeks.

While I was waiting in that dingy anteroom, the other door slowly opened and a boy stuck his head in.

"Is David Grayson here?" he asked.

"Here he is," said I, greatly astonished that any one in Kilburn should be inquiring for me, or should know where I was.

The boy came in, looked at me with jolly round eyes for a moment, and dug a letter out of his pocket. I opened it at once, and glancing at the signature discovered that it was from Mr. Vedder.

"He said I'd probably find you at strike headquarters," remarked the boy.

This was the letter: marked "Confidential."

MY DEAR GRAYSON: I think you must be something of a hypnotist. After you left me I began to think of the project you mentioned, and I have talked it over with one or two of my associates. I would gladly hold this conference, but it does not now seem wise for us to do so. The interests we represent are too important to be jeopardized. In theory you are undoubtedly right, but in this case I think you will agree with me (when you think it over), we must not show any weakness. Come and stop with us to-night: Mrs. Vedder will be overjoyed to see you and we'll have another fine talk.

I confess I was a good deal cast down as I read this letter.

"What interests are so important?" I asked myself, "that they should keep friends apart?"

But I was given only a moment for reflection for the door opened and my friend Bill, together with R—— D—— and several other members of the committee, came out. I put the letter in my pocket, and for a moment my brain never worked under higher pressure. What should I say to them now? How could I explain myself?

Bill Hahn was evidently labouring under considerable excitement, but R—— D—— was as calm as a judge. He sat down in the chair opposite and said to me:

"We've been figuring out this proposition of Mr. Vedder's. Your idea is all right, and it would be a fine thing if we could really get together as you suggest upon terms of common understanding and friendship."

"Just what Mr. Vedder said," I exclaimed.

"Yes," he continued, "it's all right in theory; but in this case it simply won't work. Don't you see it's got to be war? Your friend and I could probably understand each other—but this is a class war. It's all or nothing with us, and your friend Vedder knows it as well as we do."

After some further argument and explanation, I said:

"I see: and this is Socialism."

"Yes," said the great R—— D——, "this is Socialism."

"And it's force you would use," I said.

"It's force *they* use," he replied.

After I left the strike headquarters that evening—for it was almost dark before I parted with the committee—I walked straight out through the crowded streets, so absorbed in my thoughts that I did not know in the least where I was going. The street lights came out, the crowds began to thin away, I heard a strident song from a phonograph at the entrance to a picture show, and as I passed again in front of the great, dark, many-windowed mill which had made my friend Vedder a rich man I saw a sentinel turn slowly at the corner. The light glinted on the steel of his bayonet. He had a fresh, fine, boyish face.

"We have some distance yet to go in this world," I said to myself, "no man need repine for lack of good work ahead."

It was only a little way beyond this mill that an incident occurred which occupied probably not ten minutes of time, and yet I have thought about it since I came home as much as I have thought about any other incident of my pilgrimage. I have thought how I might have acted differently under the circumstances, how I could have said this or how I ought to have done that—all, of course, now to no purpose whatever. But I shall not attempt to tell what I ought to have done or said, but what I actually did do and say on the spur of the moment.

It was in a narrow, dark street which opened off the brightly lighted main thoroughfare of that mill neighbourhood. A girl standing in the shadows between two buildings said to me as I passed:

"Good evening."

I stopped instantly, it was such a pleasant, friendly voice.

"Good evening," I said, lifting my hat and wondering that there should be any one here in this back street who knew me.

"Where are you going?" she asked.

I stepped over quickly toward her, hat in hand. She was a

mere slip of a girl, rather comely, I thought, with small childish features and a half-timid, half-bold look in her eyes. I could not remember having seen her before.

She smiled at me—and then I knew!

Well, if some one had struck me a brutal blow in the face I could not have been more astonished.

We know of things!—and yet how little we know until they are presented to us in concrete form. Just such a little school girl as I have seen a thousand times in the country, the pathetic childish curve of the chin, a small rebellious curl hanging low on her temple.

I could not say a word. The girl evidently saw in my face that something was the matter, for she turned and began to move quickly away. Such a wave of compassion (and anger, too) swept over me as I cannot well describe. I stepped after her and asked in a low voice:

"Do you work in the mills?"

"Yes, when there's work."

"What is your name?"

"Maggie——"

"Well, Maggie," I said, "let's be friends."

She looked around at me curiously, questioningly.

"And friends," I said, "should know something about each other. You see I am a farmer from the country. I used to live in a city myself, a good many years ago, but I got tired and sick and hopeless. There was so much that was wrong about it. I tried to keep the pace and could not. I wish I could tell you what the country has done for me."

We were walking along slowly, side by side, the girl perfectly passive but glancing around at me from time to time with a wondering look. I don't know in the least now what prompted me to do it, but I began telling in a quiet, low voice—for, after all, she was only a child—I began telling her about our chickens at the farm and how Harriet had named them all, and one was Frances E. Willard, and one, a speckled one, was Martha Washington, and I told her of the curious antics of Martha Washington and of the number of eggs she laid, and of the sweet new milk we had to drink, and the honey right out of our own hives, and of the things growing in the garden.

Once she smiled a little, and once she looked around at me with a curious, timid, half-wistful expression in her eyes.

"Maggie," I said, "I wish you could go to the country."

"I wish to God I could," she replied.

We walked for a moment in silence. My head was whirling with thoughts: again I had that feeling of helplessness, of inadequacy, which I had felt so sharply on the previous evening. What could I do?

When we reached the corner, I said:

"Maggie, I will see you safely home."

She laughed—a hard, bitter laugh.

"Oh, I don't need any one to show me around these streets!"

"I will see you home," I said.

So we walked quickly along the street together.

"Here it is," she said finally, pointing to a dark, mean-looking one-story house, set in a dingy, barren areaway.

"Well, good night, Maggie," I said, "and good luck to you."

"Good night," she said faintly.

When I had walked to the corner, I stopped and looked back. She was standing stock-still just where I had left her—a figure I shall never forget.

I have hesitated about telling of a further strange thing that happened to me that night—but have decided at last to put it in. I did not accept Mr. Vedder's invitation; I could not; but I returned to the room in the tenement where I had spent the previous night with Bill Hahn the Socialist. It was a small, dark, noisy room, but I was so weary that I fell almost immediately into a heavy sleep. An hour or more later—I don't know how long indeed—I was suddenly awakened and found myself sitting bolt upright in bed. It was close and dark and warm there in the room, and from without came the muffled sounds of the city. For an instant I waited, rigid with expectancy. And then I heard as clearly and plainly as ever I heard anything:

"David! David!" in my sister Harriet's voice.

It was exactly the voice in which she has called me a thousand times. Without an instant's hesitation, I stepped out of bed and called out:

"I'm coming, Harriet! I'm coming!"

"What's the matter?" inquired Bill Hahn sleepily.

"Nothing," I replied, and crept back into bed.

It may have been the result of the strain and excitement of the previous two days. I don't explain it—I can only tell what happened.

Before I went to sleep again I determined to start straight for home in the morning: and having decided, I turned over, drew a long, comfortable breath and did not stir again, I think, until long after the morning sun shone in at the window.

XII

THE RETURN

"Everything divine runs with light feet."

Surely the chief delight of going away from home is the joy of getting back again. I shall never forget that spring morning when I walked from the city of Kilburn into the open country—my bag on my back, a song in my throat, and the gray road stretching straight before me. I remember how eagerly I looked out across the fields and meadows and rested my eyes upon the distant hills. How roomy it all was! I looked up into the clear blue of the sky. There was space here to breathe, and distances in which the spirit might spread its wings. As the old prophet says, it was a place where a man might be placed alone in the midst of the earth.

I was strangely glad that morning of every little stream that ran under the bridges, I was glad of the trees I passed, glad of every bird and squirrel in the branches, glad of the cattle grazing in the fields, glad of the jolly boys I saw on their way to school with their dinner pails, glad of the bluff, red-faced teamster I met, and of the snug farmer who waved his hand at me and wished me a friendly good morning. It seemed to me that I liked every one I saw, and that every one liked me.

So I walked onward that morning, nor ever have had such a sense of relief and escape, nor ever such a feeling of gayety.

"Here is where I belong," I said. "This is my own country. Those hills are mine, and all the fields, and the trees and the sky—and the road here belongs to me as much as it does to any one."

Coming presently to a small house near the side of the road, I saw a woman working with a trowel in her sunny garden. It was good to see her turn over the warm brown soil; it was good to see the plump green rows of lettuce and the thin green rows of onions, and the nasturtiums and sweet peas; it was good— after so many days in that desert of a city—to get a whiff of blossoming things. I stood for a moment looking quietly over the fence before the woman saw me. When at last she turned and looked up, I said:

"Good morning."

She paused, trowel in hand.

"Good morning," she replied; "you look happy."

I wasn't conscious that I was smiling outwardly.

"Well, I am," I said; "I'm going home."

"Then you *ought* to be happy," said she.

"And I'm glad to escape *that*," and I pointed toward the city.

"What?"

"Why, that old monster lying there in the valley."

I could see that she was surprised and even a little alarmed. So I began intently to admire her young cabbages and comment on the perfection of her geraniums. But I caught her eying me from time to time as I leaned there on the fence, and I knew that she would come back sooner or later to my remark about the monster. Having shocked your friend (not too unpleasantly), abide your time, and he will want to be shocked again. So I was not at all surprised to hear her ask:

"Have you travelled far?"

"I should *say* so!" I replied. "I've been on a very long journey. I've seen many strange sights and met many wonderful people."

"You may have been in California, then. I have a daughter in California."

"No," said I, "I was never in California."

"You've been a long time from home, you say?"

"A very long time from home."

"How long?"

"Three weeks."

"Three weeks! And how far did you say you had travelled?"

"At the farthest point, I should say sixty miles from home."

"But how can you say that in travelling only sixty miles and being gone three weeks that you have seen so many strange places and people?"

"Why," I exclaimed, "haven't you seen anything strange around here?"

"Why, no——" glancing quickly around her.

"Well, I'm strange, am I not?"

"Well——"

"And you're strange."

She looked at me with the utmost amazement. I could scarcely keep from laughing.

"I assure you," I said, "that if you travel a thousand miles you will find no one stranger than I am—or you are—nor anything more wonderful than all this——" and I waved my hand.

This time she looked really alarmed, glancing quickly toward the house, so that I began to laugh.

"Madam," I said, "good morning!"

So I left her standing there by the fence looking after me, and I went on down the road.

"Well," I said, "she'll have something new to talk about. It may add a month to her life. Was there ever such an amusing world!"

About noon that day I had an adventure that I have to laugh

over every time I think of it. It was unusual, too, as being almost the only incident of my journey which was of itself in the
least thrilling or out of the ordinary. Why, this might have made
an item in the country paper!

For the first time on my trip I saw a man that I really felt
like calling a tramp—a tramp in the generally accepted sense of

the term. When I left home I imagined I should meet many
tramps, and perhaps learn from them odd and curious things
about life; but when I actually came into contact with the
shabby men of the road, I began to be puzzled. What was a
tramp, anyway?

I found them all strangely different, each with his own distinctive history, and each accounting for himself as logically as
I could for myself. And save for the fact that in none of them
I met were the outward graces and virtues too prominently displayed, I have come back quite uncertain as to what a scientist
might call type-characteristics. I had thought of following Emerson in his delightfully optimistic definition of a weed. A weed,

he says, is a plant whose virtues have not been discovered. A tramp, then, is a man whose virtues have not been discovered. Or, I might follow my old friend the Professor (who dearly loves all growing things) in his even kindlier definition of a weed. He says that it is merely a plant misplaced. The virility of this definition has often impressed me when I have tried to grub the excellent and useful horseradish plants out of my asparagus bed! Let it be then—a tramp is a misplaced man, whose virtues have not been discovered.

Whether this is an adequate definition or not, it fitted admirably the man I overtook that morning on the road. He was certainly misplaced, and during my brief but exciting experience with him I discovered no virtues whatever.

In one way he was quite different from the traditional tramp. He walked with far too lively a step, too jauntily, and he had with him a small, shaggy, nondescript dog, a dog as shabby as he, trotting close at his heels. He carried a light stick, which he occasionally twirled over in his hand. As I drew nearer I could hear him whistling and even, from time to time, breaking into a lively bit of song. What a devil-may-care chap he seemed, anyway! I was greatly interested.

When at length I drew alongside he did not seem in the least surprised. He turned, glanced at me with his bold black eyes, and broke out again into the song he was singing. And these were the words of his song—at least, all I can remember of them:

> *Oh, I'm so fine and gay,*
> *I'm so fine and gay,*
> *I have to take a dog along,*
> *To kape the ga-irls away.*

What droll zest he put into it! He had a red nose, a globular red nose set on his face like an overgrown strawberry, and from under the worst derby hat in the world burst his thick curly hair.

"Oh, I'm so fine and gay," he sang, stepping to the rhythm of his song, and looking the very image of good-humoured impudence. I can't tell how amused and pleased I was—though if I had known what was to happen later I might not have been quite so friendly—yes, I would too!

We fell into conversation, and it wasn't long before I suggested that we stop for luncheon together somewhere along the road. He cast a quick appraising eye at my bag, and assented with alacrity. We climbed a fence and found a quiet spot near a little brook.

I was much astonished to observe the resources of my jovial companion. Although he carried neither bag nor pack and appeared to have nothing whatever in his pockets, he proceeded, like a professional prestidigitator, to produce from his shabby clothing an extraordinary number of curious things—a black tin can with a wire handle, a small box of matches, a soiled package which I soon learned contained tea, a miraculously big dry sausage wrapped in an old newspaper, and a clasp-knife. I watched him with breathless interest.

He cut a couple of crotched sticks to hang the pail on and in two or three minutes had a little fire, no larger than a man's hand, burning brightly under it. ("Big fires," said he wisely, "are not for us.") This he fed with dry twigs, and in a very few minutes he had a pot of tea from which he offered me the first drink. This, with my luncheon and part of his sausage, made up a very good meal.

While we were eating, the little dog sat sedately by the fire. From time to time his master would say, "Speak, Jimmy."

Jimmy would sit up on his haunches, his two front paws hanging limp, turn his head to one side in the drollest way imaginable and give a yelp. His master would toss him a bit of sausage or bread and he would catch it with a snap.

"Fine dog!" commented my companion.

"So he seems," said I.

After the meal was over my companion proceeded to produce other surprises from his pockets—a bag of tobacco, a brier pipe (which he kindly offered to me and which I kindly refused), and a soiled packet of cigarette papers. Having rolled a cigarette with practised facility, he leaned up against a tree, took off his hat, lighted the cigarette and, having taken a long draw at it, blew the smoke before him with an incredible air of satisfaction.

"Solid comfort this here—hey!" he exclaimed.

We had some further talk, but for so jovial a specimen he was surprisingly uncommunicative. Indeed, I think he soon decided that I somehow did not belong to the fraternity, that I was a "farmer"—in the most opprobrious sense—and he soon began to drowse, rousing himself once or twice to roll another cigarette, but finally dropping (apparently, at least) fast asleep.

I was glad enough of the rest and quiet after the strenuous experience of the last two days—and I, too, soon began to drowse. It didn't seem to me then that I lost consciousness at all, but I suppose I must have done so, for when I suddenly opened my eyes and sat up my companion had vanished. How he succeeded in gathering up his pail and packages so noise-lessly and getting away so quickly is a mystery to me.

"Well," I said, "that's odd."

Rousing myself deliberately I put on my hat and was about to take up my bag when I suddenly discovered that it was open. My rain-cape was missing! It wasn't a very good rain-cape, but it was missing.

At first I was inclined to be angry, but when I thought of my jovial companion and the cunning way in which he had tricked me, I couldn't help laughing. At the same time I jumped up quickly and ran down to the road.

"I may get him yet," I said.

Just as I stepped out of the woods I caught a glimpse of a man some hundreds of yards away, turning quickly from the main road into a lane or by-path. I wasn't altogether sure that he was my man, but I ran across the road and climbed the fence. I had formed the plan instantly of cutting across the field and so striking the by-road farther up the hill. I had a curious sense of amused exultation, the very spirit of the chase, and my mind dwelt with the liveliest excitement on what I should say or do if I really caught that jolly spark of impudence.

So I came by way of a thicket along an old stone fence to the by-road, and there, sure enough, only a little way ahead of me, was my man with the shaggy little dog close at his heels. He was making pretty good time, but I skirted swiftly along the edge of the road until I had nearly overtaken him. Then I slowed down to a walk and stepped out into the middle of the road. I confess my heart was pounding at a lively rate. The next time he looked behind him—guiltily enough, too!—I said in the calmest voice I could command:

"Well, brother, you almost left me behind."

He stopped and I stepped up to him.

I wish I could describe the look in his face—mingled astonishment, fear, and defiance.

"My friend," I said, "I'm disappointed in you."

He made no reply.

"Yes, I'm disappointed. You did such a very poor job."

"Poor job!" he exclaimed.

"Yes," I said, and I slipped my bag off my shoulder and began to rummage inside. My companion watched me silently and suspiciously.

"You should not have left the rubbers."

With that I handed him my old rubbers. A peculiar expression came into the man's face.

"Say, pardner, what you drivin' at?"

"Well," I said, "I don't like to see such evidences of haste and inefficiency."

He stood staring at me helplessly, holding my old rubbers at arm's length.

"Come on now," I said, "that's over. We'll walk along together."

I was about to take his arm, but quick as a flash he dodged, cast both rubbers and rain-cape away from him, and ran down the road for all he was worth, the little dog, looking exactly like a rolling ball of fur, pelting after him. He never once glanced back, but ran for his life. I stood there and laughed until the tears came, and ever since then, at the thought of the expression on the jolly rover's face when I gave him my rubbers, I've had to smile. I put the rain-cape and rubbers back into my bag and turned again to the road.

Before the afternoon was nearly spent I found myself very tired, for my two days' experience in the city had been more exhausting for me, I think, than a whole month of hard labour on my farm. I found haven with a friendly farmer, whom I joined while he was driving his cows in from the pasture. I helped him with his milking both that night and the next morning, and found his situation and family most interesting—but I shall not here enlarge upon that experience.

It was late afternoon when I finally surmounted the hill from which I knew well enough I could catch the first glimpse of my farm. For a moment after I reached the top I could not raise my eyes, and when finally I was able to raise them I could not see.

"There is a spot in Arcady—a spot in Arcady—a spot in Arcady——" So runs the old song.

There *is* a spot in Arcady, and at the centre of it there is a weather-worn old house, and not far away a perfect oak tree, and green fields all about, and a pleasant stream fringed with alders in the little valley. And out of the chimney into the sweet, still evening air rises the slow white smoke of the supper-fire.

I turned from the main road, and climbed the fence and walked across my upper field to the old wood lane. The air was heavy and sweet with clover blossoms, and along the fences I could see that the raspberry bushes were ripening their fruit.

So I came down the lane and heard the comfortable grunting of pigs in the pasture lot and saw the calves licking one another as they stood at the gate.

"How they've grown!" I said.

I stopped at the corner of the barn a moment. From within I heard the rattling of milk in a pail (a fine sound), and heard a man's voice saying:

"Whoa, there! Stiddy now!"

"Dick's milking," I said.

So I stepped in at the doorway.

"Lord, Mr. Grayson!" exclaimed Dick, rising instantly and clasping my hand like a long-lost brother.

"I'm glad to see you!"

"I'm glad to see *you!*"

The warm smell of the new milk, the pleasant sound of animals stepping about in the stable, the old mare reaching her long head over the stanchion to welcome me, and nipping at my fingers when I rubbed her nose——

And there was the old house with the late sun upon it, the vines hanging green over the porch, Harriet's trim flower bed— I crept along quietly to the corner. The kitchen door stood open.

"Well, Harriet!" I said, stepping inside.

"Mercy! David!"

I have rarely known Harriet to be in quite such a reckless mood. She kept thinking of a new kind of sauce or jam for supper (I think there were seven, or were there twelve? on the table before I got through). And there was a new rhubarb pie such as only Harriet can make, just brown enough on top, and not too brown, with just the right sort of hills and hummocks in the crust, and here and there little sugary bubbles where a suggestion of the goodness came through—such a pie——! and such an appetite to go with it!

"Harriet," I said, "you're spoiling me. Haven't you heard how dangerous it is to set such a supper as this before a man who is perishing with hunger? Have you no mercy for me?"

This remark produced the most extraordinary effect. Harriet was at that moment standing in the corner near the pump. Her shoulders suddenly began to shake convulsively.

"She's so glad I'm home that she can't help laughing," I thought, which shows how penetrating I really am.

She was crying.

"Why, Harriet!" I exclaimed.

"Hungry!" she burst out, "and j-joking about it!"

I couldn't say a single word; something—it must have been a piece of the rhubarb pie—stuck in my throat. So I sat there and watched her moving quietly about in that immaculate kitchen. After a time I walked over to where she stood by the table and put my arm around her quickly. She half turned her head, in her quick, businesslike way. I noted how firm and clean and sweet her face was.

"Harriet," I said, "you grow younger every year."

No response.

"Harriet," I said, "I haven't seen a single person anywhere on my journey that I like as much as I do you."

The quick blood came up.

"There—there—David!" she said.

So I stepped away.

"And as for rhubarb pie, Harriet——"

When I first came to my farm years ago there were mornings when I woke up with the strong impression that I had just been hearing the most exquisite music. I don't know whether this is at all a common experience, but in those days (and farther back in my early boyhood) I had it frequently. It did not seem exactly like music either, but was rather a sense of harmony, so wonderful, so pervasive that it cannot be described. I have not had it so often in recent years, but on the morning after I reached home it came to me as I awakened with a strange depth and sweetness. I lay for a moment there in my clean bed. The morning sun was up and coming in cheerfully through the vines at the window; a gentle breeze stirred the clean white curtains, and I could smell even there the odours of the garden.

I wish I had room to tell, but I cannot, of all the crowded experiences of that day—the renewal of acquaintance with the fields, the cattle, the fowls, the bees, of my long talks with Harriet and Dick Sheridan, who had cared for my work while I was away; of the wonderful visit of the Scotch Preacher, of Horace's shrewd and whimsical comments upon the general absurdity of the head of the Grayson family—oh, of a thousand things—and how when I went into my study and took up the nearest book in my favourite case—it chanced to be "The Bible in Spain"—it opened of itself at one of my favourite passages, the one beginning:

"Mistos amande, I am content——"

So it's all over! It has been a great experience; and it seems to me now that I have a firmer grip on life, and a firmer trust in that Power which orders the ages. In a book I read not long ago, called "A Modern Utopia," the writer provides in his imaginary perfect state of society a class of leaders known as Samurai. And, from time to time, it is the custom of these Samurai to cut themselves loose from the crowding world of men, and with packs on their backs go away alone to far places in the deserts or on Arctic ice caps. I am convinced that every man needs some such change as this, an opportunity to think things out, to get a new grip on life, and a new hold on God. But not for me the Arctic ice cap or the desert! I choose the Friendly Road—and all the common people who travel in it or live along it—I choose even the busy city at the end of it.

I assure you, friend, that it is a wonderful thing for a man to cast himself freely for a time upon the world, not knowing where his next meal is coming from, nor where he is going to sleep for the night. It is a surprising readjuster of values. I paid my way, I think, throughout my pilgrimage; but I discovered that stamped metal is far from being the world's only true coin. As a matter of fact, there are many things that men prize more highly—because they are rarer and more precious.

My friend, if you should chance yourself some day to follow the Friendly Road, you may catch a fleeting glimpse of a man in a rusty hat, carrying a gray bag, and sometimes humming a little song under his breath for the joy of being there. And it may actually happen, if you stop him, that he will take a tin whistle from his bag and play for you, "Money Musk," or "Old Dan Tucker," or he may produce a battered old volume of Montaigne from which he will read you a passage. If such an adventure should befall you, know that you have met

Your friend,

DAVID GRAYSON.

P. S.—Harriet bemoans most of all the unsolved mystery of the sign man. But it doesn't bother me in the least. I'm glad now I never found him. The poet sings his song and goes his way.

If we sought him out how horribly disappointed we might be! We might find him shaving, or eating sausage, or drinking a bottle of beer. We might find him shaggy and unkempt where we imagined him beautiful, weak where we thought him strong, dull where we thought him brilliant. Take then the vintage of his heart and let him go. As for me, I'm glad some mystery is left in this world. A thousand signs on my roadways are still as unexplainable, as mysterious, and as beguiling as this. And I can close my narrative with no better motto for tired spirits than that of the country roadside:

REST